T0285755

THE TRAGEDY OF EVA MOTT

THE TRAGEDY OF EVA MOTT

A NOVEL

DAVID ADAMS RICHARDS

DOUBLEDAY CANADA

Doubleday Canada and colophon are registered trademarks of
Penguin Random House Canada Limited

Library and Archives Canada Cataloguing in Publication
Title: The tragedy of Eva Mott / David Adams Richards.
Names: Richards, David Adams, author.
Identifiers: Canadiana (print) 20220196710 | Canadiana (ebook) 20220196729 |
ISBN 9780385696296 (hardcover) | ISBN 9780385696302 (EPUB)
Classification: LCC PS8585.I17 T73 2022 | DDC C813/.54—dc23

Jacket and book design: Andrew Roberts
Jacket image: Paul Taylor/Getty Images
Printed in Canada

Published in Canada by Doubleday Canada,
a division of Penguin Random House Canada Limited

www.penguinrandomhouse.ca

10 9 8 7 6 5 4 3 2 1

Penguin
Random House
DOUBLEDAY CANADA

To the mimics who dig our graves.

PROLOGUE

I HAVE THOUGHT SOMEWHAT ABOUT THE STORY OF MY friend Eva Mott, and I even painted her from memory on a number of occasions. And perhaps the best introduction to her, to her tragedy and the tragedy of those who caused hers is the comment below:

> Gradually it was disclosed to me that the line separating
> good and evil passes not through states, nor between classes,
> nor between political parties either—but right through every
> human heart—and through all human hearts.
>
> Aleksandr Solzhenitsyn
> *Gulag Archipelago*

> I am human and therefore nothing human is alien to me.
>
> Terence
> *Heauton Timorumenos*

> No great fighter ever runs from the darkness.
>
> (As said in honour of the late Johnny Tapia,
> featherweight champion of the world)

1

THE WEDDING TOOK PLACE SOME YEARS AGO, IN THE heat of the day, with the bride already pregnant, wearing a white dress. Mr. Ben Mott wanted to invite the same people who were at his brother-in-law's wedding a few months before because he was jealous of his brother-in-law's inordinate success, and also because he was a mimic. He wore a grey suit, with the sleeves too short, and the white shirt cuffs too long. His wife's dress was too small now that she was showing the round mound in her tummy, that some guests throughout the night kept patting.

There were not enough tables and chairs but even so, many people did not show. They knew Ben was too stingy and mean to sprout for anything. As some people said, they had never seen the colour of his wallet. There were also for some reason a load of big flies on the small tables that had been set up with juice and buns.

Of his friends who showed that day, Clement Ricer acted as best man, and a widow named Toomey with three children waited on the tables.

Outside, men from the mine who were not invited but heard there was a party arrived in trucks and cars to the centre where the dance was to take place, and they began to mosey in about seven or eight at night. But the band had not arrived because they had not been paid up front, and there was no alcohol, only lemonade. So two men decided to set up a record player and get a sound system going.

The brother-in-law, a Mr. Bell, chief financial advisor for the asbestos mine, and his wife finally decided they must do something, and so phoning for permission they opened the mine's mess hall far across the field and hired the cooks to make dinner for thirty-eight people.

The cook, Mr. Mountain, and two First Nations women, a Mrs. Francis and her young cousin Melissa Hammerstone, were hired to do so.

Mrs. Francis as we know cared for many people on the reserve and had studied as a nurse. She had tried to keep Melissa in her care. Melissa was still a child herself, a girl who when she was in the convent was an honours student and could play Chopin on the piano, but by this time had become, even at the age of nineteen, cynical and pessimistic about the world, and her beauty and happiness had been soured by certain men, and now she was almost never sober. People said her downfall came because of a man named Mel Stroud, and her young brother Gordon Hammerstone had tried to stop them from seeing one another.

Yes, it was the most unusual wedding, with the groom standing in line with men he didn't invite to get food he didn't pay for, with his wife in her white dress four months pregnant—the same as her sister, Mrs. Bell, who was married six months before her— standing behind him as the sky became dimmer and dimmer. There was, however, a good deal of wine hidden by the men, and soon Oscar Peterson, a man named after his uncle and not after the great Canadian musician, just as our own Winston Churchill was named after his grandfather and not the wartime prime minister, was roaring drunk and badmouthing the Dews. The Dews went at him outside and one of them hit him over the head with a bottle, and the policeman Constable Furlong tried to get Oscar in a police car to take him home, as Oscar raked them all with his feelings about the Arron Brook Dews who were not at all like other Dews, who were nicer and, he said for some reason, cleaner Dews.

At the same time Mrs. Wally and Mrs. Ricer had set up the accordion and fiddle and played old reels and jigs, and soon a few of the asbestos miners who had been alone in the old building built as a bunkhouse were trying to take advantage of certain married women. So soon jokes turned bawdy and then rebellious.

A young man, perhaps about twenty, who some girls said was *full of the devil* arrived. He drove a small convertible and wore sunglasses though it was almost night now, and small wild bats flew over the bunkhouse. Still women, certain women at any rate, cared very much for his dark curly hair, his unsettled terrible eyes, his high cowboy boots and strong body. He was the aforementioned Mr. Mel Stroud.

He grabbed a man's wife, and when the man intervened he threw him against the wall, and laughed. Then when two miners came at him he flashed a knife, and other men intervened and tried to get things settled down. He said he was here to see Mrs. Toomey—and the young First Nations girl Melissa Hammerstone. But people wanted him and his young brother gone.

The only way they could settle things down was to get Mel Stroud out of there, and they had to call Constable Furlong again, who when he heard it was Mel Stroud said he was busy.

Then the raffle was drawn and Mrs. Wally won the expensive silver watch, perhaps, they said, worth two weeks' pay, and Shane,

Mel's younger, wilder, imitative brother, said she cheated and maybe he should have the watch, though he hadn't bought a raffle ticket and did not know there was a raffle.

So then they had to get Oscar Peterson back, and he was driven back by Furlong. He came into the hall and told his distant cousins they had to go. The cousins laughed, and Shane picked up a glass to fight him with.

But just as this argument was about to take a more physical turn, the lights dimmed so the music stopped. The groom far on the other side of the hall said his best man Clement Ricer wanted to make a toast. The light was turned on. The bride looked scared to death. Clement got emotional, told people Ben was his best, lifelong friend and had many stories that he shouldn't tell here for it would be embarrassing:

"But remember when we went to the Gaspé—hey, remember that, yes, well that is what I want to say—he's a good man. I toast the bride."

By then, for some reason there were tears in his eyes.

And just as Shane was going to insult the bride—for he was even more obtrusive than his older brother, and loved to torment when his brother was there to protect him, and had all his life a desperate hatred for women, something happened.

Everyone turned, and there was Byron Raskin, the nephew of the Raskin brothers, owners of Raskin Oil and Mine. He was the person Mr. Bell had phoned. He stood with little expression watching the crowd of people. No one spoke. He had been a hero in the second war, and he had disappeared for some time. It was only recently that people had discovered he had fought at Dien Bien Phu, the last stand of the French in Vietnam. The French had fought back from one desperate position to the next, each position named after someone's girlfriend. In that battle Raskin had fought alongside French and German solders, the Germans members of the French Foreign Legion, many of them soldiers who had fought with von Paulus at Stalingrad. Most of them died in this battle of Dien Bien Phu. Byron Raskin who wanted to, did not.

Now he stood watching the festivities, and his eyes lighted on Mel Stroud.

"You had better go," he said, "and leave this celebration to those who wish to celebrate."

"I just came to see Melissa Hammerstone—she's working here. I'll see her before I go."

"No. You will go now," Byron said, without ceremony.

And Mel Stroud and his brother Shane did exactly that. They did it because Mel respected both bravery, which Byron had, and wealth, which the Raskins certainly enjoyed.

Now with the dinner almost over, and the band playing again, Byron Raskin whispered to Mr. Bell to go to the house and get a case of champagne that was there. And to tell the uncles to come to toast the bride, and to bring greetings from the asbestos mine, and to bring the beer that was in the porch and give the bottles to the men who had come to celebrate. He told him to give twenty dollars extra to Melissa Hammerstone, for he knew and had affection for her as a child.

There were another twenty deer steak in the cooler, inside the kitchen, he said. Take them out and give them to the cooks.

Then he went over and shook hands with the groom, and asked the bride to dance. The champagne came, the steak was cooked, the beer was cold. The dance went on, and the night was a night of great celebration, for the Bells, the Petersons, the Toomeys, the Motts, the Dews, the miners from the asbestos pit, for Mrs. Wally, the Raskins themselves and yes, for young Melissa Hammerstone, who Byron asked to dance.

Just before eleven the old men themselves arrived from their large house far in the trees above, and stood together at the entrance as if unsure they were welcome in their own building. They had no present to give, but they did have five hundred dollars in their pockets that they handed over to the groom, who looked flabbergasted that this wonderful shindig had gone forward in his behalf.

Everyone danced and drank, and the bride and groom did not leave until after midnight. It was a celebration to celebrate two people who were not so popular in our community but who deserved this one night of grace.

Only the next morning did the bride, the newly minted Mrs. Mott, realize that this great man Byron Raskin had been dead drunk through all of this, and would not remember a thing about the wonderful evening he had managed to create.

2

BYRON RASKIN WAS IN THE OFFICE EARLY THE NEXT DAY to rearrange his percentage of the business and to deliver the reports his uncles had requested . He had taken a pint of Scotch into the bathroom with him, and poured a drink into a glass that sat on the sink. The sink was stained with a kind of golden and rust discolouring and he looked at it as if in the still moments between the pouring and the drinking he could fathom a future for him and his wife.

He and his wife—or he at least—believed the marriage was futile. He had married her when she was alone with her young son, and had taken them in, in the same expressive way he had shown just this night before. That is, in the exact same way, no more, and no less. And that was his ultimate mistake. This was in his nature, but it at times blinded him to himself.

She was a Goya. She was a widow with a young son. He had researched her, in a way, too, that showed he was cautious. He had heard she was vain. Well who wasn't? That she had manipulated her own younger sister. Well who didn't? That she had married a man after forcing him away from his wife—that he in turn had run his motorboat into Bartibog Bridge and was nothing more than a smudge. And that this smudge should allow Byron pause. But it didn't.

She had gone to the Raskin mines after her first husband died, found herself working part-time, and going to a company picnic which was where he first saw her. Of course he had known about her before. The Goya woman, the woman who turned heads without being terribly pretty or vivacious. And yet her idea of herself, her narcissism and sense of entitlement, was well known. That is why he was attracted to her. Her very flaws made her desirable to him. She knew who he was, and in fact had known he would be where he was when she was there as well. She had been a widow five or six months when they met.

He remembered it now, while staring at the golden stain in the porcelain sink and listening to the first early birds sing outside the clouded window. He remembered her legs, her skirt, her perfume, her longish fingernails all in an instant, and realized how everything complemented her face, shaded from the afternoon. It was as if he knew he was lost at that moment—like a man who has heard of a dangerous turn on the road takes it anyway. Didn't they say she robbed her own sister? And didn't he feel—at least in a small way—that if he looked too long upon those legs, that skirt, and then to that expressive face he too would be lost? And yet he did not turn away. Now after all these moments he thought of her only as a heavy weight upon him, and of course he, one upon her.

Then turning his back to the sink he stared at the grey paper towels piled on the small white table like shrives of a damp and pedestrian world, and saw the scratches of time on the black bathroom door.

All in time to the dripping of the faucet.

The asbestos they mined was under scientific scrutiny, and he had made it explicitly clear to his uncles that the mine should turn its attention to copper and zinc, whose loads might be in abundance further into the mountain, or from the tailings of the asbestos they could recoup their losses with magnesium. He had discussions with the Indigenous council about this, knowing here in mid-century how left out they had been. Some had agreed and some had disagreed with any proposal.

And the uncles wanted to turn their mining acumen to other things, but the government needed this mine for both financial and political reasons. So the money they would get from the government both provincially and federally would offset any small litigation that might come. Nor was the government particularly interested in them mining for other ores and might fight the very jurisdiction they held.

Byron had dictated letters on the old men's behalf that he had copied, and kept asking for scientific assurances that certain men now getting sick were not getting sick because of asbestos. Certain First Nations men had become ill as well. Melissa Hammerstone's father was one.

There was bleeding, and a certain kind of stomach complaint, and trouble breathing—this and more was happening. They dictated letters to him while they sat in their chairs and were shaved in the morning, with the door opened to the early morning air, and the smell of shaving crème, the smell too of their cigars, as they sat almost back to back, looking into mirrors so it was as if they commutated to each other face to face.

The government had sent nothing back but official scientific reports of studies they had done at the larger, grander Thetford Mines. Byron knew they wanted this smaller mine to operate to legitimize the mine at Thetford—there really was no other reason. So the old men were being coerced in very subtle ways, and Byron knew that no cigar smoke or scrape of a razor on their balding faces could stop that.

While working at all of this he discovered that he and the young widow he married were not suited for each other. And he blamed himself. She had in her nature a callow dismissal of all he considered sacred. Not that she thought of it very much. It was simply that way.

Although she tried to fit in, she soon did not like Byron's uncles and would not visit them in their house, unless he insisted. Some pique of temperament made her feel that she had been made fun of. It was not easy to put his finger on.

After a few years, and again on the spur of some strange motivation, he discovered himself at Dien Bien Phu.

Byron was wounded there and evacuated by the North Vietnamese out of Béatrice. He had his hands tied and a rope around his neck. He remembered looking down out of his binoculars at the North Vietnamese who in their green uniforms had been in the trees beyond the cleared slope. There was not enough barbed wire or mines to protect Béatrice. He knew it was the same for Eliane and Dominique. Only before gangrene set into his leg was his wound cleaned with boiling water by a French medic who had been captured as well.

So now he walked with a cane, and drank and smoked three packs a day to ease the memories of it all. He told his uncles that day that he wanted to start a garage, and live differently. Perhaps this was the worst news his uncles could hear. They phoned Bell, who Byron Raskin admired, to come and talk to him.

Bell asked him what was wrong. He said Carmel and her son were "not like me." He said it simply.

Bell did not understand what he meant. "Why is that?" he asked.

"Because—it is my fault. Still, both of them are *part of the world.* I am not part of that world."

"What do you mean?"

"What do I mean?" Byron said. He turned to his friend and spoke, hushed. "My wife knows nothing. And I have discovered it is the age of knowing nothing. And this age will end, and another will begin, where all these people will turn on one another with hatred. She was alone, and I fell in love with an idea. I married her because I was sorry when I saw them at the company picnic alone. I believed she had no one. I came over to her, and she looked up at me in hope. It was the hope that I fell in love with. But even there and then I knew about her—I was no fool. I had heard about her. And yet—I succumbed to it all."

"I don't understand."

"At first she loved me. She tried and I loved her, more than she ever knew—until everything she said, everything she spoke about, I despised. I didn't mean to detest it, but I did. She believed the very people I had years ago argued with. She spoke of things— money, trips, clothes—I suppose I should have admired that. She continually was disappointed in who I was.

"We went to the company dance last year. There was a dear friend of mine and his wife. I had not seen them in a long time." Here Byron looked at Bell quietly. "She left and danced with some fellow who had worked with her. She did not come back to our table. She waltzed with him. She drank gin with him. I could never look upon her the same."

"Things will get better," Bell said.

"No. I will want the boy to have money—he too is a lost soul. Hers she will have as well. He will get his at thirty, if he has a career of some sort. He will get money if—and I want this known by him—if he gives one-fifth of it to a cause that is decent and appropriate. If he does this then he can have the rest when he is thirty."

"What cause?" Bell asked.

"I leave that up to him. I won't be around to direct him. Certainly he will think of an appropriate one. But make sure it is of some benefit to Arron Brook—that is where I have spent most of my life—so it has to be that. Once he does that the rest of my legacy will be his. I hope he does it justice. He is not a good athlete. He is not a handsome boy really. But I hope he does himself justice."

This was a strange and, as far as Bell was concerned, a somewhat self-interested declaration on his friend's part.

3

AS THE YEARS PASSED, BYRON RASKIN SPENT MONTHS and months away, was seen wandering alone through small towns in France. He did not go home often, he did not see his wife very much, did not care to. She had betrayed him in some unseen way. And that was that.

Still, he did not believe in divorce, and that was no fault of hers.

He was told what they were doing in the grand house he had built for her in 1957. She, people let him know, was now something of an intellectual. She had friends from the university and sat on a committee for the art gallery. Yet she still dressed in wide-brimmed hats and gaudy-coloured skirts, and laughed far too loudly at things that were held in reverence. Remembrance Day unfortunately being one.

She now lived a very different life than him, took courses, spoke about very wise things up at the university, read wise books, mainly of the new wave variety—new books on new religions and new diet fads. And in these books she saw many women like herself, so therefore saw her own plight far more than the plight of others. She was at the forefront of change. And she told her son he must be as well. She pushed him into things, in order to make him known as her champion.

She researched her family, found out she was a Goya, a great dynasty of ancient people. She began to write a column for the paper.

A touring opera company came in the hot August of 1965 and told her she had to leave their rehearsal because she was asking too many silly questions.

The years did pass by.

He heard that she and her son formed a group called The Wise Ears Thinking Club and held meetings at their house.

"For only the best minds," she said.

She was now the woman hating war and all its ramifications at the very moment of protests against wars and all its ramifications. Her son, depressed, somewhat overweight, was behind her in all of it.

Her hair was now becoming orange in the sun, her chin was now pointed and her eyes narrow with blue eyeliner; and all of this great life had come to her because it was whispered by those who knew her long ago that she had betrayed her younger sister.

She never thought of it as she drove her blue Cadillac up the dirt road past Arron Brook all the way to Taintville to visit her relatives. But in fact in some way she always thought of it, and tried to succeed her way out of it.

Her son often ridiculed but had no idea of the military, no concept of the Second World War. He wore bellbottoms that were too long, and wide belts that did not fit. He was picked on at school and tried to fit in by buying things for friends.

Still and all he was a youngster doing so to protect his mother. He stuttered at times, or couldn't pronounce letters, and she said it was her husband and his uncles' fault. They had continually bullied him into speechlessness. This was not true, but it did not matter. After a while it was spoken about as the only thing that could be true. So he was sent to speech therapists for two to three weeks in the summer. When he came home he could speak, as long as he deliberated on what he was saying.

His mother blamed everyone, and said his uncles put things in his food to make him speak like that.

Over the years his speech impediment lessened, he became less nervous, and his mother then said it was a sign of aristocracy. It may have been.

He was small, overweight and sad, and wanted to make his mark. His room had things he thought would attract girls, like waterbeds and hash pipes. But coming onto eighteen he still did not have one—that is, a girl.

Byron's wife had been a Goya, so her son, Albert, was also a Goya, that is, their ancient relations were the Goya clan, who had escaped from Southern France, and it had always been part of the young boy's nature, this semi-aristocratic forbearance. It was a lark on those summer days to giffle at Byron's uncles many times in inappropriate ways, and often when they were speaking, and interrupting each other, one could see the look of hilarity on his soft face as they spoke.

"I am out to change society," she told Byron once during an argument at the house.

He said nothing for a long while. He went up to his study, came out, and looking down the stairs at her replied: "Yes, and it will not be for the better."

It was during this time all the past was past, and the world was changing—and she, now in her late forties, believed in the change, and needed it, before it swept her away. Vietnam and love occupied her in the afternoons.

The last time her son asked him for a favour was one day he couldn't button his shirt.

"Could you please help—" he said.

It might have been the last time they actually met as father and son.

Byron came and went without trying to disturb or notice them too much. He still wrote to the boy a series of instructional letters:

"Think for yourself in these matters, and conduct yourself well. Honour follows virtue like a shadow."

But no one paid attention to poor Albert Raskin unless he paid for it. So he found himself doing more and more outrageous things in order to have people's attention, trying desperately for their respect.

"Would you like a movie—I can take you to a movie—I can take all of you to a movie—I can get the money from Mom."

For a while naturalists were a part of their group, young forestry majors devoted to the idea of preserving the forests and influencing Carmel about her in-laws' tracts of land, tailings ponds, clear-cutting she had no knowledge of, spills and other things, small amounts of cyanide within certain waters that had been flushed through certain rocks, the idea of toxicity.

In the huge mahogany-walled den she held her discussions on Tuesday nights, and these young men, "talented and so kind," were invited. She had a notepad. She took notes on whatever they said. So she was soon trying to solve problems of her husband's company that saddened and worried her. People would phone to tell her of certain blunders Byron's uncles had made, certain things they had neglected to do, and she told people: "No fear, no fear. I will soon be having a meeting with the minister."

No one was ever sure what minister it was.

This happened at the moment he had come home to stay. At first he did not go back to the house, feeling after so much time away he did not have the right. He walked by it late at night. He sometimes drove by it in the day.

But he listened to the stories emanating about that house, and felt something mimicking and perhaps even pathetic was happening.

He realized she was inner-lit with the idea of correcting *his* family's mistakes.

"I am planning a book," she told her friends, "about all the right things. First of all I think most women are prophetic."

This became known to him a week later. She told people she would go to the river, seclude herself for a few months, and write a book about *his* family, and how she—in a way—was the new prophet, here to adjudicate the parting of the sea.

That he did not see this as part of her nature that very first day she asked for a cigarette was something he wondered about. For now he saw it all clearly. But you see, as he explained to Bell those years before, he had seen it.

That is, he saw the very first day he had met her, far more clearly than he admitted, how she held the paper cup, how her eyes fastened on him in a predatory way. If she had hated them so long and harshly, why did she take the job with them when she was alone?

So one night he went to the house, uninvited guest in his own home, and walked in through the back basement door. Here he found himself in her son's bedroom and living quarters. He stared at the pictures of rock stars on the walls, the smell of hashish in the small tin ashtrays, the shirts all of a different colour, and he felt saddened he hadn't helped.

He had not seen either of them in two years. He was a stranger in his own home.

He walked up the carpeted stairs and came into the hallway, and stared at a painting of mother and son, done a year or so before by the artist they knew. He looked at it, the closeness of the two, hands just touching, the boy's face pudgy, and somehow surly; the mother's eyes dulled by the dabbling of the paint. The pearls he had bought her celebrating their engagement on her neck. Showing that they, mother and son, were schemers in some sense. Jealous that he was not in the painting. He heard her voice suddenly:

"I've long said something must be done with all of it."

She was in the den with her group of young boys, poets and artists. Yes, he forgot it was Tuesday. He barged through the door.

She looked at him startled, as if it was a mirage or a joke, as if he himself should realize he was a mirage. She had aged, was thinner. She wore comfortable slippers on her feet, but garish lipstick.

Her reddish hair was orange like the sunlight and she had a cigarette in her mouth. She looked at him in surprise, and also, after the shock, with aversion. He had interrupted her life. It was as if he ran into a place thinking a great upheaval was taking place, to see people in quiet repose drinking tea.

Too many of them came to these events just to see the house. To be inside the house of a Raskin. To be in a house that the owner almost never entered. To walk the floors, open the French doors, lounge about the patio, walk out to the large greenhouse among the flowers. This was revolution, but it was done with upper-middle-class decorum, soft evenings under the copse of elms. In fact it had to be, in order for them to come and be party to it. They were seen in his study going over his books, seen in the library next to it, with its bookshelves, chessboard and globe of the world. Two of his first editions—of Hemingway—were taken. Yet most of them said they disliked Hemingway. What did Hemingway know?

There was a certain hierarchy involved. Certain women she had gone to school with who came to see her. Relatives who turned up and cluttered about as if they owned his Scotch but looked pained when his name was mentioned, because he was the disappointment. But even they would not be accepted for long, and after drinking his Scotch and looking over his wardrobe— one of them stealing one of his expensive jackets—they were sent on their way.

There were many students who were entertaining and had deep concerns for the world. And one night he saw a boy, sitting all alone, listening to it all, with pale skin and deep expressionless eyes, overweight, and he trembled slightly, realizing it was her son. Who he had adopted as his son.

He had not seen him since he had been home.

The editor of *Floorboards*, the student magazine, was often there, speaking of publishing some of Carmel's "trains of thought." She told her husband the man was brilliant and had suffered.

"Ah, I see," Byron said.

That was the greatest of compliments—to be brilliant and to have suffered.

To Byron his son seemed an outcast in all of this—yes, even made light of as a lightweight by those editors and poets and brilliant philosophy students—until he suddenly spoke up one night and said he would have a party.

"A party?"

"Yes. You want something different, then we will have a party." He looked at them all with a kind of disdain, as if they had made fun of him too long. He smiled as if to tell them that this party would be the *real party*. There was a certain sustained silence.

"You're going to have a party? *You?*"

"Wait and see," he said.

If you want a party I will give you one, his eyes said. You think I am a lightweight—then come to my party, his eyes said, and his eyes admonished them while he smiled. For perhaps the first time, he felt a certain power surge through his body. His small white hands with ornaments that didn't fit and his watch that was too loose on his wrist.

He spoke about a party a young girl had had, a Donaldson girl, who tried to have a party for her graduation. She had sent out little handwritten invitations.

"I promise my party won't be like that," he said.

This was the first time he had ever spoken in the group. He was in fact quite shy, because of the impediment he had struggled with, and he was, as they knew, quite rich because of his stepfather. So he was an oddity to them. Especially when he spoke about helping the poor, which he simply said because a million others were saying it.

"All this will change," he said.

———

There was a party he had gone to a few years before, at Donaldson's house. They had become bored, and started to wreck the house, with Joanie's sister Becky Donaldson and young Clara Bell (her father worked for his family) trying to stop them, and they left and ran when Joanie's father came home. Yes, things got out of hand, but it was all in fun.

One of Albert's friends tipped over a lawn ornament of a guardian angel right in front of the girls and ran down the lane shouting obscenities.

A boy with the chip dip he had stolen, another boy with a plate of cold cuts and carrot sleeves, showed up later at Raskin's. Then others crowded into the house, their white faces beaming. They had stolen some records.

One of the records they stole had been playing when Albert's group arrived. It was "Hello Mary Lou" by the Everly Brothers.

He remembered the absurd and outmoded little record player Clara Bell and Becky Donaldson had placed in the corner so people could dance.

Later upon reflection he thought that ruining that party was not as brave as he initially imagined. However, his party would be. That is, brave.

This Clara Bell was Mr. Bell's daughter. Her first cousin was Eva Mott, the girl Mrs. Mott was pregnant with the night of her wedding.

But before his party happened, Carmel declared she was writing a book, and so was interviewed about the book she was going to write. She was a real writer, did push-ups every morning to raise her temperature, and intended to seclude herself in a room. The editor of *Floorboards* magazine published the article. *"Fed up with male convention, a courageous woman speaks her mind about woodlots and streams."*

Carmel said it was the first article of its type ever in the history of the province. Yet it was exactly like a thousand other articles about courageous women speaking their minds.

These were the early sentiments about pollution and industry that would evolve into grave discontent over the next number of years. Many academics would apply to get funds to do research to write similar articles. And where would some of these academics get this money? From the endowment of five million given to Saint Michael's by Raskin Enterprises. One demanded that if the money were given to him, he wanted no "overlord" interference from "those Raskin brothers."

The day after the article was published, Byron came into the den. She was alone. He had not spoken to her in a week or more. He said—his voice shaking slightly, as was his right hand, which held the article—"This is my family. You are mocking what we have lived and worked for. What allows you this house, this comfort, these paintings on your wall?"

But she was thinking she had hit a mark and made a wonderful impression, and believed he was jealous.

"I don't see you in so many magazines," she said.

Byron planned to leave the wife the house, and moved away before he struck her. He had hit her before, and was in agony lest he do it again. Neither of them knew the deception that would be fostered on each of them by each other, until they had married in a small gilded courthouse at the end of the street.

"Oh, your family is so chauvinist. They haven't dealt with a woman like me," she told him one day, as she walked behind him.

"Leave me alone," he kept saying. "For God's sake, leave me alone."

"Well, my son is not really a Raskin, that's what I'm pleased about."

That's when he turned and struck her. The shock and hurt in her eyes at that moment never left him, not for a moment. The worst of it, the boy was standing in the corner of the den and saw it.

He told her now, shaking and holding the article, that it was improper. To do this to old men who had not done anything to her.

"You are so old-fashioned, *improper*. I am simply following my conscience—you often told me I should—and now that I do, you are upset, aren't you."

She told him a certain professor said she was very forward thinking.

So he had the trust fund for her son; the money for his wife was intact. His only stipulation was that her son help the people of Arron Brook. He felt this would give him a motive to be honourable.

On November 11 he went to Hammerstone's house on the reserve. He did this whenever he was home on Remembrance Day because Mr. Hammerstone had fought alongside him from Juno Beach.

There they waited for him in the little white house at the end of nowhere, Melissa the daughter, Gordon the son, Mrs. Francis the sister, his wife Donalda, and Mr. Hammerstone too, all waiting for him to transport them up to the Remembrance Day ceremony, all in their poppies in a country where they had been displaced and dispossessed. The wind shook the house—the plates shook in the wind, the cramped little place was almost barren—and there they waited hopefully, their poppies shining upon their hearts.

Carmel refused to go onto the reserve and therefore never came with him.

He had for some years provided a taxi twice a week for Melissa to go to the convent and take piano lessons under the tutelage of Sister Camilla Arsenault, of the Sisters of Notre Dame. That is why he had danced with her at the wedding, but now she was remote, her lessons stopped, her brilliant talent halted, and yes, the wind would blow across their little tortured world.

So Byron had things in order and his passport in his valise. He would fly to Montreal and from there to Valencia. Then he would travel down the coast and buy a villa near Alicante. They would not find him, and he would live alone.

The only problem was Carmel came into the living room and became aware of blood spots on her new carpet. She followed them through to the grand dining room, walking gingerly on her new high heels. (Her new priorities did not negate her constant wardrobe improprieties.)

Her husband was seated on a piano stool, playing with the metronome, thinking of little Melissa and her extraordinary talent, and that nothing more seemed able to be done. He had begun the week before to bleed from the mouth. He would become a casualty of the asbestos mine that had kept his concerned and forward-thinking wife in furs.

A grand feeling came over Carmel when she read her name in the paper. She felt she would have more influence than all the writers at UNB.

4

A GRAND FEELING CAME OVER THE LITTLE GIRL EVA Mott; she was sitting on a train. She had never been on a train before—and a very kind black man gave her a chicken sandwich, wrapped in wax paper. She had never seen a black man before. And he spoke French. She didn't know French. And then he stood over her a moment to see if she opened it correctly, and when she took a bite, he smiled and said, "Good, isn't it, young lady!"

Then he opened a bottle of 7Up. In all her life she had not yet had a 7Up, and he poured it into a glass and placed it on the tray, with the green bottle beside it. And some lingering sunlight touched that bottle and made it shine.

And there was snow in the fields, and the smell of something—diesel fuel. She knew her uncle Mr. Bell had paid for everything, and one must be on their best behaviour when one went there. Of course she wasn't told this; she understood it in her mother's harried stern look as the platform disappeared.

Night was coming on, the grainy kind of twilight of midwinter, but if you asked her, *When was the first time you felt delighted?* she would have said, *It was that time—the time I went by train, to visit my cousin.*

In fact that is what she told Professor Albert Raskin years later. "I took a train ride to see Clara Bell, Mr. Raskin—that's a memory I cherish."

"Ah, dear," he said, "and you've had so little to cherish."

And she felt special when he had said that. She had felt special with Professor Raskin at that moment. Nothing bad could happen to her if she did what he said.

If her cousin Clara Bell was not rich, or not really rich, they had far, far more money than her own mother or father and were accustomed to greater *events*. Her cousin had gone skiing, and had been to New York and Toronto. Her cousin's father was an accountant, who worked out of his own office and did work for the Raskin group of mines. And her grandfather had been premier during a time they said of upheaval. Although she travelled through sparseness to get to the house that seemed perpetually dark, a wooden three-storey house off the highway by a great deal, everything looked extraordinary to her. She thought of keeping the 7Up bottle, but she forgot it on the train.

An accountant for the mines, she said. *My uncle is an important accountant.*

To her that was a very, very special thing. For her mother especially always talked so proudly about them and what they did, and they owned a sailboat. So Eva must show—*decorum*.

She was only staying two days so it seemed pointless, but with a great deal of decorum, the *decorum* of a little girl who wanted to please others, she unpacked her suitcase, hung up her blouse and skirt, put her socks in the second drawer of the dresser, folded her slacks and sweater, placed her underwear in the third drawer, and after the late-night lunch, and the game of Scrabble, went to bed in some presentiment, because of the knocking sound in the pipe far below her. And the wind that started a clicking in the iced-over trees. There were small shadows on the walls, like small dancing fingers, which made her shut her eyes tightly and say, "Clara? Clara?"

Not only, but that she might do something that would embarrass her parents—that she would not fit into the great house in some way.

Portico.

That was the word Clara put down to win the game of Scrabble. An entrance or doorway. Eva must remember it, for she had not heard it before. She had written it down, to remember, in its moment of transient meaning, its complete independence from what it actually meant. Which means she thought of it in some especial way that really had nothing to do with the word, but more to do with the very specialness of her cousin's family.

It was February, the night before Saint Valentine's Day. She said a prayer for her mother and father. Her father never knew what to do—he was always being told what to do, by his boss, or her mother—and she thought when she got married she would like someone who knew what to do, *who actually knew what they wanted to do*. Her father's bosses all wore tight grey suits with narrow ties and were younger than he was. He was now on his sixth job in eight years. He had sold furniture, he had installed windows, he had helped lay patios, he had driven a delivery truck. They lived in a two-bedroom apartment, but she heard her father saying they might have to move back to the very side road he was born on.

He didn't simply buy her a bicycle—no, not Ben Mott, he couldn't just buy her a bicycle. He ordered one from China that was cheaper. That was when she was ten years old. She waited the whole summer and into fall, every day, and finally it came in a box and it took her mother three days to put it together. Eva went out on her bicycle, smelling the new rubber tires as they got stuck in the snow, and the cold drifts made the new bike wobble.

Sooner or later with everything Ben Mott did, he would come home sad, and frustrated that people did not take him seriously. That the boss and his co-workers thought him ridiculous. But also all his life he had hit people up for money. At first

Eva did not notice this, but now she was of an age to notice, and to feel shame.

That is why she was glad to be here now, because once again her father had made a mistake, and as she thought of it she worried and curled up, and tucked her legs under her, and shut her eyes tight to make the mistake go away.

Then the old house groaned in the wind, and she looked out the window. The snow came up on the porch, but that porch seemed to be cheerful; those lights still made the wisping snow glitter. The moonlight, too, made the mounds of snow look dark and warm against the pine trees. Her cousin was happier too. It was her and her cousin's thirteenth birthday party on February 14.

They were born the same day, twelve minutes apart. Her cousin was the older by twelve whole minutes. So they always had a cake, shaped like a heart, at her cousin's house. Still this was the first time she had ever taken the train, and the first time she had travelled there alone.

This longing that came over her when her cousin spoke of things Eva did not have was really innocent envy, not spite or bitterness, but the kind that made her say to herself, *Wait until I tell Cheryl* or *Did even Mommy know that?*

But she also said: *Someday I will have everything Clara has too. You wait and see.*

Just two days later she was packing everything to leave. While packing her socks and underwear she saw the tea-coloured stain at the bottom of the dresser drawer that had looked special. Now it was simply the reminder of how little she had actually done here. She had imagined doing many fine things, and in fact she had done so little.

This trip would have a profound effect on her life. That over time she would try to compete with her cousin, and also be more and more like her.

Because of this trip she would want things in her life to be perfect—to reach a perfection, to be sublime.

There was something that was said that would bother her—not right away so much as when the months and years passed.

Her uncle dressed well, so fashionably in a button-up cardigan and a pair of grey dress slacks, with black loafers. And he was on the phone all day with the minister of finance, about the construction of the highway bypass to go into Suffers Lake where a new mine was being opened. This was a mine, she learned later, that didn't get authorized, because of problems with financing. But at the time, she did not understand all those matters.

Everyone spoke deferentially about his work. It is what she noticed as soon as she arrived at the house.

Early the day she was leaving, she had asked her cousin Clara to take her to the dollar store on the main street—she wanted to buy her mom and dad a present. Her cousin had gone outside, and she, still putting on her boots in the hallway, heard her uncle, who thought she had left as well, say: "Your sister dresses her like a goddamn little *slut*."

"Oh please, will you shhhh—she's in the hall. They have very little money."

"Still, she could be dressed appropriately. Her father couldn't spend a cent on anyone. I've never seen anyone quite so miserable, and in the end he will cause her misery in some way we do not yet know, mark my words. I feel very bad for her—very badly."

Eva didn't know what that word *slut* was, or why at that moment she felt deep, deep shame. Her own parents were happy she had been invited; of course neither of them knew her appearance would be used against them.

Her cousin that day would help buy a bra for her—pretending it was all her own idea: "Hey—here you go. You try this one and I'll get one too."

I *will be perfect*, Eva Mott thought later that night. *Because I have to be.*

5

THE 1980S. THE RASKIN FAMILY OWNED AN ASBESTOS mine here, and many other holdings as well.

The two elderly uncles were quite wise and animated in a public way. Both had served at different times as MLAs, and Chester once as deputy premier, to the aforementioned Premier Bell.

But they were in their eighties now. Their main financial advisor, William Bell, had been worried about their money, and had told them many times their pension fund was inadequate because of many insoluble and unforeseen events that Mr. Bell thought might happen.

This was the last thing Bell said to them, for he was retiring soon: "I think unless we find those letters you spoke about, you will come under very heavy scrutiny."

Sick and old, with trouble sleeping, seeing the cataclysm coming against the old men, he felt at times like an overseer of all their years, oddly responsible for them. Oh he knew they had been grouchy with him, and not always fair, and at times forgot to thank him for extra work he had done on their behalf, and once did not invite him to a very special gathering but flew off to it with someone who was trying to usurp his position and had only lasted in their employ a month. This is what Eva Mott did not recognize when she visited the house to celebrate her birthday with her cousin Clara that long-ago year. That this idea of him being important was at that moment dependent on him having a job at the end of the week. And that word he spoke rashly to his wife while she was putting on her boots was said in irritation because of that apprehension.

Now many more years had passed and it was the last day. That last day he was there, going over files and accounts. They offered him a glass of sparkling water, and felt very pleased that the maid cut some white cheese—they had no idea they had white cheese, it seemed so special. They had planned his lunch with them, but found after all this time little to speak about. They didn't know much about him.

They sat in their splendorous mahogany den, surrounded by books. Books from all kinds of authors, and on all kinds of topics. Fishing rods from all parts of the world, from bamboo to graphite. The tusk of a narwhal and paintings too, local and national, adorned the walls, from Molly Bobak to Tom Thomson. Letters of support from Lester B. Pearson, and John Diefenbaker, to keep up the good work in their asbestos mining. For there had been nothing wrong with it back then.

A picture of Allan Aitken, brother of Lord Beaverbrook. And a picture of Morrissey Raskin, founder of Raskin Enterprises.

This asbestos mine that had engulfed one side of Good Friday Mountain had made them millions both here and abroad and had kept two hundred men working. Now, in spite of everything or as some might say because of everything, it was coming to an end.

The little reserve sat at the very edge of it, the crossroads of time. When Byron went there that past Remembrance Day, all of them wearing their poppies, one could sometimes hear the trucks as they rattled the little house.

However, their oil distribution tanks, which held four hundred families' oil, would continue into the next generation if someone would take it over. They had eight trucks.

The brothers sat in splendorous solitude the both of them, not often speaking, now and then saying yes or no to a question as they carefully navigated a soup spoon from their plates to their mouths. The sound of spoons was at times their conversation.

They were used to being listened to, even when they were silent.

The silence in the rest of the huge house told one that other people were here—servants for the two men and maybe a nurse, though neither would mention this. The day was white, the great house too had a whiteness, and floodlights pierced the foggy cold outside with a yellow sheen. The asbestos mine was to close its doors soon, and like a great house where only the footman appeared, such was the silence in that pit, with one or two journeymen there during the long, cold day. The echo chamber of the years that held all the earth by its noisy galley was silenced, and now in that silence, foreboding. A truck or two that was loaded, and a railcar loaded, sitting up at the end of the pit like a solemn cast-iron dragon, seemed to complement the old men of the manor. The two secretaries arrived every morning to a huge office that was now almost silent, where somewhere at some point a phone would ring. They were doing their duty for the old men who did not remember their names.

There had been ongoing trauma in the papers over this mining operation for five years or more that was now coming to a head. It had started hesitantly and would end suddenly and harshly. The Indigenous and the environmentalist group from the university had formed a brigade against it, slowly fanning out in regimental displeasure. Yes, it was terrible, but before anyone knew how terrible, the old men had given much to the Indian band and much of course to the university. But certain men and women from that community, and certainly certain people from the university, believed restitution must be repaid.

The two old men, Chester and Dexter, were silent. They had gone to a band meeting last year and pledged to do more about the runoff on Riley Brook. They also initiated a program to build a school on the reserve, and helped supplement the incomes of two young women who taught the children in their own Mi'kmaq.

Other than this they were silent.

There was no chance at stopping what was to come, the recrimination and shaming of old men, but they awaited it in solitude, trying to figure out who amongst the world they could rely upon now. They had put a request in to their great-nephew Albert, someone they hardly knew, for a meeting late last week, but he had gone to another meeting—an environmentalist meeting with those who were determined to march against Raskin Enterprises and support the Indian blockade. They had somewhat vainly waited for his call. But he did not call. They knew he was not really their nephew but they had tried to treat him like one, even after Byron died.

However, for years they had not foreseen the power of the enemy, and now they had seen it they were too old to mount a credible defence. The enemy had outflanked them, and in a bold manoeuvre had encircled their last pocket, and in that pocket the defences were crumbling, the adversary's artillery strafed and ricocheted about their old whitened heads.

With Carmel they had always seen a reaching for prospect. That didn't sit well with them. They were too traditionalist to stand it. But Byron had been searching for someone new to protect when he married her.

Three months after the wedding of Byron and Carmel they saw her—unexpectedly walking toward them through the morning mist, with a striking red hat, a black scarf tied at its base, red hair and red high heels. The child was being held in Byron's military hands, Byron's jaw set as she spoke to him about some matter that seemed to drain his strength. That was it—they noticed it had drained his strength to be with that woman. They were both in shock.

"It has all come true," Chester said to Dexter.

"I'm afraid it has," Dexter replied.

So they bit down on their lips as they shook her hand, and as she made light of them, as if to prove her recent marriage had allowed equality and she must try and discredit the fumbling, antiquated gentlemanliness that they offered.

"Why, you're just two little bitty fellows," she said. "You're no bigger than spit. No wonder you never married."

And she laughed and looked for approval at Byron.

They laughed as well.

Little by little she became the woman who understood politics and men. To them it came from the gaudiest hat, and the parody of those heels stabbing the gravel as she approached them.

"Ah, my," Dexter said, now reading the paper that morning in the 1980s.

"Ah, my," Chester now responded.

6

HAVING MARRIED CARMEL IN 1948, BYRON BELIEVED IN hard work and duty. Albert short and pudgy came into his life on the back of that duty. She seemed helpless and alone. But he knew this was not the case. Everyone said she drove her first husband into a pier. Yet she told him how terrible was her life, how bad her persecution. And she sobbed. She sobbed to the clergy, late at night, night upon night, and then to him. He held her close, knowing she knew he knew that she in some way was lying. Yet she was fragile. Her face was filled with tears. She the redeemed victim, with the child. He could not let go of the idea, if only for a second, holding it like a wisp of a flower before the petals fell away. The idea that he as a rich man could save her—a victim. But long before he had entered that room with the article she had written about his family in his trembling hand, she had shown him her predatory side.

Perhaps she needed to in order to survive.

For some reason his uncles had offered him money to put any thoughts of marriage with her aside. In fact they took money from the safe and put it on the old field table from the First World War. When he walked upstairs into the room, with the chandelier glinting on their little bony heads, they were both smiling at him, but silent. This was in 1948 and there must have been fifty thousand dollars spread out on the table. He only shook his head sadly and said:

"Gentlemen."

So he went ahead, listened with kindness to her harsh accent and family discord, and discounted her pettiness toward her sister and her brother. Why? Because he was trapped by something elusive. Some strange moment he wished to capture.

Still, from the first month he knew it was a gross mistake and even perhaps, though he did not say this, immoral. And he had placed her in it. He tried desperately to hide these feelings of shame when he listened to her berate others, make crude jokes when someone left the table to go to the toilet, smile when she embarrassed people, clap her hands at others' pains.

Oh her nakedness was beautiful and he wanted that too. When the little boy began to talk he began to stutter, and Byron would go over the alphabet with him trying to get him to pronounce his letters.

She told his uncles at one of their infrequent meetings that she had read a book on wellness and peace, and said she would herself write one. "Last year I read a book—and this year I might write one."

For she claimed no one knew the world of men like she. And with her growing up in the dance halls and barns, she may have been right.

They looked at her, looked at each other and nodded, as if to acknowledge a private bet, looked back at her and smiled.

He despaired and began to sleep downstairs at night—even before the grand new house was built.

She realized soon something was wrong and tried hard to please him. This made matters worse, it seemed.

This act of his—for it was his act that had harmed them both— why did it come? Because he felt ennobled by it, of course. He had needed marriage, as some balm. She was the balm. Yes, so he was a self-deceiver, and a deceiver of her. He was going to show her a life that was different than anything she might imagine as a part-time secretary for his uncles. But it was only a week or two after the small ceremony in the courthouse that he felt differently—and he could not hide it. In the huge car where she often tried to ride close to him, speaking of her strange obsessions to be known, he would be silent as she spoke, as she tried to light two cigarettes at a time, like she said she had seen in the movies, and hand him one.

Finally she became his enemy. She went to the company party to see a fellow she had once worked with in the office. He knew, instinctively by the way she had jumped from her seat to rush to the dance floor, that somehow it was all planned by her and him. It should have been nothing. But to him it was everything.

It was all over the office that Byron's wife was unfaithful. Of course people did not speak about it, did not look his way.

He began to *see* her—see her not as he saw her but as she was. Or as he was. Perhaps it was *as he was*—he became more aware of who he was. He felt betrayed by the men she thought were worthy of her attention. They were silent with him, respected him at a distance but laughed that he had read so many books.

That was it—and he felt her damned in some terrible way, and wanted away from what damned her. And then he realized they were so unalike perhaps he himself had damned her. She had tried to please him, had tried to dress her son in the right way, and it was all for naught.

He would try to politely excuse himself from her life—it was immoral to have *tricked* her. He had felt such pity because he believed she was someone else. He believed she was like the woman he once loved who had died at nineteen. On the first meeting with his uncles she wore a red hat with a black sash, held by a diamond pin, a tight skirt that hugged below her knees and red high heels. He had asked her not to, but she adorned herself with the pearl necklace he had bought her on a trip to Montreal. It was her insecurity to fashion herself a model, to suddenly be wise.

Her perfume shone in the air, actually above her red hair, and she was ready for them, she said, she said she was ready for them.

"What do you mean?"

"Ha—wait and see." And she smashed her cigarette beneath her toe, and smoothed her tight skirt.

He began to ignore her. Some days she would follow behind him all day long, as if she thought he wanted her there, or as if she must do so to please him. He laid the upstairs floor of his library himself, and built the bookshelves for his many books. The snow began to fall silently against the windows.

She watched him work. Everything in the house that she brought in seemed—no, not seemed, but *was* garish. She tried to include him by these measures, she wanted him included. Hopefully she would stand near some object, or some new thing she wore, awaiting a compliment.

But then all this stopped, and she became devoted to her friends, her own car, her games of nigh time bingo, her hiring maids for the boy and rushing back to the land beyond Arron Brook, where her family was—all squabbling over five acres of land and a small beach hut. She would come back to tell him that "they are not going to pull nothing over on me!"

He tried to have humour about this, make jokes about that hut, but she remained terribly silent when he did.

Then one night suddenly, her eyes followed him with a kind of disdain. Wherever he moved those eyes were upon him. She did not speak, and he did not. They were in the library and he was filing his books on the American Civil War. He was putting soldiers along the line for Pickett's Charge on a topographical map he himself had constructed. Every time he paused to see where he should put a man, a horse, a cannon, she was staring at him. Amused, as if she understood.

"Pickett's Charge," he said, "July third, in Pennsylvania, third day of the Battle of Gettysburg—Vicksburg fell in the west on July fourth. Though the Confederacy hung on, the war was lost."

But she did not speak.

"I am sorry the Confederacy fell. You see, it is not about slavery for me—I know it should be—I am sorry it is not—but Lee, and of course Stonewall Jackson, who never lived to see Gettysburg— anyway, I think of how they fought so hard, with so little to fight with. Jeb Stuart—you—see—of course Albert—I know I agree

with him about it all—war, I do—but—I was at Dien Bien Phu."
Then he looked down at his battlefield.

He said nothing else, fumbled like a child with the soldier in
his right hand. She shrugged. He might have been talking of the
crusades, for all she knew. She did not understand why he apolo-
gized for caring about someone named Lee. She looked at him in
expectation that he would inform her. But he did not. She did not
understand he was talking about an honour greater than her own
or even his own—an honour that people must have, dignified,
and in the midst of tragic events, honourable. Where Churchill
stood against the Munich Accord.

He was telling her in fact why she and he had failed, and worse
they had both failed her son—their son.

Then he asked: "Who was that fellow—over at the Legion—
that you danced with—you held his hand and walked back to the
table with?" He said it almost apologetically.

He looked at her but she was silent at first.

"Oh I don't know," she said. "I don't remember."

Of course she lied.

He realized that he had tricked her—that the grand ignorance
in her life was left humiliated by what he had done in his life, and
so the man who thought of his books as nothing, and wouldn't
know of Gettysburg, was much better for her.

Those were the boys she was comfortable with. They had no
ambition to know the world, and expected none from others.
She danced and flirted with them to prove that his life was *not
the only life*. But now with Pickett's Charge in mind he was telling her about honour and decency in the midst of chaos and
she had no understanding. And perhaps in his anguish neither
did he.

One day as was mentioned she said something spiteful to him, and he grabbed and struck her. It was as if five years had been bottled up.

Then he fled the room and sat in the library for hours looking at Lee on Traveller. He wrote her an apology and mailed it to his own house.

"Do you want me to take my Albert and leave?" she asked.

"I don't know," he said, "I don't know——"

"Well then, if you do, the money I get and the people I tell won't be small."

"No——why——of course not. I am sorry," he said as if coming out of some terrible reverie. At that moment, one might realize it was never only her that was being tormented, it was him. Yet the world, the grave and stupidly obedient world, would not see what he saw.

Oh, but he knew she was being tormented as well.

Then the greater change came.

He sent her away to school, because she wanted to go. She went to college. And for seven months he kept the child. Or had a home nurse do so.

It was then, when she came home, that she tried to engage him in conversation, but he was appalled by it. He was appalled by what she had thought she had learned. Why? Because during his life he had been wrestling with ideas and now she came home with what he had years ago hated, or at the very least felt was affected and wrong. She had learned not who to admire but who to blame. Her professors told her she could now blame. There was nothing better than to disparage novels one could never write and then throw up one's hands before lighting one's pipe and heading into the snow. And she came home with this attitude for him to cherish.

She stroked his hair one night, speaking to him about these ideas, about who the world must get back at, and he said:

"For God sakes, woman, leave it be—please leave it be!"

She looked at his face, jumped up and ran from the room. She had learned that women had played no part in the world, and suffered, and she had added that to her arsenal against him.

So the years passed away. And she told Albert time and again who to blame.

And he became more and more lonely and more and more worried and more and more filled with angst about his uncles.

Byron had no idea about his stepson—what he did or did not do—until leaving the bar one night he saw that his son's name and picture were in the paper, standing upon a cement wall with a microphone challenging the forces of the world, with students gathered around him, wearing army vests with peace slogans, the urban warriors from rural New Brunswick.

He picked up the paper and took it home. And snow was falling on the grey streets. He had a bottle hidden in his coat—his doctor had told him to stop drinking.

He read in the paper that his stepson had become involved with the radical physicist Professor Dykes at the university, and became a spokesperson for him and made pronouncements about people in government, blaming those like former premier Bell. That they had removed books from the shelves of the university library and left them all over the halls and on the floors of the foyer to protest against *capitalistic* regulations. That is, Albert did not want to destroy the books; he wanted books to be free of the restriction of having to produce a library card. The old librarian, Miss Farmer, bent like a pretzel and grey as the back of a seal, was left to separate these books and carry them back to the shelves, under the shining library lights.

His wife told him when he complained that she agreed. He, Byron, was old-fashioned. Yes, things must change. That certain people were to be blamed.

He asked her who.

She smiled and then coyly mentioned his uncles. Then she looked up and whispered: "Albert knows it too."

Suddenly it became clearer. She had been living a life, another trajectory, and now *he* must know. All this time, from the moment she sat in his study and watched him place the cannonades on the battlefield, she had been silently striving for another method with which to crumble those soldiers.

She had become aware that she could overleap his learning with simple correct politics. And now Professor Dykes was it. That is, knowledge of the Peloponnesian War did not matter if you had someone near you saying war was useless.

Perhaps he had forced her into this horrid mimicry by having hurt her in some way.

"He will protest the books not being available without proof of identity now," Byron said, "but in twenty years he will want to remove and burn them in the street."

As time passed he shuffled about the town in a grey overcoat, with a three-day growth of beard. Of course if anyone said anything, a word about his wife, he would jump to her defence in a second, fistfights followed him and he landed in jail, a new jacket and a white shirt smattered with blood.

On one obscure night there was some kind of a terrible scene between him and Professor Dykes. Dykes, head down, coat over his arm, smiled as he left. Byron said he didn't want him to hang about his son any more. He said, "He is my son," and tears came to his eyes.

He weaved back and forth as he spoke, then became irritated and began to shout.

And young Albert tried to be a peacemaker—but finally stood and pushed his father back, with his chubby hands.

Carmel said Byron had waved his antique pistol at Dykes and her. He did wave it, at Dykes, but perhaps not at her.

But of course he didn't remember. He only remembered Dykes's smile.

The police confiscated his antique pistol, and it was impounded for months.

The pistol, a very rare and expensive antique, was returned in a small black velvet box, with five bullets kept in a side pocket of red sash.

He kept it in his closet for some months. One night he put one of those bullets in it and spun the cylinder, put it to his forehead, closed his eyes, and at the last second decided not to pull the trigger.

When he opened it he discovered the bullet was in fact inside the chamber. He looked at the bullet, and saw its lead head, its brass shell case with the tiny scratch across it, and shivered.

Best then to get rid of it.

He traded this ancient .45-calibre pistol for a salmon pool up along Arron Brook and went there in May and stayed through August. That was when he informed her of her money and his stipulation for his son's trust fund.

"You will have quite a bit—but please handle it all with care."

Then one day the doctor told Byron that he had only months to live. That his liver was gone. Not wanting to bother people, he told neither his stepson nor his wife this. He stared at the doctor's reddish knuckles, and the sun outside casting over those knuckles, and the smooth, almost too smoothly shaved face.

The doctor told him he had never in his life drunk—had had a glass of carrot juice every morning and evening, and went for bicycle trips in the summer.

Byron smiled, and went out along the cold spring street and into the bar.

Time came, time went, time passed away.

7

RASKIN'S ACCOUNTANT WILLIAM BELL CAME ONE DAY TO their house in the late sixties to let Carmel and Albert know about their husband and father. It was the first time he had seen Albert in years, and saw a pale fat young man, his blond hair falling limp over the front of his face, with a face half-covered in acne.

He had taken courses, was a socialist of some kind, and seemed now to hate everything to do with his uncle's business.

He spoke about the business like a boy trying to secure things for his mother, without knowing a thing about the business he spoke of.

Bell told him politely that all things were being taken care of.

"Yes, but as I say," he said, glancing at his mother as if in private conference, and then back at Bell, "I want assurances that I— Well, that my mother will not be left out in the cold. I am not worried about myself—but about my mother." He swiped at his hair to move it away from his blue eyes, and he had a ring on one of his short fingers, and he seemed self-conscious of how he looked.

Bell did not know the boy would fail. However, that is what he had heard from Oscar Peterson who read the tarot cards and said he had read one night to this boy.

"Oh yes, I saw it when he was young but I did not tell him. I am not like that. But if he doesn't do something to change his ways, things will get tough for him—and others. I am afraid what others just might be involved."

Bell was not prone to superstition, but now suddenly he thought of what half-mad Oscar had said.

Bell tried his level best to be polite. He realized that they both thought they were being conspired against and sat together fending off such conspiracies that never were. And he realized the boy had no real ability to fend much off.

"We are sure to lose the house," Carmel said. "They will put me out on the street."

"Nothing of the sort will happen," he assured them.

But the boy said his mother had faced enough hardship not to trust anyone. And that he was compelled to take his mother's side. Then he told his mother not to say any more.

Bell shuddered for some reason as he thought of all of this later, at this youngster determined to make an impression. Where would it all lead?

"He won't tell you this but he is dying." Bell told them about Byron Raskin.

Neither of them seemed to know for a moment how to respond. This was unimaginable to them, and they felt with him gone— they might be cut off completely.

"Oh I'm sure he will be fine," Carmel said.

"My mother has suffered a long time, and she loved her husband," Albert said, and produced papers for him to take back to the uncles. "So please give these to my uncles. I feel they are tired of us."

"Not in the least—not even a little bit."

———

Byron drank in the bars, and was in and out of the hospital. Two times, then three, then four.

When they put him in he would sign himself out. Once he was seen in his pyjamas in the lineup at the liquor store. One night in a johnny shirt down at the bar, after having been taken to the hospital in an ambulance two hours before.

Then he decided to rent a room above the bar so he could come and go in peace.

He often wandered back to the room with a bottle of gin. It is hard to imagine what life he had wanted for her and the child and what life became. It is harder to imagine how many times more he loved them than any of those who accused him of not loving. In fact he loved the boy deeply, but the boy felt he wasn't loved.

I suppose grand writers can take care of that discrepancy, though I do not know of many so brave.

Albert struggled in school, and to prove to himself and others, wrote a long essay on the struggles of those working for Greenpeace, and Penelope—a girl he liked who had been committed to an institution, and who he visited he said, with simple affection and chocolates, even though she didn't speak to him, and wouldn't see him.

He also ended this essay, which wasn't unusual for the time, by saying how innocent the drug culture was. It was published in *October Review*, a little underground paper at the university.

Many were envious of him too because he had his choice not of one, but of three cars and had a new Fender guitar that he hardly played. For a time he had his own half-hour program on the radio where he would invite people living on the street to come in and express themselves. He was a counsellor and a crusader—a person who was concerned about young people, and their mental health—especially those who wished to flee the oppressive dictates of family life. He certainly understood that and spoke often about people's mental health during these times. Young women's mental health especially. He seemed to be a young role model—a real voice for us, as certain young people said.

He became influential and worked for a while at the drug crisis centre housed in a little building on a side street in town. People began to know him, and he began to have meetings held late at night.

There were debates in the drug crisis centre where he wore an old army jacket and like others spoke to people about a variety of hash and acid and how one should take acid so their trip wouldn't be bad.

The drug centre was a small room, with a few chairs, two cots, a coffee machine and pamphlets on a variety of drugs and what they did to the psyche.

It took on the aura of grave professionalism that it wasn't and pretended needed knowledge that only rebellious experience could share. That is there was a constant concern over things one didn't have to be concerned about five years previous but now seemed to be the main emblem of the day. The idea of Aleister Crowley's maxim that *one should so do what one wilt* had suddenly come to life within him. For he had read Crowley and insisted he was a prophet. And he felt very special in being on the cutting edge of the new and impious world, of being a mental health advocate and a counsellor of sorts.

They also, because they were free, made light of all people who were not exactly like themselves and didn't smoke hash. They spoke about Frosh Week, and how young girls would be arriving from all over the country. "The best thing to do is relieve them—release them from their parents."

And then one night a person arrived in the dark rain and stood just inside the door of the drug crisis centre saying he had some mescaline. This man was Shane Stroud, and the person who got up to invite him in was Albert Raskin, dressed in a new jacket, with a new wristband. Shane Stroud looked at all of them with rather mischievous black eyes, and took out a chunk of hash. Albert was suddenly drawn to him; almost like a magnet both of them came together. It was as if suddenly they were the best of friends.

Albert was driven to do something dramatic, to release himself from the opinion of others. And he liked how they were amazed by the deferential way Shane, who terrified others, whose reputation as a cutthroat was known, treated him.

"I even heard you on the radio," Shane said. "Talking—you were even on the radio!!" He seemed amazed. Albert Raskin seemed amazed as well.

One evening a few nights later, with the lights in the tavern ebbed low, the small pinball machine reflecting those lights in its shining glass, the outside bathed in spots of comfort, the windows yellowish in the coming dark, a small round man dressed in very new clothes brought a number of files for his father to look at. His father was sitting on the chair in his room at the hotel, with the window opened to the street and the sound of cars humming along the square. One must realize that these hotels are situated over taverns and are available for short-term or long-term rent, and are seen in every town and city in Canada. This one was now Byron's home. The small round young man was doing this for his mentor, Professor Dykes. Dykes believed a community of concerned activists should take over Raskin Enterprises. Albert was sent to his father.

Albert had plotted all day what he would say and how he would say it. His stepfather sat forward pouring one glass of gin and then another.

He listened. He realized it was his stepson's attempt to show Raskin Enterprises how things could be done for the new generation. Of course Byron had already heard of these demands because his uncles had told him about them. They had themselves received them from Mr. Bell.

"Can't imagine demands like that," Dexter said.

"They are awful demanding—awful demanding demands," Chester said.

"Never saw such demands," Dexter added.

So Byron knew of them some time before. Demands to immediately close everything down, and have a new oversight committee set up directed by university students. But it didn't come really from Albert. It came, this ultimatum, from Dykes himself. Dykes whom Byron detested.

His father focused his blue eyes upon him—almost china blue in their blueness. "No, that cannot be done, son—without putting two hundred men out of work and cutting off the oil supply to almost four hundred families.

"I know it is not much, but scholarships are set up for the Indian girls and boys. I know much more could be done. Still, others talk much more and do far less. One is that imposter Dykes."

When he finished speaking he picked up the gin glass and cupped it in his hand. He smiled consciously, conscious of having hurt his son's feelings. At this moment he felt he had done a grave disservice to all mankind. He saw his stepson withdraw from what he said, his white hands, which had never done a day's manual labour, shaking. His face dabbed with alcohol because of acne, and worried about having to report back to Dykes and upset about his mother.

"Your great-uncles are old. They have done what they have done. I do not know what to say anymore on their behalf except, beyond all of it, they are decent human beings. Conquer yourself. Do not bother the dying business of two elderly men."

A year or so more passed. Young Raskin went to Europe for a month, and then to Los Angeles and San Francisco for a while. He toured the north, and travelled part way on an ice-breaker. There was a picture of him with his beard frozen. He wrote articles in the paper about his trip—about how well he understood the Inuit, and how he had taken pictures of a polar bear. He was published not because these articles were so phenomenal but because he was Albert Raskin.

Young man says we should all live off the land and do no digging underneath it.

Things went on. There were trips to the cottage, and young Raskin breaking off with a young woman who liked him. Then he tried to get her back, and Carmel realized it was she who had broken off with her son.

Her note which Carmel found in his jean pocket said:

"I can't pretend you have not disappointed me—and maybe you have disappointed yourself. No—I am not square. I understand things in life too. I am however not sure of how much you understand. Realize you will never find another woman who cares for you, and not your money—and I was the one.

"When Professor Dykes insulted me for being nothing but a middle-class white woman, you sat there and did not open your mouth—nothing proved to me more what I wanted to know less. Goodbye young Raskin—my sad little Albert—I don't know where you are going—but I fear you have already lost your way. You were given so much, so soon, for so little it will be a great struggle in the end."

He sat much alone when in town, and what he did near Arron Brook Mrs. Raskin did not know. His stutter lessened with time, and his philosophy became more bold. Small, heavy, his face pitted because of acne, he wanted to make some impression.

And then an article was written about him because he was noticed at the first protest against some effluents into the river by Raskin Enterprises. It was a cold day, the brooks very frozen, the river sluggish, and he walked about giving out hot chocolate. A young teenaged boy watched them from the edge of his property—his name was Torrent Peterson.

"He is very reflective," one of Mrs. Raskin's friends said to her.

"My son is for revolution," Carmel said. "He has a universal mind. You should hear him speak such startling, broadminded things."

"The Raskins were mostly insane—best to ignore them," some modern priest was known to have told Carmel.

Even though she did not believe in Christ anymore, she believed in gossip, and in the new priesthood, which seemed to transplant Christ as well.

Or, one might say, she believed in Christ as long as Christ believed in her.

Then:

"You will see what kind of party I will have," Raskin told his mother one night. "I know how those poets and others look at me when they come here. My party—well, let me tell you, I have been in touch with people—real honest-to-God people that would make all those guys turn pale! You and I will show them who they're dealing with."

She had no idea what he was speaking about.

She would.

8

THEY HAD THE PARTY; THERE WERE LIGHTS STRUNG AND flowers strewn across the gazebo and into the large green-house, where lights shone dimly over the many flowers and shrubs. They rallied for social change. It was not out of the ordinary to do so then. It is certainly not out of the ordinary to do so now.

Albert had spent the day hanging pictures of Jimi Hendrix and Trotsky above the patio, and he had managed to get some good hash and marijuana. He went from one group to another laughing and talking about the United States, and how their empire was doomed. It all seemed very radical to some of the frosh girls.

Dykes who had come, walked to a certain chair in the centre of the garden and sat, now and again nodding, now and again scowling, and seeming quite imposing to the youngsters who arrived. A young woman with many beads around her neck was his companion.

The editor of *Floorboards*—a man who already going bald and with a thin goatee looked ten years older than he was—was convincing students a new world was approaching, and the poetry of Wordsworth and Tennyson, the work of Keats and Browning, would soon be destroyed. It had to be—it meant nothing, compared to the poetry today. It meant nothing in the new revolution. It meant nothing to the youth who had evolved. He quoted one of his illusive poems:

"I destroy the earth
For what it's worth
And reclaim it in rebirth."

"Destroy it all—destroy everything," Albert said, passing by with a bowl of punch. "Destroy and reclaim, reclaim and destroy—destroy and fight back."

He had no idea why he was saying what he was saying—it all was simply the thing to say because everyone else seemed to be saying it too.

"Bring out the guitars," he yelled.

It was now getting quite dark in the large back yard. A luxurious warm darkness hung in the clouds. The luxurious smell of hash lingered here and there amid the dancing girls and boys.

He had at this moment a great expansiveness as he gestured in his flowered shirt, and putting the punchbowl down went into the dark toward the gate. Hair fell in front of his eyes, that he kept brushing away, as he wandered toward this gate, thinking of his lost girlfriend, the one who had written him the letter of warning. Why at this time he thought of her, and her square jaw and rather masculine face, but a face with deep honesty, he did not know. It was in fact thinking of her that caused him to turn and go in the other direction.

He had not intended to go toward the gate, he had intended to go back toward the hothouse—why (he thought in future years, why oh why a thousand times, over those years when as Bell predicted he would become more decrepit, his face filled with the result of sin) did he go toward the gate? He was also sure he felt he must do something very brave very soon. He had lied to people—the lies innocent enough—but enough lies about himself that he must now act out in some way.

He wanted people to know who he was. Why? Because they had laughed at him, at his speech, at his weight and seemingly at almost everything else. And he felt as so many young do, that he was better than they were.

At that moment a young girl walked in through the gate timidly and started toward him. She smiled at him, and he turned toward her and smiled as well—as if it had all been planned somehow, somewhere before. This was the test for this short, somewhat overweight fellow. It would take an eternity to understand that eternity mattered in this moment. The poem about destroying the earth, for what it was worth, still flickered in his mind.

He turned almost in slow motion and Shane Stroud was looking at him with meanly happy and quite clever eyes.

"Ha," Shane said, "I got it for you—"

And he held out his hand.

In the farther dark he saw a glimpse of his mother swishing her dress.

A moment or two passed—yes, just a moment or two. The girl smiled up at him, as if he was her friend.

"Yes, destroy it," Carmel yelled, looking around eagerly. But she was suddenly frightened because someone had pushed her aside when they were going for a beer; her husband had just been taken to the hospital again, and the wind had come up over the hedges and seemed to blow a warning about her husband back and forth in the trees themselves. She had been drinking and had a puff or two of hash, and saw her reflection suddenly in the hothouse glass. She shut her eyes and darkness surrounded her, with a warning.

It was in the dark as if whispering to her that she was in fact losing a great man, and his achievement towered over the people she and her little son wanted to impress. She only heard it for a slight second, but this was to become clear later in the evening.

Until that time, truth be told, she had never read a poem by Keats. Nor cared to. Or by anyone except Bliss Carman. She created a great deal of excitement by talking loudly about feelings, and sincerity. She wandered here and there about the grounds, wearing a laurel of picked flowers and a long flowered dress. Her necklace glittered under the lights, and there were shouts everywhere by people arriving through the backyard gate that they had broken down. There was a scream and a cry, and someone said someone had hit someone else—or so it seemed. Many people were arriving she did not know.

Then there was a darkness. It crept over the hilarious faces of the guests, and there was a conspiracy to do something very bold. Within the next hour things started to happen that she hadn't at all expected. One boy and girl rolled on the ground in front of her, the girl's blouse being taken off.

Now bewildered she wandered away, but where she wandered, in the dark part of the yard, someone approached her. He was wearing a cut-off sweater, and a wallet with a chain, and black motorcycle boots. He began to dance all around her—and it was as if she was compelled by his sudden dancing to dance too.

He hugged her—and suddenly she was in the arms of a stranger, a strange man. He put his tongue in her mouth, and she let him; he put his hand under her dress and under her bra cup. He held her close, so she couldn't breathe.

Then he put his face close to hers and whispered a terrible profanity in her ear.

Carmel broke free and ran upstairs, locked the door, sat on a chair and looked out the window. She became confused, and more and more the woman was becoming confused, about books and politics and some kinds of philosophy her son kept talking about. She was no longer the vivacious, hard-nosed lady of years past.

All these ideas, all this spontaneous understanding, had left her sad and perplexed. She stared down at the young people hoping they would go away. But they didn't go away for almost another four hours. In fact the yelling and laughing continued, as if all of them were falling through the cracks of a terrified, horrified mimicry. Oh of course it was fine, if you didn't mind—she wondered what it was she was looking at. And then the motorcycles arrived, people from across the province, two different motorcycle groups who had heard of this party at this grand house, and another fight started.

And after a while, it seemed the dancing and cavorting in front of the fire in the large pit looked like somewhere in hell. She realized she was in her fifties and doing what a teenager might do, and felt a cataclysm over her spirit. She saw Dykes and the man from *Floorboards* magazine quickly leave in fear—and others follow in fear as well, heading back to the university where the idea of revolution was always safe—so the yard was emptying of all but hard-drinking people she did not know. People Shane Stroud had taken the liberty to invite.

It seemed to say, *This is what you wanted.*

The students too were going home—and she was frightened like a little girl. Then a motorcycle drove right through the patio and a side window got smashed. Everyone was yelling and laughing. And then someone had cut his head and there was blood on a lawn chair.

She wanted to phone her husband, tell him to come and stop this, but the phone was in the upstairs hallway, and that strange odious man named Shane Stroud she had flirted with was lurking there. She felt for her necklace and was relieved it was still about her neck. Then she realized something very important: she had never been disrespected when her husband was with her—that was, at this moment, her actual agony. The man in the hall kept whispering that word through the door.

"Let me in, you"—then that word—"let me in."

But that was not what was bad. She had heard that word before—had used it when she herself was a girl. What was bad was—the poor girl later that she noticed, yes—that poor naked child.

Afterwards the lawn and the trees about the house were empty, the silence in midday entered a state of ennui and all things that had transpired seemed pitiless and mean. Mrs. Raskin now undressed and hid in her room. She thought the party would be filled with talk, and politics, but it had slipped those bounds very early. She thought she would be commended by everyone, about her suddenly new and brilliant mind, and everyone would glorify her in some brilliant way—that too did not happen. Dykes had run—away.

She telephoned people to ask if they had heard the noise, and was it true police had patrolled because people had reported a disturbance and the bikers from Maine were rounded up by the police?

Albert hid in the basement for a few days, and never answered the phone, and ate only ketchup sandwiches and drank warm pop.

Then the police left a card saying: *"At your earliest convenience, please contact Constable Donaldson."*

The very name seemed to wave in the trees, the heavy sky bloated by a coming storm, when he read it.

"What had happened?" he kept asking. "Dear oh dear—what had happened with that little girl and me? It was just a joke. Why did Shane come—I only met him once in my life and he shows up. Why did he hand me *it*—how was it that he was just right there and handed me *it!* At that very moment the girl entered through the gate—walked toward me—and if I had been anywhere else she would not have seen me or me her—and yet, it was all *pre-ordained*. I was not even thinking of going to the gate—"

And the answer came as a sudden emotion.

Shane showed up because you wanted to prove yourself to these friends—and to him. He came because you wanted to introduce your mother to him, you wanted to shock people. Mel and Shane will never go anywhere they aren't invited. You invited him to bring the drugs. You loved all the excitement—how people always need to notice you—how you spill yourself in all directions so everyone will say, There he is—there he is, he's— Well there you were! You don't know answers to the problems of the world, you just shout that you do. You don't know anything about your uncles, you just imply that you know.

These were the sensations—not the actual words but the sensations of shame and worry—he had about himself.

But there was something else in all of it. The idea that in order to change society he wanted to destroy himself, in fact he rushed headlong into destruction that very night, and now that it had happened there was no way to go back. In a way he had this night destroyed himself—and he would spend the rest of his life trying to put himself back. He didn't want to—but he had.

Did he attempt to have sex with that young girl when she was terrified and begging him not to?

And the answer came:

Yes. Yes—but it was a joke—it was all supposed to be—a joke.

She had been hiding from the bikers in the hothouse—behind a plant in the corner, shaking.

This is what he thought during the first day—the first morning he himself hid in the basement, shaking and spiting and trying to hide even from himself. Yes, he had wet his pants, that's why he took them off, he could tell people, yes, I wet my pants, that's why

I took them off—but hadn't meant to. Oh—it was all bad! The night had turned very bad. Who were those two rolling about in the dirt—who was it defecating on his favourite lawn chair—and yes, who stole the tools from the back garage—almost a thousand dollars' worth—no, he couldn't go to the police—he couldn't. He didn't even know what tools were really.

So he hid.

He remembered his mother running upstairs in her flowered dress, the flowered laurel coming off her red hair, and closing her bedroom door. He remembered Shane having kissed her on the mouth in the far section near the hothouse. He wanted to stop it all but he froze. At that moment, he realized that she was puzzled. There was blood and a smashed bottle and Shane had left and gone upstairs to see where she was. He had kept whispering things at her through the door.

Then coming down in the night air he punched the first boy he saw, pulled his knife and told people not to bother him. From her bedroom window poor Carmel witnessed all of it. All the shouting—the damage done to the flowerbeds and the side windows.

But that was not the worst.

At first, when he woke groggily at noon the next day, he did not remember anything, but then when he sat up on the edge of the bed, he did. Little sickly flashes of insight became clearer and clearer—little sickly moments presented themselves to him like explosions inside his head.

A young girl. Seventeen years of age. Cute. With a frosh hat. Nice dress. Happy face—where did he see her first?

He did not go see Constable Donaldson. Her name seemed ominous. And when the constable came, and knocked on the side door two days later, it was raining, and big drops fell from the shingled roof. He went to the door, and when Constable Donaldson, her cap enclosed in a rain cover, her eyes bright and merry, and a .38-calibre on her thick black belt, asked if he saw anything of this girl—showing him a graduation picture of one Annie Howl—he said:

"Man oh man, I don't know," scratching the side of his chin and looking at it, with his hair in braids which seemed to make his eyes very blue. "We had a little party—but people dropped in and out—and some only stayed a minute or two—I don't remember her." He gave a short defensive apologetic laugh.

"I see. Well, we are checking because she was here and there the other night—it was Frosh Week and she was out doing a pledge of some kind." Donaldson smiled at him, still—but when he caught them, her eyes narrowed just ever, ever so slightly, but her smile remained, and he realized it was not really as much a smile as a *portent*, a slight warning. He only knew he had seen her somewhere before—but where?

He flushed and blushed. Yes, she might have recognized him.

"You do know who I am?" he asked.

She stared at him, with no expression at all. Then looked down at her notes, made a mark and looked up again.

"No drugs of any kind?" she asked quickly, and just as her eyes had narrowed so now her smile disappeared, then returned just a bit, and he noticed when he looked down her flat black boots, that were issued to her by the department after her training, telling everyone that her life had become the life of officialdom, of preparation for service and of service. He noticed her soft blond hair just at the top of her forehead and again, at the side of her ears, telling one something of her teenaged years, recently passed, and this startled him. The black belt where her holster was positioned was buckled around her police jacket, and that jacket was buttoned to her chin. For some reason the .38 revolver, the handle of which he could just make out, showed her freshmanship. The rain kept falling, and behind her, in the driveway near the trees, her squad car sat. She had come on a mission. He could refuse this mission, her request to answer, but her standing before him was still evidence of the seriousness of her undertaking. This is now what her smile said.

"No, my mother was here," he said. "We just had a get-together—talked poetry and such. Talked about the changing world. Or I mean we talked about how the world should change." Then he heightened his speculation. "And if it did, you might not be needed." He looked reflective as the rain fell.

"Might I speak to your *mother*?"

He knew then he had made a mistake—her expression said she did not believe him, or care for his lapse into philosophy. He thought he would impress her, but he had only shown his youth—and she had recognized it instantly as veneer, even if younger than him—which made her expression so deflating to him when he saw in it a slight fascination with his own ingenuousness. This all passed between them in a second.

"Ah," he said. "What is it? Might I ask why?"

"Might I speak with your mother?" she said. Now the smile decreased but remained visible, and it unnerved him. He went and got his mother, and Carmel came to the door in her nightgown and housecoat. She began talking before she reached the dinette, her knobby knees hitting together, and came through to the door waving a cigarette. She was suddenly scared. She remembered Shane having pulled a knife. Her flimsy voice seemed to comple-ment her reddish hair, and her face had splotches because of the tanning light she had spent time under, and her red lipstick was the first thing one noticed.

Then Albert unexpectedly with much more force realized who this Becky Donaldson was. She was the young girl at her sister

Joanie's graduation party they had extravagantly crashed some
years before. He remembered she and little Clara Bell had tried to
stop them. He realized that was where he had seen her before,
trying to protect her older sister Joanie who had sent out all the
invitations. He also remembered something undefined, the force
of her personality that night when she was still hardly a teenager.
The sordid little scene of crashing a party and concocting mayhem
had in fact been relieved by *her*.

He looked at her, startled by this, and it was as if she knew why
he was startled. Suddenly, subtly, there was a different measure
between them. She handed his mother Annie Howl's graduation
picture.

The girl's graduation picture is all they had, her long hair in
a flip, with the cap jauntily to one side, the eyes a little narrow,
and the smile mischievous—as if to complement the narrowing of
the eyes. His mother looked at it.

"No," she said, handing the picture back, "she is not a relative
of ours." She said it rather flippantly, a little disrespectfully.
This was noted by the voice lisping out into the sound of the
rain, the drops falling off the shingles and onto Constable
Donaldson's hat. A dull, dismissive quality she sometimes had,
even at times unconscious.

"I know," Constable Donaldson said, "she is not. She is Annie
Howl. I played softball with her when we were in high school."

"Well, whatever happened to her?" his mother asked, with a
level of insincerity, which now seemed a condition of the universal-
minded.

"Oh God, I wouldn't read Tolstoy" she remembered she had
said at one point that night, not knowing who Tolstoy was—
perhaps a professor somewhere, but overhearing the editor of
Floorboards speak about "old-fashioned writers like Tolstoy."

"We don't know exactly what happened to her, ma'am—she fell from the Anderson Bridge. We are unsure what was going on with her—we are trying to find out. Last week she was a bright happy young woman. What happened? We tracked her back along the avenue—she was found a couple of mornings ago, without her clothes. Yesterday she fell from the Anderson Bridge."

They stood for a moment in silence. His mother looked at him as if he might have an explanation.

Albert didn't know who to look at or where to put his hands, because they seemed to him to be shaking.

"Was she here?" Carmel asked.

"I doubt it very much," he said. "Is she all right?"

"No."

"No?" his mother asked.

"She is dead," Constable Donaldson said matter of course, and she took the picture out of his mother's hand and put it back into a small leather folder with her notebook. "Thank you—this is the only picture I have, and I need to see other people."

As for Albert's stepfather, Byron was as tough as nails, had been on missions in the Second World War, had fought hand-to-hand combat, but the world had gone beyond him and he was confused. Whatever he had done and loved was now over. He planned to talk to Albert to cure him of *all of this*—before it was too late. But he was unsure of what it was.

He had dreams where he saw Albert in trouble and could not protect him. He saw that all of this was a way to one portico only—and led to sin. Perhaps it was because he was now alone, and reflected upon too many things.

"They are not like me," he had said to William Bell years before. "They are of this world, and I am not of this world." What he meant by that he wasn't quite sure. He was no less flawed than they were—but perhaps he had different flaws.

It was something that Bell had finally noticed when he was at the house.

Byron had heard about the party—even the fact that Shane Stroud had kissed his wife. The sense of betrayal was so acute it was like being burned by a stove—but it was no worse than listening to her mock him, which she had done one evening in front of a whole table of dinner guests celebrating their anniversary.

It was terrible but he was frightened to know what had actually happened, especially with his wife. Then the girl—what had happened to her?

When he asked his stepson, who finally visited him in the hospital, about this party, his stepson answered, "Oh it was nothing—some people had a little too much—but it was nothing."

"A girl went missing," Byron whispered. "Was she at the party—was wandering around the street with her nose painted and naked—everyone was concerned—she had been given drugs—yes—her parents, the poor country bumpkins that they were, wouldn't expect to see her running about with her nose painted red, stark naked, three days after she got to university."

"Where did you hear that?"

Byron stopped speaking.

"No, Dad. No—she wasn't even there," he said defensively. "She wasn't—I never saw her there—and neither did Mom."

"You promise me she wasn't at our house—at our house?"

"Nooo!" Albert said. "She wasn't. She was acting out all night— but it was at another party—people told me she was taking a lot of drugs. Things are different, Dad—thinking is different."

"Nothing is different ever under the sun," Byron said.

"Well how many times do I have to tell you she wasn't? I will go to her parents and talk to them, if you wish."

"I had a vision of it." He tried to take Albert's hand.

"A vision—"

"Well, a dream—"

Byron told him he had dreamed in a state of semi-consciousness of a young girl's death. It was certainly scattered—people seemed to come in and out of his dream—

But as conservative and out of date as he was, Byron was right. This impetuous, seemingly innocuous incident would never leave their life. No matter what he might do in the years to come, no matter how well he seemed to have hidden it—there was the rumour, a rumour that opened another door to another world.

He had given the young girl the mescaline because Shane Stroud had handed it to him seconds before—showing up at the party—and in that moment of foolishness, it was as if it had all been premeditated.

At that exact moment young Annie Howl was standing in front of him. She was enthused and happy to be a frosh, to have been accepted to university. She wore a frosh beanie on her head.

"How are you, my little brown-eyed girl!" he said.

"I have a terrible headache," he remembered her saying, just as Shane put the mescaline in his hand.

Of course he was drunk, and not thinking of the consequences. (But you see, in a way he *was* thinking of the consequences and said to himself he was bold enough not to care what these consequences were—and now that he did care it was too late. He was mimicking all those he believed he wanted to be like.)

The girl wandered off, for a while she was laughing and someone painted her nose. But for now, Constable Donaldson filed her report and did not come back and the story seemed to ebb away.

"Nothing definitive as to where she was or what party she was at—spoke to twenty-two people—as yet no clear picture of how she came to be in such a state."

9

AT CERTAIN MOMENTS WITH HIS EYES LOOKING piercingly at you, Albert Raskin believed he could take on the world and you were just another person in the way. Whether that came from his mother or the Raskins themselves one wouldn't know. And so a few months passed by.

Then one night when his stepfather was sitting up in the hospital bed and lifting a glass of water to his sad, tough but remarkably kind face, and his stepson was asking about shares and his percentage of the "hole on Good Friday," Byron just smiled most tenderly and reached over to grab Albert's hand with his large, coarse one.

"I am sorry to have ever hurt you," he said. "Be good, be kind."

He dropped stone dead. He was fifty-five—the last two years of his life had taken its toll.

He a Canadian military expert, who had known Stephenson, *the man called Intrepid*, had become expendable to everyone without knowing why. His wife was a bit shattered over it. That is, even at the end she did not believe he would actually die.

Byron was buried in the little cemetery in Saint Peter and Paul, at the back, near the fence. He never wanted a marker. Chester and Dexter were there, deeply moved. Both had tears running down their faces.

Right at the graveyard Carmel went at them, calling them cheapskates, asking them for assurances, and tried to grab Dexter's arm.

Then she strode away, still speaking loudly, her arms folded as she walked into the sun with young Albert walking behind her.

It was a cold day. They went back to the house with the library his stepfather had built over the years, with the hothouse, the gazebo, the den with the fireplace, the huge downstairs apartment where Albert himself lived.

When he went to the room above the tavern that Byron had kept, he saw an enormous amount of books, old suits and work-boots, a pocket chess set, three bottles of beer and a bottle of gin—and a rosary. He held the rosary for a moment, looking at it. It felt very strange in his hand. It was years since he had held one. There was a small statuette of the Madonna on the desk by the bed. It was years since he had seen one. He picked it up, and looked at it.

"He was a good Catholic," the man said.

" I think he was a hypocrite."

"Yes, but aren't we all." The man said, quietly busying him-self, "Aren't those who see us pray, and call us hypocrites, worse hypocrites themselves?" Then he asked, "But do you know why he rarely went to church?"

"Why, he didn't go—No. Why?"

"Because the priests have become affected by the age, preten-tious *social workers*, and no longer follow the faith—and he derided what they had become. They were frightened to stand for Christ but using what Christ taught to anoint themselves. They had all become critics of the world instead of defenders of the faith. And they will go on being that way, and become more and more like the society they preach to."

"I can't believe that"

"Your father said most of the priests—and it would surprise you—are far closer philosophically to your professors. You see, I too was once a priest; your mother, though, disapproved of me. She is my younger sister. The priests have lost their way. So I left what has become lost, and I drink too much."

Albert was upset for two reasons—first, that anyone would consider him to be close to a priest philosophically (he had discovered he was not supposed to be); secondly, this man said he was his mother's brother, his uncle.

Now he was alone, and he had to try and protect his mother. He would protect her to the end—for in his life was her, and in her was his life.

"He treated my mother *shabbily*."

"Yes. He knew he did. That is why he left her with well over a million dollars or more and moved here. And do you know, she is telling everyone she was his wife, and holds his memory and his papers, and is now his great champion."

"My mother doesn't have a brother."

"Oh yes she does. The boy who carried her on his shoulders to school—the little girl who was frightened of bears."

But then Albert took the expensive watch that was sitting on a chair, handed it to the man. "You can have this," he said quietly. "I don't want it."

Albert left and thought: *My mother's brother—what is he doing there?*

He went home with the other remnants of his stepfather's life.

———

It became apparent that his stepfather was not at all forgotten, but something of a renowned person. It was amazing what they had not known about him.

His mother then felt she must do some interviews about him. Albert assisted her in this, and they were both interviewed for the paper.

She spoke of their life together very differently now, and as if she understood him perfectly. It startled Albert, and yet he followed her lead.

Her husband had left the mine at her insistence. Her husband had worked hard to convince his uncles of the effects their mine had on generations of people.

That night sitting in the greenhouse, near the white orchids his stepfather had grown, Albert remembered what his stepfather said, but he himself had never thought of sin. Still, he went to talk to Dykes about it, and the young woman Dykes had at the party.

To them, just as it was to him and most of the people he knew, it was relative and there was no real sin at all. In fact as far as Dykes was concerned there was only class struggle. Rid the world of a class struggle and the world would correct itself.

The girl laughed at Albert, in the whimsical way young women have who know so much more than you.

"Ha," she said, looking around the room, as if the question was, like marriage and family, outdated. So Albert became embarrassed and flustered.

Dykes asked him if he was serious. And lectured him about his uncles once again.

"Yes," Albert said, "I know too much about my uncles."

Dykes himself had come from a well-to-do family in Indiana who made auto parts; he often wore a diamond ring, and gold cufflinks. But Dykes told him there was only class struggle and religion held its part in the oppression. Then Dykes asked him again if he was serious:

"In this day and age?"

So he left, embarrassed by his even broaching the question.

The thing to hate, at least for Dykes, was the Catholic church. So many Americans who taught here hated it, in a sustained, very middle-class Protestant way. After two years with Dykes, Albert mocked and hated it as well.

The best way to hate it was to imagine nothing sacred about it, and laugh at its inanity. So Albert learned it was very beneficial to go along with this, and no harm would come by being irreverent and throwing up one's hands as if to slough it all off.

Albert knew one of the Raskins had been a priest and had lived with the Natives, worked healing and bandaging wounds, poled doctors though the water to places so women could be aided in giving birth. He was an elder cousin of the two elderly uncles. His mother once told him that one of the Goyas had been as well—some said a martyr for the faith who had died during the Great Fire of 1825 trying to rescue children. He was also known as a healer.

But when they talked of changing the world in Dykes's little circle, Albert was silent about these brave men, and was too intimidated by Dykes's genius to mention them. And so no one would ever be told of these things.

He told Dykes one night that he was his intellectual father, and he promised him he would faithfully work for revolution. Some kind of revolution that would befit the place they lived in.

"Whatever it takes," Dykes said, wearing his khaki jacket and his khaki pants, and his Hush Puppies with the black heels, and wearing a tie and a black armband in protest.

"Of course," Albert answered, wearing the almost identical

clothes of his master, that never quite fit his rotund frame. That is why he had once tried to hire a prostitute when he was young.

But then with his mother's interviews it became noticeable that Byron was looked upon much differently now he was gone. For some reason over the next months he heard stories of Byron and articles were written on him in the *Globe and Mail* and *Washington Post*. People who had dismissed him when he was alive said they had known him—he had spoken to them—he had confided in them.

So suddenly almost as if by osmosis he and his mother both assumed the traits of bereavement and family ties. It was not false, for they had not known the man they lived with, or didn't live with, until others began to tell them who he was.

Yes, he was suffering from shell shock and was a real hero. That he had held off a German advance in the hills of Italy, and rushed a tank single-handed.

Albert and his mom had never been aware of this, and were stunned by this sudden historical shift. So they shifted toward it, for they could not help it, and therefore became the spokespersons for his legacy. They held a benefit in his honour and with the help of Chester and Dexter created the Byron Raskin Memorial Scholarship at the university with a two-hundred-thousand-dollar largesse. Albert himself received commendations on his stepfather's behalf that came from the Minister of Defense and the Office of the Governor General.

They also spent money on Albert's elocution lessons to overcome his slight stutter. Because of this, he rarely stuttered anymore.

His voice was far more polished, and after a year and a half, he seemed cured of his youthful affliction. He was also quite surprised that Dykes, who wore a black armband in protest against the system, wanted some money from him, and asked for what he couldn't give and would appear at Carmel's house, walking now with a cane, and smiling benignly with new false teeth, as he complimented her on her universal mind, and speaking of all his years as a radical professor of physics.

But it wasn't his obvious and fidgeting way that upset the woman. She could fend him off easily.

It was a man Albert had forgotten about—a man named Shane Stroud.

Then a few years passed, where Albert's name was hardly mentioned on our river. The town council named Byron *person of the decade*. And Carmel was given a certificate in September. There is a picture of her, holding the citation and smiling with the mayor and members of the town council.

But then there was a notice in the paper that while in the States Albert had sided with the radical Weather Underground, and had spoken to them about the best way to create a new society, and had read a statement by Dykes to a group in Chicago.

There was another picture of him, more self possessed—a man certain that revolution had to have at least some kind of trust fund. Besides, there was a rumour that he had met people like Jesse Jackson at a rally, and spoke of the evolution of the working man. All of this while he took polo lessons in Virginia.

This seemed so esoteric for us, here at home in this backwater, that he had created something of a romanticized myth among some students. Many did not know who the Weather Underground was, or really care, but seemed very proud of him nonetheless.

"He is a new hero," one of the students wrote in the university paper.

Still, Mr. Bell among others read this with anticipation and alarm.

Albert came back on a cold night in November when it was snowing. The ground was hushed, the last of the feeble leaves had fallen down, and wind blew against him as he walked along the road. Hardly anyone knew who he was. He had changed—he looked older. But he was thin and his appeal had sharpened. His hair still was long and much straighter now. He still presented you with an aristocratic glance, as if to say you didn't really matter. Or that you mattered only in relation to himself. Dykes had instilled this in him as much as anyone, and he still carried all the remnants of those tired lessons of late-sixties revolution in his heart. To change the world, but more so to be noticed doing it.

He was hurrying toward the great cottage on the bay, with the old key to the side door in his pocket. His boots were high, almost to his knees, and tied at the top.

It was a very last-moment decision to come back. He had been offered a job elsewhere, and he would have been well off. It was a job as a mental health counsellor, dealing with wayward kids, the kind of a job he had once coveted.

But like so many of us who believe we are our own masters, something compelled him to come home, and at a moment of indecision he turned eastward in the night. He prided himself on his looks now. After two years away he was thinner, and stronger. Gone were the pudgy hands and the supposed indecision. Gone was his worry about Annie Howl running naked away from him. All that must be in the past.

He should have taken that other job. For there is probably so much that would never have happened if he had.

Oscar Peterson had read his son Torrent's tarot that same day. He had quickly panicked and put the cards away. That man who he had read to when he was fourteen had come back, in the dark and sleet on a cold night. He was much different, in that he was now an adult—a Raskin—and somehow he was dangerous to everyone.

"What is it," Torrent said.

"It is the night of the wedding," Oscar said. "It has come back, all of it along the road."

His readings were most often taken as a joke. But what he divined in the cards was that everything in his son Torrent's world would be terribly altered by a wealthy man walking along a road seeking shelter in the night.

Torrent's mother had helped serve the night of Ben Mott's wedding. She was a young unmarried woman named Mary Lou Toomey, pregnant with Torrent at the time. Ben Mott's bride was that night pregnant as well, with a girl who would be known as Eva Mott.

That was long ago, and an entire age had passed, so everyone could believe things were much different now. Those young wild boys, Shane and Mel Stroud, were grown men, and besides no one thought much about them anymore.

10

ONE DAY THE SUMMER AFTER HE HAD RETURNED, Albert met a man pushing a wheelchair along the side of the wharf where his sailboat was moored. The sky was blue, almost so blue as to cause sickness, and the seagulls above were like white billowing sails. They screamed at him overhead, and the islands far away were visible, and seemed closer, much closer than they actually were.

The man turned, looked at him a second, with a rather unsettling glance, and turned his wheelchair, that looked too heavy, and pushed it away. The look disturbed him, because he did not know why it was a scathing look, and then wondered if he had just imagined that.

Well, Albert thought, *he's not the only one who can give a scathing look.*

He went back to his family's huge cottage, lay on the cot in the porch, listening to the waves against the breakwater. He thought about his mother. She was now involved in movie writing. Although she hadn't made a movie yet, she said she was certain she would, that the world would wait for it. She dabbled in it to the tune of some forty thousand dollars, and it and the script itself was left unfinished. He told her to stop spending money, and he meant it—for he had no access to it until he do that bidding about Arron Brook. But he was overseeing it and trying to control her spending.

He was worried about her extravagance, and had proposed a meeting, to try to control the finances, and she had turned pale—her red hair and her pale skin made her look ill.

"You don't trust or love me—I always sensed it!"

"That is not true at all—I love and trust you—and am here to protect you."

He felt he had to protect her from herself. The money she spent—she had had one book published by a vanity press, and the copies sat in boxes in the basement—was, he knew, a symptom of a larger problem.

By now Albert had discovered some unpleasant things.

The priest, her brother, had long ago spoken to her, had told her not to interfere with their young sister. But who could stop her. So she married her sister's fiancé.

Did it in a storm in March, and moved into a small bleak house just after the war.

Soon she was sick of him altogether. He was one of the men who never went to war but danced with all the pretty girls at dances at the Pines, who had shiny pants and black leather shoes, and danced to Benny Goodman under the waving trees. And for all of that he was as innocent as his scrub brush haircut and his heavy winter mittens. He was Albert's father.

But he was killed soon after the marriage, filled with guilt and self-doubt. Her younger sister had moved on, applied for jobs around the river. It was 1947, and work was starting up.

She was supposed to relay to her sister that a job was available at Raskin's. But she showed up herself. She took the job and betrayed her sister. And there she met Byron.

But who could blame her—for look what it brought her. It brought her a life none of her relatives could imagine. That is, she had become the widow of a well-known man, kept his papers, and was playing on publishing his biography someday. She had written to ten publishers so far but as yet had not written a word. All of this she had never thought of when he was alive, but now of course things had taken a better slant.

Albert, lying in the porch, listening to the waves, thought of all of this in a vague and uncomfortable way. He felt they were a damaged family and he was a product of it. Of a man with big mittens who danced in the halls when other boys were fighting Hitler. Albert was new, he was rich, and he didn't need the past if he could help society.

It seemed his mother was drifting somewhere away from him. And he was drifting off to sleep when there was a sudden sharp knock, and a man opened the door. A man he had not seen in some years. In fact it took him a moment or two to realize who it was. He was older and there was a touch of grey in his hair.

"Hello, Albert. You look good, I must say. God, you don't even tell your friends you're home." It was Shane Stroud. He came in so quickly it was as if Albert should be expecting all of it.

There was no way to tell how immediately offensive this man looked to him. His eyes were dark, and one was unable to see into them. His face was delighted always but only at the anxiety of others that his presence seemed to create. He had the same delighted look when he made a young child cry near the opened rink one March night by throwing his skates over the wires above them.

Shane now took something from his pocket and handed it to him. It was a joke—of course, like a sleight of hand or a magician's trick. It was the date and day of Albert's arrival home.

"You been back for months," Shane laughed, pointed his nicotine-smudged finger at him triumphantly as if Albert would share in the humour about his own guilt. "Ahh-haa," Shane said, as if he had caught him in a lie and could use it to torment him.

In Shane's life there were moments of sheer and terrible dread he had caused. There was a scar on his cheek that ran to his chin. He was Mel Stroud's younger and more dangerous brother. The torment always sooner or later started, once he discovered a weakness in a man or woman, and it widened and tightened its grasp on the victim, without Shane being completely conscious of his reasons for it all. He and his brother Mel had known Albert was home. In fact they had been watching him come and go for some time, and speaking to each other about this young man clandestinely.

He now tapped Albert on the left leg in playfulness. The touch had always a benediction to it, as if he was filling the one he touched with grace.

"Oh I meant to, I just got busy," Albert said, sitting up to light a cigarette. He forced himself to speak as the therapist had spent months teaching him. And he spoke pretty well without becoming tongue-tied. He often remembered the one time he had gone to a certain escort well-known here. Scared, he had thrown the money on the bed and run.

He had in some ways tried to put the past behind him, do new and important things, and now realizing that the past had not gone an inch. That is, no matter how he spoke, the past didn't listen.

"Busy for months—busy for months. How's your mom?" Shane asked.

"I—don't know—she is fine," Albert said.

"She is mean to me," Shane said.

"Mean—mean to you how?"

"Oh, I see her out walking down at the boardwalk—I come up to her and says hi and she doesn't even say nothing. I think she's mean."

"No," Albert said, "no—she doesn't know how to be mean."

"Great. Say hello—say Shane says hello. I want to be in that movie if she makes it—saving the seals or the moose, or some such—I could be in a movie like that there. You and I are pals and I thought I'd get a good part in that movie too."

Albert tried to speak but his mouth failed him.

"Too busy for your pals," Shane said, disappointed, looking at how young Raskin picked up the book, in panic, and held it before him, holding it up as if to hide. "Too too busy for your pals." And he watched Raskin as if he was inquiring about something.

Shane looked at him curiously for a long moment. His curiosity was of a man who expects a friend to welcome him and sees in the meeting a terrible strategy.

"Well," Shane said finally, looking around, "I gotta go. You have a great place here. A cottage—this is bigger than most people's homes. Bet this cost a pile. How much would this cost ya?"

"Don't know, I never thought about it. Don't think about money."

Shane's eyes brightened, and his smile came back, and the scar across his cheek reddened slightly. He said: "Never even thought about it—that's because you don't have to. Money is no object for you, is it—ha. But this place in nowaday money?" And he sniffed hard and looked over at Albert as if scorning him. "Six hundred thousand easy—and this a cottage—ha."

Then he stood, and suddenly without hesitation put a letter on the table, and tapped it with a finger, staring at his friend, tapped the letter again. For a moment Albert did not want to read the letter. Reflecting upon all of this later he realized that initially he did not think it was a letter. But he took it from the envelope and unfolded it.

Albert
It is not often I do this, but I feel compelled. I discovered who that girl was—do you know who it was, that girl? Annie Howl. That's who it was!!! Do you remember?? Annie Howl. What I mean is the girl at the party. Remember that girl said she had a headache and you give her mescaline. My God why did you ever do something so dangerous to a little girl?? They said the autopsy says she was violated or whatever like that there. But so far everyone is being quiet. We have our reputations to think of. All of us do!! Mel don't want nothing to do with this—I mean it's a murder—so he wants to see you. Maybe you should come clean on this or we are all in trouble.

Inside the folded letter was a card:

"Arnie and Arlo, Consultants."

Young Raskin did not know what that card did mean.

It had never happened like that. Never, never—she was willing and it was all in fun. But no—of course it had—that is, he had given her mescaline—and he had attempted to make love to her when they were alone.

He took her to the greenhouse, to the row of plants, to the smell of midnight, to the soil in jars that his stepfather had innocently worked with to save himself from memories of war. You see it was pure bedlam everywhere and he felt he had a right to do what he did.

He had started to undo her clothes, and he pushed his hand between her legs.

"*Why are you naked?*" he remembered her saying.

"Because," he whispered, "you should be naked too—can't you see your clothes are afire?"

He didn't know why he had ever ever ever said what he did; she would become hysterical. He did not know this would happen. He put his hand over her mouth, and became frightened. He offered her money to be quiet. He offered her a new bicycle.

And he had thought it must have all been forgotten by now. He suddenly thought of his mother—her universal mind, as frivolous as it was—and how she had an article on the universal mind— that a universal mind respected women, and that she relied upon young new thinking men like *him*.

"My son is the kind of man women need—he is an advocate for mental health and well being—"

This article had actually been published. Poor Carmel didn't know that many people scorned or laughed at these articles.

Carmel was frightened of a man named Shane, worried that he would come back. It was beginning to bother her to distraction.

And now he knew why. Suddenly he knew why. When he was away Shane must have harassed her.

She told Albert that he had sent her two letters two months before—she had hidden them, crunching them up. He told her to forget about it.

So this is what the party had caused, and he thought suddenly of the innocence of Joanie Donaldson's party, and wondered why had they crashed it?

"I will take care of Shane Stroud" he had told his mother. He thought of Professor Dykes and how he had run away that night, how he and the editor of *Floorboards* had run. Terrified of the very things they proposed in private.

He did not know that the man he saw in the wheelchair was Annie Howl's brother, the one who jumped in the water in a vain attempt to try and save her, smashing his legs on a rock. He did not know the man had been over these years investigating the death of his sister. That he would never give it up. That is, he too like Albert would be a professor, and teach at the same university. That the university itself would become terribly divided over a thousand different issues oscillating to a fever pitch, and he Albert would be determined to be on the right side.

The day had turned cold, and an east wind came as he walked down the shore. Sand blew up in the wind and hit his face.

Mel Stroud was sitting on a log on the beach, swiping at the sand gnats about him. He looked at Albert with a terrifying self-righteousness that lasted but a moment, but cut into Albert's heart.

"My brother just wants to do what's right," Mel said. Then Mel spoke of the liquorice he was chewing, and you could hardly get good liquorice and asked Albert if he wanted some. He held up a piece and nodded with his mouth full.

"Why—no, thank you. I mean, what has come up?"

"Well, Darren Howl is asking a lot of questions about his sister—you know, Annie Howl. Shane is some worried. He still lives with my mother—he had a girlfriend but it didn't pan out—and he is broke. He thinks of Annie Howl and he gets broken up and cries. What if mom finds out? He wanted to go and talk to your mother about it—I think he might have even wrote her something like a letter, about getting some money for the Howls—that's it, you see—he wants some money for the Howls."

Mel looked stern, even more self-righteous, as he spoke, for he wanted young Raskin to know this was no joke—things must be done to alleviate their worry. Young Raskin suddenly became aware of the situation he was in. And the situation his mother was now in. He tried not to panic. But he suddenly realized, this was always the position he was going to be in.

"A letter, my mother, talk about it—no," Albert said. He looked out at the bay water and spit again, and then tried to light a cigarette in the wind. "I can give them some money."

"No, that won't do," Mel said simply. "This is going to be between us."

"He wouldn't go to that family, would he?"

"I told him not to, but he is upset—he has a bad conscience about it—and he's dead broke—so he keeps thinking if he could get some money he would give it to them as charity or something like that."

"I plan to give him a thousand dollars," Albert blurted. "If he wasn't so impatient he would have known that today. I am writing him a cheque tomorrow—you tell him that, okay?"

Mel shrugged, perhaps at the amount offered, and the wind blew sand and old seaweed across the flat low tide. There were sand gnats in the hot seaweed, and he said: "Oh—that's the

Frontenac—" pointing lazily to the freighter far out in the waves, as if he was distracted and had not heard. In fact he was already thinking of other things to ask, and would begin to compete with his brother.

Young Raskin walked back to his cottage, not even saying hello to all the people he passed by. Not even looking at the girls in their skimpy bathing suits.

Albert did not write the cheque. He thought of going to his uncles but they had just paid for all his time away, and he had been on an allowance with them. Besides they had heard he had gone to meetings. They weren't sure what meetings—but they did know—there were meetings.

He knew right near him in a bank was thousands and thousands he could not yet access until he do something at Arron Brook. Then he would personally have about three hundred thousand—plus what would come to him from Raskin Enterprises at a certain time.

But now everything was tied up. Mel and Shane and how he had ever met them began to plague him.

He went to his mother, but just as he was about to ask she told him Shane had asked her for a lot of money.

"They never would if Byron was here," she said. "He would have handled it like a man. Now I have no one."

"Well you have me," he said, "so don't worry."

But he felt sick about all of this coming so suddenly upon them.

"I will phone the police."

"No you can't," he said quietly, "please mom—you can't. We are in trouble if we do!" Then more forcefully he almost shouted: "You can't—if you want me to be anything in this life—anything— you can't. Didn't you want to become writer in residence—how will that happen?!"

And he scared her. He truly scared her.

They were in the huge comfortable den with the huge fireplace and the three solid bookshelves.

"Why?"

For moments he was silent.

"The naked girl," he said finally.

He sat with her until dark, and all the memories of that night came back to each in a different way.

He tried to be firm.

He did not pay the money and twice Mel Stroud looked at him with sad disappointment when he passed by, in his car with the white bucket seats.

I should go to Constable Donaldson. You might not thinks so
but I's do think this is some kind of case of rape and murder—
and I am scared to my bones.

That was a note put inside his cottage porch door two weeks later. With this note was a picture of Annie Howl that had been with an article written by Darren Howl and published in the local paper about his ongoing investigation.

He went to meet them. They spoke in secret. Mel said he was upset, for Shane's sake. But his voice sounded both certain and cruel.

"I will pay you once," Raskin said.

Dykes was expelled from University Campus and was living in a house with young radicals, and for some reason, some pique against Albert, they wouldn't let him in or tell their revolutionary father that he was there. That is because some two years before Dykes said he, Albert, should be ambitious enough to rob his uncles, and use the money for projects the group was interested in.

Dykes was disappointed that this revolutionary act had never happened.

"Remember Stalin's robbery of the bank in Tbilisi?" Dykes said. 'That's the kind of man I'm after."

"Right on man," the young woman said.

Dykes, by the way, had never robbed or spent his own money, and was in litigation to get his pension.

So at this time Albert was turned away, and as he left he could hear Dykes laughing at some inane joke the young lady told.

He went and asked his uncles for the money. First they were not sure who he was. He had been away, and he had thinned and his teeth were no longer crooked.

"You want money—well let me ask you this—who are you?"

"I'm your nephew—your great-nephew—I'm Albert."

"Oh yes—of course you are—glad to see you," Dexter said, "You've done something to your face—spruced it up."

"Happy days are here again," Chester said. "But we just can't give you the money."

"No we shan't just give you the money."

"You can work for us—we'll hire you."

So they gave him a job.

"I have to get up at seven in the morning for God sake," he told his mom. "Then I have to wear a hard hat!"

"Yes—well if you wear a hard hat too long your aura will go—it will."

He went to work with a lunch bucket and a pair of workboots, and a hard hat.

All day long he had to change lightbulbs or clean couplings on pipes.

He couldn't stand it—nor could Mel stand how they were left waiting.

Things were getting desperate whenever he saw Shane's car parked outside his house.

So then one summer night, about two weeks after this, Albert was caught trying to take some money from Raskin's safe in the main office of Raskin Enterprises. Since he hadn't written the cheque it had gone from one thousand to three thousand. For the dire thing, the terrible tarot card they held, was that Darren Howl had advertised in the paper a three-thousand-dollar reward for any information. It was in fact all the money Darren Howl had at that moment.

The paper's notice read: "*Please contact Constable Becky Donaldson, 677-6767, with any information.*"

Albert should have gone to the police—to Constable Becky Donaldson.

But he couldn't bring himself to. People were thinking of him as a new force for the Raskins. A new voice.

He had been called by Doris Simpson—who wrote a gossip column:

The young Raskin, hope for our community and our planet.

Yes—the entire planet.

So in trying to hang on, there just might be a trip into hell.

The idea of that man in the wheelchair, who they informed him was Darren, Annie Howl's older brother, terrified him. The sight of the wheelchair disturbed him.

Why does he need to push it around like he does to remind me? Raskin often thought.

Because he was put into a wheelchair in trying to save his sister.

His mother hid in her house—spoke about moving away. That

is, Shane had proposed to her in one of his letters, and told her how he knew she had been "taken by him, and he by her." He wrote, "What we is, is like two little bitty peas in a pod that's what we are. Remember when we smooched right in the yard—ha—and I even for a second touched your—you know what—ha."

So Albert was in a bind, not only for himself but for his mother.

Then the worst thing happened that night.

He was caught taking the money from the huge lumbering safe with "Raskin Brothers" in faded letters on the doors, which had been left open accidentally that afternoon.

He tried to explain it all to the cleaning lady who had caught him, and he tried to stop her from going to tell his uncles. He stood at the door, with his hand on the crease of the ornate cabinet.

But the little grey-haired woman stood before him. Her eyes peered at him from small puffs of skin, and her cheeks were puffed like a chipmunk's. Her feet were noticeable because she walked so quietly and they were so small. She was only four foot eleven tall. Yet she stared at him out of those watery eyes, and her little mouth grimaced in amazement at what she had just caught him doing. Putting money down his pants.

He stared at her, at her small homely body, with a rag in her left hand and a can of Pledge in her right. She had come in to dust the table, and he suddenly remembered she did that every second day.

In the centre of the room was that military field table, a beautiful maple table that was used as an officer's dining table in the field; it had suited members of the Raskin family well from the time of the Boer War on. That is where the documents of pension payouts and other obligations had been left.

In July 1939 a German ship flying the swastika left with asbestos ore for Hitler's Germany. The last shipment to that country for seven years. The last payment came from some officious clerk in some small Hamburg office. Dated July 18, 1939. That was in the books too.

He studied all of this, rifling through his uncles' papers, to see if he could force his uncles to pay his mother all the money he believed she was owed.

There was a late nineteenth-century couch and matching chairs sitting in front of the window, and a three-tier chandelier shone down over the room.

Albert told the elderly cleaning lady that she was the guilty party. That he had caught her stealing, saying: "*You?* I didn't think you'd be grabbing at the funds."

The little Pentecostal woman almost screeched: "What are you saying, are you blaming me?"

"Well I don't see anyone else here to blame, do I?"

Dykes told him that to change the world one must not ever admit any wrong. So he said:

"I did nothing—the door was ajar because you were pilfering. I'm trying to keep the money safe, that is all."

She frantically hurried past him down the stairs and across to the house, and inflamed by his terrible words informed his uncles because she knew she was powerless against this young Raskin man if she did not. She looked distraught and held the rag in her left hand and her Pledge in her right, as if in a way these objects sanctified her.

His uncles told her to go back and finish the room.

"Dust up and polish," Chester said.

"Yes, polish and dust it up," Dexter made clear.

His uncles had to get up and come out to the office in their pyjamas, with big cigars in their mouths. Confronted by them, Albert still tried to blame her.

The Raskins had known about his mother's family too. Those ancestors who were supposed to have stolen a pot of gold lost somewhere on a ship out of the Bay of Biscay. They had tracked her life before she met Byron.

"I catch a housekeeper trying to take money and you suspect *me*?" he asked.

"I've known her for thirty-five years!" Chester said, meaning the cleaning lady. "She had a mastectomy and still took care of her crippled niece."

"Crippled niece no bigger than a little bun—little as a pea."

"That's why she took it," Albert said, "for her midget crippled niece—that was what she just told me. It was all for some dwarf crippled niece or some such."

"Her crippled niece died seven years ago," Dexter said.

"And we paid for the funeral," Chester added.

Albert tried to leave, but they grabbed him and a bundle of hundred-dollar bills fell from under his shirt and landed on the floor. He stared at the money, and then looked at them, then all of them looked at the money again.

There were no charges laid. But he was told not to come back to the mine for a year.

He tried to get the money on his credit cards, but they had been suspended. Mel had accompanied him to the bank. Had waited for him outside, looked at him eagerly when he came out, almost wantonly. Looked displeased and shocked at not getting the money there and then.

"Goddamn we're in a pickle," Mel said. "A real pickle here."

Then he stopped him and looked at him almost in bereavement saying:

"What are we going to do, Albert—what are we going to do?"

Young Raskin went back to his house, to his basement apartment, and seeing Aleister Crowley's maxim "Do what thou wilt" was overcome with anger and fear.

He sold his stereo and records to a friend, and sold his waterbed to a young woman and his guitar to a teenager to pay off the debt that no one spoke about. *Now*, he thought, *it will all be forgotten.*

"Of course, it's forgotten—it had nothing to do with me in the first place."

Shane, Mel said, was the bad apple.

"Oh he's crazy—Shane is absolutely nuts, don't ever let him near your mother, he said he was going to ask her on a date. He'll end up bedding her," he said proudly. "Wait and see."

Then he said:

"You shouldn't have asked him to your party—he's so unpredictable we almost never ask him to ours."

Albert Raskin went home, venting very much to his mother about campaigns to relieve *their* poverty.

"See what you did," he said in a frustrated moment. "Now Shane wants to go on a date with you."

"Oh! A date with me?"

"Yes. Take you to a good restaurant."

"What restaurant?"

"I don't know. Some restaurant."

"I will die first—"

"But—" He looked at her. "Why did you flirt with him? Why did you let him kiss you! It was like watching a car wreck."

She said she did not know—said it was a new age, and he, Albert, had talked her into it, talked her into wearing flowers in her hair.

"Now he'll tell everyone you are in love with him. He said he is going to star in your movie."

"No!"

"Yes—yes, yes, yes!"

"Who does he want to play?"

"Who does he want to play? Who the hell cares—he's a lunatic!"

His mother suddenly changed the subject. She spoke about his commitment to change—that in fact unlike so many other young men, he was a saint.

She knew why she couldn't call the police. It was because of that young naked girl fleeing in terror down the road.

The great adventure, whatever that was, and whoever it was for, seemed to be now over.

11

THE SECOND APARTMENT BUILDING.

What he liked, this Young Raskin, was how he was now—for better or worse, with his nose straightened, and his weight loss, quite handsome. And he had dreams of doing many grand things. He had dreams of finding a beautiful woman for himself.

He met Torrent Peterson on the beach.

The sun was shining and though the wind was brisk it was very hot. Sandflies had gathered about Torry as they were gathered around—it was revealed to him later—Eva Mott. She had swum out too far and had begun to sink in the rip. And no one on the beach was prepared or brave enough to go after her. He watched it all with some interest, some horror that he himself couldn't find the immediate strength to react, and judged later that she was too far away, and he would be no good in the attempt. He in fact was right. Few men would have been able to save her.

She was quite lucky that there was one there who could.

Two boys went to get Torrent—he had been working with his horse up in the woods, making his own house. Torrent ran down, took off his boots and shirt and swam out toward her. He grabbed her from behind, put her head into his chest and swam back, one-armed, first along the rip that was pulling her away from shore and finally in toward the shore. He could see the shore— everything looked distant, and people yelling, and two boys wading out up to their chests.

She kept saying sorry because she had lost her top. And when he got her to shore, she staggered somewhat to the beach. She had freckles and her hair was red. He took off his shirt and put it over her bared breasts. Now that she was safe, she started to laugh and cry.

"My name is Eva, my name is Eva, I'm new here—I didn't know—I'm sorry—I live up in the Raskin apartment so thanks for helping. I got tired, I'm sorry."

Albert had watched from a distance with his hands in the pockets of his white cotton pants. He had heard that Torrent was one of those lost boys, who never mentioned his father or where he lived because he was ashamed to tell. But Albert knew he lived in a trailer along Arron Brook somewhere. He was surprised to see him, startled to see his black curly hair soaking wet, and water dripping off his soaking jeans, to see his very white feet in the hot sand.

He made a note that he had seen him, and had seen that beautiful girl. Already with the sunburn on his face he was making plans in his mind, that helping a girl like that would make the memory of Annie Howl go away.

Over the years there were squabbles in that trailer where Torrent lived. The police were often called to parties where there were smashed bottles and windows. Some days when people drove by the turnoff to Upper Arron they would see Torrent's lone figure, dark against the pale evening sky, leaning against a telephone pole, smoking.

Mel Stroud disparaged the boy's father to Albert, saying Oscar *owed* him a lot, *owed* the Strouds a whole lot and the boy would turn out to be no better. He would shake his head at the shameful way they lived.

"Up in that trailer!" he said, as if living in a trailer wounded some pedantic sensibility he had acquired. "Oscar stoled a lot from us—from me and Shane, stoled a whole lot—"

"He did?"

"He hurt that boy's mother awful bad," Mel would say, scratching the knuckle of his left hand. "Albert, if you was there, you would know—you would know—I tried to do my best with them all—women deserve our help. Tried my best in my heart to take care of Mary Lou, Torrent's mother. Oscar never liked us nohow, he never liked Shane, that poor little lad—Shane's younger than me, and he had no father figure—I tried, but as you know I didn't have no help myself. Oscar did nothing but laugh at us, laugh at us when I was a young lad. He ain't much older than me but acted the big shot. I just wish I had more education like you."

"I wish you had gone to university—think of what you could have been," Albert would tell him emotionally, and not without a measure of compassion. And not without thinking he would someday mention his conversation to Professor Dykes. "I don't think I've met as many who had such a hard time, and understand so much about human nature. So much more than so many."

"I never had no chance," Mel would say, sniffing, with his hands grabbing the side of the porch where he sat and staring straight ahead, "never had no chance. Shane is someone now I try to look out for. He liked that young Eva Mott but she hurt him bad, almost destroyed him. First she is real friendly to him and everything like that there, plays him along, asks for presents, gets him running back and forth for flowers whatchacallitmums or somethin—and then she goes off with someone else—goes off with that prick Torrent Peterson, just about broke poor Shane's heart. Had it planned to take her to a dance and borrowed my car, shined it all up and everything and she walks right by him won't even say hello. Maybe you could do something about it all—"

"What could I do?"

"Don't know—but we'd be in your debt for sure. Shane needs a good girl to straighten him out—"

"When you mention Shane, I am uncertain of him. He keeps bringing up that night. That night is over."

"I've nothing to do with it," Mel replied almost softly, and then chewed some liquorice, "but Shane is certain that something happened to that poor Howl girl—you are right on that. You see, that night hurt him some bad—he was disappointed in you."

"Disappointed?"

"Well—to him you were like a counsellor or something—mental health, which was even in the paper about you—but then he went to that party—and he was scared to go with important people—and then what happened to that little girl, understand. It was the very first time he met important people. That is what it boils down to."

Mel continued: "But you see Eva Mott going out with that Torrent is his concern now—that Torrent will put a beating on her, sure as hell, and kick her arse. Poor Shane—he's the one who cares for women. He liked your mother too, and you know I tell no secrets how she was left out of the loop by yer stepdaddy—I tell no secrets that he hit her too. I tell no secrets that you got a whop of money coming to you if you play it smart. So Shane is the one who cares heaps for women, a whole lot. Just like a professor."

The wind blew against the car, and the sea was riled up. Then he added with a wink, "Hey—you got things done to you—look like some movie star now, Albert Raskin. That's what money does."

So Albert had heard Torrent's mother had left. Mel had taken her away from Oscar Peterson because he couldn't stand the way Oscar abused her, and that both of them, she and Mel, had petitioned everyone to get the child Torrent back, before Oscar as Mel said "deranged him." But that this was impossible. Then Torry's mother died, Mel tried desperately to save her but did not. He tried to help Torry but was kicked out of the yard, "on more than one occasion." He bought him presents too, and tried to help him get his education.

And when Mary Lou's heart stopped "that time there—he give her mouth-to-mouth to resuscitate her and everything else. Blew my own air into her body to help her out. Oscar wouldn't sniff in her direction, I figure."

So Albert now suspected, and talked to Professor Dykes about it, that Torry would have the same kind of horrid life as his father—the same prospects and marry and his wife would have a hard life. She would be abused. This was simply a matter of Albert's new evolvement and understanding about the lack of advantages and the chauvinists who lived here. Of course he thought this because he too had been taught to think it; where professors who came from Europe and the United States looked upon us as backward. Expatriates often left their country and applauded the country they adopted. But those who came here applauded the countries they abandoned and hated and disparaged the rural land they arrived in. And many students here instantly abdicated for their regard.

In fact to think in any other way about Torrent was to dispute his tutors. But not only that, it was to show less compassion than his tutors implied he was supposed to. And besides this, Mel, a rough but good man, thought all this as well and told him so. And to disparage Mel was to be not only hard-hearted but in error—and also it would raise the spectre of Shane, and might tarnish the reputation of his mother.

The real facts, however, were very different. And both Dykes and he were too self-consciously gullible and moreover wilfully trained in naivety to examine them.

Torrent was a sad and gentle soul, told by his father Oscar Peterson that his mother had died, that it was a heroic death; that she was saving eagles, or some other bird, Oscar didn't quite remember, but she fell off a cliff on Good Friday Mountain. And that she had even managed to fly for a little bit—not a long time, but a few incandescent flaps. "Like a little mourning dove," he said.

And Torrent believed that because his heart was good.

He believed everything then because his heart was good. Later on he would believe Eva Mott in everything because his heart was good. He believed her because he had a simple nature, and could not conceive of people lying to him. That is, when one saw his brooding strength and curly black hair one also saw gullibility, trustfulness and hope.

So Albert told his mother he was going to study sociology, take on the system, which he said would set the world straight. That he would succeed his way out of their bad luck and in a few years everything would be back to the way it should be. That he would give the money away to worthy people—some worthy young woman, and he would show his mettle in a way she would be proud of.

But what he did not know was that both Shane and Mel had heard of this money he was required to give to some worthy cause.

And one or two nights a week, Shane's black car was parked just down the street.

12

ALBERT RASKIN WAS RIGHT. HE WAS PERCEPTIVE ENOUGH to be right about Eva Mott. She was much like that young girl who had come to his party. She dressed almost the same, the voice was similar, the Miramichi accent, her means, if she had means, were about even. And what enthralled him most is she had a captivating beauty. He had already heard a dozen men who worked about the mine comment on her with that faint hope and fantasy men have.

But if he had been more perceptive he would have realized that they were, Annie Howl and Eva Mott, very much different. He would have also realized that Torrent was a hard-working rural boy, and that Mel and Shane Stroud were desperate cons, who knew nothing but how to take from others; and his mentor Dykes would miss this completely because he would look upon Torrent as a useless cog in the terrible system that must be overthrown.

Some of the young friends of Wilbur Dykes smirked at the world as they followed his lead, smirked at the army, at the navy, smirked at priests, at store managers, at railway workers—they were beyond all of that, smirkers all, and during his university years they were part of his cortège.

That is what any perceptive girl or boy on the streets of town or in Arron Brook would know by the time they were fourteen, many middle-class or well-to-do students like Raskin himself went to university to lament and study when they were twenty-four. That is, poor girls from Bartibog or from the South End of Saint John knew as much about poverty by the time they were nine as any doctoral student studying inequality at twenty-six.

Except, he came home once, and saw Carmel sitting, the whole house in twilight, the only thing noticeable at the far end of the dining room was her orange hair, and her eyes staring at him. The door into the dining room was half-closed, the dining room table was waxed and glossy but stood out as a dark form, and only her hair caught in the stove light showed where she sat, and her eyes, dark but penetrating. She had seen Shane, he was standing by the hothouse, near the door, staring in the window at her, smiling. There had been a note left in her mailbox the day before saying he would see her.

What has that night brought us? he thought, as at the same time he tried to dismiss it. But the trouble was, he hadn't dismissed it that night—and that night was the test. It was the one firm test he was to have, about revolution. And he had failed it.

If Byron was alive he would have helped. Byron might have told him that he should have thought of Torrent as a good and wise soul, and Mel and Shane as parasites, but unfortunately Albert's study of life's abandoned and marginalized ones had taught him just the opposite.

The university sat on the hill away, away from all the town.

As a young man the year after the attempted theft Albert entered those doors for the second time, determined to be his own

THE TRAGEDY OF EVA MOTT   97

man and make a mark. In fact he was the first person in his family to ever attend university.

It was a place with a number of offices with bookshelves, with notices on doors, with bulletin boards in the foyer, a fireplace in the lounge, and sometimes the dusty smell coming from those ancient *livres* on the upper floors. He wandered there, through those university quarters at night alone. Now and again picking up a small volume and placing it down again. He was embarrassed by his uncles. He tried not to say he was related. He had gone to a lecture where they were called colonialists and white supremacists, and he never raised his voice in protest. In fact this was like the Weather Underground: they never knew what they were for or who they were against either.

Often he thought of Eva Mott on those nights when he wandered from university corridor to university office wondering how to make a mark, to have others recognize him.

He had a friend at university, a non-tenured professor from Nova Scotia who he liked, who he spoke about to people, who helped him a good deal. There was even an incident where Mel Stroud showed up half-drunk and insisted Albert go somewhere, and this man stood up and said, "He is staying right here," and Mel simply turned and left.

And then one night the Nova Scotian took a knife from Albert Raskin—a six-inch hunting knife—and punched it into the table.

"Why do you have this?"

"Just to protect myself."

"If something is bothering you, tell me. I am your friend."

"It's nothing," he said. "I was in trouble once. Something— I did something I shouldn't have. But it was a very long time ago."

"Well you can tell me."

"It was nothing," Albert said. "I have seen things. For instance I have seen how a young lady was once treated. So I am determined to correct all of that."

"Is it something that man did that you saw?"

"Yes, it is something." Suddenly filled with emotion he said: "I tried my best—but I will help a young woman someday."

His friend from Nova Scotia tried to figure this out but knew that Albert was desperately frightened and probably lying.

The Nova Scotian hoped for tenure but many people didn't want him. His views were old-fashioned. He believed in literature.

He did not believe in joining the English and Sociology departments together as many here did. He did not believe that male writers like Conrad should not be taught. All the professors deciding this Nova Scotian's fate were not from Canada. No—they were from Wales and Scotland and Indiana and Maine. One night the Nova Scotian got belligerent and heatedly told them off. Then he simply stood and left the room. "He is truly conniving for a position here," Kent told Raskin in confidence later the next day, "with a belligerence we shouldn't accommodate. Well you know this better than I do." Saying so in order to flatter the one he wished to comply.

And he took Raskin's hand in his and held it. He had included young Raskin and young Raskin felt truly empowered.

"Literature must change," Kent said. "It must be more inclusive—it must be."

If anyone had told him it was because he was a Raskin he wouldn't have believed them. No matter if he and his uncles ever got along, they were terrified not to give him a position.

So after this Albert became less friendly with that man who had been his only friend.

It was as refreshing as the first day he had said "I am a non-believer" to Dykes, and was hailed as a champion.

Over time the Raskin works became a focus for the university paper, of which Albert Raskin was now associate editor. He mightn't have wanted it that way. However, it was that way. And Young Raskin himself sat in on editorial meetings when they were deciding to write articles against the mine.

Still, the university never minded taking million-dollar endowments from two old uneducated men Albert was ashamed of (Dexter had grade four and Chester had grade five), that they skewered and mocked in private discussion, and which professors in most departments spoke out against. They never offered either of them an honorary doctorate, and each time the subject came up they deflected it as well as they could by saying: "Look, they wouldn't want to get dressed up for this—come out to a setting with students."

The two old men didn't even know what honorary doctorates were.

13

EVA DIDN'T KNOW ANYONE AS IMPORTANT AS ALBERT Raskin, who seemed suddenly to be the most important person on the river (because of his weekly interviews on CBC, and a few times on national radio)was interested in her. She didn't believe in any great destiny for herself. Or the destiny she thought was grand would never be here on this river, for her. Her father was a failure, her mother henpecked her father. He sold vacuum cleaners, and then filters for stoves, encyclopedias and other things.

So they were here now, on the edge of nowhere else. So she thought she would marry and work somewhere—wherever young women worked, she supposed. Maybe in the office at the mill, or in the office at the mines, or somewhere like that. Her room had a dresser, a small single bed, a picture of her grand-mother on the dresser, a small record player, with seven or eight 33⅓-speed records, a pink bedspread with a doll set up in front of her pillow, a doll with a cracked face, stringy blond hair and one eye. Unusual songs from faraway days paraded through her mind, drifting onto the tablet of her own inner record player to be played; songs of remote summer days, of the sorrow of teenaged love.

She met Torrent later, after he had swum out that day. First she went to see him the next day at the house he was building. She let him kiss her.

Then one afternoon he was walking along the road ahead of her and she ran to catch up. She suddenly was beside him, her reddish-brown hair shining in the day's sunlight and her smiling up at him in such a way that as a young girl she had not done before. It was true she felt some grand obligation to him and he did not want her to. But she was confused too. She would ignore him or blush, sometimes even rush out of the room. Then at a commu-nity centre dance she asked him to dance, and took his hand. He was so shy that he kept her at arm's length when they waltzed. She told him, whispered in his ear, that this was providence—that it was fate and destiny for them. That she was an Aquarius and knew all of these things. Love songs flooded her memory, trips in her father's car in the rain, looking out at the shoddy fields of her youth.

They were formed from the same substance as the stars to meet where they were at this great moment.

"Do you believe that about everything?" he asked.

"Oh yes," she said quickly, affirming her youth, the horoscopes she continually monitored.

In order to facilitate this idea of their coming together she spoke endlessly about her father, and his failings.

Perhaps he understood, one not happy with her family might never be happy with his. Perhaps her reading of the horoscopes told him so. His face was handsome, his hair black. He wore new clothes to the dances, not expensive, but jeans with the cuffs turned up, polished shoes, and a white shirt and at times a bolo tie with silver studs at the ends of the straps. That is, he looked who he was at a dance where everyone could tell he was from downriver.

Since he was poor he never dressed to appear poor, which is what our middle-class kids, especially those in university, most often did. What Albert had done, without being able to accomplish it. They wore shirts with the sleeves torn and jeans with the knees out, workboots on feet that never saw a work site, or ever would. They would never say "Get the fuck up out of that" to a horse, as Torrent did the day he had saved her life, nor would they ever be expected to know anything about a horse.

They wouldn't consider the loss of industry a problem because in protesting industry they themselves had jobs secure away from it. Even if that industry in some way supported the jobs they themselves had.

The fact was, a problem for a distant time, Eva did not want workboots, and horses either. She just didn't know that she didn't at that moment. That she would turn against Torrent's type of world, a world of his own love and fancy, a world disappearing like an apparition behind us, silently drifting away to a time that would be forgot. She would turn away from all of that as surely as a young girl's blush of pride against the morning sun.

———

A few years previous, Shane Stroud had proposed to Eva Mott. He was the fellow she had let kiss her that night when she was so alone, and it had begun to rain and it was behind the dairy bar. Shane was the first boy to ever kiss her. Well, he was a man way past thirty and she was just a child.

She was a young girl in a new place, in a small apartment, and wanted to meet someone kind.

He put his hand up her blouse, under her brassiere and over her breast.

She looked at him, smelled his clothes and saw a kind of satyr, a kind of grotesque rage that made him both self-satisfied and malicious. She did not understand this, but she felt it in her soul.

He tried to push her down on her back and she escaped and ran. The next day as she started home from school he followed her. All of a sudden she realized, too late, that what she had allowed caused this attention, and it was a threat.

She had tried to tell her father and mother at supper but she couldn't bring herself to. She simply stared at the faded and worn flowers on the edge of her small plate, her fingers fumbling in front of her.

That night as she prepared to go to bed he was outside the apartment looking up at her window. She stared out at him in a kind of wonder, and then of grief and terror.

She hid behind the curtain in her room. How terrible it was that she allowed this. But she had allowed it because she was lonely and had a new pair of slacks and sneakers and went for a walk, and wanted to meet people.

———

Torrent's father was Oscar. Oscar was a man who wore a torn tweed jacket as he walked about his place feeding his four pigs. He was well over six feet tall. He had a bony frame, but hard as flint and muscular. Sometimes when people came over for a night he would beat up the dog to show he was tough. He was an expansive riddle. No one knew quite what he was doing or thinking. Yet he could quote Shakespeare and Joyce, and Cervantes, and would sometimes say: "Can't we all?"

And Torrent was his only son.

That is what Eva had found out about Torrent, because Torrent of course never told her.

She met Torrent after they had finally moved to Arron Brook because it seemed her family had nowhere else to go. Her father always had a Band-Aid somewhere, always had a strained finger or a sore toe, always shuffled about the apartment sneezing, always complained about his brother who got "the best weather" when they had to share times for a little cottage.

"Someday I will get a trailer and park it right beside him."

So she was drawn to Torry, writing his name on her books, and when someone asked her once who he was, she said: *"The boy who saved my life."*

Still, as far as Torry Peterson was concerned, others would go home to places with dens and living rooms and kitchens, bathrooms with baths and sinks, and bedrooms as well. Torrent went home to a trailer where his father sometimes held off neighbours with a shotgun poked out a window, over some absolutely silly dispute and a maniacal look on his face.

"Come and get me!" he would shout to the neighbours. "Just you come and get me!"

———

The trailer was the main spot on this side of the upper level of Arron Brook where all people converged and all things happened—smashed cars, ruined trucks, broken snowmobiles, engines littered the property, where rabbit warrens, pig sheds and doghouses found their place among wagon wheels, hay balers and a horseshoe pitch. There were things confiscated from the Raskin mine over the years, the most impressive being a two-and-a-half-ton generator, seeming rusted and obsolete, that the Raskin brothers never quite gave to him but in the ossification of our world seemed completely at home sitting in the yard behind the trailer. Just as the two pool tables sitting in the barn, and an intact oil furnace from somewhere sitting on the slope of ground near the dog kennel.

To say that Oscar Peterson wasn't a bright man might be to miss so much of what intelligence was. Oscar owned this junkyard, and people would come from all around to buy what he had. No one knew what he would charge or what he would give away, things seeming to be decided on the physiognomy of the buyer. He would stand in his tweed jacket and his orange tie, his face covered in pricks of grey beard, his eyes' rims looking red and sore, and he would talk long and intricately over the subject at hand. This intricacy was something wholly available to men and women of a certain type, seen in both the ruined artifices of large cities, small cities and towns and of course in rural domains, the absolute belief in the bartering of goods and the sale of the cannibalized parts of our earth, and the idea that when it was happening it became the most important transaction in the entire world.

Oscar in fact would spend an hour finding a screw, or a piece of copper wire, a clamp for a radiator hose. But with Oscar, the price was determined on a moment's notice, on the time he had spent searching, looking at the client with a penetrating gaze.

"Yes, but all I need, see, is not the whole snowplough, not at all. Ya see, Mr. Peterson, sir, all I need for the levelling screw is a bolt—just a bolt. You must have a bolt, Oscar, that fits on this here?"

Oscar inspected it closely. He scratched his nose. He leaned on an old fence post. He scratched his nose again. "Yes, I have a bolt—I think. I can get you a bolt for it." And Oscar would rummage around, pick up an old cardboard box, and after forty minutes—of which time he went into the trailer, came out, yelled at the dog that his food was in the tin, went into the trailer again, washed his face—he would find a bolt in a huge bin of bolts, holding it up to the light in the dooryard. Then he would walk to the barn, come out with a can, wash the bolt in oil and dry it with a rag.

Some days he would ignore the person who had come the day before—he would stride about the yard, conceitedly walk right by him, as if the man was not present, even though he had said the night before: "Come back tomorrow." It would seem he had changed his mind. He looked, at those moments, like an emissary on business for his king.

When Torrent came home from school, he changed his clothes, put his jeans and sweater in a cardboard box by his bed and put on old heavy Humphrey pants and a woollen shirt to work in the yard after dark, with a floodlight set up over the eave of the barn. He was strong, but with quiet eyes, and a gullible heart. Very few his age on any stretch of our river worked as hard. No one was seemingly as friendless or alone. He would try to study as well as he could amid the going-on, the bouts of drinking, the fights. He had a picture from New York that he had placed on the small shelf in his room. But that had been taken away by someone at one time. He had some puppies once but Oscar drowned them, and then said he didn't drown them, and then said he did but he didn't mean to.

When he was a little boy he would sit out behind the trailer and sometimes people would hear him crying. But after the age of fourteen he tried not to cry. He would go to bed and put a chair up against his door. Torrent would dream of his own home and barn, his own business of making furniture for the town. Some days he would dream that all the furniture in all the houses was made with his own hands. All children in their mad loneliness have dreams. These were his.

Once a teacher, Miss Bunt, told him his family was a disgrace. He stood before the class as she told them this: "This boy's whole family is a disgrace," she said with a smile. He held his head high, and didn't know what to say. And then she took out the strap and strapped him. Strapping was quite popular in those old heady days of learning. That's because he didn't have his lessons done and had fallen asleep. He had worked the night before until one o'clock trying to get a hole patched in the barn's roof.

Besides, people would arrive throughout the night for a variety of reasons. One, as Oscar called it, was the "forecast."

Oscar was a fortune teller and would tell the tarot. He would charge ten dollars a reading to "give you your dose of the future." He did this in an offhanded way, as if it was a joke, and everyone would have a laugh.

But underneath this taciturn display, as the greasy cards turned up there was a certain form and style he had, his hands smeared with oil across his red fingers, his face distorted against the harsh light, which made it all become deadly serious at the end. And the smell in the trailer, of bacon smoke, and the heat made it ominous. It would become more ominous as the night went on, as the tap dripped and as people stood around listening. He would lay the cards down, adjusting them with his fingertips, look at them and then look up slowly at his client.

"What does it say? What does that card mean?"

"*Death*—that card means *death!* But you—no, you—not you— are going to die probably within the next week."

"But you are not even reading my tarot. You are reading hers."

"The cards don't lie."

One night when he had the temerity to read Torrent's future he was said to have turned pale—deeply pale—and put the cards away. It was of a man coming in the night, like a squire from long ago, possessing in his hands the wherewithal to set Torrent free but at a price no one would ever wish to pay. As he had told Mr. Bell, he saw this man as if in a vision growing old before him.

Sometimes Oscar would tell Torrent stories about his youth as they sat in that little hot trailer alone. One light would glow down from the ceiling, a flycatcher would swing in the air from the little clacking fan, there would be the pungent smell of bacon fat, and now and then a soft air would come in from the window, and in this mad stillness at the end of the road Oscar would tell his tales of yesteryear.

He said he had a duty as a young boy; that during World War II he took telegrams to the parents and families of those killed over-seas. He had to wear a bowtie and carried his telegrams in a leather pouch. Every morning as he bicycled down the road, wearing his cap and bowtie and soft white gloves, people would turn and go inside, close their doors; mothers would turn from him and run. Sometimes he would ride right behind a woman, trying to hand her the telegram. Some of them would hold their hands back as they ran, and he would fold the telegram into it—and when it touched the woman's hand it was as if she had been burned by Satan. Others would simply try to disappear.

He would diligently ride down the empty dusty roads, all over Arron Brook and Dunn's Crossing, trying to locate certain families, the click of his bicycle pedals and the soft clank of his rusty chain, while they would go home, terrified, waiting for the knock on the door, the soulless sound of his bicycle pedalling toward them in the afternoon heat. All throughout the summer of 1942 and into 1945 this was a biweekly occurrence. He plodded the road on snowshoes in the winter of 1945, and people would see this somewhat angelic youngster on snowshoes plodding along the cold lonely roads, beneath the towering naked trees, with telegrams to deliver.

But his uncle, he said, Uncle Silas, had the job at night, walking the road with a wooden leg. People were panicked, left shaking, and even years later they envisioned Oscar on his bicycle or heard the sound of a wooden leg coming up the steps of those isolated farmhouses of Arron Brook where the denizens of so much Scottish, Irish and English history lived in backwoods isolation from the world.

"Yes," he said, "I was a pariah from the start and it were not my fault. That's why I live in this trailer with you. I live here and conduct my life as best I can as an outcast. I am and was and always will be an outcast. My favourite of all plays is not *King Lear*, though, it is *Antony and Cleopatra*—porpoise-backed against us all I have stood. I have found out that once one is an outcast there is nothing one might do to lessen it—but one must not be defeated by it. And never let the asp bite your nipple.

"I found professors against me, doctors against me, lawyers and sons of lawyers, police and fish wardens against me. Workers at the mines and mills smirk toward me, foul-mouthed tavern boys plot my end, hammer against me. But I am not defeated. Never defeated. Son, I do not want you to be defeated by it."

Poor Torrent did not know these people against him, did not know the humanity that plotted Oscar's overthrow, and thought it all mad and dizzying. But by and by he would come to see a measure of truth in it all.

Oscar said some people took to throwing rocks at him after the war had ended as if he too was a German and they were exercising their rights. And more than one spit on him when he was a boy, saying that he delivered letters for Hitler. He would go home to the shack they lived in and wipe the spit from his clothes.

One of these people was old Brigadier Dew, who was not a brigadier but had fought in the Boer War, wore a three-button vest and a Scottish tam. The Brigadier had lost a grandson somewhere in one of the pitiless towns in Italy in 1944, and the letter came with a small white ribbon about it, and a young boy with white gloves, who smelled of that day—of sweet heat and pollen from the fields, of the dust of the road, and trees in loving bloom—handed it to him. The Brigadier was having late breakfast on his veranda eating an egg in its shell, from an ornate egg cup, with hens pecking in the yard and four pieces of blackened toast, and hot coffee, when the boy arrived.

He was the grandfather of Carmel Goya, who became Raskin in 1948, and had the same sense of priority. Carmel's sister was inside that house on that day—the sister Carmel was to betray. Worse for Carmel was that in her heart she could not admit it.

Carmel had been one of the hauteur of our roadway, the Goya who had lived here once a century and a half before and walked the dusty road seeing palaces through the sleet and fog.

———

Torrent by fourteen was a target too. Not because of his father but because he wanted to protect his mother, who he didn't remember, who he thought had died but who had run away. She left. At the end she had wanted to come back, had begged Mel Stroud, who she had run away with, to let her. It was too late because Mel in a drunken moment had told her something about her aunt Mrs. Wally and Torrent's two young uncles Arlo and Arnie.

Oscar told Torry when he was very young that his mother had taken sick and died.

"Yes, Torrent dear, your mother took awful sick—started with a slight fever and then her temperature bounced up to about 178. Still through it all she thought of me and how she loved me—crawled to the stove to make me breakfast one little knee before the other, holding a slab of bacon in her hand. I buried her—in a hundred-thousand-dollar coffin—biggest funeral this river has ever seen. The premier wanted to come, phoned me up—twice—and I just said to him, 'Oh ya—you'll hang around me now, won't you—now that everyone is singing my praises—but before—you wouldn't give me or Mary Lou the time of day.'"

Then he put on the song "Hello Mary Lou" by the Everly Brothers and said he was the one who wrote it. He said Mary Lou was years younger than he was, and had met him one day when she needed a new chain for her bicycle.

"I took advantage of her—a little bit, just a tiny little slab of advantage, not much—she was fifteen. I was almost thirty, maybe a tad older, who knows, I forget, but she was gorgeous, son—gorgeous as a field of blossoms. Her cousin though—a bad influence on them, in and out of jail—but your mom was a saint."

Torry was six and seven when he heard these tales of woe.

———

Torrent was never sure which story was the more truthful or which story he liked better. The story of the eagle he wanted to be true.

But they were stories that often protected him when he was alone and sad, forgotten progeny of some forgotten night, and left at eight years and nine years of age with his dad in the tavern. He would hope that he would see her in a shaft of light through the great spruce trees waiting for him in the middle of the afternoon.

Then one day Torry told the story in class about his mom, and how she died when he was four years old.

The teacher did not look his way after he spoke. She had said: "Very good, Torrent, you may take your seat."

He did not feel embarrassed, or apologetic, when he had told it. He in some way was filled with defiance. He stared straight at people—one a young girl he thought liked him. He kept staring at her, wondering why she did not look his way and smile, as she had done earlier when he said he would tell the story of his mom. Now she had her head down and lifted it once to speak to the teacher about her assignment and said "Yes, Miss B" and put her head down again. There was almost a fulfilling of a prophecy in how she moved her head.

So he left the classroom, disappointed but filled with defiance. A boy came up to him, his face beaming, and said: "She weren't buried in no important coffin, nor did she die trying to protect no pigeon—but you know who she run away with?"

Torrent simply stared at him.

"The porter on the train—you know, from *darkie* town in Halifax." He grinned, his face pocked with acne.

Torrent turned to walk away, but then turned back and hit the boy hard in the face. The boy fell back, his books flying, and Torrent was ready to hit him again when he realized if he did the boy would be desperately hurt, that his right hand was able to deliver a punch that until that moment he was quite unaware of.

All that night Torrent asked questions and Oscar became more and more confused—until there was only one train track, one train, and a hot, sticky day when she packed a bag and left. And it wasn't with the porter on the train as people liked to think. It was a man named Mel Stroud. It was then Torrent discovered that he had uncles as well—uncles he did not remember, except in a faint and vague way.

That his uncles were two Toomey boys, little creatures, harmless, kind and helpful, who Mel Stroud had working for him selling acid, mescaline and hash.

When they were caught by Constable Furlong, Furlong gave them an ultimatum: tell him who they worked for, or face jail.

Terrified of going to jail, more terrified of Mr. Stroud and what he might do to their mother and sister, a man who often talked about loyalty and betrayal as long as it was *they who were loyal*, they were found dead on the barrens. Stroud told Mary Lou that he himself had nothing to do with the boys' deaths, but that Oscar had informed on them and therefore sent her brothers to their demise.

"They run away, dear," he told her. "I were out all night looking for them, poor little vagabonds."

"Poor little what?"

"Poor little vagabonds, dear—vagabonds. Anyway I couldn't find them, I cried aloud and cursed and swore, which I usually never do."

"Well who told on them?"

"Oscar—your so-called husband."

"Oscar?"

"Yes, dear—Oscar."

So that is how it came about that she left with Mel Stroud, Oscar told him.

"I told her she couldn't take you—I said you were not going to live with Mel Stroud, and Mel did not want you near him—he hated you. Please, please don't ask me no more questions! Too many questions spoil the broth or will make me start drinking it."

So Torrent began to understand certain dark things about his mother's life that had been kept from him in this little cluttered trailer.

Oscar said she had gone to hell, to *a land of mythic imps that plague our conscience late at night. As miserable as I am I will not enter that world—*

It was then our Torrent, after believing for years and being told his mom had died, and was asleep in a coffin with big silver handles, the grave which he actually visited and put flowers on every Mother's Day in a solemn ceremony, he realized now that she lived somewhere else, woke when he woke, had a life that had little or nothing to do with him. Yes, they had walked up to the gate of the graveyard, the little boy with flowers in his hand, his father, a stubble of greying beard, a look not entirely sane, with the boy by the hand, waiting for all others to leave, not understanding why no one spoke to them, and then when they were alone placing flowers on a grave that was unmarked.

What he also remembered is, as gruff as his father was, his father never forgot his birthday, never missed a Christmas dinner. Put money away in a little tin box for him. Then he heard one day that his mother actually *had died*, and was going to be buried after the spring thaw. He was still very young and did not understand how his mother was dead, then alive, now dead again.

However, he did not go to the funeral, he went out behind the old trailer and hid near the oil tank. He shook all day, and thought wildly of dreams in which the world was pure.

There was a picture of the Holy Family that his mother had left pinned on the wall above his bed, a picture of three holy people in darkened shadow, against an open window. So he said a prayer to it. But he did not go to the funeral.

Torrent had kept a pair of white high-heel shoes that were owned by his mother, scuffed on the sides with long dark streaks, and a broken buckle on the left shoe, along with the birthday card he had gotten when he was four years old. The card had stayed where it was, wrapped in the plastic that covered it, a white card with silver writing adorned with a cowboy hat, the cowboy hat with golden sparkles upon its top. So it sat through years of other birthdays and hidden personal storms.

For years Torrent was alone, almost friendless, and had dreams no one else knew about or shared.

So when Eva Mott presented herself—rashly trying to dislodge herself from her own kind of hell—well, Eva presented herself. She appeared one night in his shed, that is, she *appeared* to stay. It was after an argument at the apartment. She had told them about Shane, and her father said it was not his fault if she had flirted. That it was her fault.

"It's a woman's job to know how far a flirt should go," he said. "You most likely went too far with the flirt."

Then he took a piece of baloney and went into the TV room.

So she packed a bag of clothes, a small overnight bag, and her makeup kit. This is what made his heart go out to her—yes, within a month after he had saved her life by rescuing her from the tickle, she had stolen his heart away.

14

THE ASBESTOS MINE, ITS GIANT WHITE PITS GLARING under large fluorescent lights, had stayed aloft because the federal government not only wanted it to be successful but convinced the brothers to stay the course. Why did the Canadian government want this? *Because of Thetford Mines.* That is what Byron had known. It was necessary to placate the Liberal government in Quebec because of their world dominance in asbestos. To slight Quebec might bleed away support for Canadian sovereignty itself.

Both Quebec and Canada knew this, and were silent. This in itself was the arrogance of the hauteur transplanted to our shores, the incomprehensible dissertation in departments and authorities that lapsed into posture with a flick of the hand of some signatory. So the Raskins' little mine became the so-called *legitimate counterbalance* to Thetford—to show all was equal in this decision-making process. But from the late 1950s on, the two brothers were questioning the damned wisdom of it all.

Because it was then, one day—when they were more robust than now, one day when they were still taking acreage away from others to build their empire—a man stood at the door of their house—at the back door—or to be frank a ghost stood at their door.

Yes, he was a ghost—a shadow of what had once been a man, a shadow of a former form. He had not been to a doctor, he had been nowhere, he had withered away, he had travelled like a hobo, or a homeless man, across the country and back, thinking the air out west, or the air in the American Southwest would triumph over what ailed him. It did not. He had worked for them, and yet they hardly recognized to whom they were speaking, so shallow and weak was his voice.

He was Vince Toomey—Arlo and Arnie and Mary Lou Toomey's father—and he had trusted the pit he had dug in, the asbestos they blasted, the rocks of it they shovelled: never realizing the fibres he breathed into his very lungs would metastasize. He had moved his family here to live in the apartment, and now it was as if his bones stuck out of his skull and he looked at them as if to say:

See—

See

See

They brought him in, they wrestled him into a pair of Dexter's pyjamas, they called their doctor, they made him broth, and yet in a telltale way he ignored what they did—they were objects in a room and he was drifting to some other place. His wife and children were brought to him, little Arlo and Arnie as sweet and as white as ghosts themselves, and the daughter Mary Lou with her braided hair.

They all sat in hope thinking the doctor would do what was right. They were sitting in a room so large it echoed, on chairs they seemed unfit to sit upon. All little vagabonds in vagabond clothes, with hope-filled eyes, looking once more expectantly at the doctor, the next at their father.

The doctor could do nothing, and stated almost with tears in his eyes that he could not, and that evening, just before dark when the house lights were coming on, Vince Toomey died.

They wrote to the scientists, and after a lengthy delay the scientists wrote back.

Still the brothers, business-minded but unsophisticated, actually believed these government-hired scientists, for the scientists wore white coats and told white lies.

Now as we approach this story the government was backing away slowly but surely. The government in Quebec had changed and wanted out of Thetford, and everyone was leaving these two rustic brothers to deal with the horrendous onslaught to come on their own. That is, they had been used, finessed in a way, like a card player is finessed at cards by a cardsharp, into asbestos and now were left to the fallout. Their hand cobbers sick, the backhoe drivers ill, the grand conveyers coming to a slow halt.

Left to deal with both the hatred and the animosity, while the government would be silent. First Nations men had come to them with a plan to take control of all the land from the field just beyond their estate to the headwaters of Riley Brook, and miles beyond.

The two old men were too proud to be impolite, and too proud to make any response.

Some years before, on the night Albert was caught at the safe, they took him from the ornate room. If he had had his hands tied behind his back he would have smiled. He had the arrogance of some men going to the gallows. Like his ancestor in the carriage—that is, the father of the little boy earlier mentioned—his face had an impetuously aristocratic look, bordering on perplexity.

His uncles took him out of the upstairs office and back to the house. They took him to the big office, with its huge elk head on the wall above the large oak desk, the two phones, the Teletype on the counter.

Dexter put on his pants over his pyjama bottoms. Then Chester went and did the same. Then they stood before him, looking up at him, both of them shrunken a little by this time, their zippers half-undone and the pyjama bottoms sticking out the front.

Dexter put his hand in his pants pocket and hauled out a huge wad of money—twenties, fifties, hundreds—there must have been three thousand dollars in this wad—and took off three one-hundred-dollar bills and four fifty-dollar bills and stuffed them into Albert's pocket.

"Go home and don't come back for a month," Dexter said.

"And mend your ways," Chester said.

"Yes, do some mending," Dexter said.

Then the both of them turned and went to bed.

They did not speak of him for a while.

The two Raskin brothers had their business structured around the mines of Good Friday Mountain. Each drove their giant half-ton trucks back and forth to the site. There was because of this mine an oil pipeline, tanks and mercury deposits in the soil, asbestos shards, zinc and copper drifts, and tailing ponds from those, and a white sky in the morning. They still brought in about a million a year. In the heady days back in the 1950s they earned about four million.

But the Canadian investors knew better than to invest in asbestos now. And though they wanted out of it, they still had obligations to fulfill.

So they were old and forgotten, and everything they had done for the community, everything they had wanted to do, now seemed to be heading toward inevitable failure. But they did not relent. They continued. And on their travels they would sometimes meet at certain economic meetings representatives from other industries who still desperately needed their product, as fire retardant and insulation, and kept urging the government to make asbestos more accessible. It was also in the interest of certain First Nations families who received money for a lease of a field near the head pond of Dawn Stream that emptied fifteen miles away into Riley Brook. Riley Brook was at the very outer border of the reserve. But in the months and years to come it would become the epicentre of the conflagration, where some First Nations band members supported the Raskin payouts to them, and many others, ruined by time and circumstance, did not.

The field where three sheds sat was used as ground zero for lime purifying the stream. Each year the First Nations were sceptical that this did not run foul into Riley Brook proper, or do any good whatsoever, and each three to five years the payment was increased. But the First Nations (they were not known as First Nations then, but, as the old men said, Indians) *had suffered* under debilitating neglect for many generations. *They had had land and streams poisoned before and had a right to be suspicious.* They had had dreams themselves unfulfilled and were desperately aware of it.

So now it did not matter to them that it was or was not Raskin's fault. They needed someone to blame. What they said they wanted to happen, a complete shutdown of all activity, lumber and mining, in the entire area, would actually destroy or compromise the very economy they themselves had much depended on, the roads they travelled on, the skidoos and trucks they bought. Still, they were angry men and women. It had been too, too long a sacrifice for the Indigenous. So they were now demanding consultation.

15

I HAD BEEN HIRED TO PAINT THE RASKINS' PORTRAIT, to paint their brother's (Albert's grandfather's) portrait, from a photograph, to paint their dog Snub, and their trucks, to do a mural along the wall of a backhoe and grader. It seemed to be a retardant against the insults now occurring against them.

So I was busy doing so in the heat of one summer, through the long evenings of sweet July and into August, when in that summer it rarely rained, and the asbestos was ripped and blown from the pit beyond me.

There was also a bust of both of them, and a statue that the board of commerce commissioned me to do. So I overheard them speak, in the office and when they stood for me. They stood bickering as I painted them, and often I did not know who was who. I would say Dexter when I meant Chester or Chester when I meant Dexter. Then they had an old gardener and handyman named Lester, who looked like they did. I was more puzzled than anything else at those voices as they stood in their ancient and heavy military uniforms from World War I. I could hear them whispering back and forth; they were talking about their nephew in unpleasant ways, not meaning to perhaps but like old men at times unable to stop.

"Gentlemen," I'd say, "I just want you to keep your faces straight for a second—look this way—thanks."

Their faces would turn toward me as I dabbed a touch of brown, a darker shade for the collar of the uniform, a moulted white for the chins and diminishing hairline, all expressing in their physiognomy a fury against the world that age and science had betrayed them. They would look almost chagrined that I had heard something of the unpleasant family squabble as they turned back toward me. As if thinking:

"You were talking!"

"No, you was."

"No, you!"

It was strange that I, hardly religious, thought this, but the church would never have betrayed them as the science they relied upon had. Now clad in uniforms of battle that existed on a pitch of earth well over a half-century before, they called out to me sheepishly:

"Would you like a drink of tea or sumpin?"

"Maybe some Kool-Aid—we made grape Kool-Aid—would you like that?"

They asked me if I knew Albert. I told them I had seen him now and again. They asked me what I thought of him. I said I didn't know him that well.

They asked me if I thought he was cracked. "You think he's cracked?"

"Pardon?"

"Our Albert—is he cracked?"

"I'm not sure," I said.

They looked at each other and nodded. "We both think he's cracked." They said he was for something called "bortions." They wrote him a letter: "We are not completely sure what abortions are, but we are both against them."

After this, as I mentioned, Albert within a few years became a professor.

"Albert Raskin—newly appointed. 'I will help put an end to the mayhem' says new professor of sociology. The Raskin name is familiar—his devotion to equality is not."

So then everything had been prepared for him, and he didn't even know why.

This was about the time Shane was put in jail, for an incident that will be explained later.

I met Albert a few times in the summer after he became associated with the university. He played bridge with a group, and belonged to a shuffleboard club.

At this time he was very interested in the pistol his stepfather had owned, the one his stepfather had put to his head that night, and wondered if anyone here had ever heard of it. His father had traded it for the salmon pool, and Albert wanted, if he could, to buy it back. It was an heirloom, and he wanted it in his family.

Over that particular summer Mel Stroud had become aware of how much money that pistol was worth and had gone to him one night, saying he could find it for him, for a price.

Dykes and his other soldiers (as he called them now) were very interested in Albert's inheritance too, for it was their one chance to take some of this money for their campaign against money.

They all swam around him, this handsome, articulate young man, who no longer stuttered.

One night Albert was sitting in the dark of the hospital, with his hat in his hand, because his mother had been taken there. He wore a pair of soft white shoes, and white slacks, with a white sweater.

People said his mom was acting bizarre, threatening suicide or to go on vacation—he didn't know which, and he had taken her there as a precaution.

That was the first night I ever met him. He looked up at me extremely worried, and his expression was peculiar. He had seemed to mistake me for having an answer to his problems as he watched me come into the main entrance. Later I realized he thought I was the Nova Scotian poet because we looked similar. He blinked and nodded, as if I had something to tell him, coming toward him from the late twilight. Then recognizing me he asked me if I might paint his picture.

So I did so.

His ancient ancestors had made it to the shores of Bouctouche and lived there in the woods. They became a family no longer set apart, the wife and mistress, the three sons, and a daughter all together. After the Reign of Terror two of the family members went back to France, served in Napoleon's army. The mistress died in childbirth in Bay du Vin, the wife remained alive, and the son, the youngest boy, married a Hache woman here in 1812 and moved with her to the land of lumber and fish, the Miramichi.

There was a painting of him, this child, in a house in Eastern Quebec, that Albert had never seen, but which showed the same chin and almost offended eyes. It was a painting situated at the end of a hallway when one turned a corner to go along the west side of the old stone house—one looked straight ahead and it was there above an end table that was covered in a white cloth. The long hair, the jaunty blue tasselled cap, made one think of a young girl, but the masculine eyes looked out at you from a white, boyish face that was not facing the viewer but looking toward some imaginary incident that may have never taken place.

How the picture that I did not know of until recently ended up in Quebec I can only surmise. They had dealings in Montreal and in Quebec City, so perhaps that was why.

"Did you know of a girl named Annie Howl?" he asked me.

At that time, though it seems strange now, I hadn't. "I don't think so," I said. "Is she a girl you want to help?"

"In a way," he said, and his voice drifted off as he spoke. Then he said, "Do you know anything about fuses?"

"A bit."

"I know nothing about fuses at all," he confessed. "They went out the other night and I think my mom thought we were being attacked. I have no idea about fuses." Then he added, "I don't know—but I think my mom has gone crazy."

Why I don't know, but I felt sorry for him.

I think at that moment, with his warm smile, he could have gone back and started over. He might have gone to Darren Howl and spoken the truth that he had hidden so many years. He might even have told the many parasites now surrounding him, like Dykes and his revolutionary friends, to go fuck themselves.

16

THE WATER WAS DARK AND BRACKISH. IT IS WHAT EVA remembered. She had changed behind the trees, and walked to the beach alone. She was angry at her mother and father, and she knew no one here. They had moved in the spring, she had to move schools, she had no friends, and it was all their fault, and she had no one to talk to, and she wished she was dead, and she had no money and had a package of menthol cigarettes but couldn't inhale and she would stand on the side of the road puffing and hiding the cigarette behind her when a car passed. And sometimes boys looked at her and she was queasy and didn't know how to react, and at other times there was a sensation she was frightened of. And then that night came.

A moment in that night. A night where she was supposed to be studying and the curtain blew and warm air came into her room, and she snuck out and went down into the small village. She was alone on the sidewalk, all seemed pleasant and deserted at that moment, the white buildings in shadow, and their back sheds shaded by trees, and there, in the shadows of an old staggered building with only one small light on at the back, a strange man grabbed her. And he hustled her behind the dairy bar and kissed her and put his hand under her sweater, and she said *no don't* and then she ran. In a way it was a terrible thing, that this was the first boy she had met on that backstreet. The first boy who had ever kissed her.

It was where her father had brought her, with a dip dip dip and a tip tip tip in his walk up the stairs jauntily into a worn two-bedroom apartment, the hallway carpeted with green carpet and smelling of cat piss. It was as if he was providing her a *portico* into a new, exciting world. And this was the world he had brought her to.

The next day that Shane man phoned her.

She hung up on him. She sat by the window looking out over the old parking lot with crabgrass withered at the edge of the cement. She had no one, she knew no one at all. A fan blew, and an old, old picture of the Fab Four sat on her small dresser.

Then glowing little flowers came by way of a deliveryman in a white truck. Then a question:

"If you don't have a date for the prom I will be your beau."

Then he met her on the street, and said: "Here's a card for you—it shows a flower, see—" And he showed her the flower. He looked scared that she would not accept him for who he was. His nicotine-stained finger shook as he pointed at the flower.

It was a young girl's romanticism that had caught her first, saying to herself, that night: *What if I even would let him kiss me?*

But what had happened because of that kiss, and that wondrous ideal that was still bathed in the scent of naivety with the trees waving coming unto dark?

"No, thank you," she said when he offered the flower.

He began to follow her.

Then, after a time, he began to threaten her, in phone calls. He told other boys not to talk to her. He told her not to ever talk to other boys.

Once by the candy store, with the tinkling bell over the black door, and in the rain he said: "What did you talk to *him* for?"

A chilling feeling and a dreadful realization that he was right behind her, wearing his torn leather jacket and his cuffs turned up above his worn black boots, and she ran.

One day an Indian boy was kicked and hit, because he had spoken to Shane and said: "Leave her alone—don't bother the young girl, have some sense, she's a lot younger than you are."

He was Gordon Hammerstone, Melissa's younger brother.

"You are not being very nice to me—not very nice. What other fellow sends you flowers?" he said after he had punched and kicked that boy.

So she hid, and then in late June the heat became insufferable and the apartment bled away her resolve to hide. She could hardly breathe, and the sunlight came in on the old shag carpet and made her ill. So she went out to swim.

The sand was soft and hot, and she wanted to swim to the red marker and back, to the laconic drift of water to one side of it, coming out from what was called the Arron Tickle.

She got out to the red marker but couldn't get back, and pieces of bark floated by her. She could smell dreary summer pulpwood— that is what she remembered, that she would die with the smell of pulpwood in her nose. And she realized at this moment if no one else in the world did realize it, her life had been so ordinary, so sad. She had never been anyplace farther than Moncton and had two pairs of sneakers, an old pair and a new pair that were becoming old.

You see she had moved with her parents to Dunn's Road, a small side road off a side road between Arron Brook proper and Good Friday Mountain, where from her bedroom window she saw three transformer towers, the bulbs and steel of godawful progress, and the giant oil tanks where oil for the whole north of our province sat in isolation, like some round whitish leviathans, owned by Raskin Asbestos Mining and Trucking. She moved to where her parents had nowhere else to go, with all her small dreams enclosed in a small bedroom in a corner apartment.

She and her parents lived on that side road in a ten-unit apartment building sitting on a scraggy lot of grass and shale rock, a few pitiless starving trees, hallways carpeted with dirty carpet, the perpetual smell of cigarettes and hash, the sound of people yelling upstairs and down, and she went for a walk. Many of these people worked for the asbestos mine, drifted in and out.

Some years before this apartment building was built, a little square wooden apartment building stood, and that was where even more hopeful and poorer Mary Lou Toomey grew up, with her two brothers, Arlo and Arnie. (They were twins also.) That apartment had been bulldozed away by the Raskins and another, grander apartment was built. But by the time Eva Mott got there, it had gone to seed, to the perfidy of time, motes of sunlight on carpets fading, and men in boots and work hats.

It was during her walks where she, Eva Mott, could pretend that her father hadn't failed again. That he had not gone back to school, tried to take a course, failed again.

"Never never will I live like this, never ever, ever never!"

So they had fallen all the way down to Arron Brook siding, not knowing where they would go next because there was nowhere left to go. It was an asbestos desert without the sand, a mountain without a peak, and a roaring wild brook where children when young were lost.

And then she became silent as if she was broken, and said nothing. She would go for a walk and find a nice boy, and he would take her dancing and to a restaurant. And this is who she found, Shane Stroud, in the darkness of a building late at night. When she got to see him in the light, she realized he was a grown man. But he would not stop bothering her.

He once told her he had a watch to give her, a silver watch worth two hundred dollars, if she would go with him to a dance in Boiestown, and she stayed inside and hid until she could not suffer it anymore.

So that day in June she went swimming, and felt the tug of the riptide hauling the top of her bathing suit away—until Torrent Peterson was there. It seemed it was destiny. She, after the terror of almost drowning, felt very important to him.

Torrent went back to work in the woods, bare-chested, his pants soaking wet, and she came to thank him the next day. She stood hidden in the small maple trees behind him for almost an hour watching him, and then he saw her, almost hidden, her face looking at him in wonder and curiosity.

She then came forward, and her back was covered in welts from deer flies; so he took some pitch he had made earlier that morning and rubbed it on her back.

"I am sorry my top came off."

It took him a long while to answer. "Nah," he said. "Didn't notice."

"You didn't?"

"Well, a tad."

But if he thought of it at all, it was with compassion at that moment, for her, that he had noticed her nakedness; even perhaps as if they were in the garden before the fall. He noticed her as a human being, needing assistance to become *well*. And he knew that she had to become *well*—that she was asking him to help her become *well*. This was now the unspoken question in the soft summer air, her smile of curiosity when she was hidden in the trees. She knew she would also use him for protection against that man Shane Stroud. He, Torrent, knew nothing of this yet. That she picked him almost unconsciously to aid her, to rid herself of the dread that the world creates.

"I knew you from school," she said. "Are you really Oscar Peterson's son?"

There was a dead quiet. He quit rubbing the ointment and then he started again.

"Yes," he said.

"Well, we are both damned—right?" she said.

She told him about this boy—actually a man—who bothered her. She didn't tell him right away, but at the end of the day, toward evening, when he kissed her softly. She told him.

"Do you know who he is? I don't even know him."

"His name is Shane Stroud," he said.

So the Strouds, those who had influenced his life through his father and mother, were suddenly back in it.

"Never mind him," he said.

Yet Stroud would mind her. He would drive his car behind her. He would shout out the window at her, "Come here—no, now just come here for a moment."

And when she didn't he would yell, "Stuck-up cunt," and roar off in a trail of dust and smell of gas, the car wresting around the turn in a fatal way, the fox tail waving shadowlike on the aerial.

"I will make sure he doesn't hurt you ever," Torrent said. And he meant it. For, kind and gentle, Torry Peterson was no one to mess with either.

When Torrent went home the night after he had hauled her from the tickle, Oscar looked very impressed. The day was ending, the sky was filled with smoky rays of late sunlight, and Oscar Peterson, the youngest son of Morrissey Peterson, his father named after the

Raskin industry creator, asked him to come and sit with him on the porch.

He smiled at some unknown thought, staring gravely ahead into the twilight. But he had heard of the noble bravery of his son.

"Imagine—right up to the tickle," he said. And he patted his son's arm.

His son Torrent could hardly read or write and had been going once or twice a month to Clara Bell who was teaching him his words. So Oscar was very proud of this young boy.

Oscar hadn't meant to be an absent father, but all his life he was. He loved his son, but all his life other things happened to make others question it. Since he was a child Torry would go down at night to the tavern, and wait outside with snow falling over his khaki coat, walking in the snow in wet, torn boots, waiting for his father. The lights inside the fogged windows would illuminate a world he did not know; he would hear laughter and cursing, the sound of glass, the door opening with a wet smell of beer and heat. Everyone knew it was Torry Peterson waiting and some men coming out would go back inside and say: "For God sake, Oscar, your little boy is waiting for you out in the cold."

"Yes, well, I'll be along in a moment."

The tavern would close at eleven and by eleven thirty Oscar would appear, dishevelled and unsteady. They would start their trek back to the small out-of-the-way trailer, the snow falling into their open coats and torn boots, and sometimes his father would fall into the drifts of snow. Torry at ten or eleven years of age would be bent over him, trying to pick him up.

"I'm getting up, son—don't you worry about me—go get Pete."

And Torry would run and get the horse Pete and walk him along the old snowed-over road to where Oscar slumbered. Then with Torry helping, Oscar would make it onto the horse's back and Torry would lead them home. That is, he would simply walk ahead of the horse and the horse would plod behind, the snow flying up from the horse's hooves, with Oscar holding on to the mane, and on clear nights the great sky cast in glinting flint like stars interspersed in endless black. Those glinting balls of fire so far, far away from such a small, humble scene that silently revealed the traits of men and beast. Then came the soft, faraway smell of smoke, then the last ice-slicked turn, and then the great silent yard, with the barn like a huge silent being, almost hidden in the black night, but its form like a heavy presence, ominous of the endless coming days of drudgery and work.

The horse would clomp toward the barn's open door, but stop just before the entrance, and Oscar would fall off. Then the horse would continue to its stall, the sound of its great unshod hooves thumping on the cold floor telling of its denizen now home to bed, so if you met the grand horse at that moment he would look at you with bold, upturning eyes, as no more than a speck of curiosity, for this was his barn and it was now night.

Yet for all of Oscar's own reading ability—some said he had read Balzac and Dickens—he had no idea that Torrent could not yet read. He had known, but he had forgotten. And his usual excuse was: "I had no idea—imagine that."

There was a rival.

Albert was taken by that girl and convinced himself over the next week that this Eva would need him. He had begun to daydream about it all. He would be instrumental in saving her from a terrible life that living and being with Torrent would have in store for her.

I have a real opportunity to help someone here, he thought. He would make it all up.

How would he approach her?

They would go for walks. He would speak to her about poetry and social injustice, and Laurence's Hagar Shipley. He would speak to her about Black sound poets, about Eldridge Cleaver who had signed a book to him, and the renegades of the left like Allen Ginsberg who he had met twice, and Germaine Greer. He would speak to her about going to Pittsburgh and having his picture taken with Simon and Garfunkel. He knew how much this would impress her.

Then, when she left her husband (for she would have to leave her husband), he would be there for her. There would be a scene, but he would stand firm. She would come to him, want to make love, he would say, "No—"

She would be the one person he would tell about Annie Howl, and she would be the person he asked forgiveness from. Why? Because she was to him another Annie. So he was desperate to do this.

She would cry—give him a note. The note would say: "You have made me free because you have taught me—you have freed my soul and saved my life." (Well, he had different scenarios about how it would work.)

She would realize he was noble. A cut above the dreary boys she knew. They would part as friends. She would hug him and say goodbye. Her husband would be devastated.

"I now know how I should have acted," he might say.

"Yes, well perhaps now you can change your ways," Albert would say sternly. "Life is more than hunting and carousing. Think of what she had to go through with a man like you."

The man would turn away and then he would come back and shake Albert's hand, and finally he would say: "Thank you."

And Albert would say, "Do not thank me—thank her."

In doing this Annie Howl would go away.

Then he too would be free.

Shane was very morose and unhappy, and he wandered about town very lovesick. First he thought that woman Carmel loved him. He was sure she did. She was just scared because she was respectable. So he wrote her love letters and asked her to meet him secretly. Near a tree—he had even picked the tree out. "The little one right beside the big one near the bush—thirty-two steps from Miller's Brook, that's where we will lie down. It will be night and no one has to see you—come as you are—wear that peach dress, the one with the zipper—you know why—!!!"

But she wouldn't even allow him in the house.

Still, that was okay, because seeing Eva at the picnic, he decided he loved Eva again.

He went all to pieces over Eva all over again.

He went to the tavern. But soon an altercation occurred with a crippled man. He was thrown out. He got in his Mustang and drove toward Dunn's Crossing by Load Road.

That very moment there was a young girl getting ready to pick berries with Eva Mott. She lived on Load Road. She would take the bicycle Eva had given her last May—the bike Eva's father had sent away for years before, packed in a box with Chinese writing on it, the cardboard box buckled down with brass rivets, with assembly instructions inside, in English, French, Spanish and Chinese. The bike was green, pale green and flimsy, and its tires were thin. It was not like the bike Eva had dreamed of.

The box had sat at the train station for a week in October, and then sat in the Motts' back room for almost a month. Eva's mother then put it together, with a spoon, butter knife and Allen wrench. Eva tried to ride it that first day in the snow and rain. That was some years ago, when she was thirteen.

The girl had gotten a new brake pedal and a new front basket, which Torrent had put on for her. He had tightened the spokes and made sure the chain was oiled. He had fixed the little bell that rang so people would know she was coming.

Shane left the tavern, driving his Mustang, and he went up Load Lane so he could cross to Dunn's Crossing to see if she, Eva, was at her apartment. His licence had been suspended, and his car always pulled to the right. He wasn't thinking of anyone but Eva Mott and how she had used him, and he was drunk. He had a .22-calibre rifle on the back seat.

He said he did not see the young girl on a bicycle going down the hill ahead of him. He said he didn't even know he had hit her.

"Surprised me," he said.

She had been invited to visit Eva Mott—they were going to pick strawberries for the men who were about to hay. The hay was not only for Torry but for this girl's father as well. She was sixteen years of age.

When she got the call from Eva, Shane was being told to leave the tavern, barred for a month. When she got on her bicycle, which she proudly kept in the porch of her house, she had eleven minutes left to live. There were rocks and ruts on Load Lane; she had to ride her bike carefully when she went over the hill. So she was very careful.

She thought a boy named Danny liked her, and she would pick some of the strawberries for him. That was her last thought before she thought she heard *a car* and tried to pull over just to be safe. She rang her bell to tell people she was there.

The suggestion was Shane had intentionally run into this young woman thinking she was Eva Mott. For it had been her bicycle. Whatever he thought, he did not stop but left the scene of an accident, while this child lay bleeding on the road. No one found her for twenty minutes. Then Becky Donaldson drove by in her police cruiser. She had been called to the tavern because Shane had thrown a chair at the waiter.

The girl lay on her side, almost as if she was sleeping. Her left foot was jammed between the frame and the front wheel, and her eyes were slightly opened. There was blood from her nose, and her right hand was still on the little bell, ringing it so she would be safe.

Shane was sent away to Dorchester Penitentiary in August. Even his brother Mel said it was the best place for him.

"Can't do much with him. Momma and me tried."

Though he had intended to, Albert became busy with various things, and didn't get to the young girl's wake, but Torrent and Eva Mott attended, in the pale evening, after supper, with the heat still beating down, and the sound of the great Arron babbling incessantly, as if calling out in time to the sweet, careful sobs of parents who had rashly separated from one another just a few months before.

The coffin was closed.

Their daughter was dead.

When he visited his mother, Albert discovered she had these three women terribly confused: Eva herself, the young woman who was killed on her bicycle, and Annie Howl who flew from a bridge to her death.

She began to believe their death was her fault.

One day when he came in, she was seen packing all her clothes— she was going away and she would never come back! Her son was at a loss, and could do nothing with her. He spoke to her about getting help.

"Help—I need no help. I need to be listened to—something happened."

"What?"

"Kisses and everything," she said, throwing a blouse into a suitcase. "And my sister—do you understand? No, you don't—my sister."

"I did not know you had a sister."

"Yes—I told—no one." She said, "If Byron was here—goddamn it—if Byron was here, no man would bother me—but I have no man here—I have no man here anymore. Can you imagine what he would do to men who bothered me! A man who fought hand-to-hand combat—ha."

"Mom," he said. "I am here!"

"You," she said in despair, "are a boy, you can't do anything for me—and—"

"And what?"

She glared at him like the old Carmel Goya she once was, and lighting a cigarette said: "And your Professor Dykes is an arsehole."

So her brother came back into her life at this time. She kept saying something bad was all her fault. But she wouldn't tell him. She said her son would have to do so.

"I want Albert to go to confession, and when he does everything will be good again."

Yes, she had lied, to her mother, to her husband when he had asked her who that man she had danced with was, to her friends in Taintville, arrogantly driving her new Cadillac up to their small crumbling houses, with a sudden look of rapacious ego and stepping gingerly across the spring mud holding her hat against the wind and her drizzle of perfume on the air.

All came flooding back when her brother who had warned her of all of this anguish she was causing clutched her hand.

"I want Byron," she said, looking at him, almost accusatory. "I want Byron to help me—to help my son—he is the only man I ever knew."

She had given forty-eight hundred dollars to the Strouds, and her son had given by now some thousands, all because they were helping the poor.

"What did your son do?"

"Murder," she whispered, "murder. Though he will never admit it now. *And perhaps he keeps telling himself he never did.*"

17

THE FIRST APARTMENT.

Arlo came into the snack bar with a big silver tea tray, came up to me as I was sketching and asked if I wanted to buy it—then taking a look over his shoulder he picked up the silver tea tray, nodded goodbye and rushed out the back door. In came Constable Furlong:

"Did you see Arlo?"

"Yes."

"Did he have a silver tea tray?"

"I'm not sure."

"He stoled it from a wedding," Furlong said. He gave me a quizzically angered look, and out he went after him, down over the hard embankment toward Arron and watched as Arlo started wading across with the tea tray above his head.

"Arlo—put the tea tray down or you will drown. I am not going in after you—that is rough water—I can't swim and I am not going in after you, you little sawed-off prick. Put the tea tray down or turn around now and come back."

"I'm about to lose my balance, Constable Furlong—"

"Put the goddamn tea tray down—"

"Stop yelling! I am trying to turn around—it is difficult conditions—stop yelling or it's your fault."

"I am not yelling—"

"I am not losing this tea tray—I almost had a buyer for it."

"It is not your tea tray, Arlo."

"It is very difficult conditions here—*very difficult conditions*—so if I drown it is your fault!"

"Is not."

"Is too."

Arlo turned and came back, dropped the tea tray and ran, so Constable Furlong, well over two hundred pounds and only five foot seven, could not catch him.

Constable Furlong was our only village constable here (there was supposed to be two for the village of Arron Side) and he tried to do his job. Arlo and Arnie were trouble for him. Living in the white apartment building with their simple-minded mother and their sister Mary Lou they were constantly snatching things. But both of them were likeable. And Oscar Peterson liked both of them and tried as best he could with them, especially after he began to hang out with Mary. But even before then he had a soft spot for them, gave them work in his hay field or yard, some days buying them Dixie Lee fried chicken.

Arlo and Arnie had razor-sharp, almost photographic memories—and this came into play in many ways. They knew the combination of every lock in our stores along here, knew the exact key for any truck in the Forestry lot, knew every television show or newscast, and what time it would be on, at any time of week. Knew to the minute when Constable Furlong would make his traumatic tour in his old second-hand paddy wagon—had it down to the minute. They knew what guards were at the asbestos plant, where they would be at any time of night, and they could open the tool shed or the machine shop or any of the trucks at will. And they did all of this as a lark, not to injure or hurt anyone, but simply because they could, and they made up contests for each other.

One contest came the day after they saw a milkshake being made at the centre snack bar. They spoke of how it was made almost the entire day. And then:

"Arlo."

"Yes."

"Get up—get dressed, hot-wire one of the Raskin trucks, go into town, sneak into the centre snack bar, make two cheeseburgers—and—"

"And?"

"And a milkshake—chocolate—and get back here by—3:25 and you win."

"What time is it now?"

"Two o'clock."

"What do I win?"

"My undying respect."

"What else?"

"You like those cowboy boots—you can have my tan leather boots. But if you don't get back in time, I take—"

"What?"

"Your transistor radio. And your pillow—I get your good pillow. That's if you don't get back. But think, think—cowboy boots."

"I need 3:40"

"Okay—3:40. Go now!"

And this was done almost to perfection, except the milkshake wasn't as chocolaty as Arnie preferred and he did mention this in passing.

Many said Arnie was smarter, but it was almost impossible to tell. Both were brilliant little minds who lived on a dustbin heap at the edge of Arron Side—farther away from the main Arron Brook than any other dwelling, certainly miles from any other apartment—a desolate affair where one would question the wisdom of putting four families together, isolated from all else around.

But the Raskins had built it for company men, who came with their families and never lived there but went to the new apartment complex upriver. So these apartments were rented to those who had nowhere else to go and little money to take them. Most were on some sort of societal aid; more than a few had been in small-time trouble. Their heroes were all darker than them—that is, their heroes had disobeyed the moral law of the world, and managed to say it was a moral surety to do so. A few did work for the Raskins, but drifted in and out over the years.

This is where they were left alone, because their mother worked at the asbestos plant doing laundry in the big industrial machine, and walked out of the blue laundry room in the evening toward the Gall Road that took her toward the apartment.

It was where young Mary Lou tried her best to dress them, and keep them clean, but she was a child wanderer as well.

It was mid-June of a particular year when they were awoken by a party, out in the hall, and stood at the door in their underwear listening to unfamiliar voices of men and women, and saw under the weak parking floodlight a giant convertible car that to those two children was a strange emblem of success.

The two of them had just stolen the questions for the math and social studies exams from Sister Beazley and had been up late looking them over.

"Pretty breezy exams, I would say, Arlo."

"Pretty breezy, Arnie—but can Mary Lou pass it?" (Mary Lou had already missed two grades, and was back with them.)

"I will sit beside her—"

"Yes, but sitting beside her is no guarantee."

They had not slept very long when the noise from the street climbed the stairs and became bedlam outside their apartment. This had often happened, but tonight it seemed different. It did not go away, it did not diminish. And there was some insistence in the yelling that said, "*We are the young who demand to be heard, in spite of law or order.*" That is what it said. Who this noise was addressed to was anyone who disagreed with the premise.

It was dark and silent and very hot in their living room, with only one light from the fish tank they shared.

"What do you think we should do, then?" Arlo said, wearing tan leather cowboy boots, even when he was in bed, so every night Arnie was reminded what he had lost when he looked over and saw the toes of the boots pointed in the air.

"I think we should go out and see them—and tell them we are in bed, and that we are waiting for our mother and have a social studies exam. And that there is no need at all to wake us at this godawful hour."

"Yes, that's sure to wise them up," Arlo said.

But just then someone banged on the door and the both of them ran into the kitchen and stood behind the small breakfast bar.

"Ya, so what you want?" Arlo said.

"Is Donna there?" came a voice.

"Out."

"Out where?"

"Out and about," Arnie said. "Who are you?"

There was silence.

Then, "I'm your long-lost cousin."

He asked to be let in, this cousin, and Arlo went to go to the door, but Arnie held him back.

"Come back tomorrow—"

But just as he said this, there was a kerfuffle and Mary Lou said: "Hey, let me in—Arnie—Arlo—"

And a loud laugh.

"Hey boys, your pretty sister is out here—with all us wolves."

And the boys, those dearly loved little specimens, who lived in the smallest of apartments in this white clapboard building, opened the door to someone who couldn't love, because they loved their sister.

His name was Stroud. He was dark-complected. He had been out of jail for three weeks, and drunk almost every night.

He was Arnie's and Arlo's long-lost cousin, fourth removed. But he was a closer relation to Oscar Peterson who he never liked. Oscar was older, and once in a while babysat him as a boy. He tried to get him to stay in school. He bought him a red bookbag with a leather strap that Mel sold. He bought him a pair of jeans and a plaid shirt, socks and shoes, and Mel had sold them all.

Stroud didn't like Oscar's old-fashioned ways—and ridiculed him incessantly, mocked him when he saw him.

Everyone in this community knew Mel Stroud's name. Feared this name. He liked the idea of people pointing to him and saying: "There he is—Mel Stroud." He liked it too when people called him dangerous. He liked the idea of being dangerous—and having cars stop for him so he could cross the street anywhere he wanted in our small village. He liked his mother imploring people to pay no attention to what others said, that he was a good man much misunderstood.

He liked the pretence of being a good man misunderstood because of his having a rough life. He liked it when people said he had a rough life and he would smile sadly as if he knew he could not describe the pain, but didn't want to anyway, for their sakes. He was always giving testimony about his youth, about all the people he had helped, and about the men he had fought. But sometimes, in noticing his eyes one saw a glint of desperate resentment that no citation could quell.

The absolute disregard for Raskin Enterprises, his fury at anyone who had something, was increasingly obvious over the years. Or he especially disliked someone who worked for something.

By sheer happenstance and luck, this night would lead to Albert Raskin himself.

The criminal element cannot be underestimated in any movement toward political or economic change.

Mel came to their apartment because some four years before he had loaned their mother Donna Toomey three hundred dollars so she could move here and take up residence, after their father died—and he now had remembered this money. He needed it back. When he came in, it was almost as dark as ink. He walked over to the fish tank, and combed his hair under the white tank light while looking at the small tiger fish, and said:

"Boys, it will be great to see your mommy again. Did she ever mention me?"

———

No one knows how it happened, except perhaps for Oscar Peterson, who finally went to the police; but presently Arnie and Arlo were seen running errands, driving in the back seat of the huge Pontiac Coupe de Ville, so that only their heads were visible. And soon their names became familiar as the youngsters to go to if you needed something from Mr. Mel Stroud. For he had cards printed that said just that: *Mr. Mel Stroud, advocate for rights of the individual.*

These rights had to do with the marijuana laws at the time. Or so people said. And the boys had cards printed as well: *Arnie and Arlo, consultants.*

Mel had a lifetime of misconduct, but had taken everything he could from the idea of being a target.

"They target me—no one else—Furlong targeted me many times—and up in Newcastle and Chatham it was worse—so I have a lot to forgive, lot to forgive." He told this to the young boys one afternoon, as they were driving around in his second-hand Coupe de Ville.

He looked and acted as a rural boy gone urban, with that cologne he preferred, the hair always neat, the shirts well pressed, the jeans with a crease. He thought these little boys were nuisances, wanting to sit in his car, playing with the eight-track, trying all the buttons, looking under the hood checking the wiring and the plugs. But he desperately liked Mary Lou, and as he often said about girls, something that came from some small thought: "Old enough to bleed, old enough to butcher."

This was the same thing Shane Stroud said.

This prurient ideal showed in his bold stare and his slick pants and high boots, the three rings on his fingers and his dull lack of appreciation of the glory of the world.

Little did any of these people know—Albert, his mother, a woman called Henrietta, a woman named Faye Sackville and Mel Stroud—that someday one cap of mescaline would link them all together on the bridge where young Annie Howl fell, link them together in a way none of them would wish.

So these boys were nuisances. Yet Mel one day suddenly realized that these boys were more than boys, they were brilliant little fellows—never forgetting who came in and out of the apartment, never once losing track of Constable Furlong. Not once forgetting a penny during a negotiation over anything their mother bought, from groceries to a toaster. In fact it was these boys who held the money, handed it out to their mom or their sister as the need arose, paid the bills, worried about the heating and lights, argued with the superintendent when he happened to come around. They were the ones who fixed Mary Lou's bicycle, helped her with her homework, washed the clothes, fed their fish, cleaned the fish tank, took care of the three stray cats. They were the ones who ran a lemonade stand near the asbestos mine, sold sandwiches to truckers, baloney and tuna fish.

Soon with the same innocence and perspicacious thrift they were selling amphetamines to the truckers, Dexedrine and Benzedrine, had them in little packages of seven, and had hashish and marijuana, had names and addresses they kept in their little heads, and each bought a new pair of blue jeans, and a cowboy hat.

They were capping mescaline, and had bought Mary Lou her own stereo record player for her room. They were children, and did not know that these might be harmful things. They in fact had been infatuated with the idea that it was only people like Constable Furlong who might be upset with ingredients like these, and it was harmless enterprise.

"*A new generation has finally come,*" Mel told them. He said this with the tone, the manner of a visionary, putting hash on a pin, as fine as an idealistic boy.

"*A new generation*—yes of course," Arnie said, "that's what it is."

"What does Jerry owe us, Arlo?"

"Thirty-seven dollars and ninety-eight cents."

"You have that list of buyers?"

"In my head."

"In your head—who can vouch for your head?"

"Arnie will vouch for my head—he has the same list in his head too."

So they would sew the pills under their cowboy hats, and in their coats, and tuck them in their boots. And no one was nicer than Mel. No one was kinder, no one more perspicacious, no one less demanding. Sometimes his brother Shane would come around, and pick up some ingredients to sell.

"The fixins," Arlo would say.

The one man concerned about all of this, the one who in the best way he could stood up to Mel Stroud and Shane Stroud, was Oscar.

But now Oscar had the love of his life to take care of, Mary Lou Toomey. Yes, he was much older than she was, but she had never had a chance. She came to him one night some years before, and said she was in trouble. She didn't even know what sex was really—but she was with two or three boys, down at the beach, and now she was in trouble. And her mother had told her the year before, "You get your arse in trouble you are on your own," and so here she was, worried and desperate.

"Then I will take care of you—and the child," Oscar said. This was not unreasonable since Oscar had tried to take care of her and the boys for ten years.

And so as if to have a white wedding, at the age of sixteen she moved to live with Oscar Peterson.

"She shouldn't be there," Mel complained to Donna, "she should be here in the apartment—that child should have been decently aborted and she should be home. Bring her home and I will take care of her." Then he left the table. He spoke sorrowfully about the sorrow of women, as fine and as decent as anyone could, or would. As fine as a writer of popular novels.

"No, I don't want no peach cobbler," he said with sad moral discretion. "I waited for it all day—but now I don't think I want no peach cobbler at all."

In that distant time, when things like this were more common, people still remembered the little girl in a maternity smock, sitting on a wooden chair, husking corn near a pile of truck tires, living with Oscar Peterson. Everyone thought he had knocked her up, and everyone whispered about it. But she was sixteen, the age of consent. And what they did not know is that Oscar had not and would never sleep with her. But knowing she was not bright—knowing she was the object of lust and stupidity— he would protect her.

What they did not know was Oscar would never in his life have sex—though he tried once, and shook so bad, and teared up so much, he never tried again. The First Nations woman he had tried to have sex with, a woman who cared for him, finally put her arms around him and held him as he cried.

But Oscar knew what the boys were doing, her little brothers packed with brains.

So it was Oscar who asked to see Mel. He had to see him, was in fact compelled by some feeling—some secondary foreboding that came over him whenever he heard the name of that young cousin.

The meeting happened at the trailer, sometime in August of that year, and Oscar proposed that Mel leave the Toomey family alone and he would pay him money. Mel paid no attention to this request. Then he stood and patted who he called "Old Oscar" on his hard and bony shoulder, but he kept his hand there, squeezing the shoulder hard, so Oscar winced, but pretended he didn't feel it.

"And what are you going to do, play hockey with that boy? Build him a rink? Come on, you know nothing at all about children—you shouldn't be allowed to have one. Besides that, I will steal Mary Lou from you—you're just an old man." Then he laughed as if it was a joke.

When Oscar told Mary Lou to stay away from Mel she said, at that time, that she hated Mel Stroud, and would have nothing to do with him, and didn't like the way he looked at her.

Oscar was relieved about that, and went outside and pitched horseshoes. Mary Lou sat inside the trailer listening to the sound of the horseshoes clink.

Poor Oscar, she did love him at that time, but he could, poor Oscar, not make love. But poor Oscar was no fool. He discovered what had happened to Mary Lou, little by little—backtracking until he discovered a burnt-out shore fire, too many drinks of wine, a trip up the back entrance of a big white cottage, two boys hauling a local girl by her arms up to the spare bedroom with its seashells and white walls, and there having their way with her with four or five younger boys standing around the bed.

And when he discovered that, to keep it as quiet as possible, the father, a judge in our local court, and his wife, who had connections with an MP, Oscar was given what was generally given in those days to young girls in trouble, six hundred dollars.

Oscar stood in the doorway of that white cottage, with Mary

Lou beside him, in the soft heat of the day, with the foyer leading to the back stairs, looking domestically summerlike with the sunlight on the white banister, where she had been carried up that night, the boys taking her pants off her as they went.

Oscar always frightened to enter such a grand place, stood ashamed—not in the way he was dressed, like the country bumpkin he was, and not in the way he spoke, the sputtering hope of a rural man trying to protect a ragamuffin child, and washed out by upper-middle-class silence—but he was ashamed of the earth itself and of those who stood before him with the smell of flowers and damp earth in large pots outside. They were the Lampkey family from the south side of the river.

The little girl went back to the trailer with him, that long-ago day, pregnant with six hundred dollars in her hand.

"That's a whole lot of money," she said, hopefully. "I'm going to give some to Mom. And," she added, "I want a rabbit. Oscar, can I get a pet rabbit?"

Her delivery was difficult. Arlo and Arnie, her mom and Oscar were there. Oscar, six foot three inches, with short cropped hair, half-mad eyes and a bouquet of yellow roses, the boys sitting in cowboy hats and jean jackets, and their mother unable to keep silent but talking to everyone who ventured in.

"Here's her husband here—but he's scared to go into delivery—he's just a nervous man." Then she would break out laughing hilariously. Then as the labour went on, she said: "Oscar—go see! Oscar—go in!"

But poor Oscar, all six foot three, sat like a stone, tears in his eyes.

That same night in another birthing room a First Nations boy named Roderick Hammerstone was born, twenty minutes before Mary Lou gave birth to Torrent Peterson.

That he would have something of a strange parallel destiny to Mary Lou's child Torrent was of course not known at that time. He was Melissa Hammerstone's only child. The young girl Byron had once hired taxis for to take her to piano lessons.

Mary Lou wanted to call her son Terrance, but wrote Torrent, for she did not know how to spell.

But she was not strong, filled with sneezes and fevers. So shortly after the birth of her own son, Mary Lou developed severe diabetes, and was so afraid of needles that Oscar had to give her insulin each afternoon. She would close her eyes, grit her teeth, and Oscar would sing to her about the Big Rock Candy Mountains where:

All the jails are made of tin
And you can walk right out again
As soon as you are in.

That always made her smile.
And then after a little *"ouch"* the needle would be taken away.

18

FOR A FEW YEARS MEL CAME AND WENT, WITH MUCH going for him, more money—a bigger car, a better smile—it seemed to the Toomey family. And little by little—well, when Mary Lou came over with Torrent for a visit, or to do laundry in the laundry room downstairs, Mel would help carry the baskets, or lift the stroller, or hand out cigarettes. One day he gave her twenty dollars for the child. His smile revealed a secret but she did not catch it.

Then he simply turned away and in another vein declared: "I think I'll have some upside-down pineapple cake—your mom made it for me. You need a piece? I certainly do."

"A change is in order for you, my girl," he said one certain summer night. That night he took her to the swimming pool in town, and bought her a yellow bikini. And said: "You look AMAZING."

Mel then bought her a friendship ring, and told her he loved her so much that he might commit suicide. "I could and no one would ever care. I would—I really, really would."

She had left Torrent with Oscar that evening. She said she would be back in an hour, and was gone all night. Oscar was frantic and was sitting in the dark with the boy on his lap when she got home.

One night Mel was having a birthday party for Shane Stroud. Oscar was so furious that Mary Lou had dressed to go out without telling him that he slapped her, and gave her a black eye, and locked her in the back room. She held her white shoes in her hand saying: "Let me out."

And little Torrent said, "Let her out, Daddy, let her out!"

The next week Oscar had been hired by Chester and Dexter Raskin to pick up containers along the barren road, containers of waste that had been collected near one of the tailing ponds, and he was away. He would sleep at a small camp far up at Mile 37, alone, and take one of the Raskin trucks, the barrels would be put in a waste dump beyond the great mine and be left in hundreds of those black drums, for no one knew what else to do with them.

It was then that Mary Lou decided to leave him. She was going to go with Mel, who now roved around in a Coupe de Ville.

But before Mel could act on anything else—on the biggest deal of his life, with a biker group in Maine—he was sent to jail for nine months for a fight at KO=2 bar. He had hauled an army issue knife on the wrong man—Packet Terri.

It was then that little Arlo and Arnie made their mistake. Except in their innocence they did not consider it such.

They had both broken into stores, both capped mescaline, both had stolen stereos from cars. Now and again they took the whole car. They had not been caught by poor Furlong, who seemed incapable of an arrest.

Now and again Mel would hand them some money—take them for a treat at China House food. But their mother was ill— she had washed clothing and other laundry from men at the asbestos mine for twenty years, and now had a hard time breathing. She would sit in a big chair with swollen legs and a puffer, looking at everyone who came in as if they were the one person who might alleviate her problems.

Therefore, on their own Arlo and Arnie began dipping into the money that Mel would actually consider his. Money that was sacrosanct for Mr. Mel. They bought their mother a new dining room set, a new dishwasher, brand-new dishes, and walked around with pencils behind their ears. They got a new filter for their fish tank and seven new guppies.

They even thought they might get into real estate, buy a blueberry field or two and plant marijuana.

"We can always make it up to him," Arlo said, happily and full of vigour as he shook some fish food onto the top of the tank.

They had it mostly figured out—mostly.

But when Mel got out of jail, early on good behaviour, for he was a man who was good, he asked, very politely: "I need my four thousand—where is it?"

That is when the little apartment became anguish, and quite seriously, a vision of hell.

Once Mel threw the new dishes his dinner was on across the room. It startled their mother so much she started to shake. She had made him his favourite dinner and he seemed so thankful. But then he threw it. She ran into the bedroom and was crawling about on her knees trying to find her puffer. He walked into the room and kicked her puffer under the dresser. And then walked out.

Arlo and Arnie ran in and moved the dresser, all of them shouting and crying. Finally Arnie got the puffer to her and she got a few puffs in and they laid her on the bed. Her lips were blue and her eyes buggy.

Which is what Arlo said.

"Her eyes are somewhat protruded—I don't like that sign at all."

Arnie sat with her until she finally fell asleep, wheezing and coughing.

They had to sell their guppies.

They doled them out a few guppies at a time until they were all gone back to the pet store and only one fat goldfish swam about in their big tank. Of course it was at a loss—they made almost no money from it. The tanks of the pet store, with its hamsters and snakes, once so inviting, now became a symbol of failure, and the owner, a snappy little man with small wire glasses and a goatee, smiled whenever they came in—and managed to get in the end almost everything back.

They capped extra mescaline and put dark soil from the asbestos mine in it, to be able to make more caps, and sold it at the beach and the new mall. On September 5 Arlo capped thirteen mescaline with some soil. Shane took it to a party at Albert Raskin's, because Albert had believed Shane's presence would shock those he wanted to impress.

That night it was given to a young freshman girl from Napan— and the result was a young girl running naked. That was the moment, long ago now, that caused fear in a handful of dust.

I have heard that Arlo and Arnie were hoping to go to Saint Michael's University as well—Arlo said he would become a doctor, and cure his mom. Arnie said he would become a lawyer, and keep them from jail.

They had it all tabulated—money for tuition, books, and courses picked out. And how much they could put away for Mary Lou and her child Torrent.

Still, in order to facilitate what must be, in order to make something up to Mel, Arlo and Arnie had to drive a van across the blueberry flats to the border. In fact this is what was bound to happen from the first time Mel ever knocked on their apartment door. The two had been warned on a number of occasions—always subtly. A look, a nod, a shrug, a stare from Mel's brother Shane, who tormented them—all of which now manifested itself in their memories as being ominous, and yet when they were being driven to the drive-in theatre to see *Green Monster from Outer Space* and eat fish and chips, and slurp pop, they had dismissed such omens.

They told him, both of them, that they didn't want to go. It was too *sketchy*.

So he answered: "*I give you my friendship*—what have either of you ever really done for me?"

(And that is why Arlo had stolen the silver tea tray, thinking it might be half-helpful in relieving the debt).

———

By the time everything was in order it was the winter. Snow had fallen out in the daytime, against the naked black branches of small trees, against the fiery alders along great Arron Brook. A darkness in the earth had certainly descended and the earth was covered in early snow that had not yet concealed the harsh cold stubble, the dead branches and the long, endless cold ditches, but left streaks of black and brown between the pencil-thin white that had just fallen.

And so these two frightened boys, without a chance in the world, it seemed, started across blueberry flats under a full moon, the ice slick beneath old bald tires, with bags and bags of amphetamines, mescaline and acid tabs in the panels of their van, and were stopped by Constable Furlong. He stopped Arlo, who wore a night light on his cowboy hat, reading a map, and licence-less Arnie driving the stick shift.

Furlong was given the information by a person on a pay phone down at Ball Shore. Years later I discovered that it was Oscar Peterson—in fact he was trying to protect them. They would never have gotten across the border, and the American border guards would have taken them to Washington County Jail. If they did succeed in delivery there might have been no guarantee they would be allowed to leave Portland by that biker gang they were delivering the goods to.

Furlong brought the boys to the little office and began to interrogate them, one at a time and then both at once. He knew it was Mel Stroud's doing, but without cooperation there was no proof.

"If you don't tell me right now who is who, and who you are selling for—you will go to jail," Furlong said. "I could charge you with murder—for a trucker has died of a heart attack while taking those uppers."

"Tell what you know," Oscar pleaded with them, for he was asked to help, because it seemed Furlong had no idea how to handle it. "You must tell—now, for your own good."

But you see he had been their *best friend*, Mel Stroud. They bought cowboy hats to look just like he did, and Arlo wore those leather cowboy boots to bed. How great it had been when he was angry with them, and they were worried lest they had done something wrong, that suddenly after a time he would look at them and wink. Then their hearts would be glad.

As their mother Donna had got sicker, Mel Stroud was always there, driving her to and from Outpatients and getting her prescriptions filled, even saying he would get her a hospital bed for her bedroom, making sure her mask was placed right and her oxygen tank was full. (But it was Chester and Dexter who had actually done all of this. It was Mel who took the credit.)

And now he said they had all *betrayed* him.

Mel is a killer, Oscar had told them a year ago. *He kills people, I am sure.*

They ran and told Mel what Oscar had said, and he looked startled, astonished, ashamed and sorry. Then the next day Mel tweaked both of their ears and they broke out grinning.

Now there was an empty feeling where all his kindness once had been.

Oscar posted their bail and promised they would be in court. They sat in the bedroom, and spoke.

When they went out that night, just after Furlong had interviewed them, and walked into the broken parking lot in the desperate cold to feed the stray cats, Mr. Stroud drove his car up the drive and didn't even look at them, so used and betrayed he felt.

They knew they had to help Mel Stroud, because he had helped them.

"That's the least we can do," Arnie said.

On the table was their report cards, 98 percent for Arlo, and 98.5 for Arnie.

They had both graduated when they were fifteen.

Constable Furlong had sat the boys down, walking back and forth in front of them, while he ate a big bag of chips and sipped on a Coke.

He said: "It will be nice for you two, going up to Dorchester. They like pretty boys like you. There are rough men in there, and you two little lads will be tidy morsels for them. You will see how it goes. Now jail instead of giving someone up—prison for a loyalty that wouldn't matter a damn to him. So give us his name and we will protect you. If you don't tell me, to prison you will go."

"Tell them," Oscar pleaded, "I will protect you."

"That poor trucker," Furlong said, "had a wife and four children—do you know that? I guess he coughed and died right in his truck."

Furlong remembered this for years after. He remembered sitting back in a chair and putting a handful of chips in his mouth, and then shaking the chips up, he offered the bag over. He remembered telling Oscar: "Those little buggers are scared to death of me. They have no way out now. Soon they will talk."

He remembered all of this, did Constable Furlong.

It was the day before they were scheduled to appear in the courthouse in Newcastle, when a phone call came. They had not heard from their friend Mel Stroud in weeks.

"I will drive you out to the barrens—near the blueberry flats. It's marked on a pole—Mile 17. But we have to wait there."

"I know where that is," Arnie said.

"But we have to wait—a package is coming to prove our innocence."

"How—what?"

"I am not going to tell you over the phone." Here there was a long pause. "You want to go to Dorchester"—another pause— "take this offer—take it. It is the only offer they are going to give. But we'll wait there—I'll wait with you—don't worry."

"Who has to see us?"

"Oh I can't say"—pause—"over the phone."

Click.

All day they moped around, and then Arnie cleaned the fish tank, even though they had only one fish. They had their pants, shirt and ties laid out on the couch, to wear to court the next morning. Then they cleaned the elements on the stove, and washed the vinyl flooring.

"We had better go—if we are going—he will drive us—so if we want to show our loyalty we have to wait with him. After that the charges will be dismissed."

So as far as anyone now knows, trying to fathom all of this, the minds of two young boys in that long-ago time, they left at five that evening with Mel Stroud. They told no one where they were going, The smell of mid-winter cold rested on the grey roofs and small spruce, on the entranceway to the apartment building, on lumber and creosote poles. The waff of cold and the stink from the mill, the heat from generators and the macabre-looking lights.

Mel dropped them off at Mile 17. As soon as they left the car, he started to turn around.

"Aren't you staying with us?"

"No. I have to do something to help—I'll be back—we will get home by midnight. Tomorrow with the evidence he gives you, you will walk out of that court."

"What evidence though—what evidence?"

"You don't believe me?" Mel said, looking up at them from behind the wheel.

"No, we believe you—it just seems a bit perpendicular."

"Ha—a bit perpendicular," Mel said, shaking his head and pointing a finger at them. And drove off and it was already dark.

That night the temperature dipped to minus thirty-five. And they waited exactly where they were told. At about eleven they realized there must have been a mistake. Their feet were numb—numb with pain. Now they could no longer feel their faces. The air had penetrated their small jackets and caps, and left their blood to clot. So they thought, desperately as children who do not recognize peril, they could cut across from Riley Brook by taking a compass reading, off the stars, the trees and the cold light moon above them.

They started back toward Arron Brook. They had no matches—and had a long way to walk before they even got to the Riley Brook. There at the far end would be the house of the First Nations boy Gordon Hammerstone who had always been kind to them.

But after a while they no longer felt the cold. They no longer felt their legs, and Arlo opened his coat and pulled off his cap.

They were discovered huddled together the next afternoon, covered in a glaze of snow. It was hard to tell who was Arnie and who was Arlo. They had been loyal to the end.

———

Mel was frantic. The day after the funeral he paced the hallway outside the apartment. He told Mary Lou they had to go, now. *Now.* He lighted a cigarette and put it out on the carpet, and then another. He screamed at Mary Lou, saying that Oscar had betrayed everyone, and the boys were scared and ran away.

"Phone the police—tell him he beat you—get that son of a bitch in jail now!"

So, her hands shaking, her eyes watering, her nose running, she did.

In the end she would rather go with Mel, who, crying and holding her hand, had sat in the pew at church beside her, the two little coffins side by side and the priest going over everything in their lives as if trying to find something to rest upon.

In point of fact, as Clara said later, Oscar was actually trying to save not only the boys but Mary Lou as well.

Oscar went to church and lighted a candle every day so Mary Lou would come back. He spoke to the priest, who tried to understand his flailing and wailing about—and finally gave up on him, and wouldn't open the rectory door. Oscar rolled about in ashes from the barrel at the side of his trailer and went along to the priest covered in ashes.

"Some kind of priest you are," Oscar complained. "You're good at molesting boys—but why don't you try to fulfill your other just as important priestly duties," he yelled. "No fuckin wonder why I'm leaning toward the Pentecostals."

After a time he invented her death, as one of a child who wanted to save eagles, and told Torrent to lay flowers on her grave.

Furlong never forgave himself about those boys. Ever. He simply drove the paddy wagon to and from work until he was retired. And he died of a heart attack at age fifty-one. No one knew of

Mel's involvement in this for a long while. Everyone believed Oscar had told on them and they ran away.

Every day Furlong remembered little Arlo, looking at little Arnie, and then nervously glancing at him and saying *Thank you, dear sir*, when he took a chip.

19

AFTER A TIME THE APARTMENT BUILDING WAS BULLDOZED to the ground. The boys were buried and forgotten, their mother died sometime later, and little Mary Lou was gone to Saint John where Mel Stroud tried to pick up work on the docks, working on the frigates. It was a time of great change for Dexter and Chester's business. Though they still had markets in India and Pakistan, they had fewer markets in Canada and Europe. Dexter had taken a trip to Europe, trying to keep the doors opened in West Germany. He got lost for a whole day in the airport in Frankfurt. He spoke personally to Willy Brandt. Then he had travelled into Pakistan, just about the time of the outbreak of war with India. He was jostled about on a street in Lahore. He came home saying all the buildings were old and everyone dressed funny and were nuts.

They would often be seen sitting in the great den, looking over the papers.

Dexter would say: "They are—making trouble."

"Who?"

"Students. All over the place, marching up and down."

"Of course they are. Education gets the best of them."

They had torn the small white clapboard apartment down and built a square brick apartment building. Two miles to the south was the east gate of Raskin Enterprises, with its floodlights shining twenty-four hours a day.

Five miles away, over broken and patched roads, the KO=2 bar sat. In the summer one could hear crickets in the weeds by the gravel parking lot. There men played slot machines, shuffleboard on the glazed pine table, and drank draft beer, rum and hermit wine, and ate pickled wieners.

Beyond that the long road across the barrens and blueberry flats, where those two luckless kids got caught out and froze.

"No matches," Dexter said. "Should have had some matches. I always have matches when I'm out and about."

They looked at each other with the same narrow, malignly bright eyes.

So the second apartment was where Eva Mott came to live with her luckless father, with the windows opened in the heat, and the smell of tar and wire, of sweet grey birds, and if it wasn't for a boy named Torrent Peterson she would have drowned three weeks after she arrived.

Kaput.

Albert wanted to give some money away.

His lawyer insisted Byron actually wanted him to give it as a loan. So finally he said he would. But it had to be a worthwhile project.

He decided upon one person—actually one couple.

Both of them had come at night in the fall to his door sometime after that young girl from Load Lane was killed. Eva and Torrent had asked him if he might help them with a loan.

They had been to every bank, and every credit union, and must now try Household Finance if their dream was to come true. But he, haying for them, told them if they ever needed help, come to him.

So Albert said, to the two youngsters standing there, "I will see. There are many people here who would benefit from some money."

"Yes, please think about it, sir," Eva pleaded.

They went away, and the man, young Torry Peterson, said to his wife, young Eva Mott, that he no longer thought this a good idea, to start a cabinetmaking business, to make renovations to his barn, and to buy the timberland from Clement Ricer might be a pipe dream for him.

"No no no," she said, "it's our one chance—it is our one damn chance. We have to take it."

"I am not good at asking for money."

But it was a pipe dream Eva would not let go. She could be like her cousin Clara Bell after all.

Albert could get the money easily now. In fact even without Byron's money he was quite rich because of certain payments from his uncles.

He would publicize it also, to make people aware of what he was doing.

He could loan the money to Eva, in order to empower her. (He did not really think of Torry here.) It would be a business venture.

Her wedding was a year or so before. She had married the man who had saved her life, the luckless Torrent Peterson.

There was a woodlot, a stand of timber above Riley Brook belonging to Clement Ricer that had remained untouched in the fire of four years before. And Torrent and Eva wanted it.

Torrent had all his grandfather's tools—ancient tools, all types of saws, chisels, wood drills, a vise grip, planes, hammers, mauls. He was an exceptional carpenter but he worked for his father, in the junkyard under those lights that shone out from the barn.

At times Eva would be there as well, helping him move tin and iron, old stove parts and electric motors, in that grand frozen inventory of Oscar's life. During summer gnats and mosquitoes spread their blood, and in winter the wind lashed upon them, and Eva's hair froze against her cheek, her leggings under her heavy woollen skirt, and her heavy-soled boots tied with leather laces.

Oh, Albert thought, driving by one day, if only he could take a picture and show people who he intended to help.

He believed Eva was his ticket to redemption. But he needed Eva to help by him helping her.

Because if she succeeded *without his help* then his *sociological* book, which he told people he would publish, about Arron Brook, would *fail*. He must himself play a part, of supervision to prove himself. He would loan money and supervise what was done.

If she and Torrent were happy as they seemed to be now, then his thesis would be a moot point. He knew this too, as a seed in the forest of a million trillion seeds.

Once when he was driving down the hill of Load Road he came to the spot that young woman was hit and killed by Shane Stroud.

At the place where she was struck down the family had put a marker and a note from the Bible. The wind had blown the marker sideways.

There was only one problem. He was no longer that unattractive teenaged boy. He was now handsome and many women liked him, and it had made him vain. And this vanity was to play a devastating part in his attempt at redemption. And Eva Mott was beautiful. In fact she was both beautiful and susceptible.

That summer he made sure he walked along the gravel road toward his cottage instead of along the beach, he made sure he was at the beach where she still swam.

In the evening he wrote sketches of her, what she wore, how she dressed and spoke.

She often blushed when he spoke and often said: "Sorry, sir, I get some confused. Sometimes I could just die 'cause you make me confused."

"I am not *sir*—"

"Well, I could not call you Albert."

"Professor Raskin," he said, picking up a piece of grass and putting it in his mouth.

"Yes, Professor Raskin. I never spoke to a professor so much before."

A few days would go by, and he would decide not to see her. She was, as so many country girls are, disarming in her beauty.

"I won't see her again—I will—yes, I will go to confession, I will just give the money to the Arron Brook Community Centre— Why oh why did that night happen—leave me alone!" he would sometimes say aloud to the clouds passing by.

Then he would come forward when he saw her alone. He would wave, walk up and speak to her.

One morning he told her that he was "thinking hard on your proposal."

"Oh sir! Really? Do you know what that would mean to Torry?"

"And to you?"

"Yes, sir, to me too—to us all the way around."

One day she came to him. He was sitting on the giant white drift log that was up the shore a way from the tickle and suddenly she was there. For a moment he didn't know if she was laughing or crying, and she pressed a piece of paper in his hand, her face still with the same beaming red expression, and turned and ran up the pathway toward her home.

On the paper was a heart drawn in crayon like a child of eight
might have done, with the words inscribed inside it: "Thank you
so very much sir." And signed: "Me and Torry."

But there was a problem.

Who was this problem?

Well, the problem was—*Church Bell*. That was what people
in his department called Clara Bell. An old-fashioned Catholic
girl. God Almighty. She said the rosary; she had an aunt who
was a nun! Her grandfather had been premier at a time when his
uncles became rich. She infuriated Dykes, Dykes hated her—
and Albert was influenced by Dykes.

Each time Clara saw him with her cousin Eva she would in
some way try to intervene. She would call Eva to her, or try to
catch up to them on the beach. She even stepped in between them
twice, gingerly making Eva back away.

Then one night, lying alone in the dark, he thought: *It's that—
she knows something about that!*

Darren Howl and Clara Bell were married.

And a deep unease over came him. A deep fear. And he went to
a bookshelf and picked up a book at random, and it was T. S. Eliot,
and closing his eyes he opened it to a line. Opening them he read:

   "I will show you fear in a handful of dust."

Albert and Clara met because Clara Bell's father worked for Raskin
Enterprises, and there were certain things that Albert was now
asked to do.

For three or four days over the course of a summer he found
himself at Clara Bell's. One afternoon they began talking about
pregnancy and women, because of three unmarried women who

were having children along the Load Road, and the two young girls here who were pregnant and only teenagers.

"Abortion is the only adequate solution," Albert said ardently. "Even noble. Then the child doesn't suffer." Then looking at Clara he said, "I know Catholics might disagree."

Clara responded: "Yes, the best way you have not to have a child suffer is not to give them a chance at it. But none of them that I know would give up a moment of their lives for your opinion about their lives."

"Well, as I said, I know Catholics would always disagree."

"So many along this road too did not have the luxury of being wanted either—Catholics or otherwise—but they made out okay," Clara said.

"But you must admit, many are better off not born?" Albert said. "Look at Torry Peterson."

"Torry Peterson?" someone said. "What's wrong with him?"

"Nothing is *wrong* with him, it's just I see his life—the life of his wife—"

"What's wrong with his wife?" the same person asked, confused.

"Nothing," he said suddenly, and felt embarrassed. Then he looked over at the woman sitting beside Clara Bell. She had not spoken at all.

He had seen her somewhere before but he was uncertain where. He kept trying to picture her someplace else, kept thinking of some feature he recognized. At this point she turned and looked at him as well, and gave the same slight smile he had seen before, tense and knowing. Then he knew, and his face flattened out to one of shock.

It was the police officer Constable Becky Donaldson—a good friend of Clara and her husband Darren Howl.

He looked toward the corner of the room and his eyes lighted on the small record player with the black ink stain—the record player that Becky Donaldson's sister had at her little party years before.

Clara was now talking about two boys, Arnie and Arlo, who had frozen to death in each other's arms, out on the barrens, in a scowl of wind one February years ago. It was a topic that had come up now and again, in the way elusive things do, because her husband Darren Howl believed that they were mixed up with someone at that time, and sent to their deaths.

Though Clara did not and would not tell this part of her husband's theory, he believed they had to appear in court. They had been selling mescaline. Her husband's contention, also not spoken of here, was not that Arlo and Arnie were trying to run away—as the police file stated from that long-ago night—but *someone* they must have really trusted had deceived them into going out there.

This was her husband's theory, but it was also Constable Donaldson's theory and Oscar Peterson's theory as well—and Oscar was pivotal in the research being done by her husband Darren Howl. You see, a quarter horse can do a good deal—and in this case it made a connection between Oscar's and Darren's family. Oscar had rescued a quarter horse named Piny Wood and rode it back to them years before. It had been Annie Howl's quarter horse. They had been in touch ever since.

Clara did not tell very much of this ancient story.

"You see," Albert said, "you see—well that's my point—and my point is this—that if they had not been born, their lives wouldn't have been a torture for them or others!"

"Why is that?" someone asked. "I knew them and they were pretty good young lads."

"My reasons are"—and here he counted on his fingers—"poverty, early pregnancy, lack of knowledge or understanding. Fatherless, probably—"

"Poverty for sure," Clara said. "Lack of knowledge I doubt very much. Both had incredible intelligence."

"You know, Albert, both of them were brighter than you," Clara's sister Joanie, the one who had the graduation party an age ago, said. And he hadn't even seen her sitting in the room, at the very back near the stairs.

People began to laugh at this. The woman sitting beside him, who knew nothing of the ongoing war between him and Clara over Catholicism, who was on vacation from Nova Scotia, who left all religion to others, who was studying to be a veterinarian and who was Becky Donaldson's lover, punched him on the arm as if it was a great joke.

"There you go, lad—you've been told!"

He laughed too. But he left his beer unfinished.

He passed the church. It was four o'clock on Saturday, the time the confessional was opened.

20

THE INVESTIGATION INTO ARLO AND ARNIE WAS BEING conducted by Clara's husband (a lame man in a wheelchair) who was the brother of that child who had taken the mescaline at that party some years before. He had been in touch with one person especially about this—Oscar Peterson, who knew those boys were selling drugs at that time and who in his own way had tried to protect them.

The evening after his sister had taken the drugs Darren had tried to rescue her. When they were driving her home she had left the car at a traffic stop, and jumped onto the bridge rail to see what she said were thousands of goldfish in the water. It had rained very heavily early that day, and putting her legs on the second rail she suddenly slipped. Without a sound the little girl, full of hope two nights before, fell. At that moment none of them knew anything about drugs—had no idea about them at all.

Without a thought, Darren, strong and athletic, had jumped in after her, crushing his legs on a lay of rocks.

His sister died that night. She simply did not surface for an hour, caught up in a bale of chicken wire. Clara's boyfriend Darren Howl was left disabled. The investigation had gone on for a long while now and then petered out; whispers about drugs were simply spoken about in retrospect, and over time forgotten. *Young kid got on drugs and died over at the university.* Others said that Darren had accosted his sister in the car and she was trying to get away from him. Others said she knew they were taking her home to whip her, and they had before. Others said they found out she had been selling drugs and was involved with a married man.

So Darren, spurred on by these accusations, interviewed people, and on a hot, lazy day in August last year someone he contacted said: "Oh, Shane used to bring drugs down to the parties here."

"Shane who?" Darren asked.

"Shane Stroud."

He contacted Constable Becky Donaldson and she renewed her interest in the case, but as yet had not come up with any definite results. Becky would let people at the university solve the problems of the world. She had no interest in them. She had her twenty-six-year-old lover, the young veterinarian Sandra Poke from Nova Scotia. She had her dog Muscles, she had her banjo that she played quite well. She had a four handicap in golf. She would solve the case.

Darren hardly knew who to speak to, and then someone came to see him about it all. Like many Mi'kmaq men he arrived after many years of silence.

His name was Gordon Hammerstone. He had fought for the rights of his sister and her daughter to have their band cards. His wonderful happy-go-lucky sister Melissa, who Byron had sent to music lessons long ago, on the third floor of the convent in Newcastle, had been addicted to drugs and alcohol the whole time she was pregnant with Roderick, the boy who had been born the same evening as Torrent Peterson. Taking drugs and wine, she had a son who was diagnosed as having severe fetal alcohol syndrome. She died in shame and hatred of the world.

This and other matters plagued Gordon, and one day he showed up at Darren's office to talk about Mel Stroud.

Gordon was an excellent carver, maker of small figurines he sold, tied a hundred dozen salmon flies a year to sell in town, had a good grasp of history, never to be outraged easily. He also made bows, and was a furrier of some reputation. The reserve was to him hectares of misery given to them by another people. But he also felt the Mi'kmaq or anyone else had to decide their own lives by their own conscience. In fact he felt they had to concentrate on schools and universities. They had built New York and Toronto walking on skyscrapers above the earth—why not partake in the glory of them? They had to move into the world.

So one night listening to certain band members speaking of how much they were owed and how much was taken, he spoke out, thinking he was doing nothing wrong. But the wrong he did was not able to be mended:

"Who is not subsidized for their oil? I know you want to protect the land but remember some of us exploit it just as much as others. The world is going to the stars—get your kids educated. Our kids are more important than anything else. I think of what my sister might have been—I think of little Roderick."

There was silence and the silence remained, and remained.

Now his nephew Roderick had found other friends and could not be handled anymore, and was told his own uncle was a traitor. That his mother had died because of racism, that the young First Nations men must take action. It was now time to retake the land. Gordon heard all of this in dribs and drabs over the last few years. He and some others continually tried to protect Roderick from the one who harmed him most—himself.

Gordon went to see Darren on a windy cold day in late August. For many moments he did not speak of anything in particular and then he said almost out of the blue: "I think Albert Raskin gave your sister the drugs, just as his friend Mel gave my sister drugs." But Hammerstone said, if he remembered, she asked for them, and he couldn't be positive of anything.

"Why?" Darren asked. "Why? She wouldn't even know what they were—why?"

"I was on my way home when she arrived. She said she had a headache."

So then Darren after ten years knew what had happened. And yet in the trauma of it all he had all but forgotten what had plagued his sister: *migraines*.

She had developed them at the age of fourteen. At times coming back to the farm, in youthful exuberance over a ball game, the soft sweet nights of late May, with daylight still clinging in the air, the house would be silent and dark, smelling of spring in the evening, the last twittering of birds before silence, and yet in silence not reposed, the drapes of her room drawn, and not a sound allowed. It was Annie—she had been in her room since three that afternoon because of her headache. She couldn't go to the game, and she was still in her room in the dark.

Later she would come from her room, pale, thin and trembling.

This was the spell put on her by young womanhood that had come with her first menstrual cycle she could not escape.

So it was after many years that he, Darren Howl, had discovered why all of this had happened.

Oscar at this same time was going to Saint John to ask questions, and discovered that in the early seventies Mary Lou desperately wanted to come home, back to her child. She was taking cocaine, was thin and ragged. They lived on Britain Street in Saint John, and Mel made friends among very strange people, some of whom she was terrified of.

She missed her mommy, who was ill, and she cried often over Arlo and Arnie, and Stroud would say:

"That's enough crying now, I know but we can do nothing about what Oscar did to them, they are dead and gone. That's why I brought you here, to forget."

She sent letters, addressed to Torrent, in her childlike handwriting. *To Master Torrent V Peterson, 175 1/2 Arron Turn, Back Settlement, Lower Newcastle, Miramichi.*

Oscar had told Torrent his mother had died, so he hid these letters in the back wall.

In one of the letters she placed a picture of herself and Mel Stroud near the Saint John Harbour. And in another envelope the day she turned twenty-one, she placed something else—a little silver watch;

the one Mrs. Wally had won in the raffle the night of the wedding—
chipped a little, but still ticking away the seconds of time.

"Give this to your girlfriend, Torry—when you get big and tell
her it is from your mom who loves you stronger than four hundred
push ups."

The day after she sent the watch away Mel asked her where it
was. She was eating her cereal. She remembered the loud music,
Mrs. Wally's "Oh dear" when she had discovered she won the
watch, the accordion music.

"How did you ever get that watch?" she suddenly asked with
her mouth full of cornflakes so she looked like a chipmunk.

"It just turned up. Where is it?"

"I don't know," she said.

He realized she had been giving the landlady letters to mail.

"No more of that," he said. "I don't need people from up on the
river knowing where we are."

"Why, for heaven sakes."

"Just be quiet—eat your cornflakes. It's bad if they know—I'm
working for the government."

"You're working for the government? What are you doing working for the government?"

"You'd be very surprised."

She was unsure what it all meant. But she wanted to go home.
She sat in the room and listened to the wind over the great Fundy
bay and wanted to go home.

She didn't know how to hide things well. She didn't know how
to outsmart anyone, except poor Oscar. And Arlo and Arnie were
no longer there to help her.

He had her too scared to talk to anyone. And twice the nice
coloured man (for that's what she called him) who they had met at

the market came to ask about her, because he had seen her and had worried how she was.

"Oh don't worry about her—worry about your own," Mel said.

The landlady was told to mind her own business as well, that poor Mary had escaped from a brutal husband, who was looking for her with a hatchet.

"Poor little thing," the landlady said.

Mary didn't know how to escape and had no one to help her plan. So most of the day she sat in the chair, the window nailed and the curtain closed. Now she said she wanted to know what had happened to Mrs. Wally.

"I want to know what happened to Mrs. Wally."

"Whatever for?"

"Because of her watch."

"What watch?"

"The watch you give me—after Shane give it to you—I'm not so stupid."

"You're pretty stupid."

"Yes—but not that stupid. I'm starting to figure things out. So if you don't tell me, I will tell Mr. Freeze."

"Who is Mr. Freeze?"

"The coloured man—"

"Strange name for a coloured man."

"I don't care—he told me to see him if I wanted. So I will go to Mr. Freeze—he told me to is what he did, and he calls me Miss Mary Lou—not all the mean names you call me. And I want you to tell me about Arlo and Arnie—and I want you to tell me too."

So she closed her little fists and closed her eyes, and stamped her left foot.

That's why other plans were devised for her. They had to be. Soon she would say something to someone about something that would cause trouble.

That last letter was delivered the very day Mel Stroud discovered she was pregnant.

"That's the last thing we need. I told you—didn't I tell you— you have to get rid of it."

"No, I will not—I won't. It'll be like Torry—it'll be Torry Two."

"I have no need for a Torry Two," Mel said. He started screaming and yelling.

And she went and hid in the closet for the rest of the day.

These arguments took place in a cold foggy city. In a place of torment, where she worried for the child she was carrying and some days planned her escape out the window.

But she didn't escape out the window. She didn't escape out the door.

One day, after Mel gave Mary Lou her insulin, she felt so weak, and her heart seemed to fade little by little. She tried to sing the Big Rock Candy Mountain but forgot the words, and Mel had never sung it to her. It was dear half-mad Oscar who always sang her that song. Mel sat in a chair, and when she reached out her hand toward him he didn't take her hand. It was such a betrayal— you see he didn't take her hand.

They sent her body home for burial.

The landlady stood out in the hall, the ambulance came. Mel had gone out and came back up the stairs as if he had just gotten home from the dock.

"Oh my good God," he said, and he fell—poor man he fell to his knees. The landlady never given to emotional outbursts nonetheless put her hand on his shoulder and wept.

The birds too wept in the trees, as they seemed to all take flight together across the dispassionate sky toward the dark water beyond.

Mary Lou was now gone, and forgotten by almost everyone in the world.

It was two months later Mel's other family came to live with him, a docile woman named Glena Brewer, and her younger, wild, abused and violent half-sister Henrietta Saffy who had been released from a Saint John halfway house two weeks before. She in fact was exceptionally bright, not extremely pretty, but with small penetrating, somewhat beautifully intelligent eyes, blond hair, a flattened nose, white skin with small orange freckles and hated most of the things Stroud hated. Still she had a macabre and vicious humour, and could see through most things with remarkable ease. When she had done cognitive tests for the psychiatrist at the institution she had been committed to when she was fourteen he discovered her IQ to be about 170. That is, she was forty points higher than he and fifty points higher than most of the staff. He tucked this document away.

Mel was deeply attracted to her intelligence, just as he had been to Arlo's and Arnie's.

He told her of the pistol Albert Raskin wanted .He said someone *owed* him that pistol—he would sell that to Albert Raskin for twenty-five thousand. That he had a deal to make with Albert himself. It was the pistol that had killed Jesse James. This stunning grasp of mythology was not unusual. It was a way to compare himself to Jesse James. He had compared himself to men of danger, gunslingers of old, and heroes of war, even detectives in the night.

Henrietta said nothing. She had no reason to. She knew he actually meant blackmail. For that was his best quality. She knew he had someone on the hook who lived up there. She knew something else too. One day when she was combing her hair in her bra and panties, and he glanced at her.

That is, she would replace Glena her sister, tic tac toe.

She was incredibly bright, had forged cheques, mailed false insurance claims and burned cars for the insurance by the time she was eighteen. The last thing she ever thought about was a soul. She had never yet met a person who believed in one who was half as brilliant as she was.

21

UNIVERSITY AT A GLANCE: A PLACE ALBERT RASKIN entered where people believed they knew exactly what must be done for the world. And much of this suited Albert. Especially the idea that the best critics of writers were sociologists, like him; since he had tried to write ten novels and failed, he realized he could slam or dismiss any novel in the world and still be accepted for his deep understanding.

Albert became a professor, and was intricately involved in all that the university now was, including the idea that books must be banned. He didn't state this until it became quite evident that the most important of people thought this way too.

"Yes, I entirely approve," he said in an interview on the CBC. "I do—I entirely approve. Some tomes gravely concern me—yes, some tomes do."

Books by a journeyman writer from New Brunswick, who had had many articles written against him, about his backward regionalism (in fact Albert had written two scathing reviews about them), and other less-than-compassionate books, like *Jude the Obscure*, *Heart of Darkness*, *Middlemarch* and *A Bend in the River* as well.

"Their decommission is long coming," Albert said.

The one man who had earlier stood against this was the poet from Nova Scotia, so Professor Raskin was forced to make a hard and difficult choice when it came to him. This was at the start of his career. *"Many masterpieces now re-evaluated, considered sexist and homophobic, says new young professor."*

Therefore the Nova Scotian was let go.

However, the administration had discovered that a *startlingly brilliant woman* from northern England was available and had applied for the same position—a *woman* who had written two books, the first a discourse on the entrapment and lessening of the feminist voice in 1930s literature, and a second book stating emphatically that there was *no truth*—that truth was simply a *male construct* used to devalue women.

One would never think this, seeing her, the new professor, walk down the hall in her longish skirt toward the office on the second floor, her eyes behind thick glasses, looking neither here nor there, and smiling quickly and slightly at people she passed, that is, that she had infected people. That she had caused a young protégé of hers to attempt suicide. But that was the very strange rumour.

Her name was Faye Sackville. She had been a nun, but left all of that some thirteen years prior. She was a social activist—that is what her CV stated—had been reviewed in the *Times Literary Supplement*.

She deplored violence, but she used manipulation to great advantage. With manipulation there was no sin attached, no violence, and the truth was relative.

After being here two weeks, before the first departmental meeting, or the reception honouring her arrival, she berated the backwardness of the place. And too the lack of restaurants. In *Where to Eat in Canada* she found only one New Brunswick restaurant seemed suitable, and that was on the other side of the province.

From the moment of the reception in her honour, which both Clara and Darren attended, it was quite evident she was highly displeased and offended by many people here.

Two days later she appeared in the dean's office and spoke about being sexually harassed.

At first there was great silence over this, until Professor Sackville threatened to go to the London *Times*.

Then it became a matter of some concern.

Professor Eliot Slaggy was fifty-three years old, a man who had never married, who played the piano and had taken violin lessons, who wrote poems about wildflowers, and elms, and an actual deer that he once saw in his lettuce patch. He had very few friends.

His glasses glinted under the ceiling light, and his little face beamed a sweaty welcome. He was beside the table of cold cuts and punch. He almost ran up to her, extended his hand and asked how she was.

"Welcome, welcome," he said.

She did not answer. His glasses still glinted in their silver frames and his small mouth spoke.

"England, my God, England, I always wished to go—never got there yet—Mommie, you see—but I've read—I've read the

Brontës, the lasses of the moors—the girls of Piccadilly—Virginia Woolf, that old doll, and Anaïs Nin—it's so romantic, Byron and Shelley—Mary Shelley, now there was a lady—did my master's on Keats, wouldn't go to the castle—Shelley you know loved him—'Have you ever seen someone die, Severn—then I will do it as quickly as possible to cause you the least amount of pain.' Wisdom, wisdom."

She glared down at him. She held her glass up as if for protection.

"Come to my house tomorrow night—I have recordings of Thomas and Yeats! And a special brandy—we can sit together and be philosophical—I'll read you my article on Chatterton."

She couldn't really see his eyes, only his glasses lenses, and his small shaven face. He was speaking so quickly because he was so shy, and felt so inferior he had to try and get everything out at once. Also his breath was bad.

"Brave lady," he said. "Brave lady—you must be a brave old girl saying what you did. Yes—*no truth*—*just constructs*—*all is relative—even sin*—not sure I agree—sin will be sin—boys will be boys—get my meaning—but brave—brave girl."

He wore a bowtie and a flower in his lapel. The flower, the lapel, the corduroy jacket a bit wrinkled, a bit small, a bit old, the shoes freshly polished all except one or two small spots, the pants slightly too long so they drooped over the top of the shoes, the blond hair combed back so you could see the individual teeth marks of the comb, and one small strand of hair sticking up at the crown. The wind blew outside, all was damp and cold.

"Yes, yes, yes, delightful—I know your concern—but you girls have a secret way, don't you. You get yours. You and I have to have a secret meeting soon. Yes, yes, yes."

————

When Professor Eliot Slaggy went into the common room the next Monday, with a book of Matthew Arnold as a present for her, he found he was facing a sexual harassment charge. Filed by Faye Sackville.

Everyone knew this was nonsense, everyone knew. *That is, everyone knew.*

Yet her students lined up to sign a petition and had a sit-in, in the president's front office.

They were pushed forward like a crowd trying to enter a single door. The president, smooth as a butter pat, was pugnaciously pushed forward and could not stop. No one could seem to stop.

McLeish cornered young Raskin and said: "Come with me."

With Raskin beside him, they walked into the president's office, and with great dignity said: "Address this! Address this immediately."

Other girls came forward to say Eliot had winked at them. Even once asked one of them to help him pin on his flower!

Eliot Slaggy walked the hallways, and people on seeing him would go back into their office.

He had nowhere else to go. This university, like a cloister, was his refuge, the only place in the world where he could feel at home. He was frightened his eighty-two-year-old mother would hear of this.

Like a shell fired from a gun the bullet has its own trajectory, and on it went toward its destination with deft precision no one was willing to stop. In fact Faye's student Tracy McCaustere became adamant that her research showed this had been systemic in the university for many years.

Eliot Slaggy lost the appeal because this vortex had covered him over, and he was ordered to write a letter of apology.

"Kindly go into your office and write a note of apology—a sincere one," the vice-president told him.

But surprisingly Professor Slaggy declined to do so. He sat in the room at his desk, with the white paper before him, and the pen, a rather exclusive pen from Halifax he liked, and the wind blowing the fall leaves against the window, and suddenly he wrote: "Ms. Sackville, you can go to hell."

It was the first time he had ever written something so harsh.

Professor Eliot Slaggy was suspended until such time as he relented and wrote the letter of apology.

"Professor must write letter of apology before being reinstated," the local press reported.

It was a terrible incident at the university, heart-rending actually. It left an emptiness in those vague book-learned hallways.

Ms. Sackville looked quite refreshed the next day and ready to go to work.

"The highest level or the lowest, every well will sooner or later be poisoned," Clara Bell wrote.

Raskin and Sackville became close; they remained friendly with Dykes. Young Tracy McCaustere and McLeish were often seen with them. They were the vanguard. They were called the famous five. They were called the indomitable ones. Their students gathered by them, spoke of social justice. They were the excitedly defiant.

Since they knew of all the problems of the world, they were never the ones to create any.

It was on a particular Sunday that Raskin, who had become her chaperone, was driving Ms. Sackville, who was looking for property to rent to buy. As they drove up along the Arron Brook one day, she noticed a rather disjointed house and barn. She touched his arm and smiled. He did not ever touch her—so he was suddenly inspired by this. She was older than he was by some years, but he didn't mind that. She had convinced him that men only used fissures of truth to benefit themselves; church was a mythology whose time had come and gone. Churches would soon be burned—especially Catholic ones—and no one would complain. He complimented her on her wisdom a lot.

"A tower of wisdom—like Dykes."

"Oh, I am much more clever than Dykes."

"Yes, of course you are."

"Much more clever. And you know, Dykes is yikes, don't you think?"

"Yes."

"And he smells. He does. He smells—and I as a woman have failed. I have come here to do important work and I have failed."

"No," said Raskin passionately, "you have not—you have not even begun to fail—you are a genius."

"You think?"

"Absolutely."

"Thank you."

"You're welcome."

Albert had never been so enthralled nor had he ever been so influenced. Some young women, Sackville said, should be taught some lessons. She smiled remotely at this and then continued.

She found the Committee on Peace and Equality that they had formed far too fainthearted to be much good, and she told them so. Political action was the mandate now. Tear things down, especially the patriarchy.

"Yes—you mean men?" he would ask.

"Of course, *oui, oui,* my little Canuck. We don't need one more book by men—I refuse to teach them."

"Yes," he said.

And twice though very subtly she mentioned his uncles.

"Stop dottering and tottering! Come to grips with them, please—they've ruined the lives of many here. They think they are kings and we are all peasants—do you like being considered a peasant?"

"No—I do not—I do not whatsoever!"

"*Oui.*"

She had been in her life here two semesters.

"*Oui,*" he said in reply.

"*Oui,*" she said.

She also said that if the group on equality wanted equality they would need certain elderly men to give up their property to the cause. "Lots of old white men have money and have lived a life of indulgence," she said. "It's time to take back the land."

Then she added: "Do you know, my little Canuck, how many animals have died?"

"The puffin—"

"A lot more than just the puffin."

"*Oui.*"

"Revolution, my boy. Women will rise."

"*Oui.*"

This particular Sunday when she noticed that particular farm-house she said, "Now that house might be worth having—well, not the makeshift house but the property."

"Oh, that belongs to people I know," he said.

"Well, it's certainly in a privileged spot on the river."

"Yes it is."

And suddenly they saw Eva walking along the side of the road.

"Oh—what a pretty thing," Sackville said as they came close to her. She touched his arm. "Slow down, my dear man, and let me look at this *pretty* thing. A wildflower in the middle of a barren field."

So he slowed down.

"My, she is pretty."

"Oh—yes. Better without her top," Albert said, passing her by in evening dust that Eva tried to swipe away. He did not know why he had said this. Perhaps it was the word *pretty*. Perhaps it was because she had touched his arm.

"Yes," Sackville said completely unexpectedly, lazily looking over at him, "I really would think she must be beautiful with her clothes taken off. If you know what I mean. Oh, she would protest it happening, but if I know women like her, be in ecstasy when it did. Finally someone would have her." And she took time to light a cigarette, and toss her head back a bit completely at sophisticated ease, then turning her head toward him as it lay on the back of the seat she added, "What do you think, my dear young Canadian man—am I right or wrong? Don't be shy with me."

"Yes, yes—of course—right, I would say."

"Of course I am right."

Then she said: "Tell me about her—if you do know her."

He told her about the money—and he said he would be making them a business proposition.

"God, that would be something. But wouldn't you be taking a chance?"

"Yes—but I want to help people in this backhole. I need to. You know that—"

She sighed and shrugged, told him he was being admirable, and looked back again to see if she could see Eva.

"Good God how seductive she is, without even trying; exquisite—married to some brute of a man, I suspect."

"Yes she is—and do you know who her cousin is?"

"Who is her cousin, pray?"

"You're right—Church Bell—Clara Bell."

"That horrible bitch, that odious Catholic, who is on the board of governors and tried to protest the firing of Slaggy?"

"Yes."

"God, there is no hope then, is there?"

So they spoke about Eva, not about what was true, but of what might be perceived to be true by people like themselves.

"Think of that gorgeous girl—to be used up in a hole like this."

"Yes, I—a mental health counsellor at a drug crisis centre—know that."

"Of course—you are at least trying to learn—but she will have no hope—until people like us intervene—"

Sackville spoke. Albert listened. All that she said proved that Torry shouldn't be any concern of theirs.

She was quite animated. They must protect that girl—from Clara, and anyone else.

This is what she said: First one must look at the university setting as the only setting with which to exercise the rights of a broader humanity, and these two did think this. Second, one must think that young women had little chance to advance in this humanity if they were confined to rural areas, and these two did think this as well. Thirdly, it was not at all improper to influence these women away from this reality to further advance their learning and understanding of the world. Fourthly, this learning must be the kind of learning that these two believed in, and this was true also. And all of these things were discussed now as they spoke about this beautiful young woman.

The other point was this: she had been saved from drowning by her *now* husband—that was looked upon so often as something pre-ordained and meant to be—but Sackville suddenly realized it was a *prison* sentence for this young woman, who out of *simple gratitude* was staying with a man who had no future. So to Faye Sackville the worst trait Eva had was loyalty.

"We have to take her under our wing," she said.

Then as they advanced past Oscar Peterson's trailer, Albert nodded at it and said with a deft contempt: "This is where her so-called husband comes from."

"Oh—fuck me," Sackville said, tossing her cigarette out the window. Then she said: "We must find a way to pluck that wildflower up, and make it ours."

So everything was actually put into universal context that very day.

Sackville would use whatever manipulation she might to change the course of Eva Mott—and do it for Eva Mott's benefit. To her it was simply an intellectual exercise now she was in this backward New Brunswick place. And good God it was a horrid place. The first thing she'd seen when she arrived was a dead moose in the bed of a truck.

She would begin a new challenge. It would be fun. It would be a good deal of commitment, and, she believed, fun.

However, it was Eva Mott's life.

All wells would be poisoned.

22

OSCAR WANTED TO LEAVE ABOUT THIS TIME AND LIVE WITH a relative in Manitoba because he was afraid he'd insulted so many people that they *would* poison his well. That is, he had forebodings of his demise and just did not know where to place his cannons.

He tried to stay awake to vouchsafe this did not occur but it was often hard to stay awake days on end and he would slip into a coma sooner or later, sometimes on the porch, sometimes in his old Chevy truck, sometimes standing against the barn. There Torrent would find him, wake him, sometimes carry him into the trailer— a place he had lived in for years, a verity of boxes and crates and old metal tables, a two-burner stove, and un-level shelves and cup-boards. A picture of Don Quixote on the wall.

"Thank you," he would say. "Torrent, you're an awful good young lad. Yes, a little glass of water, please, to take my pills—I am hoping to get off my pills someday. I miss her, son."

"Who do you miss"?

"Mary Lou."

"Dad, I know you do—but she is gone now—you have to real-ize it."

"I know—and I'm a grandfather."

"Yes, you are."

"And how old is your little one today?"

"Today she is two months, Dad."

"I mean exactly—"

"Sixty-seven days."

"Sixty-seven days. And tomorrow she will be sixty-eight days."

"Yes, she will."

"Time passes."

"Yes, it does."

"I am sorry."

"Dad, what are you sorry about?"

"I am sorry about how I treated you. I hit you—remember?"

"Don't be—you treated me very well. I know that—does it matter if others don't? Yes, you hit me—and yes, sometimes I did not deserve it—but sometimes I did."

"Someday I will make it up to you."

"You have nothing to make up."

"Someday I will find out what happened to Arlo and Arnie—find out what happened to your mother—I will—I will."

"You shouldn't get so upset about it all. Time passes."

"Time passes—that's right. How old is she now?"

"Sixty-seven days."

"You see, he was double fussy over his car."

"Who?"

"Our Mr. Stroud—our mad engineer of human souls."

"What about him?"

"Bothered me here for years, the man who committed crimes. Well, he loved his car—and one must take care of it here in the winter—and how worried he was about it stalling—outside after dark with a cold snap. So I went to the lad I bought the Massey Ferguson from, Mr. Benson, who is actually a German. He was captured outside of Caen and sent to the prisoner of war camp here in Minto. Some say he remained a Nazi, and complained that we didn't applaud him for fighting against Stalin. So I went to see him. I thought about the car. They did not walk out there alone—someone had to have driven them.

"Benson told me Stroud took his car to Benson's garage on two occasions within a day. He had the battery looked at, the antifreeze changed, the oil too. He kept worrying about the temperature, and kept an extra battery with him. He kept saying, 'Is it really going to drop? It better drop.'

"'Why?' Benson asked.

"Stroud said he had two snares set for rabbits, and set them with the idea that the temperature would drop. 'Poor little lonely beasts, I want them to die soon—hate to see things suffer.'

"The next day he came back his windshield smashed by a tree limb and mud and frozen ice over the side of his car. And his gas was almost gone," Oscar said.

"Why might that be?"

"Because he kept turning the car on, warming it, waiting for something." Oscar sniffed. "And he was parked in a hidden area— and he left that hidden area without turning his lights on and cracked his windshield on a branch." Then he picked up his bottle of wine and poured a glass, looking out at the stony junk-filled yard.

"It makes me think of Shakespeare—"

"In what way, Dad?"

"There are no more devils in hell. They have all escaped to earth."

Torry sat down beside him now, and put his arm around him for a moment. And Torry remembered when he was very young and the social worker came to take him away. The problem was, there wasn't a clean shirt. All his shirts had Oscar's big oily hand marks where he had given little Torrent Peterson hugs. But the only thing the social worker saw was soiled shirts, which proved Oscar didn't love his son. Much like Ms. Sackville, she didn't realize the hand marks were from hugs given over two days.

Torrent had that day come to leave off the coroner's report about his mother, Mary Lou, which after all this time was available to her son.

As he left, Albert Raskin was driving by in his car with a remarkable-looking woman. He saw this woman toss her cigarette out and it lay on the branches. He went over and stepped on it, and put it out.

Mary Lou was three months pregnant. This is what Torrent learned from the coroner's report—a complication with that pregnancy, a problem with insulin. It was perhaps in her weakened state a heart failure caused by insulin shock.

Two weeks later Oscar phoned him about the coroner's report.

———

Before the phone call is recounted, *something else* must be.

Torrent was ecstatic, though hesitant and confused. Secretly if he *searched* his soul some spark about what was happening could signal disaster for him. But it was too mercurial for him to put his finger on, the pulse of it all too elusive and the thrill of something else too significant. They now had a little girl to think of. Her name was Polly.

Out of the blue there was a phone call, where Albert spoke of actually going into a partnership.

The day Albert went haying, the heat, the great horseflies, the terrible sharp sticks of hay that cut his arms, the sun that blistered his back, the heaviness of the bales, the undeniable thirst throughout the long, hot day—little did he know that haying was like this, he had only seen it as a youngster, in a pastoral setting with the sun going down, and the wagon topped with hay bales, hauled to the barn by some endearing vintage horse.

That day when Eva came out into the field with strawberries and bread at noon in a halter top and white shorts, did he say:

"Perhaps I need a bandage here—"

Torrent overheard him, and said nothing. And Albert held up his bleeding forearm. Though most of the men would have thought a cut such as his didn't warrant it, Torrent asked Eva if she might take him back into the house.

"It is a beautiful place, a beautiful piece of land. I love how it lobs up to the trees in the distance, and then passes through giant pines down to Arron Brook on one side and the bay on the other. The kind I always dreamed of. Is it yours?"

"Maybe—if I marry him." She looked at Albert and smiled as she taped the cotton around his arm.

"Torry?"

"Yes—Oscar gave him this land and he was building this

house the day he rescued me—he ran down from here—no one else had the wits or the strength, though I know some of the youngsters were frantically searching for a boat."

"I was there," Albert said.

"You were where?"

"Well, at the beach. I saw—you."

She looked at him quickly and blushed.

He looked at her quizzically, waiting for her to say more.

"Naked. Yes, I was—my top was gone, my bottoms was pulled down, so everyone could see."

"You were very beautiful—well—it was a great moment for me—"

"For me too," she said. "Torry was my hero that day fer sure."

She wrapped his arm, with a shimmering whiteness of the cloth against his dark left forearm, and caught his blue eyes.

Eva felt a disquieting—a strange slight desire, with this, as he looked at her.

This was the problem. He was no longer who he had been, he was now who he was—and his good looks, which he had not had at sixteen, now having, were unmanageable to himself.

She also caught how he had looked at her house, which until that moment she had loved. Oh it was a beautiful house, with new hardwood floors. Still, there were things in it unfinished. One whole wall was left unfinished. He must have noticed that!

"Can I pay you?" he said, taking his wallet out.

"Go on—get out of here," she snapped, and turned away, and to prove her mastery of the moment, moved with undeniable beautiful and sudden *seeming* submissiveness of her form to the sink.

The truth was, no one from the U.S.A. or England or anywhere else wanted to be here—they simply *were here*, found themselves here, found the hellish winters too long, the summers too hot and fly-infested, the people too coarse, the world too unsophisticated, and so every visitor, every speaker or poet who came to visit the university on those drab February days, these professors dressing almost identically, all with certain accents that did not match, would privately complain about why they were stuck here and why they should be somewhere else more important. Albert took up a love of baseball because so many of them had such, he listened astutely, complained about what they complained about, and sighed about what they sighed at.

He was seen most frequently with Ms. Sackville.

Ms. Sackville walked to class from the apartment she had moved into, covered with heavy black boots and scarf, a winter coat with the collar turned up. You would see her knocking on the Saint Michael's janitor's door, with a little quiet tap.

"You must transfer some of the heat you seem to have, through the pipes you seem to operate, to my room which seems to have none."

More and more he and Ms. Sackville were known for their solitude, knowledge of the world and great intellectual defiance.

He loved the idea of being defiant. But more, he loved people saying he was.

The little tap on the door went on all winter; the little boot marks were seen in the snow, waiting for Albert in his proper Volvo to drive her home. The little office window was opened an inch, the little tea cup hanging by a thread from a brass hook and now and again her little notice that she, Dr. Faye Sackville, would be attending a meeting in Ireland. And the little sticky to Albert about the plight of Eva Denise Mott and her "arrangement."

The concealed feeling both had, to free her from herself. *"Think of how free she would be if we tore such terrible tethers away"* was written on one sticky. He waited for those stickies almost every day.

And on another: *"My plan is quite delicious. And if it frees her, I would never say—malicious."*

Albert had heard Eva Mott was studying for her graduation equivalency. And that meeting him had spurred her on to do so. So *he* had already succeeded. She had left school in grade twelve, had gotten married, as a way to escape Ben Mott. A few months ago they had a child, Polly.

Torrent, who knew nothing of these internecine machinations, told Eva he saw Professor Raskin one day at the wharf alone, staring out toward the far buoy, his hands in his pockets, his hat tilted back on his head. It's as if that very stance signified a grand departure.

"Poor fellow," Eva said. "He's fighting his battle all alone. His uncles are so mean to the Indians and everyone else around here, bullies and thieves they are known for is what my teacher told me—and are polluting places, going around polluting all the places. And there is an ozone layer too, and they pretty well diluted that all by themselves. And he is not a polluter himself. He gives his money away to help the poor, that's what all the students say! He is what you call altruistic—I wrote that word there down, to explain him."

"Ah," Torry said, nodding.

"I sometimes in my heart of hearts—not that it matters—wish upon a star that I were a student too," she said, "and could learn from people like Professor Raskin—who is altruistic—for he would know so much."

"Ah," Torry said.

But he knew Eva knew nothing about the poor, knew nothing about the rich, knew nothing about polluters or those who fought for environmental laws. He had seen them on a dozen job sites already, they had harassed, and ruined equipment, and he felt that many of them demanded you listen to them while they did not listen to you, and knew themselves little or nothing of the world they demanded be changed. And they used the Indians' plight to gain attention to themselves.

He was thinking of Dykes here—though he did not know who the old white-haired man with the crazy anger was, who now wore First Nations beads and chanted. All he seemed to do one day was go "*Ahhhhh*" and point at Torrent who was busy digging a ditch for a small gas line.

"*Ahhhhhhh*," said Dykes. "*Ahhhhhhhhhh.*"

"Destroyer!" Dykes yelled, and those with him did as well.

They stood in front of road construction and jumped up on a front-end loader, and put him out of a job that day, when Eva was pregnant, and now some months later took the road; they yelled at oil trucks and a year later made sure their tanks were filled.

Torrent knew this because in the variety of jobs he had, he had had to face them. Eva wanted things to be nice—and as long as they were, or as long as she thought they were, in her own way, then she would be happy. Anything too unsettled, that made her less than happy. He knew she had to be happy. In fact when he got into an argument with another farmer one day—Torrent knowing he was right, knowing she knew he was right—saw her run back into the house, lock the door and stare out the window.

She couldn't stand to have people not think she was perfect. She could not stand not to be liked. But Torry had never been liked—had always been alone.

So she took a ceramics course, she took a painting course from an artist I knew. She went to night school and talked very guilelessly about the world. In fact at times, during the evening after Polly was in bed, she would speak to Torrent about her life ambition, about what men and women were now doing, how they were now thinking, how terrible men had been throughout history, boiling people in oil and cutting their noses off, and how the teachers at night school were handsome.

"Oh not that handsome, Torry—it's just that they know things."

"What—things do they know?"

"Well, one of them was to Indonesia. I figure that's something."

"It is—yes it is."

"Well that's what I mean. And I found that out, well, from Georgina Preston, who left her husband and now goes with a supervisor and everything. She told me her husband was fine, but he didn't have a romantic side is what she said, and a woman has a desire of the heart—and a desire of the head—it's what I learned from her, she sits beside me in class—so I learned that from her."

"You did?"

"Yes—so I spoke to Georgina last night and she comes up with that you are my desire of the head—you are and I will remain with you because of that. But there is a desire of the heart—a very secret desire of the heart is what a real woman searches for—and often never finds."

"Well that is too bad."

"Yes," she continued, as she ate her supper, cutting her pork chop and thinking aloud, "yes, that is the women's sorrow—I guess is what Georgina told me. Do you member Georgina, she was in that talent show last Christmas?"

"Yes, I know Georgina, she plays the accordion."

"Yes—they call her Accordion George. Well I guess that is just as true for me. I mean a desire of the heart and a desire of the head."

She looked up quickly and looked back at her plate, and cut her pork chop again.

"I guess," Torry said.

"Yes—so many women suffer between the head and the heart. I have Polly and you and that is my head for sure—but somewhere is my heart."

"Ah—well, you and Polly are my head."

"How do you know that?" she asked, looking up at him and blinking.

"My heart told me so."

These new theories, doctrines picked up in the labyrinth of current sentiment, were what separated her now from him, like an aura, a sheen around her temperament. It began to engulf her without her knowing she was being immersed. She would never have been dissatisfied until she was instructed to be.

And yes, the instruction was mainly from people who demanded she be dissatisfied.

Unknown to Torry she wrote Albert a letter:

I know you sometimes give money away sir—people said to me that—because you are in a fight for the little man—but I wouldn't allow you to just give us money—I would only ask for a loan upon my soul to God. Don't tell Torry I wrote or he would skin me but he is almost like an artist and it would be so good if someone could help him And you said you wanted to help the artists—so I send you this letter. Either that or we have to go out west to work.

He showed the letter to Faye Sackville. She read it, lighted a cigarette and looked up at him with wonderfully expressive dark eyes:

"Well, let's do something for her, or she'll escape and live a life of drudgery." And she folded the letter and gave him a quick kiss.

So at that moment Faye placed her as being a greedy and backward country girl, just like those men she had seen at the airport, but with, as she said, "an exquisite shape."

Then opening and reading the letter again said, "She thinks her husband is an artist."

Sackville said he wasn't to give money away—he was to loan it. It was simply preposterous to do it any other way. In fact she would recuse herself from the whole venture if he did.

"Your stepfather—well, he was oblivious most of the time—"

They came a few nights later, with an offer of partnership and fifty thousand dollars. This would all be done in haste. The partnership would be in the form of a loan—twenty-six thousand for the acres of oak and maple Torrent wanted along the ridge leading to Good Friday, and twenty-four thousand for the barn and supplies. They had to sign two documents. The first document spoke of advancing money for equipment and upgrading the barn, winterizing it, and bringing wood into a space to dry. The second document was for the land.

"Are you sure you want this?" Albert asked her.

"Oh yes sir."

"A loan—it will be a loan then," he said.

"Oh for sure."

"Well, there will be little pressure—"

Then Ms. Sackville said that if by the end of fifty months this money was still not paid, the guarantor of the loan would be able to sell the property and the hardwood ridge as he saw fit to recoup any monies. That was the only stipulation, but it was nothing to be worried about. Fifteen pieces priced right would get the fifty thousand repaid, and all would be well. Twenty pieces and they'd begin to make real money.

Raskin was looking at her as if wondering if Eva was the right person to have this money. That is what she recognized, and she did not want to disappoint. She lowered her eyes and kept nodding, kept hoping to impress as much as possible.

"Okay, I will sign for him," she said, excitedly. "I have a security number. I could call him—"

"Call him after you sign," Sackville said amiably. She looked at Eva with bright and somehow gorgeous eyes that assumed a sudden liaison and a partnership. And her accent was so different, it felt like she was from a different world—it cut the air of the kitchen so.

Eva nodded, said, "Here I go," and signed with her hand shaking. She closed her eyes and handed them the paper. "There," she said, smiling with her eyes still closed, her eyelids fluttering slightly in the warmth of the evening room.

"You keep this, and have *him* initial it all. How many pieces can he do in a year?" he asked.

She tried to think, and she counted on her fingers, her eyes still closed, and when opening them saw Faye Sackville staring at her from behind Albert's shoulder.

"Let's say as far as cabinets maybe five, but desks and chairs too—maybe a half-dozen"—she exaggerated—"and his best is grandfather clocks."

She knew Torry would never discuss his work with them. She was in fact doing all of this without his knowledge. She began to realize this, and felt queasy—no, she had not discussed this with him.

"Wonderful," Faye Sackville said.

"Yes," Raskin said, but he seemed dissatisfied.

Raskin was studying the contract. He looked at it, looked at her and said: "This too has to be signed—the *bad faith* clause— you have to sign here—just if something you told us was not really true. The rest I do not care about—the money will be paid when it is—but the *bad faith* has to be signed here, Eva."

"Oh—it's all true, sir—it is." She looked frightened.

Sackville smiled and put her hand on Eva's arm and stroked it. "Oh, we know—we know that, dear."

So she had to sign again. Her hand shook again, she felt dishonest.

The day was coming to an end, the birds tweeted. There was the on-again, off-again sound of traffic, and the light was now fading in the windows, making the room duller with sudden diminishing bursts of evening sunshine.

Sackville reached out, put her hand on Eva's shoulder and said: "Congratulations. Well done, young lady. You did it on your own. You took matters into your own hands. Did anyone ever tell you— you are very, very pretty. My God, you are a diamond in the rough."

She blushed and stood before them rocking slightly back and forth with Polly in her arms.

"Oh, you are embarrassing her," Albert said with concern. "She's already had enough of us."

She felt like sitting down on a chair and looking away from Professor Sackville.

Because in the awkward silence that followed they were examining her, examining every part of her, and wondering why she looked perplexed and sad.

Like so many things in life that are wrong, she told herself that it was right if looked at it in another way. Like the teacher who put his arm on her back and bent over her when she was writing her exam, took her pen from her hand, and holding his hand over hers, made a correction on her text, squeezing her hand as he did—and brushed her hair with his face, which she did not tell Torry about.

Then they left, they walked out, their somewhat special foot-steps on her gravel. Matilda the sow lay on her side in some half-dried mud.

She hoped he would turn around and wave but he did not. She hoped she had not said something wrong. She hoped that the way he had turned that showed a sudden kind of victory over her whole life wasn't real. She ran out to the porch trying to shake their hands. But they had gone.

She went into the little den, and sat at the window watching as they drove off. She waved even though they weren't looking.

She realized quite suddenly that she had done something ter-rible. She had not even considered Torry or cared to let him know. Because she was frightened of what he might think.

Sackville knew something too. Far smarter than Raskin, she knew exactly how that lien would come into play, months before it did. That is why she smiled a beguiling smile when she sat in the car, reached over and stroked his cheek. She believed, here less than a year, she had bested them all. She simply did not know quite how the tragedy would unfold. If she had would she have stopped? In the years to come she often asked herself this.

23

EVA WAITED UNTIL TORRENT CAME HOME THAT WEEKEND. She met him at the wharf. She drove him in her dilapidated Honda, and then suddenly inside the door of the house she began crying, half-hysterical, for fear this would *not* happen. So she began to tell him, she blurted out that they had a new partner. But he could not go back to work on the dredge. He had to quit a job and work in his shop. She told him she signed for him, and he could write his initials on the side of the pages. If he did not, the contract would be moot.

She ran and got him the documents. He asked if they should take it to Clara. "Clara has everything—she is a lawyer married to a professor," Eva said to Torrent. Because she was instantly terrified Clara would find a ruse in this agreement, and Eva wanted to convince herself and him that there was no ruse.

She shut her eyes tightly as if she was a child, and stopped breathing, and then said: "Listen to me, will you, please! Listen to me. He will sell your furniture all over the place—okay?"

There was something frantic about her that issued an alarm in him, an idea that he wasn't her ideal—that something or someone else must have been, that she had been waiting for him to change—that her life was one of an obligation she now needed to escape from. Polly sat in the highchair looking at both of them, her simple kind eyes seeming to wonder at her mother.

He was exhausted, and he began to wash up.

"Oh yer not even listening and it's such a big thing—and I told you—I told you."

"I am listening. I thought you had forgotten all about this—it's too much money."

"But he will do everything—he will sell them for us—you won't have to—and he will find buyers—we will be able to do what you said you wanted to—own your own business!"

"But I work alone—I told you that a hundred times—it'll not make the money back and we'll be stuck with the loan. For that's what this boils down to—a loan. It might sound different, but it is just a loan!"

"What—are you crazy?"

Then she closed her eyes again and held her breath and when he didn't answer she stamped her feet, twice.

"What about Polly?" she said. "Do you want Polly to grow up like me or you, with not even a pair of pants to put over our arse?"

He now remembered Professor Raskin on the wharf standing alone—a figure so removed from him, the lobster traps piled up on one side of him. All was quiet, below him the green waters of the bay. Why was he suddenly frightened when he thought of it?

Because he *briefly* (not fully yet) saw how *he* had taken shape in her mind, how she had been determined from the very first moment he, Torry, mentioned that he would like to have his own business and he wished he could buy the lot on the ridge. It became her portico into the world she believed she wanted.

She was the one who had talked him into going to the banks, to fulfill this dream.

From that moment on, this dream constantly trumped any other wish in her. She refused to drive by Clara's house and refused as well to speak to their old friends. She was planning a life commensurate with her older cousin's—fourteen minutes older.

One evening after they had come home from haying she had berated him for not wanting more.

He said nothing as she spoke. And finally she said:

"Yesterday Clara's name was in the paper—someday, if my name was in the paper once, I would—just faint, I suppose."

So he now knew he must move in her channel in order to stay with her. All of this was controlled by tethers invisible to the naked eye, and flashed before him so fleetingly that he almost did not catch it.

How when they went to the banks, her fists were closed and her little knuckles were white, hoping against hope as the loan officer went over their application. She was on the verge of tears, her face pleading without her voice speaking.

How one bank and then another satisfied themselves as to their penury. Then—and this was the point—what if Albert hadn't took it upon himself to come haying, to tell them he could help—might she have forgotten it? Or if Albert had been someone else—might she then have forgotten it?

Now she was someone else.

Slowly she opened her eyes and stared up at him, with an almost cold otherworldly look as if she had just caught on to what he was thinking, and as if he had *caught* her because of her insistence; that she did not want him any longer—she wanted others. She had been overtaken already by Albert Raskin, already she had tried not to think about him—already she had dreamed about him, and didn't know why.

"You promised," she whispered. "You promised."

"Yes," he said, "I know. But let's go out west like we planned—I'll find the money—in three or four years we can come back and start it up by ourselves."

"I am so, so sick of living like this here," she said quietly. "You said you wanted it. You said."

"I wanted a business—but, well, what say will he have?"

"I don't know what say—you are the carpenter, the craftsman, not him! Think of how you took me up to that ridge—those are the trees you wanted, that is the timber you want—"

He sat on a kitchen chair and looked at her, his large hands on his knees, his shirt torn at the collar and the top of the right sleeve. She was in a housedress, bluish white with a button missing, and worn sneakers on her feet, with a small dark hole near the right baby toe, and white socks to her ankles.

It was night now, and outside they could hear the croak of frogs down over the hill in the pond. They could smell the fresh pine night through the side screen, and hear the bluebottle fly buzz.

"Your idea was to have your own furniture business—it is what you always said."

"Yes—it is what I said, yes. But I have to make a living doing other things at the moment."

"Not if you get that money."

"It won't work like that, Eva."

"Why won't it! You never ever take no chance. What about Polly—what about our little girl!"

He looked at her sadly, with this new knowledge of *who she was*. She had distanced herself now by the curious craving to have him succeed. How their eyes met at that very moment said in some way she had deeply betrayed him.

"When will we have to pay it back?" he asked.

"Well—he will get his money back over the course of a few years—as long as you make your furniture. Torry, he's a Raskin—for God sake—a real honest-to-God Raskin."

"A few years—fifty thousand—how is that possible?"

"But it is—I know it is!" she said. "Fifteen pieces of work will do it—and it'll be our business and our timber."

"What are these signatures here?"

"I already signed—you just have to initial—so you just initial!" She tapped the page where the ink marks were a little smudged, and walked to the counter, looked out at the black hole of the night and then turned to him.

She did not tell him about the lien on the house if it was signed in *bad faith*, for that was mentioned to her so quickly and as such an afterthought and seemed to her so unlikely and so untrue it didn't matter.

Torrent signed as best as he could. She watched over his shoulder as he struggled. Outside that night there was the smell of new-mown hay, the stars came out, the trees waved in the warm breeze from off the bay.

The phone call the next morning was from Oscar. He told Torry he did not believe the coroner report. He said: "Son, your mother was murdered."

Mel Stroud telephoned Albert the next day as well.

"You gived all that money away—that's a little disappointing. Shane and I had long expected you would give it to us—as your good friends and partners—"

The first few months everything went well with the partnership. As always things at first looked rosy and promising. They got together and Albert stood and watched Torrent work. Eva would sit on a bench and talk too much. Sackville at times would drop by. They even went to Albert's cottage once, and met certain people from the university.

"*Helping out: A Raskin promises changes*" was an article that appeared in our paper.

Then more than a few times Sackville insisted Eva go somewhere with them, sitting in the middle of the front seat.

"Let's go and do something," Sackville would say, then hesitating she would add, "Come with us, my dear, and leave your manly macho man to chisel. We will go back to our place and have a glass of wine."

They took her twice to the university and showed her around the campus.

Once in a while, out of the blue Sackville would buy her something nice to wear, and give her advice on university.

"Woman studies for you, my lady. You're being picked upon, you know—yes—don't speak—you are—you have to overcome it."

She, Eva, was overwhelmed by this attention and yet frightened by it—because there was something wrong with it that she didn't quite know. Well, she did. They were leaving Torry completely out. She had to be in the barn with him for at least part of the day, even if it was just to clean and sweep up.

One night she came home late, Torry had left off working on a cabinet. It looked so lonely, that cabinet, in the middle of the barn, the tools on the bench; the air was still, the evening going dark in the opened barn.

Yet in the moment it all seemed—for her among these bright people—impossible with Torry there.

Once when they were alone Ms. Sackville—she insisted Eva call her Faye, but Eva refused—grabbed her, put her head on her lap and said: "I'm going to massage your temples—just lie here and relax—yes, relax. No, close your eyes—yes—yes—yes."

They were supposed to go to Chatham for a few minutes but were all the way down in Escuminac and the wind buffeted the car. Still Eva almost fell asleep, as she felt the woman's hands upon her. Sackville then stroked her shoulder, and then her breasts, and slowly down along her leg to her knee, and giving her a little slap on the thigh said: "There. Now arise, madam, you are a new woman—under my control. My job is done. Anytime I want you—I can have you. I can always tell, you know. Do you want me to have you—do you?—say it—"

Eva didn't want to.

"Say it—my little bitch."

"Yes," Eva said, her eyes still closed, "Yes yes. Have me"

"Take you?"

"Yes."

But then coming out of a daze she sat up straight, blushed and looked straight ahead. Hoping it was all a joke. She told Ms. Sackville she wanted now to go home.

She knew Torry resented Ms. Sackville too. She called him macho man. She said once: "No wonder Clara Howl likes you."

He felt embarrassed. Only Eva knew he went to Clara's to learn how to read—so how did Ms. Sackville suddenly know?

Within two months Albert was giving him suggestions, and Eva would be seated between them in the car when they drove back to the barn. And she herself had started smoking again.

One night he said: "This can't last."

"Why?"

"They don't—"

"Don't what, Torry? Things are nice."

"They don't respect my work!"

So little by little Torrent was upset with Albert, with Ms. Sackville and with Eva.

He hated it when Albert said "Oh come now" and patted his shoulder.

And there was something else. Raskin berated Torry one day in front of a buyer.

"Oh damnit, Torry, you are so precious—you are going to lose this sale."

"Fine, then I am not selling to him."

"But he has come over from Woodstock."

"Well I am sorry but he can go back to Woodstock."

Torry came from the barn, closed it up padlocked it, and told Albert to go to hell.

"Stop taking Eva away—she has duties here," he said.

"Are you jealous?"

Torry didn't answer.

"She comes with us by her own volition," Albert said.

"Whatever that is," Torrent said, and suddenly smashing a fence board with his fist.

Afterwards nothing could go back to the way it was.

———

Then Mel phoned Albert from Saint John.

A friend catching up, a man concerned about him and asking about his health, for he had a health scare—his blood pressure had risen a few weeks before and he couldn't stop his palpitations. So he had been sent to the hospital. And Mel seemed quite concerned.

Then he said: "I know why you got so sick—all that money gone to that Torrent Peterson. Peterson who stoled that Eva Mott from my brother too."

Then he phoned again a week later. "I told you Eva was up in love with Shane and then Torry come along—I thought you understood."

"Look, it's a small business arrangement."

"I don't like it at all," Mel said.

The third phone call came a day later. Mel was agitated and angered.

"You come and give me the money and be partners—I will get that pistol for you too at a good price—just like you want—but I don't like being cheated out of money. I want to start up a bottle exchange. I was your partner long before him—so I want my money too. I need it to protect Shane in jail—and I want as much as Torry Peterson. You do that and it will be okay—I promise. No more small change."

Albert sat all night in the dark smoking one cigarette after the other. He knew why he wanted Byron's pistol. Though he had never fired a gun, he wanted, and needed, to protect himself.

When he finally mentioned the Strouds to Ms. Sackville two days later she said: "Do you want to kill them?"

"No, of course I don't."

"Then shut up about them." And she lighted a cigarette and went back to correcting papers. She looked up, suddenly took his hand and put it under her shirt, under her bra next to her heart and said, "Feel that, feel my heart—yes—I know what you desire. And you will have it soon. But I have long ago stopped being afraid."

Things went on and became more and more depressing for the business. Both for Torrent and him. One night they met in the big field below Raskin Enterprises to iron out what they might do. It was called Bloody field. Named so by the great Byron Jamison when he was scouting Good Friday Mountain. But Torry said he had done all that he could—he had worked to exhaustion, and had at that moment not slept for thirty-four hours.

24

THEN SOMETHING HAPPENED. SOMETHING SACKVILLE had been told would happen months before. And was quietly waiting for. It was something she had plotted secretly with Tracy McCaustere within the confines of that silent university. That is, Tracy had told her to go see certain people on the reserve. All of this she believed was her design to help Eva, to allow her to be free.

Late one afternoon as he sat in the den, representatives of a First Nations group, Justice and Recompense, came to him. It took the representatives a half an hour or more to come to the point— telling him the acres Torrent Peterson bought and was now care-fully culling for his business was actually *theirs*. That it was *unceded land, a part of their nation*—they told him that the person Torrent bought the land from, Clement Ricer, was not the owner, they were. They didn't dislike Torrent but he had done something illegal.

"Aren't you his business partner?"

"Only in a sense—they have a loan."

"Well," one of the men said, "I thought you were on our side. Are you on our side or what?"

Yes, the wonderful thing about reconciliation was you had to be on someone's side.

But it was this interview with the band, in the paper the next week, that he couldn't abide:

Furniture business illegally culling trees of local
Native band, Albert Raskin partner.
Well-known environmentalist, indiscriminately cutting on Indian ground?
Professor Raskin, benefactor, champion of all
that is, must answer to who he is now.

The committee meetings on Peace and Equality which had been held at his cottage were cancelled. McLeish was as disappointed as Dykes—or just about.

Faye Sackville herself told him she was surprised he had not looked into all of this more carefully. She kept from him her secret that she had.

Albert went around the house throwing chairs.

Dykes too refused to see him. He banged on Dykes's door. Sackville said she was too busy for him. He cancelled his classes and sat in the dark. Though he was not being called a racist yet he was being called one who was unaware of his racist tendencies.

All of this happened within a week.

"I am in despair," he wrote to Sackville on a little yellow sticky. "I will do whatever you say—whatever you think is right—tell me what to do and I will do it. My God, how can they ever call me a racist—me—*moi*—who fought for justice—you saw how I fought—me—*moi*."

He kept leaving stickies all over her door, and they would disappear, and he would go by and leave more.

She was silent for five long days. Then she wrote:

"I will get back to you."

Two days later came her response.

"My boy—what if you make a statement that under my direction the property will be turned over to me as a centre for peace and justice? That's what I would do—look how you would fare among our mutual friends—we who want equality and justice to triumph in this godforsaken hole called Canada? You know how fond I am of you—you have already touched my breasts—can't imagine what you may touch next."

And she drew a funny face to go with it all.

"What if people don't forgive me?" he wrote back.

"Oh—my pet—I will simply demand that they do."

Torrent, working sometimes fifteen hours a day, could not sell as much as he needed to offset expenses. And for some days after the accusations started, he didn't even hear of them. Eva knew, however. She suddenly read her name in the paper.

Then Mr. John from the reserve came to see him, and asked Eva to be present as well. They were in the house. Outside some men stood, in First Nations dress. One played with little Polly and gave her a sucker.

Mr. John told them that the deed to the land Torrent was culling was bogus. It did not belong to Mr. Ricer. It was distinguished from British holdings by an 1853 treaty—just as the asbestos mine itself was.

"We own the mine—we always have—and it's time to take it back."

In fact they were thinking of blockading both the mine and Torrent's new land. Eva kept her head down, fumbling with her fingers, tears in her eyes, the same as she had done one day in grade eleven when she had to go see the principal. Mr. John saw this and said:

"But perhaps things will be okay—we can come to some compromise."

Still, from the moment of that visit on, nothing was the same. For Mr. John did not control the band any more than a commander controls a battalion once the battle has begun.

The next few months Albert set the process in motion, the clause that allowed him out of the contract and the recoup of his losses, if good faith was broken.

Indian men said they were prepared to confiscate the lumber in Torrent's barn, and the timber he had drying in its stall.

Eva had gone to the doctor, and was prescribed pills to help her sleep. Everything seemed to be unravelling and she did not know how to stop it. Still, she clutched her little knuckles in hope.

One night he told her, "We will owe him fifty thousand and I have no way of paying it back—and if I'm sued by the band, what then? I can't begin to think—I can't think anymore. We will lose the damn house—oh, if it was all for Polly—where will our little girl sleep?"

"How much have you paid back so far?"

"Fifteen thousand—and it left us almost penniless," he told her. "It is all wrong—everything is wrong. I should never have done it—why oh why?"

"Well everyone says you work too slow, so why did you leave

that job on the dredge if you work so slow. I told you it was up to you—I told you." And she ran upstairs.

Albert had to start formal proceedings against false pretences and bad faith.

"Be the man you were meant to be," Dykes told him, raising his fist in salute, in some measure of uncompromising, in some measure of solidarity with the masses, in some tribute to the Indian band, in some instant moment of vanity and self-gratification.

"Go for your uncles. Side with the Indians to show who you are."

"Right on—wow, motherfucker," the young woman said, her legs in a lotus position, and not so young anymore.

To Dykes the world was filled with conspiracies—and he was seeking evidence. He told his protégé this unequivocally—he was now seeking evidence, against Raskin Conspiracies. And of course the CIA—the CIA was always, always involved.

He went back to the house—he went along the lanes, he walked with one great moment of being resolute.

"You do look angry," Sackville said. "Oh my God, you are finally your own man!" And she kissed him passionately, and let him touch the inside of her thigh, "I have waited a long time for this—"

Some months before, Torry had gone with Eva to a party in Judge Lampkey's large cottage. He had never been inside before—only on the outside when he was hired to do the shutters in the fall, to paint an outbuilding in the spring, and to plant flowers.

Eva collected things from the party to bring home; she took a small placemat that Mrs. Lampkey had given her. The MP Edgar Lampkey was there, and she had rushed back in to have her picture taken with him at the last moment. Now that picture was on the wall in their living room. Never had Torry seen her act with such sycophancy, though he didn't understand it.

The party at Lampkey's was a catastrophe. Torrent was so shy he didn't want to talk about his cabinets to anyone, or couldn't.

Ms. Sackville standing beside Albert said: "Male stupidity. Get rid of him, I'd say."

So that day, Eva was humiliated; rushing around trying to tell people about the furniture that her husband made, "*ta fit real snug in all yer houses*," and Torrent was embarrassed by her, left early while people drifted off in the summer sun.

Later that day Albert had sat on the veranda of his cottage smoking, looking over the pale water as it was growing dark, and she, who had gone back to her house, suddenly appeared, in a halter top and very tight white shorts. She suddenly bent over, put both arms around his neck, hugged him and said:

"Thanks for today, Mr. Raskin sir—I met an MP and got a placemat from Mrs. Lampkey and everything. And look—one of the invitations that you made."

He laughed at that innocence, and kissed her quickly.

And then in bared feet she ran off the warm veranda and disappeared, by the darkening hedges, while he watched. He turned his head and saw Ms. Faye watching him.

No one was more disappointed in Torrent than Eva. She was both embarrassed and furious. She didn't speak to him. And this caused her to suddenly forget, or want to forget, who he was.

Eva left Polly alone the next day, and went to the cottage, walking down to Arron then across to the bay, and up along the beach. It was pouring rain. She thought others would be there, for they usually were (or did she think this), but he was alone, and the rain fell and lashed all the windows.

Her clothes were so tight and wet they seemed to make apparent every part of her. Her hair was damp on her face.

Some crow cried too and the sound of the rain sounded comforting on the roof, made everything more enclosed, as if it separated them from the world.

"You have to help me," she said, crying. "You must help me. Torry is not the same Torry." And suddenly she clung to him, her face both scared and tragic.

It was the last thing he ever thought he would do again to a woman. He gave her two Valium that his mother used to quiet her nerves. He spoke to her about being her guide. He spoke to her as she clung to him.

He looked at her, kissed her very suddenly.

"Your clothes are wet."

He then began to take them off.

It was—her destiny—not Torry's or even Polly's but hers alone. She was exclusive—and was meant to be with different people. Sackville had bought her a blouse and had given her a book too.

She would be with Professor Raskin, and be like Clara, yes, just like her.

That first day the air remained still in the room they had left, the couches with their blankets, the chairs with their old cushions, the fireplace mantel with its small seashells and crafts, the black soot that had over the years crawled up the orange brick, the wood in the wood box sat alone in the sound of rain, while murmuring came from somewhere up those stairs, and along the hall.

This moment, this very moment would be the height of their relationship, the high-water mark.

Nothing else would ever be the same. For anyone, really, in Arron Brook.

Darkness called, waves, and sky birds sang. The rain was over.

And Torrent was alone with Polly when she made it home that evening at ebb tide. He didn't even ask where she had gone because he had been trying to find buyers on the phone.

The birds sang in the willow branches, and the gravel drive had spots of clear mirror-like puddles. She ran upstairs, she hid without him knowing why she would ever want to hide. There she shook both in pleasure and dread at what she had done. Why didn't she tell Albert that Torrent was putting money aside for her education?

She remembered how she had stumbled to put on her wet clothes and ran from the cottage. She thought of the line from Genesis. "How do you know you are naked?" seemed to hang in the dank air, in the towels and the smell of pink soap.

Then it all came out—that is, who the land belonged to. People no longer spoke to her at the grocery store. That is because too many were against them, too many were saying they were greedy. Too many others—like the beekeeper Jessop, and the maple syrup guy—had hoped to get that money and had never gotten it, to have much sympathy for those who had. They walked by Eva as if distraught by everything she had brought to the world. And there were now rumours too and she could not dispel them.

When Torry was away Eva drank, and wandered from one end of the house to the other, crying, with little Polly following her, holding her doll Mo Mo in her hand. Finally she telephoned him. But Ms. Sackville answered the phone.

"It's Torry's fault," she said, holding back Polly who wanted to talk on the phone. "It is, Professor Sackville—it's not me, it's Torry's fault."

It was raining now too. The rain came down on Matilda, on the old horse in the paddock. It came down on the window like some kind of curse. And she was weeping and hoping to run away.

25

ON THE EVENING OF THAT PHONE CALL, SOMETIME before dark and after the rains had stopped, Oscar Peterson, lay preacher, pig farmer, bolt seller, mechanic, merchant, mortuary worker and harmonica player, a man who loved his son Torrent Peterson and did not know that Torrent's wife had lain naked five times with someone else, was pushing Darren Howl over the ruts of the barrens.

In the rural proclivity that defined both their natures, and the natures of so many around them, Oscar wore a pair of workboots, tied midway, an old pair of grey pants, a white T-shirt ripped and stained, a wallet with a chain in his back pocket, and having in his mouth a bolt of black Copenhagen snuff, while Darren, no less rural, was this evening dressed in a pair of white slacks, with braces on his legs, a blue short-sleeved shirt and a red bowtie, and a yellow fedora with a grey ribbon around its base. In his shirt pocket he carried a pen, in a white plastic pen holder with a logo from Benson's garage.

They were both being plagued by flies—horseflies and blackflies that in hotter climes don't multiply so rapidly. Darren was rocked by the journey but his bright eyes squinted at the sodden ground Oscar pointed to.

"Here is where they were found," Oscar said, stopping beside the weeds along the side of the dirt road, in a seemingly endless area of nowhere at all. A sky hawk flew in the brilliant night, and a little bat flitted out almost beside them. Above to the left was a huge rainbow in the evening sky, as if Arlo and Arnie were telling them they were fine and at peace forever.

"Arnie was down on this side. Arlo was somewhat beneath him, we figure. Arlo fell first and Arnie fell soon after. But his arm was out—Arnie's left arm was out—hooked up, in a fashion like *this*." And Oscar crooked his arm. "I was the one who came out to identify the boys. So I figure even if Constable Furlong didn't notice it—and the bodies were removed before any other police came— that Arnie had his arm up in a gesture."

"Trying to stop the cold?" Darren said.

"No, no sir, not at all, sir. Trying—to get someone to stop."

"Someone to stop?"

"The car to stop—someone who watched them. Look—up there—that pole—just up at the turn—Mile 17."

"Yes."

"Come along, I will push you there. I want you to see something."

"How long has it been that you have been trying to solve this?"

"Years."

"And will you?"

"Yes."

"Are you sure?"

There was no answer for a moment. They came to a muck hole and Oscar had to push around it, to the left side. Finally he said: "Yes."

"Are you dealing with dangerous people?"

"Yes," Oscar said. "I'm dealing with the very most dangerous—the worst. A man who would defile himself and God by killing young boys."

Then he said: "I want you to believe me—that I never intended to hurt anyone."

"I know."

"Well I will find out what happened to Arlo and Arnie and after that I will be recognized like Sherlock Holmes—or someone as big."

"Yes."

"I found something here last week—it had been here for a long time. Most of the evidence is long gone, but miraculously, I suppose, not this."

They came to a birch windfall that lay out over the road, with its branches still shimmering softly in the coming evening. All was quieted by a jay bird somewhere now, making it quiet with her chirp, and then the small rustle of some small animal going home made it longing and sad.

"One thinks of murder in a place so quiet," Oscar Peterson said.

"Did you know that was a thought in a poem by Alden Nowlan?"

"No," Oscar said, "but one doesn't have to write a poem to know that it is true—I have been here too many times. I have followed him with my mind's eye. Or love—"

"Yes, that too."

"*Splendour in the Grass.*"

"Yes."

"Who with your mind's eye—"

"Stroud, of course. Stroud. As I told you, Stroud, who had these boys rushing about for him, Stroud, who had them believing he was doing it all for them, Stroud, who hoodwinked my Mary Lou into thinking it was me who had those boys run away—Stroud, who that cold night waited—*here*."

He stopped the wheelchair with a jar, and Darren Howl went forward, and Oscar held him in the chair with his right hand, his broken fingernails black with dirt.

Then he turned the wheelchair to the left, up a small nineteenth-century wagon lane, hidden from the empty dirt road.

"Here," he said, "here is where he waited—one hundred yards away from two freezing-to-death children and watched them—*die*. He drove them out here, put them out of the car—the cold was thick, and he said he would be back in an hour or so. Never left—just went here, and waited. But you see, he had the knife on the seat beside him in case they did not—die."

Oscar bit at his fingernails—he was always doing so—and then, in the sleeping quiet of evening he said: "Here, let me show you—what I found."

And he went to the woods nearby and looked about here and there, and then picked up some piece of old poplar stump, brought it out, and holding it up he took out of his pocket a pair of tweezers.

"Embedded—I saw it glint—it was embedded. Most of it I suppose has melted away, but not this—a few pieces are left."

"What is left of what?"

"Now," he said, wiping his mouth quickly, "you will see."

And within a second he had taken with his tweezers, from the little pile of orange and reddish poplar rot, a small sliver of bluish glass.

"There," he said, and he held it for Darren Howl to inspect. "Oh—I have a tiny bit more of it in a basket at home. These are the shards of glass from his windshield that went through the air in a thousand ways on a dark night—and were embedded in the earth, where man continually embeds his misery. You can tell where that branch was—on that maple there"—he pointed to the left where a branch had been broken away some years before, its stump blackened by weather. "Right through the car—and out he goes following those boys. Later, worried and a little brilliant, he came out and chopped that branch away."

"Can you prove it?"

"No—of course not. Nor can I prove that they sold that mescaline to he who gave it to your sister—who killed herself by accident—and when you jumped in after her you smashed your legs on the rocks below, as if they were awaiting you for eight thousand years. I cannot prove that either. But perhaps your Becky Donaldson can, for she has not let it go. I believe Stroud is working himself up to the biggest crime—the enormous one—you see, men have to do so, once they start out—all sin is an imitation of the greatest sin—and the greatest sin, the sin which all other sin aspires to, is *murder*. And all people who need power, sooner or later need *murder*, in some way or the other—in some way or the other. Maybe more the mental kind than the physical kind. It is what plagues mankind from top to bottom. And the smaller, more intense devil with him is his brother Shane Stroud. He attacked my son one night on the road—furious over Torry and Eva. You see he believed Eva was his girl. But he just did not know how strong Torry was. Right in the middle of the road. And then the next night he got in a car and raced up Load Road to try and find Eva, and runs over a girl, a child—then heads to Moncton. All of this surrounds our family like the Black Death."

"I see—I think I see."

Oscar was now in the mood to talk.

"You see, elderly matriarch Mrs. Lampkey long ago demonstrated this to me. For she is no different than Stroud. Oh she might think so—but wait, until I explain—"

"Explain what?"

"There was a young girl who was pregnant—her name was Mary Lou. The night she waited on tables at Ben Mott's wedding she was already knocked up. She was a simple girl—maybe not very bright. Whenever they had a test in school Arnie or Arlo would make sure they sat beside her or behind her and whisper the answers to her in code. The only problem was, she sometimes disremembered the code they had worked out with her. She was scared and alone and became pregnant, soon she was big as a butterball—but by who, we didn't know."

"Not by you?"

"No! I am so sorry not by me. People wanted to think that and torment me still, for being an old man and knocking up a youngster, but not by me. I never told anyone it was not by me—for her sake. And maybe if I want to tell the truth, for my sake as well.

"You see they told her she was going to a party with them—the kind of children that come here in the summer. But this night they turned a corner in their car, and were driving back to the wharf, and there she was picking flowers by the Ladies Auxiliary hall, with the sun just going down. To them she was an hilarity, a girl of fifteen growing into a young woman who did not know enough to as yet wear a bra, whose underwear was ripped, who had a T-shirt with a picture of Minnie Mouse on it. *Oh their concern now—for women's rights.*

"They put her in the middle of the back seat, with two shining young boys on either side, and drove away, she still with the smell of earth on her body, and hay straw in her beautiful hair. And that is how Torrent Peterson came into being after a bottle and a half of golden nut wine."

"Is that so?"

"Yes. Now one of those boys at that party was Edgar Lampkey— son of the judge and he now an MP."

"Is that right?"

"What I discovered, yes."

"Was he the father?"

"Who in hell knows," Oscar said, irritated. "Still, I was discovering who it was that might be involved. I went to Judge Lampkey's house. I stood before them in old boots, my hat in my hand, with her beside me.

"But they offered what people did in those days, six hundred dollars—and God forgive me I took it. I took it for her. But you see they did not want to profit by it any more than I did. The father was ashamed, the priest I consulted was useless, and the boys were scared. The terror of an unborn child had drifted over us—but by *whose authority* does terror come? Christ you see was born almost in the same manner—an unwed mother and a father who knew the truth—in a stable—like my old trailer—and yet there was joy to the world. So who caused the terror?"

"I don't know," Howl said.

"Ha—the devil causes the terror—Satan—Satan wants our children in garbage cans."

"You believe it?"

"On certain days I might. Sometime after, Mrs. Lampkey came to me, to the old trailer, and offers to take the girl away. Now she came without anyone else knowing—she came by herself up the back path, with a hat over her eyes, and asked to take the girl."

"Where to?"

"She didn't say. She smiled and asked me if I wanted a job. She said if I allowed Mary Lou to go with her I would have a job as junior supervisor at asbestos mine because she knew people there. She asked me what I earned now—I mean when she spoke—and I told her I earned forty-eight hundred a year and earned every penny. 'Give the girl to me for a week and you will have twenty-four thousand a year,' she said. '*I will make sure you get a job.*'

"Now she wanted, with her learning from McGill, to take the child away. To do what? I didn't even want to ask. The child was almost five months along—so what would she do. I think I froze at the suggestion that the world she had been trained in could be that open-minded. To throw the unborn child in the garbage.

"It was an unfamiliar world to me. In some ways I'd rather have the Pentecostals browbeating me. I stared at her flat white shoes, her rather thick legs, and couldn't lift my head for a time. She looked at me and asked if I minded that she smoke.

"'Smoke. Oh God, smoke,' I said, as if this natural plea was the only good thing said in this moment. She stared at me quite coldly—and who was I to go against a person like her? I was nothing—well a flea—compared to them.

"'God Almighty,' she said, glaring at me, 'this is a disaster waiting to happen. You can't let this happen to this child.' She was almost hysterical. Her eyes showed desperation. Christ does not cause such.

"How I found my voice I do not know, but I did find it. I was shaking, but I found my voice. You see I relied on the Raskins for about three thousand of that forty-eight hundred by extracting waste from that tailings pond and pouring ten thousand pounds of bulldog lime into the surrounding area or it would all seep into Riley Brook. I did not want to lose that job. Now I was suddenly frightened of her.

"'You can see what I am saying?' she said, calmly. The little girl was in the back bedroom, and was poking her nose out, listening to the conversation about her and shaking.

"'But you see—here is something you do not seem to understand, Mrs. Lampkey. It already has happened, but I will not allow anything else to happen.'

"'What do you mean?'

"'I mean I will not allow it to happen to the child she is carrying—that would be a crime.'

"'A crime—my soul, it is not a child yet,' she said.

"'It is not?'

"'No, of course not.' Here her smile was conciliatory and bemused. She wanted her look to reveal how less cultured I was.

"'Then you really believe in miracles, don't you.'

"'How is that?' She was startled. I think surely she had given all miracles up.

"'Because the way a child is made is so unimportant to you. It is never a child until it flies full-formed from the cunt of woman.'

"With that she was utterly mortified—I utterly mortified her, I guess. That is, abortion at five months was a fine and noble thing for a middle-class Protestant lady to offer poor ignorant Catholic Mary Lou, but never dare ever say the word *cunt*."

"But Lampkey was never mentioned by you?"

"Never. Still it happened in Judge Lampkey's summer place. But they were kids too—it is the adults who washed it away. You see I am not angry at boys trying to take a piece of tail—but the girl must be wise to what is being asked. In her case and in your sister's case, neither did know. Both were helpless. Now, after this time, all must be atoned, they must come back *now* and say *we are sorry*, and if they do, well I would gladly forgive the world, but if not, if they do not now come back and say *I apologize, I was a stupid young boy* there is no hope for them."

"That is my problem too," Howl said. "Who do we blame for my sister—who was seventeen. A boy of nineteen who was callow and vain? I too think of God and wonder why."

Oscar took the brake off the wheelchair, and swung it around.

"I have two caps of mescaline for you—it came from the batch Arlo and Arnie did for Mel Stroud. It was what I was going to take to the police, but after they died I didn't, for there was no longer proof. If you want those responsible for your sister, start with them."

"I will—yes, I will," Howl said.

Then Oscar pushed his friend along on the silent road, and tears came down his eyes, and he said: "But she is gone now, the love of my life—she is gone. And there was no reason for any of it, if only she had listened to me. Of course I gave her a big black eye—and I know I was a fool, but that was to get her to stay."

And the sweet night descended over the winding weed-strewn road.

26

A. T. RASKIN HAD HIS LAWYER WRITE TORRENT AND tell him to pay off the loan or his property would be forfeited.

Torrent, who had come in from helping his father dig a trench for a new electrical line to the barn, and had spent all day away from the cabinets he was making, did not know this would happen. Now it seemed entirely natural to him. What was more telling, and even ominous, was the friendship Albert had cultivated with one of the carpenters who he had tried to introduce into the business, Brian Moor. They were now friends.

Torrent had to get his father to read the letter, and then he phoned.

Albert said while he had him on the phone: "Maybe if it's so stressful you should give up carpentry."

Torrent remembered Eva's little white knuckles in the loan office of the bank.

Things were returned to the barn that retailers couldn't or wouldn't sell. One vanity was broken, and a chair had a leg missing.

One of the best secretary desks had taken him four months. It was simply hauled in and left on the barn floor, as if it was nothing.

Now First Nations men were asking for some twenty-six thousand dollars, and he did not have it, told them he did not owe it for he had bought the land from Ricer in good faith so had used his own wood, and not theirs. So now they said they would sue Torrent, Clement Ricer and Albert Raskin.

Professor Raskin went to the paper and said he had ceased all business transaction with Torrent Peterson, that the business was now null and void.

There was a picture of the farmhouse in the paper, and in the background Matilda the sow wandering along the fence.

Torrent would discover what a lien was that day. That night he sat in the dark out in the barn, looked at the night light on in his little girl's upstairs room, and he began to shake. The trouble was, Raskin was a Raskin—he was such a gentleman in how he dressed, and what he said, and the blue eyes of hauteur, poor Torry couldn't face him. He only told Eva:

"He didn't need to pay for anything—we didn't even need to take the money. Why in God's name were we so stupid as to take the money."

"But I never wanted the money," Eva said, suddenly frightened. "You wanted to quit your job and do cabinets. I was doing it for you, and you're so mean to me you don't even speak to me no more!"

He got up to leave the room.

"Don't leave this room," Eva said, panicky. "Don't leave this room."

Eva ran to the dining room and looking into the desk she found the contract that detailed exactly what was happening. The most telling clause was one that spoke of false pretences.

"I didn't know," she said, her hands shaking, "I didn't know—look—that there—I didn't see that there—did you see it—why didn't you see it, oh you were sneaking over to Clara's to feel her beautiful tits, so what I don't know—so why didn't she teach you enough to see it?"

"What in God's name are you going on about—what in God's name?"

But she just slumped down in the corner, trying in some desperate way to blame it on him, holding a whole fistful of papers in her hand. Clara had always been the problem, and Clara she knew had been teaching him to read.

She read the contract over again and again—now it was not a delightful paper that had Mr. Raskin's signature and solved all her problems—it was an edict of dread.

Torry still went forward, still culled his wood, still worked late into the night.

Once she said: "That is so good for you, but what about me? My life is over. We will lose the house and my life is over."

She went to the registrar's office at the university and got all the information she could on the fall courses.

Now she had to prove to *him* that he had made the right choice when he helped her. For she still believed he had helped her. Yes, they had both helped her.

She now felt that this was all Torrent's fault. If he had just paid more attention—more attention—done his work the way Mr. Raskin asked him to—but no, he was just too stubborn. That was not what she wanted in a marriage, she decided—no, you bet your boots!

She would tell Mr. Raskin that the next time she saw him too—that she knew he only meant to do nice things for her, and her husband wasn't as grateful as she was—and she didn't want him to think bad things about her. And once when Polly was crying she shook her and said: "Oh if it wasn't for you I'd be happy but you ruined my whole life."

The little girl continued to cry and Eva said she would make her pudding if she just stopped, and she would buy her a kitten, yes a kitten, so there you go.

And then she walked about the kitchen biting her nails and crying too. And saying "Holy oh cow—" Which was almost as bad a swear word as she ever said.

On many evenings the shy boy, as she knew him, Torrent Peterson, would walk up the main road to the house on the main river, near where the old ferry the *Romeo and Juliet* once ran, and in a brick house he would climb the stairs, and Clara Bell would be waiting. The blackboard, the desk with sharp pencils, the young readers' anthology, stories about the three bears and Little Red Riding Hood, and now, clipped stories from magazines and papers (but not, intentionally, the one in which Raskin or Chief John was interviewed) where he could begin to follow politics of the day, and see in a way what he had never known before, what a shy boy like him was facing in the world that was turning against them.

Clara was always waiting, even when she was ill, and even when the night did not go well, she was there. Did she love him? Yes. Did she think of him *that way?* Only in the briefest of ways, the fantasies that come unaided to the soul, and to the heart, on cold nights when one is alone. Loneliness being the terrible passion maker, and creating a well of longing in every man and woman that no man or woman can escape. Did she know there were rumours that hurt her and her husband, and put a strain on their relationship? Yes, she did know.

They went over the primary grades, went over the alphabet, phonetics, went over angles on geometric instruments where she found he knew them as if an angel had come to him when he was young and put them in the air before his eyes, squares, rectangles and all the many symmetrical and algebraic signets he already seemed to know. And slowly over the two years he began to read. For one reason only: so Eva would be proud of him. She didn't seem to be proud that he could make a clock or cabinet better than ninety percent of humanity, or she never seemed to be. But perhaps on a cold night if he opened a book and surprised her under the glow of the kitchen light?

One night as he left the house, and walked back to his truck, he met a strange figure who needed a drive. A strange little elf who wanted to go home, and seemed not to have a home to go to, a strange sad little fellow whose friends made him act out for them. He was on his way to the reserve, and no one in an hour, in the sleet and cold, had divined to be kind enough to stop for him. And so Torrent did. They had been born in opposite worlds on the same night, almost at the same moment seven metres apart.

The reserve where he lived was barren, the soil bad, the sea wall crumbling, the houses dilapidated, the streetlights broken, the dogs half-starved. He who had been born with severe fetal alcohol syndrome knew no other world or place. Nor did he know where he wanted Torry to leave him, but finally they saw the lights on in a trailer behind the reserve's community hall, and the light drifted out into the sleet-drenched night, and the little elf jumped from the truck and said, "Thank you I love you whole bunch goodbye."

His name was Roderick Hammerstone, and as the boys all said, he was always either hammered or stoned.

——

Nineteen seventy-four. Some of the boys would say to Roderick Hammerstone, "Go into the school and wag your wiener."

And he would. The boys would grin. His uncle Gordon would desperately try to stop him, but it was almost impossible. Other First Nations boys would look out for him, call him over, give him lectures, tell him he shouldn't do what such-and-such wanted him to, and he would listen and nod and say:

"Yes I love you whole bunch—I love everyone whole bunch— even white people."

But then some others would whisper: "Roderick, go kick Constable Furlong in the nuts—how about it?"

And Roderick would do so, and Constable Furlong, bent over outside the centre snack bar would say: "You little bastard—why did you do that? Why did you—do—that?"

But poor Roderick wouldn't know why. He was just compelled to do so. So the boys would tell him to run naked across the street. And he would. And others would try to stop this. And it would stop. Then at some point something else would happen.

He was born with fetal alcohol syndrome and some of the boys had made a game of it, like a medical condition formed in the womb was a jest of God, that showed no life was unimportant, even as a warning to others. The warning of neglect and poverty on the reserves; years of being considered less than others, of being forced to an area given to you by government bureaucrats. All of this while Gordon's sister went from a gentle brilliant child who played Mozart at recital when she was eleven to suddenly looking at him one night with wild hurt eyes, with a drunken glare that hated the world.

Gordon more than anyone tried to keep his nephew safe from the mindless ones who took advantage of the boy, but as he grew, and as he became more independent and as he wandered, he became more and more a worry. Many days would go by and no event would occur, and nothing would happen, and Gordon would think, *He is better now*, and then all of a sudden one day in the afternoon, sometime after three o'clock, Roderick would appear, with a car stereo, an eight-track tape, and seven cans of premium-grade oil.

"Where did you get those?"

"They are mine."

"Yes, where did you get them?"

"They are mine—for my part."

"What part?"

"The part I played."

"In what?"

"In the robbery."

"What robbery?"

"Of the fire station."

"Who was with you?"

"My pals."

"You have no pals, Roderick—don't you understand, you have no pals—just people telling you to do things and running away when you get caught—you have *NO PALS*."

"Everyone has pals, Gordon, except an Indian like you."

This had gone on since Roderick was six years old.

Now that he was in his twenties the fear of him committing a horrid crime kept Gordon awake, and isolated, and alone. It caused resentments and fights, and made Gordon remote and silent in front of those he once considered his friends. There were many First Nations men and women who looked out for Roderick and tried to keep him safe, but there were those who played with his mental state. And Gordon was the only family Roderick had left. Gordon with years of political wars under his belt had to fight another one to keep Roderick from doing something simply because he was told to do so.

One summer evening soon after the lien on his house, Torrent went out to move his four oak trees, that he had cut and limbed early in June, and was stopped by a gathering of seven First Nations men who startled him coming out of the side road that would have led back to both his house and Oscar's. They told him they wanted the twenty-six thousand dollars and had a right to it. That he himself had no right to the wood he cut. He told them the deed he had was registered at the court, and that he had bought the land from Mr. Ricer.

"The court means nothing to us," one of the men told him, and he held up his own deed, with his own family's signatures, the appropriate stamp and arrowhead. It was he said authentic and over a hundred and fifty years old.

He told them he did not know what was authentic and what was not but he had paid for the land from Ricer.

Three of them stood on one side of the horse, three on the other, and one dressed in a mask stood in front of the horse. This man with the mask Torry would easily be able to identify as Roderick Hammerstone, the boy he had given a drive home some months before. He was not really a part of the group but had simply decided to follow them up the ridge, with a mask on and telling them he had come to help.

The men said they needed to take their wood back. He said the wood was his. They said they had an understanding with his partner, that this was unceded land. He told them he had no partner anymore. There was silence. The red sky hung over them; the horse waited. Roger looked from one to the other, and was silent. Torrent said he was going home with his logs.

Then two other men spoke. They told him the land had been unceded, and belonged to them.

The land, Torrent said, had belonged for generations to the Ricers and he had cut these oaks that he had watched grow since he was a child. That no one disputed Mr. Ricer before and the deed was now his.

After this there was no talk, only a stalemate. For ten minutes or more two men spoke in Mi'kmaq.

Torry had the long oak chained to the horse. The horse, Pete's Kind—sired from Grand Pete—a small but tough Belgian, listened docilely to the argument, wondering whether he was to go or not, his tail trying to measure the horseflies on his back, the smell of manure rich at his hind hooves.

Torrent said he wanted no trouble, but he was going home. Roderick decided to stand in the horse's way and each time the horse started, Roderick would jump in front of it, once almost slipping and falling on the downgrade.

Finally Torry tried to move the horse around him toward the lower maple trees, but Roderick grabbed at the halter, and his fingers accidentally went into the horse's left eye. Pete's Kind flinched, stepped back into the dung, and then bolted sideways, running down into the trees, with Roderick hanging off its bridle and Torrent, who fell when trying to get to the front, caught under the heaviest oak, crushing his left foot.

The First Nations men did not mean for this to happen, but it had happened. They did not mean for Roderick to act the way he did, but he had come with them to help. It is what Gordon was trying to protect him from.

Everyone was solemn. One of the First Nations men went down to the spring and got water, two more lifted Torrent onto the wagon, and one man got up on the horse's back, calmed it down, was able to turn it out of the trees. And they started down the hill toward Torrent's house, bathed now in twilight and the smell of strawberry blossoms.

"We are sorry," one of the men said.

"Much damage will be done," Torrent said, as if looking into the hills, toward the asbestos mine and great oval oil tanks, he saw suddenly the destruction of their entire world.

He did not press charges and the men did not take the lumber. Other litigation was coming against the Peterson couple.

27

I WAS NOW ARTIST IN RESIDENCE AT THIS SMALL UNIVERSITY, so though I had my own studio in an almost vacant floor at the back part of the arts building, and though I kept to myself so I would not have to listen to how people said they could not afford an artist in residence, I was still aware of certain things emanating from those hallways and offices on the grounds below me.

Little Eliot Slaggy brought a lawsuit against the university about the same time Mr. Oscar Peterson started his lawsuits against the police, and the medical officers, for the cover-up in the deaths of Arlo, Arnie and Mary Lou Toomey.

Oscar's petitions and outbursts were dismissed, but he was now determined to widen his confrontations. He would show up at the Raskins' magnificent house driving his scooter, wearing a huge helmet with an American eagle emblazoned across the top he had traded a spinning rod and lure for. He would walk about outside with his helmet on, his boots on the soft pavement, the slanted cedar shingles shading him, a pair of huge goggles covering his eyes. They would finally open the door, and step out into the sunshine.

"Do you know who I am?"

"I think so," Chester would say.

"It's Oscar."

"Oh yes. Oscar. Well, your goggles make you look something like a big bug. You look like a Martian."

"I know it," Oscar would answer without taking off those goggles. Then he would start in about the police reports, medical reports on three young people Dexter and Chester had for the most part no knowledge of. He would hand them a batch of four hundred pieces of paper, tied with ribbon.

"See what you can do," he would say.

"Oh yes we will."

"See how it goes."

"We will."

"With you in the picture something will get done."

"Sure it will."

"*The conspiracy,*" he stated, "*stinks to high heaven.*"

"Yes, that's what you say."

"Glad you're on board."

"Thank you."

"Crazy as a bedbug," Dexter would say as he left.

"Certainly is," Chester would answer.

But the two elderly brothers had their own problems now. Their family had taken over Good Friday Mountain, from Lower Riley Brook to the forks of Arron Falls—and they had cleared the land and dug out zinc and copper little by little, and had deposits of gold. They had a fight in the 1930s with both the Sloan and Jamison families over the area of great timber. But then the government came to their aid in 1938, because of asbestos—which everyone believed was a super-element, an ore that would allow electricity to run, pipelines to function, houses to be insulated. It was in homes and buildings and stoves, in filters for the cigarettes people smoked. They had white chrysotile that many scientists touted as being safe. It was a super-element, a fire retardant and insulation. The government opened the mine for them, and money to mine it. They had first-rate hand cobbers, and good strains of fibre, and conveyor belts and sifters, then as time passed hand cobbers and shovels were replaced by backhoes and crushers.

So they had their contracts during the Second World War and after the war became wealthy. But the two brothers did not marry. They stayed together.

For years they made money, sold to suppliers in Canada and the U.S., contracted to the Navy and Air Force to build the war houses of servicemen across our land. And treated their employees well. But things happened to dismay them. And every time they went to the government in those years with concerns about asbestos fibres being breathed, like had been in the case of Mary Toomey's mother and father, their own concerns were dismissed.

"The asbestos is needed so the asbestos is good."

The letters they wrote to the governmental bureaucrats on concerns they had were actually considered counterproductive to the safety of their workers.

But then came the seventies, and little by little the government changed, started relenting to international scientific pressure— and though Raskin hung on, still employing seventy men, and though they still had contracts, they had to fight for every morsel they got.

Now the governments had changed again, the scientists were proved false, and these two old gentlemen were caught up in a terrible battle. Environmentalists, of which their nephew was one, were telling them they were the culprits. And the longer they held on looking for this explanation, the harder and harsher it would become.

By the 1980s some men who had worked for them in the late 1950s and early '60s died, slowly. And by the time of this last inquiry 36 percent of men who had worked for them had contracted some type of respiratory ailment. Others had lesions on their lungs. Boys who dug in the soil and used backhoes and loaders, boys who flushed out lines and packed crates, and diligently protected their industry, those boys whose hands they shook at July 1 barbecues—those boys once strong and able could very well be dead in two years. It was why Chester and Dexter wanted to stop mining asbestos and mine copper ore. It is what they petitioned the government for in 1969, and were refused.

Now when they petitioned once again to do this, word got out, and they were looked upon as predatory, ambivalent to the welfare of others, and greedily looking for a way out.

This is what McLeish wrote an op-ed piece about—vowing to shut them down. So certain of the smaller equipment was sabotaged, and a truck was burned. Yes, all revolution started at the universities spread to the workers and was handled in the end by criminals willing and able to do the job.

The old men, who had been the first to say they wanted out of asbestos, were now the first targeted as the ones to blame. So they decided they would stay the course. Of course all kinds of secret talk revolved about them among the men who drank in taverns and ruined their lives in schemes that went nowhere: one, the men were gay; two (and the most prevalent), they were child molesters and had a secret cabal with the village priests and hid children in their house.

None of this was even remotely true, but in the world, as Ms. Sackville said, there was no truth, only constructs. These old men wouldn't know of constructs or books that spoke of them.

At times, both driving their own huge half-ton trucks at fifty kilometres an hour, one black and silver, the other silver and black, one behind the other, they went to visit those sick boys too—don't think they didn't. They entered small houses in Neguac and Lagacéville, and saw Acadian men they had relied on in their twenties who spoke French and were instrumental in those days moving into Quebec, now in their late forties already sick, and they held their hands, saying: "That's some real bad luck, isn't it," and they hugged the wives of those men, and spoke of how wonderful they worked. And they sat the children on their knees, as they were supposed to do. And their eyes were dark and shining—and they both could stare down a pole. And people were frightened of them, and reverential. And they stood silently together with their hats in hand. They spoke of hunting to those who hunted and fishing to those who fished, and they said:

"If he is up for it, he can be fishing at our camp next July."

"Oh, that would be wonderful."

"Well, why not. We can have the helicopter come pick him up."

"Did you hear that, Antony—did you? A helicopter to pick you up."

"Now he worked for us for eleven years, didn't he?"

"Fifteen," his wife would answer. "He worked out at the tailing pond, and with the zinc, and he lifted asbestos rock with a backhoe."

242 DAVID ADAMS RICHARDS

They would both look down at the man in the bed.

"Ah, fifteen years," Chester would say. "Well, well. I knew he was a loyal employee—a very loyal employee."

"We'll take care of him now," Dexter would say. "Any bills for treatment, you send to us."

"It's just the oxygen. We have to—well, oxygen costs a lot. And the night nurse. And he has broken out in some sores here—look on his buttocks."

There would be general almost embarrassed silence, for they never themselves spoke of money or needed to discuss the illness.

"Well send the bill to the office and we will take care of it," Chester would say abruptly, and then quietly they would start for the door.

"Did you hear that, Antony? Did you hear?"

But you see, both of them would be confused—puzzled—and it would show on their perplexed faces, it would all show. A tank of oxygen is nothing, but three thousand tanks of oxygen is something else again, for it signified something these old men—who had given what they could to the workers—did not understand. They did not understand what was happening, or why it was happening to them. They built their empire like other salt-of-the-earth men had built their empires, so why was theirs the one chosen for this calamity, this pandemic on their house? What horrid anxiety had now come?

So they called Albert, and asked him to help his mother find the copies of letters they had written about these concerns many years before. They were sure they would be in Albert's father's study.

"We asked the government in 1959, if there was any danger then to stop it all," Chester would say. "But the man come and said he had never seen such clean asbestos in my life."

"I know it, boys oh boys," Dexter would answer. "Where is the copy of that letter that we wrote? We must have filed it. We wrote ten of them letters—you can tell the paper that."

He could not help his uncles. Even if he wanted to there was nothing he could do. He listened to their complaints against his friends and colleagues and then left them. He didn't say a word. His friends were waiting for him at the other end of Bloody Field, where the university grounds started. He had to go—and make a statement, introduce a guest speaker. So he left quickly and went to them. For there was nothing much left to say.

"We are getting older, we need some help straightening this out," they told him. "If we found those copies, you could try to drum up some support for us with the Indian bands. We have given a good deal to their community—"

"Aboriginal peoples," Albert corrected.

"Oh yes," Chester replied, "those peoples."

"Done all we could," Dexter added.

"Yes—that's right. Done all we could."

In the grand old house the nurses took the old men's blood pressure and gave them their morning pills, and the maid tried to keep the paper away from their coffee table. First Nations men and women stood outside their property with many signs.

They could not see them but they knew they were there.

"He doesn't believe us—he does not believe us," Dexter said as Albert left.

"But didn't we have good times together?"

"Of course! Took him fishing."

"Yes . . . Did we?"

"We must have . . . Didn't we?"

"Went to Disneyland too—went to Disneyland."

"Yes, we did . . . Or did we? Did we go, or did just he go by himself?"

"At five? No, he didn't go by himself at five. I thought we all went—got on that rollercoaster—"

"I thought we got on that rollercoaster—yes. Well, there you have it. How many kids get to Disneyland?"

"Not so many."

They were silent. For a long moment.

"We took him to Disneyland, that's a fact."

"I have a picture of it—you have on a pair of Mickey Mouse ears. Right in the picture, a pair of Mickey Mouse ears."

"Mickey's ears?"

"Yes. You said, 'Damn if I won't try them on.'"

"Don't remember."

Staring at each other across the room, Dexter was silent and so was Chester. Except Chester rubbed the butt of his cane on the floor. When the housekeeper rang for soup, both of them, hurt and confused, refused to answer the bell.

By the 1980s the sadness and hopelessly lonely confusion, the scorn now beginning to be heaped on them by government officials who once came to dinner, the absence of invitations to political meetings, the silence when they asked for advice, the missing letters of inquiry they themselves said they sent, was seen in every teetering step they took. However old they were, in the coming years they would begin to see in their dreams the sad, sandy terror and the reality of dying men—and they themselves would step out of the shadows into the light and try to make restitution as best they could. First it was greater salary, then it was extra pay, then it was money from their accounts, then it was selling holdings to give workers what they could. Then it was a new wing of a hospital.

They both walked with canes, their legs shaky and their eyes misty, yet still afire. Though no one believed them, though they had stalled and procrastinated their final destinies, they had no idea that asbestos in the hidden vales of those white cliffs would cause this; that it would scorn them, ridicule them, and make them targets of the wrath of the new generation. They had relied on science, and science had killed them. If they had trusted in what they had prayed for, the truth, they might have done better.

Now, in penance, they allowed the scorn to wash over them, and were silent.

The person they later hired to help them make fair restitution was Clara Bell. That is why she became so famous in our country.

"Those silly sons of bitches from the university."

"Yes, I know."

"Surrounding our property last night, for they say that we are poisoning Riley Brook. We are not poisoning Riley Brook—or are we? Maybe we are. But we gave them four million, eleven million, whatever it was—and now they are back. And every oil pipeline they hate—but they use oil, don't seem to be using wood."

"I know."

"Who is among them?"

"Ladies and men. White and—Indian."

"Well, we can't fight ladies—we can't."

"I know."

"Still, I will never give in."

"Either will I."

"We will die together."

"Absolutely."

———

So Torrent's house became the fierce focal point. To get to all the area the Natives claimed, one would have to acquire it as well. Because of his arrogance they would take it over and use it as a centre for peace and justice. He would not speak to them, refused to speak to the Indian band. It was also land that was now under lien because of money from false pretences.

Albert, being pushed forward by others, by Dykes who he still was obligated to impress, was unable to stop, to turn against the current and go back. He would face unbridled ridicule if he did.

"I will burn it first," Torry said when he heard they planned to confiscate his whole farm.

"Not wishing justice for all. Torrent Peterson says he will burn his house."

How wise those reporters, who wouldn't give up a sniff of their salary let alone their house to anyone. They sat in the newsroom and barked soliloquies at one another, looked at the AP and Reuters wires, and went for a pint at the end of the day.

Until this time the Raskin brothers were able to keep a lid on developments against their enterprises. But now they were, as Chester said, "being pissed in the face."

Later I will tell you about how they watched as their statues I had done and erected in the front of their main office were torn down (pretty good statues, if I do say so myself). Stoically, without comment, together leaning on their canes. I will explain that later.

Their empire, their legacy, gone, they stood against those cheering boys and girls who had ropes around the necks of their bronze statues that were commissioned in our town with such reverence years ago. They had given in salary some twenty-seven million dollars over the years. And when two young men, both in second-year sociology, said they would spit on them, they stood up both of them, both of them stood straight and leaned on their brown oak canes and stared at those boys, and those boys turned and walked away.

For that I will always admire them.

I had liked Oscar, and Darren was helping him as much as he could. Sometimes I would tag along. He would come to the door, without opening it. And when we told him who it was, who I was, the local painter, he would slowly open the door a crack to look out.

"Okay—come in for a moment or two. But I want everyone out by dark—by dark. Tomorrow I want you to come and show me your paintings."

So I brought in a painting I had done of his trailer, with a group of buyers standing in his junkyard on a summer day, with Arron Falls to be seen in the far background in lush summer afternoon, with the high oaks off on the hill that Torrent said belonged to him, shaded in a slight mist. He seemed very appreciative of it—asked me how much I wanted. I told him it was his, and he placed it on the shelf over the kitchen table, near the picture of Cervantes's Don Quixote. I believe that was the last time I was in his place.

We know now (and should have known earlier) that there was possibly only one thing Mel Stroud was looking for. That is when he lived here, and doted on the boys and Mary Lou. But he did not find it.

He was looking for the pistol, the 1908 New York Police issue Colt .45 that had once belonged to Byron Raskin. Oscar now and again would take it out and show it. And he showed it to Stroud when Stroud was a boy of sixteen.

Stroud had not forgotten that in among all that junk, all those cannibalized cars and parts of scrapped engines, a pistol he believed was worth thousands of dollars just sat somewhere there, immobile. A pristine oak-handled pistol owned at one time by a detective who searched Little Italy for the Black Hand. That too was terror.

The pistol's history showed the diaspora of living. It was given to the detective's nephew in 1912, a man who traded it for a set of grandiose moose horns in New Brunswick in 1926. It was later bought by old Mr. Raskin in 1936, and then given to his only grandson, Byron.

Byron traded it years before, for the salmon pool now being blockaded by the First Nations.

The man who traded the salmon pool for the pistol, a Mr. Hiram Welt, traded the pistol for a second-hand car from Oscar Peterson. So Oscar had it.

He told Stroud when Stroud was a boy he could have it for the right price.

"When he was sixteen, did you tell him you would sell it?" I asked.

"Yes. I said, 'Get a thousand and I might sell it.'"

"But I believe at any auction it is worth so much more."

He looked at us and said, "I know it killed Jesse James—that day."

"It did?" Darren said.

"Pretty sure it killed Jesse."

"When was it made?" I asked.

"I have a paper says it was made in 1908."

"Yes, that is what I thought. But you know, Oscar, that Bobby Ford shot Jesse James in the back on April third, 1882."

"Did he?" Oscar said. "Imagine—in the back."

"Yes. Betrayal is always in the back."

"Well, that might make it less," Oscar said. "I had figured a thousand. Maybe some more."

"I tell you what," I said. "On auction sites it is worth in the vicinity of twenty thousand to fifty thousand dollars, and a private sale might get that. So maybe you should keep it safe. Maybe you should get a gun cabinet, and bolt it down. Because I am sure Mel Stroud knows what it's worth. I am sure he knew as a boy it was worth a lot. But perhaps he has someone who will buy it from him."

"Fifty thousand . . ."

"I think you might get that," I said. "That's why Stroud was so eager to get it."

Oscar went into the back room, and opened a hole in the wall, and brought out the pistol wrapped in oilcloth. He brought it forward and lay it on the table, opened the cloth, and there it was—the kind of Colt 45 that Theodore Roosevelt made a New York City Police issue in 1895.

Oscar had fired it three or four times, but for years had hidden it away. Very few people knew he had it. Stroud told Albert he could get it for him some years before.

Albert, like most people, had no idea who had that pistol now.

Mel Stroud entered the back of Oscar's trailer one day and asked to buy the pistol for three hundred dollars.

That was the only news we have about Mel Stroud and this affair. But all of us knew that on dark wild nights in Saint John lifting weights with other men of his kind, he would not forget the pistol. In fact he was obsessed with it, drove Henrietta crazy and became like a little boy when he spoke of it. It was his dream, the portico he wished to go through to a new world.

28

IF YOU ASKED MOST OF THE MEN IN PRIVATE WHAT THEY thought of her they would simply say, those who were open to it, that Ms. Sackville was both deceptive and prone to grudges that she carried along with her smile and her quite bright nature.

She wore big square glasses and had her hair in a bun. She had a long silver pin thrust into that bun, and she was known to have hauled it out against some ruffians who made fun of her one night.

"Disperse," she said, holding that pin between two fingers of her closed fist. The ruffians were startled not only by her defiance but by how her hair fell lovingly over one cheek and gave her a moment of true beauty.

She wore long grey skirts and small black boots. She had a brooch on her blouse that depicted a maiden carrying spring water. Of course she was intolerant now that intolerance was allowed as a matter of liberation. But no one should be measured simply by that. At her bravest moments she was utterly fascinating.

Still, she simply believed Ms. Bell was having an affair with Torry Peterson, because she thrived on illicitness, and loved gossip in private meetings. That, and other things, got her expelled from the convent.

Why was Ms. Bell disliked by Ms. Sackville? They had had an argument one day when Clara was visiting her husband. Right in the hallway by the photocopier and people gathered to listen.

Albert told Ms. Sackville that she had won the argument but both knew this wasn't at all true.

"Oh, you won it fair and square. Forget it—you won it." But he could not get away with that lie.

The day of the argument Clara had simply said: "You are myopically self-interested, callow—and you will not stop until someone dies in this town."

Albert said, at the end of the tirade, "Never mind her."

Until one night last year he saw Clara on television. Bell was the lawyer defending a certain Professor Eliot Slaggy, in a civil suit against the university and Ms. Sackville herself. There were seven people named in the suit. The main person was Ms. Sackville.

It caused a furore over the entire campus. Sackville kept to herself, and sent private messages to Raskin and a couple of her fellow professors that she thought she could trust. They must come out now and support her. She worked late into the night alone. She told people she was in the fight of her life. Albert's name was mentioned as having been an early supporter of Sackville. He tried desperately to hide one moment and be on her side the next.

Because now people were saying she should lose her position or retire.

Clara wanted Eliot Slaggy reinstated with four years' back pay. Over the next six months the tribunal was disbelieved, the account of the assault was read in court, former students now gone on in life did not come forward, and Sackville had to take the stand.

The dean and the president had both retired, and both had re-evaluated the case now that they had. And as Sackville said to Raskin with a curt smile: "Both of them bald, and both ball-less."

Three other people were called on behalf of Sackville who were now living in other provinces. All of them sent written statements saying they were not at the party and did not remember the incident. In fact Professor Sackville did not fully remember the incident either.

This was a grave crime, Bell maintained, but one not perpetrated by Professor Slaggy.

Little Eliot was reinstated with four years' back pay, and went around the department ignored and apologizing to everyone. Sackville would not sit in the same room with him. Her students shunned him with their heads down, moved their seats in the cafeteria if he sat too close.

She said to her students, "I, *like a thousand other women, have been victimized by policy.*"

No matter that, he dedicated a poem to her, called "We are Wise to Forgive":

We are wise to forgive with the days turning cold
With all that has happened
All that unfolds,
We are wise to forgive
Before we grow old.
So forgive me, my child,
As I forgive you
As the days turn to darkness
It is all we can do.

The poem was left in her essay box in room 199.

Bell's husband was in the Department of Criminology. He rarely if ever saw the English professors and had little to say to the sociologists, but once when Albert passed his door he waved and asked him in. Albert felt obligated to answer the request by a man who was disabled. And he went in and sat down.

"McLeish wants to start a war with your uncles. Are you with him on that?"

"No—not with McLeish so much, but with the war maybe."

He said he knew his uncles, and knew much of the problems and though he cared for them now had to stand firm.

"But do you think that when everyone leaves them when they are being blockaded, now is the time to stand firm against two elderly men?"

Albert flushed and said nothing.

Howl then asked: "Did you ever know, Albert, a girl named Mary Lou Toomey?"

"The Toomeys—oh, something about them. Pretty sorry lot. No idea who they are, really. Lived in squalor. Feel bad people have to live in squalor. My whole life has been pitched against squalor."

Howl nodded. "She had a child when she was fifteen or sixteen."

"Who?"

"Mary Lou."

"Terrible." Here Albert shook his head, lowered his eyes.

"But what should have happened to those boys?"

"What boys?" Albert asked.

"The boys who got her so terribly drunk she fell asleep and then stripped her naked, and had their fun with her—or some of them, not all of them. I can only imagine a few of the youngsters—some of them wouldn't have been able to get it up, some of them wouldn't have been able to complete the act. Kids themselves. Don't think I don't feel some empathy for some of them too—but I have to ask this question of you. It has taken me a long while to get up the gumption to ask you."

"It did? Get up the gumption?"

"Yes."

Albert looked at poor Howl sitting in his chair, one of his hands twisted, and a lever to ride him about.

"Why do you ask, Howl?"

"You know, I don't know why I ask, really. It is just conversation, I think. Maybe it is time we had a conversation about what happened some time ago."

Again Raskin found nothing to say.

"I am teaching a course called Higher Virtue in Our Legal Affairs next semester—I am writing a book on it, with the help of Clara. You know Clara, my wife?"

"Oh yes, of course. Nice lady."

"You think?"

"Oh yes—wonderful lady." Raskin flushed.

"She got six hundred dollars."

"Who—Clara? For what?"

"No, little Mary Lou Toomey. Six hundred dollars from the parents of those boys, the standard payment for devil-may-care. And that's all it was, to the boys."

"No!"

"Yes."

"Six hundred—that's all?"

"Yes. Back in the day this was still the accepted level of response, you see."

"Horrible!"

Then Albert spied his book on the asbestos mining, which he had published the year before, along with his friend Ms. Sackville, and said: "Can I sign this for you?"

"Oh—if you would like. It does have certain wrong—very wrong things about Premier Bell in it."

"But fair, I think."

"You think it's fair? I'm not sure it came close to being fair. He cannot answer once he is dead. And you seem to make yourself as important to the province as he was."

"I do—?"

"I think so."

"Not at all—"

"Well then, your book does one thing—it holds a light to a kind of voguish academic thinking that usually hides in classrooms in front of impressionable young students, in faculty lounges, or always in like-minded journals of higher thinking where academics publish each other to earn points for tenure. That's what I thought reading it."

"It's an independent book, Howl."

"Oh come now—if it was, Ted and Bill and Nancy and Kent wouldn't have invited you to dinner—they would have treated you like they treated the Nova Scotian. You see, you are being played, Raskin—by all of them—McLeish and the rest—even Sackville a little—they need you with them—just like—well like—"

"Like who?"

"Like Mel and Shane—you might know them, I'm not sure."

"Mel and Shane—not really."

"Well you have a name—the Raskin name—so anyway in a way—you are being used."

Raskin thought this over, looked at Howl's twisted feet which seemed to mitigate what he had just said, and shrugged.

"No one uses me," he said.

At any rate Dykes and some of the more revolutionary students liked the book. But still he knew, secretly, he had hurt people. He remembered that after he had written it, or Sackville did, standing over him, peering down over his shoulder, with her big square glasses, directing him on what and what not to write—how articles called him brave and level-headed, but one review in the paper was not too kind.

"The body snatcher," the review called him, "digging up the bones of our greatest premier to promote his career."

He told Clara that the book was not about the premier but about the Raskins. He telephoned his uncles to tell them the book wasn't about them but about the awful premier.

His uncles pretended they hadn't heard a word about it.

"What a book—well isn't that something—a book—good for you—a book—what did them rock 'n' roll fellas say: 'Paperback writer'—well that's something—good for you!!'"

But he knew he had hurt them terribly. He knew he had hurt Clara's family terribly too. He hadn't meant to—no he had not meant to. In fact he had always hurt his friends—he hadn't meant to—it was just that way. He'd always thought he was brighter than those his money allowed him to feel superior to. He didn't mean to be. People like him could say grand and wondrous things and turn on anyone in a moment. Sackville and he interviewed people and then wrote what they wanted. He didn't mean that either.

Howl said: "Yes—please do sign it."

So he picked it up, thought for a moment what he should say, and wrote: *For you, Howl, a man of many parts, Albert T. Raskin PhD.*

And as he was signing the book Howl kept speaking: "Yes, it was a different age, so she was left all alone—except for one poor man, who brought her to his home and claimed the child as his own. The others all fled. That is, the parents of those boys, affluent and well—well-adjusted. I mean, so many people here talk about being well-adjusted, seeking a new road. A new world. I sometimes wonder what that ever had to do with the human soul."

"Human soul—what do you mean?" Albert said, closing the book slowly and putting it back on the desk.

"Thanks," Howl said, about the book, and continued quickly: "Well, who had the most integrity? Who had the most love? That deranged man—and he is a tad deranged—who took the child in, or the parents of those boys? That is what I am asking in my course. I am asking if integrity in the matter of human dealings will destroy the need for courts."

"You are saying that in your course?"

"Yes."

"That's very strange—very strange—"

"Yes, I know. But are there greater lessons to be learned?"

"What lessons? Don't understand."

"The lessons—well, about the seeds of right and wrong, not in the law but in our very souls."

"In our souls—here you go with souls again. It doesn't work like that."

"It doesn't?"

"No, never!"

"But then, where was God in all of this?"

"*God*—"

"Yes."

"Hiding, as usual," Professor Raskin said.

"Perhaps. But just perhaps God was with the broken-down derelict who took Mary Lou in. You see, perhaps that is where the idea of right and wrong superseding the law and the courts and the obligation back then of six hundred dollars comes in."

"Really?"

"Perhaps it is not money or education that will ever stop this—and boys will be boys and who knows what we might have done at the moment, kids of fifteen, for God sake, all drinking themselves and with a young girl naked on a bed. How would I have acted as a kid? But perhaps as I have thought since the day I was twenty and lying in the hospital with my crippled legs, what we do is never a matter of the law so much as a matter of the conscience. That is the first order—the law always attempts to adjust that to fit individual circumstance. But integrity comes first."

"Yes, well, whatever. I am sorry about your accident. I remember you played baseball."

"And my sister was a very decent barrel racer."

"Oh, your sister? What's a barrel racer?"

"Horses," Darren said. He paused, looked into Albert's sudden mystified face for a second, now showing its age, his age, and his ears and chin struck one as having gotten larger and sharper, and his head was now balding.

"But I have thought, if here and there, during those nights, those two nights, someone really for a moment thought those children should have been protected. But you see, certain people did—an older man wounded in his own soul, who delivered telegrams as a child and suffered because of it, who took her to his little trailer and kept the child, and a First Nations boy, Gordon Hammerstone, who was ashamed at what he saw at a party, and recently wrote me a letter about it. Over time I have come to some conclusions about it."

"What conclusions?"

"Well, the test was not Mary Lou's test. It was those who maybe stood by and watched it—it was their test, for some of them knew it was deeply wrong. That she was a little girl passed out. God, if he exists, wanted them to pass the test, and they in their souls did not."

Darren cleared his throat, and his left arm began to shake as it did at times so the chair rattled just a tad.

"You said two?" Albert stated, looking up at him.

"Two?"

"Two cases."

"Oh yes. Well, I was thinking of two. The letter I just received from Gordon Hammerstone is about the second case. It is why I asked you in here."

"He was Catholic, I think."

"Who?"

"Daddy," he said. "At least he took me to church now and again, and the priest with his hocus-pocus did his rituals."

"Yes."

"Sins of omission. What man has *not done* that causes turmoil. That's what he told me. Sins of omission. You see, it was the war—I mean the war destroyed him in some way. Gave up his position at Raskin Enterprises and became a wanderer."

"Ah yes, sins of omission. Those are the daily ones, the real ones," Darren said. "Did you know that your uncles realize that too. Since you mention them."

They were both very silent for a long moment.

"Have you come to terms, Howl?"

"What do you mean?"

"About your condition?"

"Oh, I suppose, in a way. As best I can."

"That is very heartening," Albert said. "Very heartening."

So Howl continued. "Still, I believe your uncles did want to move away from asbestos in the sixties and get into potash, but there was immense governmental pressure for them not to. Now the government is mute on the subject, and other younger men have taken over the potash mining here. So should these two old men pay for other people's sins, even our country's sins, for it was our country's sin of omission? And when they realized something was amiss they did donate much to the reserve for the last fifteen years. They are just two old men who believed they were doing good things for their country until their country turned against what they were doing. They wrote letters asking for explanations."

"But I have looked and I can't find those letters," Albert said. "I know Clara's father works for them, and Clara is one of the lawyers over there, but I know as much as she does. I did look for those letters—I did!" He was very passionate about this because he had looked for those letters some years before.

"But what if the letters did exist?"

"What if they did?"

"Would you have a different opinion of your uncles?"

"It's hard to say. We need reconciliation now."

"Perhaps. Perhaps. But it all smacks of revenge—revenge rather than reconciliation. At least to me."

"You can never say that about the Indigenous."

"Of course you can—they have no instant moral higher ground. Many are no more protectors of the land than you are," Darren said. Here his left hand began to shake again.

"Can you actually say that?"

"Chester and Dexter gave more and cared more for the Natives than Professor McLeish or Professor Sackville who until four years ago had never seen a Native man or woman."

Albert, bothered by all of this, began to look about the room as if quite suddenly interested in different things.

To him the books here were very alien—not the ones so much on criminology, the study of everything from tort law to civil litigation that defined two walls of the office, but on the far bookshelves: paperbacks of historical texts. *Gettysburg, Vicksburg and Antietam* was one book. *Von Paulus and Stalingrad* was another. *The Fighting Farm Boys: History of Our North Shore Regiment* was a third. *Beaverbrook* by A. J. P. Taylor was another.

Raskin had lived in such a different world. Trips to Europe paid for and even his protests in Washington paid for by his family. He stayed at the Hilton in Washington when he went there to protest, and appeared the next day with others who had slept on the street. He was the only one in the group with a credit card. The second night there certain students sleeping in a van noticed him and Dykes dining at a restaurant near the Canadian Embassy. Dykes pontificated about the CIA, ate his shrimp and complained about the students not being dedicated enough.

Annie had a pet dog named Corley who for over two years waited at the front of the lane for her to come home. Every night she went to Annie's bedroom door and slept.

Suddenly thinking of all of this, Howl's leg began to tremble so the chair began to rattle.

"I am sorry—could you hold my left leg?"

"Pardon me?"

"Could you hold my left leg, please?"

"Yes—sure." And Albert got up and kindly did so and after a moment the leg stopped shaking.

He was prepared to leave now, but Howl asked him to sit again. So he did. Then he thought a second.

"Is it because of your dire illness?" he said with sudden concern.

"My dire illness?"

"Well, someone gets ill, or has a blowout, and gets all religious on us, maybe a little scared of sex, becomes all moral. I notice those things."

Darren Howl seemed to bend forward in his chair, as if he was trying to catch this statement better, and not quite understanding what was being said, as if both of them had been speaking on two different planes. Raskin could see the hair in Darren Howl's ears as he bent forward.

"It happened in a split second. My sister ran over in the rain, she wanted to see the water. She said, 'Oh look—let me out—I have to see the goldfish.' She ran to it, climbed, slipped and fell off a fifty-foot bridge, and I went in after her. It all happened in twenty or thirty seconds. Her life was over, my life was changed."

"She was at a party, and there was mescaline, young men being very cool. You know the time of being cool with drugs, we both lived through it, you and I."

"So she got into the drugs. Lots of people did back then—I know that."

"No, she had a headache."

"Headache?"

"I am positive. She had migraines since she was fourteen years of age. There was an Indian boy there—Gordon Hammerstone. I think he became ashamed."

"Oh," Raskin said, startled suddenly.

"Yes, she had sex that night—or at least someone tried to—so I am going to say it was murder. Someday someone will come forward. No one knew where she was. Until her clothes were found all over the street. She was seventeen years old. But you see it all comes down to Shane Stroud," Darren said.

"Shane Stroud, for God sake—why him?"

"He watched this man leaning over her, and she was extremely agitated, then she said, '*Why are you naked?*'"

"Let me ask, if you found this man who tried to get fresh with your sister, what would you do?"

"I would ask him to change—for nothing else can happen until he does."

———

Sometimes when he looked in his wallet and saw his credit cards, he thought of Annie Howl, and realized her humble means, and her determination to go to university and everything he wanted for himself or others would stop.

He never again went down the hallway by Howl's office. One day in the Sobeys parking lot he began handing out hundred-dollar bills. He didn't know why. And suddenly someone was there, going to people and getting the money and handing it back to him. He looked at her, startled when she put the money back into his coat pocket.

She gave a slight grimace of exasperated love. Yes, he knew her, the girl who had broken up with him long ago. The one who said she didn't love him for his money. The girl who had gone away.

"I will start a charity," Raskin thought later that day. "A big one—"

29

HIS MOTHER HAD WRITTEN HIM ONCE AGAIN. SHE SAID she would be going to the cottage for a while and make tape recordings of her poems and her songs. Then she would get in touch with Leonard Cohen or Joni Mitchell. His mother said she was now religious and had a premonition she would be visited and told the truth. She asked him again if he had gone to confession.

He often wondered if that little girl Annie was religious too. He often thought what might she have become. Those were the worst moments. The moments when his heart palpitations came back and he had to use a puffer, and would go to Outpatients.

He tried to forget Mel and Shane, and spent days trying to forget them.

———

One night he came home and Sackville was crying. She had lost the court case, lost everything, it seemed. And she remembered when she herself had been escorted from a university in England by two men with her books in cardboard boxes. Because that is what she was remembering as she sobbed. That young protégé who she drove to attempt suicide, bossing her, dominating her, demanding she wear certain clothes, buying her a certain blouse to wear in the office, insisting she drive her home, insisting they go to a restaurant, insisting they go to a conference, insisting they stay in the same hotel room, refusing her master's thesis and never being able to admit in her desperate sternness that she loved.

She was remembering all that Clara had said when she, Faye, was on the stand:

"Mr. Eliot Slaggy has never even been on a date with a woman. He wouldn't know how to approach one."

"I cannot help that."

"You see, if he did not go on a date with Ms. Lockhart, who asked him to, he would I believe not go on a date with you. He was only being, as he always has been, kind, and your position and credentials made him nervous when he spoke."

"Well he made me very nervous."

"Could you show anyone in this room mercy?"

"Of course I show mercy—I am showing mercy by being here, though it is a strain to speak. You see, mercy has cost women all our lives."

And Clara answered: "But Portia, a woman, does say: 'The quality of mercy is not strain'd, it droppeth as the gentle rain.'" And asked Faye if she agreed.

"Why should I agree? One of your quips. Who's Portia?"

"But it is not one of my quips. Portia from *The Merchant of Venice*. I thought you might know."

But then she told Clara she had been a nun, and saw no mercy there in that dreary convent, in northern England with that Irish mother superior, and she was now studying to be a Muslim.

Then Clara said: "But then surely you know what the Prophet saith: 'If anyone lacks Mercy and reveals the flaws of others, Allah will seek him out and reveal his faults, and he will be shamed even though he hideth in his house.'" And Clara asked her what she had done her doctorate on.

And she said: "Women's menstrual moments in nineteenth-century literature."

Clara then produced Eliot's love, the love of his life—little Mr. Beansworthy. A man who had had Eliot's affections for thirty years, a man who was even more withdrawn than Eliot. Who grew flowers in his hothouse, and hardly was seen in public. A man who was married and could not tell his wife or his two little Beansworthy children what he was up to.

Tonight she sobbed and she sobbed, and Albert was beside himself as he watched. And finally they stood there holding each other as if they were in some bunker at the end of the war.

That same night in Ottawa, in one of the offices of Centre Block, along a long hallway, to the left and past one of the out-of-date washrooms, with the sun glinting off the great brass railings, and a long row, an inestimable row of dignitaries on the walls, behind all that quaint and notable artifice, an MP of a certain calibre was talking now to his executive assistant.

There would be an election soon, and this was on his mind. He must in some way show deference to his career, and be careful, most careful with how he acted. The letters the old gentlemen sought were somewhere—but there was silence, and he realized neither major party here wanted to reveal them.

You see, people were lambasting old white males, and he must too. He must yell shame the same as others. It was impossible not to do so. In fact it was opportune if he did. If he tried to protect them he too would be singled out just like those old men were now being. He would be ostracized just the same as they. He thought his motives were well hidden. But even the woman helping him with paintings from the Art Bank to decorate his new office knew him exactly, knew him, exactly. Fastidious and wary of being wrong.

"If they were in the archives, where would they be?" he said. "I have no idea what these old men are talking about, but these letters were written to someone in some portfolio during the age of Diefenbaker or Pearson. Can I be expected to know where they are? Well wherever they are I have not been able to find them."

He had done a cursory search but to no avail.

The MP from New Brunswick put the letter in his briefcase, the imploring letter about a quest that was undertaken by Raskin Enterprises to discover the harmful effects of asbestos in the years between 1959 and 1962, and again in 1965. But he went out into the coming night, walking by a picture of both Diefenbaker and Pearson along the hallway where bits of sun still managed to shine. There was nothing he could do. The Parliament Building itself was greyish in tone, beautiful and greyish as was Canada on this date and at this time.

He imagined the information in these letters would have been redacted, and in a way subject to regulations. So he felt better not sending a letter either to the ethics commissioner or the clerk.

The grand library centred at the far end of the great hall, one of the great structures in Centre Block, one of the finest libraries in the country, was closed, the lights off. He turned and walked down the broad stairs, past the two security guards, and went into the late afternoon.

Now in the evening when the sun disappeared the street was busy near the Château. His desire was to drink, and to remain obscure in the shade of the building. His name was Edgar Lampkey, and he had had a problem; they had come to him for help, but his family had had a problem with the Raskins all their lives—they came from opposite sides of the river, opposite political parties and opposite interests, though they vacationed side by side.

The two prominent families—not the greatest in our province by any means, but prominent nonetheless—sat side by side. Lampkey pondered this. One family Liberal, one family Conservative. Never really helping each other. Eyeing each other warily. But now the old Raskins were asking for help. He could send his research assistant into that library or over to the national archives building and she would most likely be able to find some evidence that letters had been sent. The Raskins had written him pleas in shaky hands with smudged ink.

But there was a problem. If there were letters, if he revealed them, then his long publicized four-year fight to get Native land reinstated would be compromised—for he would be revealing a government who had turned their back on the Raskins' own desperate concerns about the land, the Natives and the entire Arron Brook years before. This would become known at the very time he wanted to take the Raskins on.

To help would mean the Raskin mine would be less a flashpoint for dissension, the government would, and what he had already said about the Raskins, that they were unthinking industrialists, the worst on the river, would come to haunt him. That is what he realized as he drank his Scotch. A small sliver of his own mendacity filled him, his own sudden lack of moral fibre, and he shuddered. He realized that Robert Glendarren had just passed by without acknowledging him.

Glendarren had proposed an amendment to a bill. The amendment was sound and practical. Still, Lampkey had voted against this amendment. He had stood against it because his party did, not because the amendment wasn't good, put forward by a decent man, but because one must in these times be careful to say the right things in the right way.

Edgar Lampkey had come to Ottawa to follow his conscience, until he saw where his conscience would lead.

The beacon of his displeasure was in fact Albert. He had sparred with Albert all his life, disliked him, and thought he was a poseur. Especially when he wrote his sound poems, and talked sociology as if he knew the poor. Still, Albert had sided with the Lampkeys over this.

It made it all difficult. The very sides of the world were shifting. Even crumbling. Loyalties were falling all away. You see, Edgar Lampkey was the main MP in Ottawa wanting an inquiry into Atlantic province mines. All of them for unenvironmental working conditions, the befouling of drinking water and the pollution of the land.

Perhaps that was why he had received this request from the old men.

Yes these old men had written him an imploring letter to seek the letters of protest they themselves had sent wisely years before. If he found the proof of those letters they declared they had sent, the letters would expose him as well, for being partisan.

Then there was the recent turmoil with Torrent. That was the real devil in it.

He had been hearing about Torrent in connection to some small bit of unceded land, and some kind of furniture shop. The woods, the streams, the land, no one here would care about except for the new social activists who would condemn Edgar himself if he didn't side with the Indians themselves.

Then he thought suddenly with a pang of elapsed fatherhood. So this is what *the boy* was up to?

Edgar could step in now and change the direction of this young man's life. He could do it with a shift of concern. And he should stand up and do so. But what might happen? Everything that had got him elected would be rendered moot. His entire agenda had been the environment, the ruin of Raskin, and his own Indigenous connections and charitable dealings.

You see, Edgar knew that Torrent was his son. He was the only one able to cum inside her.

But what might he do about it now? The papers were always put on his desk every morning by nine o'clock so he knew what was happening at home—and the idea that *his son* was now considered acting in bad faith, and had bought and claimed unceded land, was bothersome, if anyone discovered *he was the father*. In fact there were times when he was contemplating coming to some acceptance of it all. But now? Now was not the time.

Besides, it was just a party, and she was willing—or so he believed. She had gone somewhere and he thought she was dead. He hardly remembered her face, only her nakedness, her small beautiful breasts and dark wonderful mysterious pubic hair, for a bit.

Now and then he would hear about *him*. Once in a while his heart would go out to him. Once in a while he would see him. Once he gave him a drive to his trailer, in a snowfall in February.

Torry was about fourteen, and had been in a fight at school, his hand was swollen and his chin cut. He told Edgar someone had made fun of his mother that day.

Edgar hardly spoke to him, because he didn't know what to say. Edgar remembered that his own mother said she would take care of it, and had gone to see Oscar. He had sat at the cottage waiting for her to come back, watching the little TV they had, wearing his sandals and shorts, his black hair long, and a silver chain on his brown neck. There was a Monopoly board on the card table, and a fan blew.

She came back incensed at something. A few months later the boy was born. Now these years later Lampkey was driving him home. The boy's hand was swollen because he was forced to fight others alone. Edgar had never done such.

Strangely they looked so much alike—except Torry was much stronger looking, and had the sweetest smile he had ever seen.

But he could not claim the boy, ever. He wanted to. He gave the boy twenty dollars that day, and when he turned and drove back home, there were tears in his eyes. But he could not claim him— even if it meant sacrificing him now. You see, he had to sacrifice him now.

Anything else would implicate Lampkey and change the entire direction of his career. He was not at all a dull man, he knew what Albert Raskin was doing, how he was manufacturing his outrage against this young man to position himself. Subtly he knew he was sacrificing his own child to the career and ambition of that poseur Albert Raskin. And of course to his own.

So he kept the letter of inquiry in his briefcase, and moved off along the street.

The night was filled with shade and noise, and then darkness near the Tomb of the Unknown Soldier. No one in his family had

fought. In the world he was now in, this was considered a fine
thing, even a brave example of pacifist resistance. Perhaps that's
why the Raskins hated them. The Lampkeys had not fought.
They were the judicial branches of our world.

All wells would be poisoned.

Torrent's ankle healed. The split in the bone mended with three
screws placed inside the bone in Saint John. Over time he came
back home, and to work. Over time he sawed the oak, and left
it in stables to dry against the sun. Each board, each side, would
dry for three years. Though his leg pained, he searched the
great hills for the right timber, carrying a backpack, and at
times Polly in it.

Then after the drying outside he would move the timber into
his workshop where it would be laid out on his giant work table
and let dry for another four or five months. He would work with
chisel and ballpeen hammer, curved flat axe, hand sander, bow
saw and lathe, the way he had seen his grandfather do. The air
would smell of sleeves of wood, of varnish and sawdust piles
gone orange in the twilight. The light would filter in through
the windows, the light itself filled with motes of dust.

He did not go back to the timber on the land he had bought.
He used the wood he had at this moment. Covered in sawdust,
with a tool belt on his waist, his overalls tied with twine at the
shoulders, his hands large and fingers strong and nimble, he still
looked quite amazingly like his father who sat in Ottawa. There
were rumours of who his father was since he was fifteen. Most
people thought it was Mel Stroud. Yet some, some in the know,
some people from farther upriver and along the Saint John River
Valley had heard rumours, in a way hoping someday to still Edgar
Lampkey's career. But Torry always said, sitting in the back room

of his little trailer, that Oscar was his dad. That he would and should have no other.

It was amazing how this gentle young man, who had done nothing except be born, had caused so much terror in the world.

With the oak he had already dried—some of the oak and pine he had cut the month he had saved Eva Mott—he built his oak cabinets and pine shelves, with old square-head nails he searched downriver for, among old barn timbers and old skeletal remains of drifters and lobster boats sunken into the sands of far-off shores.

But now he was in desperate trouble with money, now the empty barn at eight in the evening after a day's long work looked sombre and melancholy, with a small echo of nostalgia in all that would not get done. He could not go back on the dredge as a sounder, and he had not asked to be hired on as a carpenter to do renovation work in town.

Now he looked about the barn, and realized what a desperate moment it was in their lives. He had to protect Eva and Polly. Like so many men that was what he constantly worried about. He had to make peace with Mr. Raskin in some way.

The barn was where Eva also sat sometimes in the evenings when she was alone, wondering what in the world would become of them now.

30

BAD FAITH. EVEN THE PAPER SAID SO, WITH A PICTURE of their barn, and the old horse.

Then there were phone calls by many young female students to Eva and Torrent's home, calling them racists and bigots and thieves. They didn't even care that it was little Polly who picked up the phone.

Eva tried to hide. Sometimes she put her hands over her ears and put her head between her legs and would yell "Go away!" At nothing.

She would sit in the barn for hours sometimes, when he was away with Polly, looking at the clean, brilliant lines of work that had enticed no buyer and found no home. She remembered talking to him about the boys in her night class, how smart they were, how she spoke about going on a trip, and maybe just leaving him and Polly behind. How women were no fools now. That was her line. *Women are no fools now.* She could abandon her child and have no guilt. Why she had wanted to treat him like this she did not know, except he had frustrated her life—and she had just found it out. She ridiculed him in front of others, especially other men, and it humiliated him. She had said many terrible things to him over those many months, and now it came back like sharp spikes being driven into her head as she remembered verbatim.

"We're no fools now," she had said.

"I never thought you were a fool," he said.

"Oh, but you did. But Professor Raskin says I'm smart. He says men take advantage and sometimes the woman is far smarter than the man—lots of times."

"I would agree."

"You would agree?"

"Of course I would."

"Well, I never thought you would."

"That's because you listen to Professor Raskin more than you ever listened to me."

"That is not fair," she said. "No, that is not fair, and far as I'm concerned I never had one friend—never one—in my life, and you have about a million. I am always alone, trying to figure things out—trying to decide what I should do to change my life."

"What about that friend—that man you went to see just before we were married to talk to. Was he your friend?"

"Yes—he was and I just went to talk and explain something," she said.

"There is no other woman I ever had to explain anything to," he said.

"A bully," she said. "That's what I think you are at times—and I'm tired of being pushed about by a bully."

And she ran upstairs.

Suddenly, for some unknown reason, Eva Mott got sick and was taken to the hospital in an ambulance. People were now saying what a terrible life Eva Mott had with Torrent Peterson.

But there was one little thing she had done. In order to facilitate her meetings with Professor Raskin, she would give Polly sleeping pills in her milk. Then with the child asleep she would carry her to her bed, lock the big front door, and when Torry was away, sneak to her lover's house. Then coming home she would lift the child from the bed and put her in the cold bath to wake her before her husband got home. This made her own life a misery, a misery now of both cooking sherry and pills, and Torry didn't know what was wrong.

"You are acting crazy," he said to her one night, when he came upon her sitting in the loft of the barn, with her legs dangling over.

"Yes, and I will cut my wrists and everything else if you don't watch it—wait and see," she said.

In August he and Gordon Hammerstone were hired to pour bull-dog lime into the tailings pond north of Riley Brook.

At night he would sit in the hot cabin, and down over the long hill Riley Brook glimmered like a bracelet in the twilight sky, and birds cheeped out their evening songs, and the smell of tar and roofing tin permeated the old cabin, while the Coleman stove cooked their meal of baloney, beans and potatoes. There they would sit with a pungent mug of tea, and large slabs of brown bread, while the four-wheeler, battered by trees along the windshield, covered in loose lime, would sit silent in the half-overgrown yard, like a bludgeoned animal, while the wagon that they dragged behind was loaded with the morning lime bags. That is, the last load was the load for the next morning.

With his socks off, his feet looked a mess. Huge burns covered them, and where the tibia in his left leg had been soldered there was and always would be a grey displacement, the bone protruding almost nakedly out against his skin, and the calf muscle of his leg almost gone. His arms huge, dark, the hands large, lay across his knees, and he stared silently at the coming night. The flies were terrible and the bulldog lime shrank his boots and lime and sweat burned his skin, so that both ankles had open sores. When Gordon saw that he said: "You can't stay out here working—it'll ruin your feet."

"No, it's okay. I only have to think I am doing it as I should have done before, for Eva and Polly. I will pay the money back over time, and they will not take my house."

"Do you have any money left?"

"I have eighteen thousand. I never did any work on the barn—I put it away for Eva. I'll make him an offer. Take that, and take the rest over five years."

"Okay. But will he go for it?"

"Not in the slightest," Torry said. "I was wanting it for Eva's education—I had kept it a secret for that," he said, and smiled again. "But I think I have to make an offer of some kind."

Gordon Hammerstone, a Mi'kmaq man who said little but knew much more, knew Torrent had been placed into this abyss—this purgatory—by his own wondrous naivety.

The naivety of Torry was seen earlier in the year when Gordon noticed him on the back road, making his way with little Polly in the sunset. He walked on crutches with the cast on his leg, the little girl walking beside him as the last of the sunlight shone on the road beyond.

Oscar had offered to sell the pistol for what he might get, but Torry said no, he didn't need the money.

The pistol that Byron Raskin had traded and that Oscar now possessed.

But long ago Mel Stroud decided with his girl Henrietta Saffy that they would simply steal it. He spoke about it so much he made her crazy. When they drove anywhere he spoke about it. He even took her to a gun show in Maine and was elated talking to gun dealers.

"Worth almost a million," Mel told her. "I can sell it to a dozen people and then we will be free. Free, Henrietta. Just a simple theft from a simpleton, and we will be free."

That, and their trip to the river to do so, was now being planned.

She already knew he got money from that Raskin man. She simply had no idea how much.

But at times she thought to herself:

"Why do I deal with such boring cunts?"

Torrent came home. He was about to make the offer to Professor Raskin when, checking their account at the credit union, he discovered that the eighteen thousand was mostly gone.

He asked Eva about it. He thought she might have given it back to Professor Raskin. But she wouldn't answer.

At first, for two days, she said nothing. She kept her head down as she ate, she took her plate into the porch. She ran and hid outside.

"I didn't do anything whatsoever with it."

"Well where is it?"

"You could have spent it and not known."

"That's not true. I had it saved for you and your university. But I was going to offer it to him."

"Oh I see—well then, you didn't want me to go."

"Don't be ridiculous. Of course—it was for your tuition for four years. But you and I know we are facing ruin here."

He finally found it out. Benny Mott, deep in debt to Household Finance for the new recreational trailer, had asked his daughter for the money. She wrote him a cheque for a promissory note two weeks before.

"He couldn't sell a pair of socks—he's an idiot."

"Don't call my father an idiot. I never called Oscar one."

"You called him everything but."

They would now certainly lose the house and the field and barn. He told her this as he stood at the sink. He told her this and stared past her at the wall. Her face turned almost to ash. She tried to think of what to say. That she had kept Polly on pills, that she didn't know what to do, or why she had done that for her father. That she had lost who she was, and who she was supposed to be. That she wanted to ask forgiveness and did not know how. But she said none of this.

Above them dark was coming, the trees blew and night descended. Shadows played behind her. All suddenly seemed ethereal and ghostly as she stood in her summer dress and bare feet, the underside of her toes reddish.

"I am sorry," she said, "I am sorry. He's my father." Then she added: "You never wanted me to go to university anyway and to become educated. You were afraid I would leave you, because I'm smart, so don't say anything about the money for that there!"

She ran into the living room and turned the television on, picked up a magazine, and kicked a cushion.

The eighteen thousand he had put in a separate account for that very reason seemed to be held against him. And so the little promissory note was now under a magnet on the fridge.

They did not speak the next day.

When he came out from Riley Brook the next week he told her there was a job at Zellers that she must apply for.

"Zellers?" she said. "No—I can't work at Zellers. I will not work there."

"But if we are going to get out from under it, you have to— just for a year—six months to a year. And then I promise university it is."

He said a Toomey woman who worked there who was a cousin of his could get Eva a job.

"But I am not like her," Eva said. "No, I am *not like her*. I am like other people."

"What other people? Eva, what other people are you like? She is a kind, good-hearted soul who knitted a suit for Polly. Who are you like?"

"Just other people."

"Who are you like, Eva? All your life you are embarrassed by me."

"That is not true. I read where men like you are too sensitive because you are too emotional and don't understand women's rights. And I read that there is a left-brained person and a right-brained person, and I am on the side of equality and women's rights because I am on the most sensitive side."

"Women's rights? Does that mean you don't have to be kind enough to say hello? You have friends and they don't speak to me and you get your picture taken, and you go to dances and dance with men, and I sit at a table and watch you—and they feel sorry for you—but not fucking one of them could pull you from the water when you fucking drown."

"Is that all you think of?"

"No. I think of all kinds of things. I think you put on airs to impress people who look down on me."

"I didn't put on airs—not even a smidgeon of an air."

"Well, who are you like?"

"I'm like Clara is who I am like."

"No—no, you aren't like Clara, Eva. I am sorry, but you are not like her. You are not as kind as her, you don't have as big a soul. And you *have to work at Zellers*. it is the only chance we have to save the house. You have to help me save our house! It is the only way we have now."

She tried to think, she got flustered, then she said as if weakly inspired: "Not as good as Clara—no, no. But Professor Raskin doesn't want the money back from *me*—he only wants it from *you*—not from me. So I could get a student loan and still go to university."

"What do you mean?"

"I mean he told me when it all blew up, I don't have to pay. It's what he told me."

"But I have to pay?"

"But yes. And because he says men like you always take advantage, and he is not like that, is what he says. He says that to me, that it's your debt!"

"But not yours?"

"No." She started to cry. "I don't have to pay. I could still get a student loan and go to university and live in my own room in town and everything. And see Polly on the weekends."

"And the money your father took?"

"Dad is willing to pay you back."

"Oh. Your father is willing to pay me back?"

"Yes."

"That is so nice of him."

She thought for a second, and then relying on her ability to deflect whatever was said, a well-established strength she had, she said peevishly: "It was your loan, and if you were greedy enough to take it, what am I supposed to do? Why did you spend it all on yourself, which is what my father said you did?"

He looked at her stunned. "Except for the eighteen thousand," he said.

His hands lay on the table. The skin between his thumbs and forefingers on both hands were burned raw, and two blisters had formed on his thick neck. His hands, deeply painful, started to shake. He wanted to hit her, but he did not.

"Well if you want to know what it was, Mr. Raskin said to me too, he says you did all of this for yourself. Professor Sackville said if you were any kind of husband you would have given me half of it to go to university last year. But you didn't—so I think you just saved that money not for me but as a contingency in case all yer plans went awry and you had to take off somewhere. But now you say it was for me. 'Cause I don't know what yer plan was. I just know everyone says you are being greedy."

"When did they tell you that?"

"They just did—over time kind of let me know. They didn't belt it out all at once. But you used it all for yourself and your cabinets! Mr. Raskin told me to go to women's studies and everything and see Ms. Sackville and everything, and start my own life and everything—knocked up at nineteen by you, only because I felt I owed you because you saved my life, and then and there you came inside me—so I want a new start. Mrs. Lampkey gave me her placemats and everything—ha, can't even read right." She looked at him startled, her face in astonishment at what she just said. She always called Albert Mr. Raskin, even now. She could not think of calling him anything else.

Torrent looked down at the table ashamed. Deep, deep shame flooded him. And she never told Professor Raskin that he had put money aside. That is what was so revealing. She had not told them that he had loved her that much because *he* must be the reason for *her* disloyalty.

"He will take the house," he whispered, almost crying (she had never seen him cry, even when his head was cut open by Shane Stroud's rock). But not to her—he whispered it to himself.

She looked at him, and turned to run. She ran all around the room, looking for something, grabbed her purse and then ran up the stairs.

"And don't come in my room!" she screeched. "And I shouldn't have given you what I gave you last night, a blow job and everything like that there. *And don't you think I ever will again!* Go to Clara if she is so nice. So whatever I did weren't none of my fault and if I was roped into doing something—well I won't tell you what—it weren't my fault!"

"That's a goddamn lie—you know that's a lie. Who started that lie?"

"I am only saying it is what people are saying so don't yell at me for saying it back."

"It's a lie about her. She is the kindest person I ever met."

"Kindness is as kindness does is what I say."

He had to drive back to work, and Gordon was waiting for him outside, pretending not to listen to the squabble, but digging at the dirt with his feet.

"Listen," Torrent said, going to the door. "Next year—next year you can go to university."

"I don't care if I ever never go. It's just a dream. Like my father you are, the same. But everyone said I should go this year, this year, and they said I should have gone last year, and be a lawyer, which is what I want to be and put men in jail—and don't you think I won't. I'll put a good batch of them right in jail for what they do around this place."

"Yes, well, your father should be in jail for taking my money."

"It was my money too," she screeched. "That is the big problem. You never thought it was my money too. Mr. Raskin, he said to me that he thought I would have some say in everything, so I end up with nothing at all."

"Go to university, I don't give a damn. Leave Polly—you have been wanting to do that for months."

She didn't answer. She began to sing under her breath, which she always did to ignore something painful. So he simply turned and went back down the stairs.

Torrent was gone. The Raskin brothers had asked him to drive a load of asbestos down to the shipyard in Saint John.

Something strange came over Eva that night. It was this. She could only be with the bright, glittering people, the people who were concerned, if she left him. That is what the people wanted. She knew that. And Torrent knew it too. There would be no debt for her if she left. And maybe the debt for him would be relieved as well if they just got rid of the awful house. Or say she just left—perhaps all would be forgiven him. For his biggest crime involved the trapping of her.

Also if she left there would be nothing to stop her from *finding out who she was*. The word had gone out that she was both beautiful and hoped for better, and had tried to start a business with her husband who did not care for her. That is what she hoped they would all realize. Her expression now was always one of sadness and regret, and an attempt to be happy.

Over the last year and a half she actually saw her life as dark and hopeless. The house they lived in was still unfinished—the walls of one whole room were covered in sheets of stapled plastic. He had no time because he was always doing other things. Now he was disabled.

She did not know how it happened—well, of course she did. She took three of her sedatives and a glass of wine, left the house alone, walking, and then remembered she was at Mr. Raskin's cottage again. She was in the doorway by the kitchen, and a woman was sitting in a seat—she did not know it was Mrs. Raskin, Albert's mother, who had come to record her songs and get in touch with Joni Mitchell. Eva was talking to someone—it wasn't Albert, it was Mrs. Raskin's male companion, a wispy-haired gentleman with soft, well-rehearsed manners, and she, Eva, had pissed herself. It had run bitterly down her leg. How had that happened? She had tried to get to the bathroom. Mrs. Raskin looked scared and worried—she kept asking Eva if she was *the girl*. What girl was she?

"Oh yes, Professor Raskin and I are *real close*," she remembered saying. "If you only knew how close. Two peas in a pod.

"Yes, he accepts me as a person. I will owe nothing. It's not my problem. Professor Raskin just has to come forward and tell the truth—tell the truth and I will be paid off. Eighteen thousand and then we will see. Professor Raskin and I have a whole bunch of secrets. It's almost like a secret love, if you want to know. I sometimes simply wear a pair of shorts—just shorts and top—just to please him. Yes, and the real culprits will be taken care of, let me tell you. And Professor Raskin and I will go away—and maybe get a movie of it made over in Hollywood, it's that important a story. For there is criminals, and I've come here to tell you I'm the one who knows who they are."

She did not know how horribly she was upsetting the now elderly woman, who couldn't comprehend who this girl was, or why her son had to *tell the truth*. You see, what was unknown is that Carmel was worried the police would come. She believed she would have a visitation of some kind.

Now she was alone, and scared. And thought that *this was the girl*.

"Can't you see you are bothering Mrs. Raskin," the man said. "Perhaps you should go."

And then Eva remembered pee running down her leg. But she only remembered this the next morning. The shame was unbearable, and she wanted to die.

31

SHE WAS LEFT WITH THE LITTLE GIRL WHILE TORRY WAS away. She would walk with the little girl and talk with her, and they were seen together at the ice-cream stand. She still had a prescription for antibiotics and sleeping pills in her purse. Someday perhaps she would fill it, and that would relieve everything.

Eva left the house and went to live at her parents' while he was away. The little kitten they had gotten Polly was left inside the locked house and wasn't fed until she got home.

Knowing that he had just taken thousands of their monies, Mr. Ben Mott said nothing to her, but plied her with obsequious grinning compliments. Told her she and Torrent—who he always talked down to, disrespected and laughed at when others did— could use the recreational trailer any time they wanted.

But now looking at her father saying grace at supper, she realized the horror she had helped cause—the innocence of the boy she had married, and the way she had betrayed him. But the problem in part was that innocence—and the corruption she wanted in order to prove that she was grander than the innocence and more important than the one who had saved her life.

Her father had a giant bandage slathered on his forehead, right beneath the mole. He had banged his head on the cupboard door just the day before. Now with his small, flappy red tie, his pale shirt, his black ankle-high boots over his thin little ankles, he was out looking for a job, with what looked like a Kotex taped right across his forehead.

The dismal smell of soggy turnip, the piles of wash, the loose cupboard where he had banged his head, his antiquated "cheerio" to his wife made her feel as if she was thirteen years old again, sitting on her bed, wanting to escape. She remembered when she had told them she and Torrent might be in trouble with the business, how her father had supressed a grin.

Again the fights and broken dishes and squabbles in other apartments kept her awake, and the lights of the asbestos mine trickled in past her window.

She sat in the apartment with Polly for five long days. The young girl kept asking for her daddy, for the kitten named Peaches, and Eva kept trying to find things for her to do. The name *MOTT* scratched in ink on their apartment door was slanted and almost hidden. And the door itself had been banged at by people wanting money, so some of the wood was splintered.

"We're here for our money."

"Go away. There is no one here."

"You're here—because I hear you."

"We are not home."

"Where are you then?"

"We are out and about."

"You aren't out and about, you're just behind the door."

"No one is home. Go away now, please."

The money she had allowed them had alleviated that at last.

Her little second-hand Honda was hidden in behind the building.

And then one day coming back to the apartment, with Polly in her arms, and a plastic bag of groceries in her hand, a young woman passed by her in a rush, carrying a box, going up the flight of stairs. She looked preoccupied, and stared through or past Eva Mott, with a certain kind of hilarity, as if Eva Mott did not exist, and in some way would never exist. Her name was Henrietta Saffy. Looking into her brilliant impenetrable eyes, Eva knew she would be more than a match for Faye Sackville.

She hoped no one would be told she had been at the cottage, speaking with those important people.

But unfortunately she found out differently. Professor Raskin was furious. He phoned her and told her never to come there again.

"I am so sorry," she whispered into the phone. But not to Mr. Raskin. Perhaps to God.

Later that night she took the little Honda and drove up to town to see him. She wanted to talk to him about everything— but more importantly to get some relief for Torrent Peterson, the man who had saved her life.

"But you was our friend."

"Oh of course I was your friend. But Torry did not tell me, Eva—he did not tell me he was culling on Native land. It put me in an untenable position."

"What's that?" she asked.

She grabbed him by the arm and asked him what was happening with *them*.

"Happening? What do you mean, happening?"

She had even worn a button that day made by some of his students: "I'm a Friend of Albert Raskin."

Two days later, unable to sleep, even with the pills, Eva wrote him a letter; in it she said: "I am not going to university so there. I have to help Torry pay things back—so there."

She was hoping for an answer, for him to run to her. She waited by the window, near the phone. But he did not come. But not one phone call came.

Albert went to see his mom a few days later. He knew that his mother had been worried that Shane was now out of jail. He had just heard it himself.

He entered the back of the house. All was dark. The place was dark—all was quiet too, and there was an odour, somewhat sweet and deep and offensive. She was sitting in her chair, her head tilted sideways, her neck wrinkled and blue. Her eyes were slightly opened. There was no movement at all.

"Hello," he said. "Mother?"

She had argued with her male companion and caregiver, who gave up the position.

Dark pools of blood lay on the floor, some on the letters themselves. The blue stencilled copies of the letters the old uncles were looking for were spread around her—she had discovered them finally, rooted them out in her box of miscellaneous papers. For a while she had kept in touch with her brother, the defrocked priest, but that ebbed away, and no one knew where he was.

She had looked for the letters, found them to give to him.

She had sliced her wrists two days before. Perhaps it had been an accident. But she had phoned him, Albert Raskin, asking him to come and see her, that she had found something that would solve it, and wanted to give these things to him, but he had been busy.

The place had the ugly scent of sweet decay that was almost unnoticeable and then suddenly overpowering.

He picked the letters up. The earliest date was November 3, 1959.

He picked the stencilled copies up, put them in his briefcase and phoned the ambulance and the police.

To destroy the letters would leave his uncles with no last vestige of hope.

What had Tracy McCaustere said to the reporter last week? *"We plan to make a stand, a new way forward, in hope and reconciliation. We plan to march across the field to show solidarity with our Native brothers and sisters whose Wigwam Blockade has been ordered down. We plan to show that protest is more just than power or police presence. No one wishes to destroy, we wish to raise people up, so all voices can finally be heard."*

He thought of his enemy Lampkey in Ottawa. Lampkey would end up on the best side—the side the professors were on, the revolutionary side of things.

He, in living his free life, had no choice in the matter at all.

It was strange she had only twenty people at her funeral, one her brother, the man who he had given the watch to years before.

So the house would be his; so would the assets. So would some remaining four hundred thousand dollars.

And then Shane Stroud appeared. He came in the night looking for something. It was two weeks after the funeral.

Shane was always looking for something. Even as a child he would wait to take advantage of someone. He had always done so. Then there was that moment when he had decided to get the watch Mrs. Wally had won. One night he saw her leaving bingo and walking home. That is when he went after the watch. Then, frightened what he had done, he had given his brother what he had stolen. Mary Lou had the watch, and unaware of its history, sent it to her child.

Torrent by a strange coincidence had been given these letters from his mother by Oscar just two weeks before Shane was released from prison. In one of these letters was Mrs. Wally's watch.

Not knowing what the watch signified, he gave it to the planned recipient. That is, Eva Mott now wore it. No one knew that in this circuitous route the very emblem of crime and murder would find its way back to the intended love of his life.

It was stunning to see a vague shadow against the backyard tree. Albert thought nothing of it for a moment—and then he realized it was Shane Stroud, who suddenly began to move toward him, still in shadow, still almost unrecognized, except for the cringing way he moved across the lawn.

He was now on parole.

And seeing Albert closing the drapes, he simply walked to the door. He opened it and walked in.

"Who was that?" he said.

"Who was whom?" Albert asked.

"That woman who just left?"

"A friend," he said. "A Professor Sackville."

He tried to sound at ease but he was trembling. And Shane Stroud knew he was trembling. Shane was very well attired, in a new coat, and new black boots, and black leather gloves. He was incredibly happy at this moment. He was out and the world was free and he wanted money.

Then Shane said quickly: "Bad mescaline all those years ago. That's what caused all your trouble—that's what caused it all. You gave it to Annie Howl—how could you do it—I mean that you were so low to do that, an important person like you, going to those depths and everything like that there. It shows where the depths are, don't it?"

"Where?"

"In the human heart," Shane said. "Darren Howl contacted me, a few days ago. I told him to *let it go.*

"'*Let it go*,' he said, 'no—*let it go never.*' So I'm worried about you." Shane sniffed and looked about the room.

"I gave you and Mel a lot of money. I don't have more."

"Oh you give Mel money. That's what I wonder about. You just give Torry money—whosoever stoled my girl. You give Mel money, why not me? You give Mel fifteen thousand to keep quiet last month."

This was true, he had done so. And now he knew it would not end. That they could accuse him now over the very fact that he treated one brother better than the other. That they would argue with each other over who had the most right to use him. This was the true con.

Shane kept looking at the dining room table, and then up at his victim. His coat was soaking wet as well as his boots. Albert could smell the dampness and sweat off of him.

"I have suffered enough," Albert said. "I have not done one good thing since that night."

And that was true.

"Ah, but suffering is the human condition," Shane said. "I know a man from here who wrote that in a book. He writes books—you only pretend to. I used to drink with him at the tavern—he could drink for months, not like a piss-ass like you. He might write a book someday about this here murder. He said to me suffering is the human condition."

"Yes, I know," Albert said, who had laughed at this writer. He was suddenly ashamed that he had to hear this from Shane Stroud. He was suddenly every bit as ashamed of himself as poor Eva Mott.

"But Mel and I know this too—you know nothing—those people you are saying you are in with, to protect the environment, they are just going to cut every tree on Good Friday."

"Why?"

"For stove pellets—ha. That Professor McLeish, a horse's arse—that's what he's up to. He wants a lot of money to go back to Scotland—so the runoff in the spring will wash houses away, then the dry in summer will make Arron Brook a puddle. And he'll go back to Scotland and pretend he did something wonderful here."

Albert was stunned that Shane would know this. Shane smiled at him being stunned. Shane and Mel knew far more than Albert about the world he pretended he wanted to save, and the smile said as much.

Shane picked up Faye's scarf, the one she had left, and looked at it while saying Darren now wanted to question him.

"I will go and see Darren—tell him what I know."

"I never did a thing to her. I never meant anything!"

But Shane didn't miss a beat. "And you with Eva too, love of my life. Don't think I haven't kept tabs."

"What do you want?" Albert had never fired a gun. But if he could find that pistol, if he could—

"Ten thousand and it is forgot, swear to God Almighty."

"Ten thousand?"

"Yes."

"Ten thousand."

"Yes, what I said. I'm going out west—I have lots of girlfriends out west—so out I will go."

"Okay. Next week, ten thousand. But that has to be it. That has to be it! Or I will go to the police myself."

"Oh, and *her*."

"Who?" he asked, astonished and unbelieving.

"Her. I haven't had sex in a long time neither—not real sex."

"Ms. Sackville?"

"No, not her. I wouldn't fuck her."

"Who, then?" Again Albert was panicky and astonished.

"Eva Mott," he said.

"Eva Mott?"

"Yes. Get me Eva for a day, and that will be it."

"I can't do that."

"I want her—so do it, or you will be in jail. Or ruined. One or the other. I will go to the paper. You always go to the paper."

"I will deny it."

"Okay, fine. Deny it," Stroud said very simply as he got up to leave. "Yes, I will go to the paper and you can deny it."

Eva Mott, even more than she thought when she saw Albert Raskin and Ms. Sackville drive by without noticing her as she carried Polly through the rain, was now absolutely alone.

Albert needed her now to excise the demons playing in his soul. *"Why are you naked?"*

Now he would make Eva terrified, and it was the only way to save himself.

So he knew what he must do. Either kill himself, or confess.

He walked to the police station. He stood outside for an hour and a half. He went up to a police car, to the officer sitting inside, and almost said what he wanted to say. But the officer was eating a chicken sandwich and looked at him with his cheeks full and smiled, and Raskin, so handsome now it was a plague upon young girls, only managed to smile back.

When he was young and pudgy he had always wanted to be handsome. Now looking into the mirror in the morning he often wanted to cut open his face.

He spoke to Sackville later. He said he needed her advice. He said he was being bothered by a man named Shane. What could he do?

"It's an old incident—it should have been forgotten," he said.

"From your youth?"

"Yes."

"And not from Eva—who you had in ecstasy?"

"No—well no, not really."

"I see. I see! Well then—he threatened you? My dear man, what are you little Canuks made of, mush? Get one of those fucking pistols you spoke so often about—and shoot him."

But he had already tried to get the pistol. He had already paid money and was promised a delivery that did not come.

He went the next morning and tried to buy a shotgun; a double-barreled twelve-gauge pump. He had never fired a gun before, and unfortunately he had not taken his required safety test, and moreover he didn't know how to hold it. So the clerk told him to take his test, learn how to use the gun safely and come back.

"If I had to use it safely I wouldn't need to buy it," he said.

But if he could get the pistol—if he could find the pistol—that would change everything.

32

TORRENT HAD GONE TO SAINT JOHN WITH THE LOAD OF scrap and asbestos from the mine. One of the last trucks. And all the way down he thought of his mom, of how she was, and who she was. A tiny little girl—that's how he thought of her. So when he got to the docks he left the truck and taking the address he had found in the wall—for he had been given the letters from Mary Lou two weeks before—he walked toward it. There in the fog and cold of a late summer day, past Queen's Park, past a small corner store with a neon sign, past the gloom of faded brick and asphalt, was an old clapboard apartment half-hidden down a side street. He went there, thinking calmly that he would confront Mr. Mel Stroud. He would have it out with him, just as he had had it out with his brother Shane some years before.

He had the letters from his mother, though the letters were so cramped he didn't know what they said. He had been given a watch that he thought was hers, so he had given it to his wife, Eva. But then he realized that the letters might be important, so he had left them in a box at the trailer. Maybe the police might need them. He was thinking this as he walked.

The night of the wedding of Ben Mott and his bride they all danced as if dancing through hell. They were jiving, the men with broad backs and plain expressions, not knowing how to react to the music that came from Detroit and London, used always until then to music from Nashville and P.E.I., and the women—yes, Mrs. Wally who had won that watch, and women in the kitchen and on the dance floor almost an age ago now. All of them together that night. She, Mrs. Wally, would be Torrent's aunt. He at that time was in Mary Lou's belly, just as Eva was in her mom's. They, Mrs. Mott and Mary Lou, at one point danced side by side.

Torry was walking the street toward this backstreet apartment building when he was stopped by a man seated on a bench in a small little park near a bus stop. The man called him over.

"You are him?"

He looked and saw the Black man sitting there.

"You are him?" he asked again.

"I'm Torry Peterson."

"Yes. Your mother spoke to me about you. He is gone."

"Who is gone?"

"Mr. Stroud. I came to see him get arrested, but no such luck. I didn't know how much he controlled her, or I would have gotten her away."

"I came to see him too."

"Well, it's best if the police handle it."

Years ago this man was the porter who had given little Eva Mott that 7Up, and years before he tried to befriend the frightened girl who lived in the apartment across the street from him. He disliked Mel, and the brother who sometimes came around. Of course Shane called him the N-word but never clear enough to react.

So he waited today because he had heard Mel would be arrested.

A police officer, Corporal Becky Donaldson, her blond hair tucked up under her cap, with just a slight tinge of greying, her boots solid and her gun belt snug around her waist, had been after Mel Stroud for some time. She had come here with a City of Saint John detective and an RCMP officer.

This had all been set it in motion some little while ago. But Corporal Becky Donaldson, the woman at the cottage on vacation who had smiled at Albert with that same knowing smile she had at his door that rainy afternoon, knew if she arrested Mel for the overdose of Mary Lou, he might give Shane up for Mrs. Wally. This is what she had been working on, since that child was killed in a hit-and-run and Shane fled to Moncton.

Eva went and stayed with her parents, thinking she would run away. But then she went back home the night before Torrent returned from Saint John. The little kitten half-starved jumped at her out of thirst and fear. So little Polly sat beside the kitten as they fed it, and Eva wandered through the house. After she put Polly to bed, she came into the hallway and saw her darkened evening reflection in the mirror far down at the end of the hall. Suddenly she remembered Mr. Raskin's exultant look when she kept trying to do favours for him, and remembered where she had seen this look before. It was in the look of hilarity on the face of that strange woman, Henrietta Saffy.

She sat in the chair deeply chastened. She had eaten nothing in four or five days.

The drawer of the desk Torrent had made her was opened. He had been trying to find the contract that he had signed.

Later that night going through the papers in the old desk in the dining room, looking at pictures from the birthday party she had at Clara's when they had turned thirteen, tears flooded her eyes. She found a picture of Torrent taken when he was working on the house—the day before he saved her. She placed the pictures on the table. The floor was still unfinished here, and the table was one he had made. She took out their insurance policy and set it on the desk, and taking a glass of white wine sat back and read it. The phone rang in the upstairs hallway. The evening was dark.

Professor Raskin was on the phone. Yes, he was going to apologize to her finally, and she would tell him off.

He said he had a proposition for her. It would release her and Torry of all they had ever owed him, and her world would be back the way it was. If she did this he would go to the paper and say he would not take their house, as a gesture of fidelity and good conscience, and leave it at that. Nothing more would be mentioned about their house and they could live in peace. He would intercede with the First Nations, have a sit-down with them and see if it couldn't be ironed out. He would never ask for any of his money back.

"What is it? What is it I have to do?"

There was in the past a moment that evoked the future, that foretold it—that telegraphed what it might be for Torry and her.

You see, I was the one she had come to see the week before she was married. I had gone to school with her (she was three grades behind, however) and I knew her very well. I knew her father and her mother, and when she was a young woman in grade twelve, I sketched her one afternoon sitting on a drift log on the shore. I tried to catch the whimsical sadness of her face, in her smile.

But that day, long ago, before her marriage to Torry, she had come to see me. It was a strange moment. The idea that she just turned up at my door showed something of her inner makeup, something that in fact *was* made up: *she had to have a good male friend* because this is what someone told her, that in this age a male friend she could confide in was a notable part of one's attire, but more than that, someone she could hold up to her boyfriend was the optimum tactic. In her own country way she had to do what she had been led to believe. So I was chosen, and in she came, to speak to me about her impending marriage and her worries about Torry.

Oh, she said he had many flaws, many of them, and wanted my advice. He was uncouth and didn't know the least thing. When they went to a restaurant he talked too loud. And when she wanted him to be sensitive he didn't know how. What did I think? I was a painter, so I should know what she meant. I was startled she was there. I had not seen her in eighteen months, and I did not know why she chose me, except I might have made a little bit of a name as an artist. My work had sold well enough here.

But I saw suddenly—not instantly but suddenly—the *invention* as she spoke. I was the *devised* male friend. The device that was ultimately cruel but sad as well. Her childlike sadness was also a part of this. Right in the moment of planning the wedding at the small Saint Peter and Paul church, she said to Torry: "I have to meet a friend."

"Oh? Who?"

"It's just a friend." She looked at him seriously, searching his face. "You don't know *him*."

"I don't know *him*. Well, who is *him*?"

She looked at him again with an immensurable potency that lasted only a brief second. "He is a friend."

Suddenly what dawned inside him was exactly what she had wanted to create: the realization that she had another life, a parallel world. How instantaneously this was given to him was what was so overwhelming.

"I did not know you had a friend," he stammered.

She wore a white blouse and a locket from her mother, a blue skirt and a pair of white nylon stockings. She had a pair of loafers on her feet, and a small bracelet on her arm. Yes, what effect it all must have had, for he too could *almost* see through it, and *almost* knew it was a sham. More worrisome with her little purse in her hand because it was a sham. That it might have predicted a future time and place where it would not be.

She again looked very solemn. She did not smile. She took his hand and squeezed it. "I will be back in a while."

"But where—where is this friend of yours?"

"You don't know him. I will be back in a while."

He went down and sat on an old scow at Savage's Shore, staring in glum and numb forbearance. What was this unexpected turn of events in Torrent's life, two days before a wedding, where it showed that he did not know her?

And so she came to see me in my small house at the back of two houses, on a side street, with a pleasant enough stone fence, and an old garden with dry, blackened soil and some ceramic pots that were cracked. And I believed she would never see or count me as her dear friend again, that in fact this was an imitation of something she had told herself about *liberation*. Worse, she knew she could do it to him and to me.

We sat for forty minutes in the back patio that was shaded by poplar and elm trees, and where an old broken lane passed just behind the house. There she told me about him, and I realized I was very gullible before—that is, very gullible in how I thought she perceived me as somewhat wise.

"What do you think, after all those flaws he has?" She smiled. Her smile was delightful, as if she and I had a bond against the brutishness of the world. "Should I still marry him?" Then she sighed, put both her hands out in front of her, spread out her fingers as if inspecting them.

"No," I said.

"No? Oh! Why not?" She was astonished. She thought I would say *yes*. That is what she was waiting for. That is what the *male* friend was obligated to do.

"Because," I said, "you came here to see me. You do not love him enough. Not to marry him—and you will never forgive him if you do. He is not educated and you want someone who is. It will hurt him, and maybe you too. Shane Stroud is a bad man. He followed you in his car, he tracked down where you lived, and all because of a *kiss*. But you see, you were alone along Arron Ridge and Dunn's Crossing, but you allowed *him* to kiss you. You could not tell who he was. So I am afraid for you."

"Afraid for me?"

"You allowed Shane to kiss you. That is a telling moment.

Torry protected you from Shane Stroud—and I hope you know this. But you will either know or don't know, and if you don't know, especially here in this sometimes dangerous place, you will make a mistake somewhere along the line."

"I don't understand. I am talking about his flaws. I came here to seek advice—"

"Shane would still be seeking you if it wasn't for him. Torry is in awe of you. He wants to know things. He wants to be better. See, his mother left, and he had Oscar for a father. But he was not destroyed by that. He has never betrayed anyone. But he would be destroyed by betrayal."

She looked at me insightfully, carefully nodded and left.

She went back to who he was, flaws and all. She went forward, took his hand, swung her arm with his as they walked up the lane.

"You saw yer friend?" he asked now.

"Oh . . . yes . . . I did," she said slowly and mysteriously. And then looked over her shoulder once, twice, and then stared straight ahead.

I have become convinced that this is what started her on the road to Mr. Raskin. It was the beginning of their mutual despair.

Before he had left for Saint John, he spoke of *bankruptcy*. It was not only a new word, it was a revelation, a paradigm of exotic monies and travel, the kind which she had never experienced in her life.

"Bankruptcy?"

"Yes," he said. "I will ask Mr. Raskin to take the house. He can have it. I can't pay back that money. And I will never think of cabinets or chairs again. I will lose everything in the shop. I can sell the oak though, I think, or maybe I will just give it away. No one wants the old tools I work with but I will sell off my truck. There it is. I will simply work for Chester and Dexter Raskin.

You'll have to put up with me smelling like a piece of asbestos or a lime bag. But you can go to university—you can do better than I did. You get along with those people anyway. Then after a little while I will go away and leave you to it. I can't even pay the taxes now that the eighteen thousand is gone."

When he said this, she was not happy. Mr. Raskin had told her to go away. She had been so certain the future had been opened to her, like a portico she would squeeze through.

Desperately she had tried to make it up to Mr. Raskin (this was before his phone call). She drove by his house. She sat on his doorstep. She snuck to a party where he was, and sat at a table, and ordered a glass of red wine.

But no one knew her at the university. No one spoke to her when she went to the registrar's office the next day. No one waited for her. She found Professor Raskin's door. It was closed and locked as well; on the chair outside the door was an article left by someone: *Trotsky, Societal Revolution, and Its New Vanguard.*

She did not know what that meant, and perhaps she would never know.

Now, Mr. Raskin had phoned her, clandestinely, and asked her to meet him to discuss something. A proposition. At first she had been happy about a proposition, of any kind—but now again a feeling of trepidation crept over her.

Suddenly she took Torry's hand, covered in lime burns still, and kissed it. She kissed it with tears in her eyes. Perhaps the tears were not for him, but for her.

"I am so sorry," she said.

"About what?"

"About those old lime burns whatever," she said.

He laughed at this, and then he took out a book, a small copy of *Tom Sawyer*, and opening it he began to read to little Polly. (He had been saving this up now for three months.) Now and then he looked over at Eva, and then swiftly looked back at the page. Little Polly, her blond hair in braids, sat on his knee, and suddenly as if sensing something immaculate and precious and even holy in her mother's gaze, a newness of expectation, she clapped her hands.

I had not thought she would ever come to me again. But she brought the contract over for me to look at. The contract that said the loan of fifty thousand would become *active* after three years, and that payment would be sought if financial returns from the business were inadequate. That any false disclosure would result in the contract being nullified and the money being repaid.

The only thing I told her was that they might be able to challenge the word *inadequate*. But there was a dispute over the land he cut, and that was the problem. To keep heart I told her even that might be resolved. It might be a compassionate reason to drop it if they had not known what they were signing.

But looking carefully at the contract, seeing they had both initialled this, even Torrent, and witnessed by the lawyer, I knew that there was no recourse with this. That clause about false pretences was also *italicized*. The entire river was saying they had stolen timber. The money would have to be paid back. She spoke about the taxes on the house and land, and how she had not thought of them. He would even have to pay taxes on the disputed land to keep his claims on this land valid.

"Raskin wants our house. He is giving us a month more. He says that is fair. He plans to give the land to the Peace and Security people," she said. "Then he said he would give the land on the hills back to the Mi'kmaq."

"Well, Clara could help you, maybe. I can loan you three thousand dollars. That would take care of the taxes, or some of them.

Pay it back when you can—in twenty years. I can't speak for them, but maybe just maybe Clara and Darren will loan you the money to pay back. They are well off, or at least doing okay."

"No," she said. "I have to save him—from me—from all I got us into now. I have to save him."

"Who?"

"Torrent. Yes, I swear I will save him, even if I have to kill myself and get the insurance and never harm him again. You know," she said, "they are so important and so intellectual they don't even care for Polly. They think I should have aborted her, because we couldn't give her the life they said they could give her. This is what Ms. Sackville said to me. Yes—she even said that as she was massaging my shoulders. And like that there too. How can one deal with people like that? And yet I tried to deal with them and I will tell you a secret. I did bad things with Mr. Raskin."

Her eyes were burning bright, self-fascinated, anxious and filled with tears.

"Please, we won't talk about it."

"But I did bad things, sir. I am sorry."

"Yes. Please—I know—we won't speak of it."

And so she left me. Gone was the earlier triumphalism; now she was a sad little creature who had been used by her friends and her father, and was yet still cherished by her husband and her daughter. I saw her walking to her small red Honda. Nothing in the world seemed more sorrowful.

I did not know at that moment, as the wind blew her dress, that she was planning to save her husband by meeting Shane Stroud. And that she was hoping all would be well.

Their argument that came that very night came because of Torrent insisting she go to university.

Now she was adamant that she would not go. She would never go. He kept asking her why. He had a final four thousand he could give her and she could take a student loan for the rest. The taxes would not be paid, and the land and house would be open for sale.

If they were going to lose everything, what did it matter? This would help her pay her first year.

He kept walking behind her in the house. He kept imploring her to tell him what it was, that was wrong.

Finally she went to the very corner of the house, the smallest, tiniest corner, and slumping down after eight in the evening with the very last twitter of the birds, she said:

"I've had an affair or something. I am not sure what you call it, maybe or something like that there."

He had been walking toward her, and he stopped. There was the tick of the stove, the smell of sweet pickles in a jar, the sound and then the silence from the last bird, and then rain started to hit the window.

"With your friend," he said after ten minutes.

"Yes. I thought he was my friend."

"The friend you went to see before we were married?"

"Yes," she said, and then realized something. "No, not him. No, someone else."

He said nothing. He sat in the chair. Rain came down against the flat window.

There was silence except for the rain. The stove ticked. The jars of pickles she had made. She had tortured him—even his notion of himself had been shattered now.

"The one with all the money," she said. "I sold myself to him, I was his, and am humiliated. I was going to say it was because of you, and you were always away—or you was with Clara. I want to run away into the ocean. It wouldn't take long for me to drown in the ocean."

He said nothing.

"I am real stupid," she said. "And he did nothing but laugh at us—laughed at me. Nothing but laugh. But I will take care of it, I want you to know. I will take care of everything. I promise I will."

For two weeks he went to work at Raskin works pouring lime again, and when he came back he discovered she had gone to work at Zellers. Sometimes when Clara came into the house to see how she was, she would try to hide. She did not eat, except when Torrent made her soup when he came home.

But she refused to see Clara, and Clara would leave the food on the counter.

One night he came home he saw a Band-Aid on her wrist, where she had attempted to cut it. So he hid the knives and took his rifles and locked them away.

She hid on Torrent as well, in various closets in the house. And she phoned Mr. Raskin for one last time for some explanation about the money. How much did they still owe? And she was amazed that they still owed it all. They only had a few more weeks to pay the taxes. But if she helped him with Mr. Stroud, and no one had to know, *nothing would be charged.*

It would make her free.

So as a last resort or retort, the last hope at dignity, she said: "And I'm not going to university, so there. I wouldn't go to your old university, so there. And you can tell Ms. Sackville who I think— well, I just think is a big bully, so there, and she leers at me as if she wants me to take all my clothes off in front of her, if you think I don't know. And you—you are a bully too, and I'm sorry I got to know you—so there. Because I don't even know if you even knows you is a bully—I think you is too unthinking to knows."

In fact this was as mean as she could ever manage.

"I wanted a catharsis for you and we've all been betrayed," Albert said.

And all poor Eva could say to that, as she was blinded by tears and rubbed her nose, was: "Well, I'm sorry. I'm very sorry and so is Torrent—so there. And you use big words and I don't even know what catharsis is but if it means a heart attack over you and your handsomeness, *I DID NOT HAVE ONE.* So there!"

Torrent never spoke to her about the affair.

That night he was in Polly's room, and when she went to him his eyes were filled with tears.

"We have lost everything, Eva," he whispered. "I shouldn't have gotten us into this. I can't even pay the taxes now."

"I will save you," she said.

"How?"

"I will save you because I love you and let people say mean things about you—and I heard them mean things and laughed right along with them people and I am so, so sorry. I will do whatever it is I have to do. And I will save you—and we will live together in peace." And her eyes blazed, blazed suddenly in deep sacrifice and love.

The next day she walked to Professor Raskin's cottage:

"Where will he be?"

"I will ask him."

"No. He will be here, here in this place. Once. Then the debt is all over! And you pay our property taxes for this here year too, and the vet bill for Pete the Second because Torry can't even pay that," she said, not looking at him but staring into the hallway that led to the bedroom.

"Fine. Okay."

"Well fine, okay. I am not telling Torrent ever," she said, still not looking his way.

"No, of course not."

"Because he would kill you, he'd snap your neck like a twig, and he would kill Shane Stroud—and I don't want my *sin* on him anymore."

He tried to touch her but she backed away. He comforted her by saying she must understand that from his reading and researching he had discovered there was no real sin. That he had come to that conclusion.

"Well then, if there isn't, stop committing so fucking, fucking many."

33

McLEISH WAS A SCOTS, AND HATED THE UPPER CLASSES of Britain. Lord Halifax's assertion that the lower classes should go to school because England needed more butlers was never lost on him. Except for the fact that he was much closer to Lord Halifax than most others here. He prided himself on his position just as Halifax, his brilliance, as Halifax, his versatility, as Halifax. He did not think others deserved what he had worked for, like Halifax.

And he was, with his great beard and red hair, every bit as protective, about his position and who had rights at the university and who should not enjoy those rights. But to tell him this would make him howl. He did not like Albert because after so much work, first in Glasgow, then in Manchester, then in Belfast, then here, with the underclasses (which is a term he himself used) he didn't believe Albert. He thought he was a squeamish momma's boy. He even called him a puke to his face one time.

And too, he had a trait that was very widespread among professors: he was petty and jealous. He was furious that beautiful Clara Bell, who sat on the board of governors, did not respond to him, and his flirting, with her husband a cripple.

So the idea of this meeting this day, that had finally come to fruition, of the group interested in supporting the First Nations and their claims to unceded territories, was remarkable in this fact: McLeish had organized it, and here Albert was.

Because it was a meeting to generate white support no First Nations were there. One had been invited, a Mr. Roderick Hammerstone—who they had heard had tried to commandeer the horse, but no one knew really who he was. Nor did he find his way there.

It had white people, and white women, accusing white people, mainly white men. It talked about the slave trade, talked about Indigenous suffering, and talked about standing up for rights of visible minorities and starting a rainbow coalition, of women and African-Canadians, gays and First Nations. (As if these people would forever get along.)

McLeish read part of his article from the *Glasgow Herald* about suffering single mothers in 1950s Scotland. His voice trembled in self-reverence. A student of his spoke about the deplorable idea of home children sent to our shores just a short hundred years before. They spoke of teenage pregnancy, incest and the AIDS epidemic, the treatment of gays by the religious right. And the demonic Catholics. And all or most of this, as Tracy McCaustere, with her head shaved, her quite beautiful angelic face complemented with large, dark eyes, said, was somehow linked to the Raskin Company and what they had done here.

And there was no need to speak of the right to do something; it was a moral obligation to do something. And sitting there with

Sackville—not directly beside her, they never did so, but close to her—was Professor Raskin who, it was long noted, had taken welfare rather than his uncle's money, though McLeish believed he wouldn't be there except for his name.

"If it wasn't for his name he wouldn't be here."

But Albert, having heard of this, spoke to it, forcefully.

"I am here because of my conscience and for no other reason. I have more right to be here than anyone else. I have been trying through back channels for years to get my uncles to do the right thing." Here he looked about, especially at Tracy McCaustere, hoping she would nod, and she did. "Two years ago I started a business with a man here, but when I realized he too was taking lumber from unceded Mi'kmaq land, I am now in the process of terminating the arrangement."

He looked at McLeish and added, "We have MP Lampkey shouting off in Ottawa, but nothing is being done. *Nothing.* What voice is needed here, more than any other, is a voice from their own family—is my voice."

This penitent revelation moved many a person.

It was suddenly mentioned that he had a lawsuit started against a man who was using part of Good Friday Mountain as his own that the First Nations were concerned about, that this man had tried to run over some First Nations men with his horse, and Professor Raskin was now taking court action.

Not knowing this was going to be revealed—Tracy McCaustere revealed it—Albert suddenly looked put out, sad, and determined all at once, and angry as well, and people nodded and didn't meet his eyes as he glared.

"Exactly," McLeish said, in his deep, unpleasant Scottish brogue, after a suitable silence. "Exactly. And let me tell you, anyone who is at this moment prejudiced or intolerant of others, no

matter who they are, better leave this room. I have had enough of
that in my lifetime, with the fuckin English."

Ms. Sackville gave a little start, glared a bit, and was silent.

No one left the room, though some did look at each other.
McLeish was an old-time socialist, drearily leftist, and prided himself on the mean intolerance for cant that was supposedly a part of
the jovial working classes. He came from that school, as did his
father and grandfather, but the world had gone on. So the old-time
labour unionist was suffering under the pale of young men and
women fraught with egocentric self-interest, modified sexuality
and self righteous expressions of victimhood and bigotry. And
none could now stop this onslaught into the abyss, and politicians
from all walks of life would go along with it signalling their virtue
and myopic struggles, and people like McLeish would be now
tossed aside. And this committee meeting for social justice and
equality, so obscure as never to be mentioned but by a few in this
university, the university obscure in itself and most professors
longing to be somewhere else—what was happening would in fact
be an indication of many things to come.

No one spoke as McLeish took the floor and talked about
great strides being made to be inclusive, but one could not be
inclusive if one had any feelings of bigotry or superiority in
their hearts.

"I am not saying that Albert's uncles are the most responsible.
They are unwitting dupes of a system they profited from. This
is a systemic racism that cannot be cured in an instant. But I say
it starts here, and now." He looked quickly at Sackville, hoping
she would agree. She did, but this was not what he really wished
to talk about. But he couldn't talk about unions and boots and
shovels, because not one of them had ever worn boots or picked
up a shovel. So he talked of systemic racism and sexism. And

because of the women present, sexism mainly. He forgot his own peccadilloes at this moment. His red beard shone under the fluorescent lights. No one said anything for a while.

"Racism and sexism go hand in hand," a young female student said.

"Yes," answered a boy notable for being a rugby player, looking around for approval, his cheeks fat and well fed.

"Yes," said Albert. "The person I worked with and signed on to help with money was unfortunately both, a racist and a sexist to his wife."

One man sat listening to them in the farthest back corner, speechless for a long time. He simply now and then looked out the dark window at the darkness. He had come here knowing they had invited Roderick Hammerstone and was hoping he would show up—to show them what had happened to the child Roderick. What fetal alcohol syndrome actually did. What the world, what Mel himself, had done to his beautiful sister, and what Byron Raskin had tried to prevent. This was his way as an honest man to try and pay a debt.

Then someone made a joke about Peterson, and his father Oscar, and a few guffawed. The rugby player guffawed the most, and shook his head and looked around. Professor Dykes—who had taken many down to Washington to protest, now blind, sitting with long, stringy white hair, and a white cane, which he at times lifted—asked people to speak louder please.

But then some realized what had been said was in bad taste.

The man at the very back, the silent witness who had come alone, finally did speak when Oscar and Torry were mentioned. People had to turn in their seats to listen. And his face was in shadow because the row of lights above his head weren't on.

"I've known Torry Peterson since he was a boy. I worked with him, I like him, he would do anything for anyone. I don't think he was trying to run over them, I think he was trying to go home. I think he believed the wood was his—it's that simple. I believe he is caught up in something he doesn't understand."

"Oh well, he did run them down," McLeish said, turning toward him. "Whether he wanted to run them out or not is beside the point."

"No. The horse bolted. Torry was the one who had his logs spilled over the road."

"It is not his logs," a young dark-haired woman said.

"How do you know? He was the one who in innocence paid for them. In innocence he tried to start a business. The land deed was legitimate as far as he knew. He never had a business before— he was doing something he had never done. He was even talked into doing it by others. The land might be in dispute, but he had a right to believe he had bought it in good faith."

He spoke very quietly and people tried to figure out who he was.

"Yes—and he wanted to take over *their* ridge," a young woman lashed out, disgusted.

"Where are you from, ma'am?"

Some of the people tittered at the word *ma'am*. They did not know old-age etiquette still existed among good people.

"Halifax, Nova Scotia."

"Then you were never up on the ridge, you know nothing of his work. No First Nations man was ever up on that part of the ridge until Clement Ricer sold it off to Torry Peterson. I helped Torry map out what he wanted and what he could buy—because I know the treaties here too."

The blind Professor Dykes was noticeable because of his serpentine smile, his eyes turned inward so they were white, and his long white hair falling over the corduroy jacket he always wore.

"Haah," he said. "Haah," and everyone looked his way. Faye Sackville looked his way as well, with a particular interest, strangely waiting for him to say more. Since he did not she finally turned her attention back to those conversing.

The one defending Torrent, the person they did not know, continued, his voice still very quiet.

"How many here have been on the reserve? How many of you gave five truckloads of oil to the reserve last winter? Oh yes, the Raskin twins in their eighties did. Let me ask this—have you ever spent a weekend there, seen the desolation and disaster among the families? The fathers too drunk to walk? No, it is not their fault. They have suffered enough. They have suffered too much, they have tried to fit into a world that has scorned them,. Their world exploited and a new world has to come—but it is only in *their power* to correct. It is not in the white man's power, not in a young girl's from Halifax who arrived here last month. And asking for more land around Riley Brook or more governmental payouts, for a ridge they don't care about, won't do it."

"That is the white man's fault," the dark-haired woman said. "That's why it's systemic." (She had just learned that word.)

"In the past, yes. Not now. Don't demand from others, do for yourself."

This man was Gordon Hammerstone, a First Nations man, an outcast who told his people if they wanted to be successful stop asking only for land and start demanding education for their children. He said: "A man's reach must exceed his grasp or what's a heaven for."

His face was toughened by this terribly uneven struggle, and there was no woman or man in this room who had ever come close to that.

"You sound terribly upset—maybe upset because the Indian

people are beginning, just beginning, to show their mettle," the young woman said, smiling triumphantly, as young privileged women were often accustomed to doing.

"Yes," another young woman said, wearing black with a red balaclava around her neck, and black tights with big green sneakers. "Yes, you just don't consider them as people."

"Racist! Racist!" came the shouts from all sides. "Racist! Racist!" came three young women's almost gleefully hysterical shouts.

Gordon left and continued his myriad search for his nephew, continued his dramatic and lonely quest to honour his hidden lonely commitment for a person of his blood, his even greater commitment to his own people no matter the consequences.

A possibility of endless virtues and vibrant obligations, they sat at night, bivouacked near Riley Brook in the summer, with a few tents and transistor radios, barbecues and coolers. These were old issues, and old wounds, and it did not matter what else was offered, for they now wanted all things on Good Friday theirs. And this concern in demonstrations and truck burnings and standing up to the police was slowly approaching, masticating like a beast whose time comes round at last, the frozen gates of Raskin works, where the two old men sat playing checkers in the spacious, glorious mahogany room that held the narwhal tusk. After years of being who they were, they now awaited the mail from Ottawa to set them free.

The mail that could not come.

"King me, Chester. King me now."

"You forgot to king me."

"Did I?"

"Yes, you did. I'm a king as well."

"We did all we could, goddamn it."

This is what the two old men had said when they pushed the reporter a month before. And now all eyes were on the conflagration soon to erupt.

"*They have shown complete lack of moral credibility—a dearth of ethical integrity*," the reporter did report.

"What's dearth?" Dexter asked.

"Lack thereof," Lester, their butler, or handyman, said.

"Ahh," Chester said, "that's what that word is."

Gordon did not find Roderick. He had been in jail but they had let him out at eight the morning previous to the evening meeting Gordon had attended. Gordon was fraught with worry, terrified his nephew would do something so unthinking that he, Gordon, would never forgive himself for being unable to protect him from the ruthless demons in his way. That is what this machination came down to: the dread of his nephew, unable to know right from wrong, being channelled by the demons in other people's souls. He drove his old bicycle on the streets of Arron Cove all the way to the crossroad where Oscar Peterson lived. He rode his bike on a lonely trek, knocking on doors and asking people if they had seen five-foot-two little crazy-eyed Roderick in the last few days. But no one had.

At a certain point a car passed by, racing over the hill toward Oscar's trailer. It was a stolen car. A little red Honda Henrietta Saffy had taken to pick up her new friend Roderick Hammerstone who had phoned her from the centre snack bar.

"Hey," Roderick said, as they flew by Gordon, "there's my uncle. Henrietta, we'll have to do something for him special too. Okay, Henrietta? Okay, okay?"

"Okay, my boy—just don't be so antsy. I've gotta get this car back before Miss Prissy Cunt misses it."

And Roderick, his hair mussed up and his eyes shining, and a brand-new Team Canada cap in his hand that Henrietta had just bought him, and a chocolate bar, and a new package of smokes, and his torn sneakers showing half his dirty toes, laughed and nodded and said: "Oh boy."

The old car rattled and Roderick, his little imp-like head seen out the window by passing cars, yelled, "Houston, we have a problem!" and laughed.

"Get your fuckin head in the car, Rocket Man," Henrietta said.

And they drove past Oscar's, around the turn and across the bridge.

The car was returned before Eva even knew it was gone.

34

IT WAS EARLY IN SEPTEMBER WHEN HE RECEIVED A letter that he told no one about. He was surprised when it came and more surprised by what it said.

It was a letter from Clara Bell.

My dear Albert Raskin,
It has been a while since I have spoken to you, so I hope you and your friend Professor Sackville are well. I do hope so.
People told me how you helped take care of children when you were a boy, and your father (I think of Byron as your father) was away, and would bring them in to the large cottage for treats. That was very kind and noble, and I wanted to tell you that one day. I was one of those children, and you played Scrabble with me. In fact you were the young boy who taught me how to play. I wanted to tell you that I remember your

kindness to me when playing Scrabble. We both had to go to
the reserve to go to church on those summer days, and one
time both of us, sitting in the back seat of my dad's car, passed
a lane of houses with nothing. There was a horse caught up
in the swamp and I remember you were overcome with grief,

I am appealing to you as that young boy. I am appealing
to you to help Eva and Torrent. I am not appealing to you to
confess to something you did as an immature young man, but
to help Torrent, and in that way make recompense in this
life. If that is done, I am sure Darren and I can come to some
closure about the rest. I am begging you to help save my
dear cousin in distress.

But if you do so, if you forgive the debt, it will not go
easy on you—they will smear your name. If you stand
with Torrent now it will be very harsh. If you refuse to
sit with those protesting the two old men, harshness will
follow disgrace. You know them and so do I. You know them
as compatriots now. They all want his blood, and blood will
flow, I am certain. I am just uncertain as to whose blood
it will be. Yet Torrent is innocent and an innocent soul.
I know in your heart that you know this is the right decision
but it will not be easy. It will be the right decision not to
march with them against your uncles too, but it will not
seem so. Especially for you.

You will be shunned at the university as I am now shunned,
and Darren is shunned. Many of the best professors, professors
who were left out to dry, are shunned. Good men and women
have to accept that. Still, it is the hardest and the noblest
of ways. You have tenure—you can say tomorrow that you
believe Torrent acted in good faith, that you will not march
against him, and you believe that your uncles did write those

letters of concern. Because my father swears they did. If you do this, and publicly do so in the press, it will be heroic. It will not be the false heroics that so many students parade now. It will be truly brave.

Darren and I will go on with our lives knowing the mistake of a young man was the mistake of a young man. A mistake that will be forgiven.

I am sorry that you are in this position, but the decision is yours. And time is now passing.

With kind regards to both you and Faye,

Clara

He hid the letter upstairs, in a box. In that box were many of the soldiers his dad had set up during his reconstruction of the Battle of Gettysburg.

"*Honour follows virtue like a shadow.*" The man who they had replaced, the Nova Scotian, had just published his verses and was up for a major award in Britain and the U.S. They had not even published his poems in their magazine here.

Everyone like Nancy and Kent and Bill was once again singing his praises and saying how wonderful he was.

"It's too bad he couldn't have stayed," Nancy said with the false diplomacy university wives often had.

He telephoned Stroud and told him Eva would not be available. He told him he had just heard Darren would not press about that night any longer. He told him it was over. He told Shane he would not comply.

He was ready to hang up when Shane said: "Oh, but it's not Darren I would tell. He already knows. It's the university— it's the papers. It won't just be about Annie. It will be about Eva too."

In the end he set the toy solders back in the chest and tore the letter up. What was to come he felt was cast in stone.

At the university in the early fall of that year, I learned that a strange event had happened. It was a week or two after our good Raskin had his conversation with Professor Howl. A week after Albert reminded Faye Sackville of her embarrassment on the stand.

Ms. Sackville went into Darren Howl's office and simply began to take books off his shelf, while musing over the titles as she did, picking them up, holding them out to see the titles and then dropping them into a wastebasket she carried under her arm, then brushing her long, immaculate fingers on a white handkerchief as if the books themselves were too odious to touch.

It was considered by many of her more vocal students to be a sacred duty. To them she was a Mother Teresa. News of it went across the university like wildfire. It made the news and was the lead two nights running.

Raskin had handed Sackville a list of books he had seen on those shelves, and those books which had been banned from the curriculum over the last five or six years: *Othello*, *Huckleberry Finn*, *Heart of Darkness*, *Darkness at Noon* and *Blood Ties*, along with the works of Flannery O'Connor, Ernest Hemingway and Philip Roth; and when she had taken them off his shelves, along with the book on the life of Beaverbrook and a book on Churchill (replaced by a book on Gandhi), believing she was correcting an injustice, she looked at her fingers, wiped them with the handkerchief once more and started to leave, just as Professor Howl came in.

One might know that she had not read one of these books, not even *Huckleberry Finn*. That is, it was the dangerous age of arresting books rather than people. She was hoping, of course, in a mild and even mischievous way, that people would follow. In fact, if you made a list of your favourite twenty-five books, it might just be possible that Ms. Faye Sackville would not have read one of them.

It was said, and it was probably true, that Darren chased her about the room with his wheelchair trying to corner her, and she dodged one way and the other with little squeaks coming from her, little footsy sidesteps, explanation being these books were banned, and like *pistols* they shouldn't be made available in any way to children. These books were *repulsive*, she explained.

This was a woman, after years in the convent, now bulging with fire and fury. And somewhat cute dancing slippers with little silver buckles, that she wore in the office.

Tracy McCaustere, a young woman, was interviewed for the student paper, calm and almost serene, with the brushcut and the pierced nose.

"I can see both sides," she said. She was too diplomatic to say more. That would come with time.

But Tracy did assure us that the banning of books had its origin not in censorship but in freedom. It was a new freedom, *unchaining the cerebellum* it was called. Using positive models to be a new source of a new provocative enlightenment.

Unchaining the Cerebellum was an essay explaining all of this, published in our Saint Michael's University paper.

Tracy was applauded, just as she had manoeuvred herself into so being. She had mainly set her sights on being an advocate and white female champion of First Nations concerns. She knew there were many of those and she was determined to be the most effective.

Sackville also commented on the banning of books: "I am after a more vibrant understanding of our obligation," she said, "not to break our trust with parents who send their children to us. Oh, this male autonomy has got to stop—I think there is a song about it somewhere. Where *every man is a king*. Well, every man is not a king, even those who subject others to their lordly presence, like certain professors I won't mention—one who took me to court, who I won't mention."

She was, as our student paper said, a former nun, a woman studying both Islam and Buddhism, a woman of qualifications.

But give her her due, she never read the press about herself, good or bad. And when some of the students said they must make a reverential button to pin on their blouses for her, she cited much more work must be done, and declined.

She made sure she spoke this in front of Albert, who was standing beside her, with his brown corduroy jacket supporting just such a button about himself.

Eva went home from work on September 15 and looked out over the fields. Here was where her husband planted the rows of potatoes, beets and turnips. Here is where he hayed, and reroofed the shed; here is where he made the chair for Polly. But she had run pell-mell to the land of professors. And why had she done so? The feeling of having committed a grave error, an offence against who she was supposed to be, had finally come over her. That is, books and learning and understanding had to, in some sense, come at first from inside oneself. And she had been led along only by her desire to be rid of this.

She wandered about her house, the house he had built for her, and thought of her betrayal. Was there any way to cure it? Her own misery came in knowing her collusion, knowing the bases on which it happened were self-propelled, clandestine and dreamlike but developed within her own soul, not his—not Mr. Raskin's. She had all the time in the world to say *no* as she knew where they were headed. She knew from the moment she turned and walked to the sink after bandaging his arm that his feeling for her was not to help, or not only to help, and that his feeling even was by then by her reciprocated, and waiting for a time to ripen, though she denied it. In fact in her heart she did not care about university. She only cared about *seeming to care.*

When he was taking action against her husband, she felt the nuance of his blame was not directed at her, and she might escape if she was silent, if she gave her own husband less support. And so she was silent, as he went out working day and night to try and save them. All of this added to the eventual shame she was bearing, without knowing the exactness of it all.

The problem was, her shame was not factored into the equation until the price for this equation became due. Shame then became due as a penalty, a deepening wound. She tried to go forward but walked in mire, and she wanted to die. She wanted to die because of what he, Raskin, actually had thought of her when he smiled and told her how much he cared. But she knew she could have simply said *no.*

Worse, that first morning she went along the shore road to visit him, the country-and-western song "Heaven's Just a Sin Away" was on the radio. And no one could encapsulate the world both of guilt and desire more than a country-and-western song. And yet within it all, within the very expressiveness of his face, all things had been revealed even before he began to strip her naked, if she only wanted to see. They had been revealed totally as far back as the day she had bandaged his arm. The bright shiny moment was one of falseness. Both of them knew this.

So he was the conduit for her dissatisfaction, and now the cosignatory of her unhappiness for her own misdeed. She knew this now, and she wanted to correct it. She wanted to scrub the world clean and be clean and clear of all she thought she had needed from him.

The talk of her freedom was so appealing a year ago, just when their liaison was ratcheting up, that she had thought of leaving her child. She thought she would be complimented by him, she would do something he had called "*revolutionary.*"

She had begun to think that the one right a woman must exercise was to leave her child behind. But what was more painful—unknown to anyone but her, not the pills she gave the child to go to sleep so she could have meetings with him who did not care for her or her child (always telling herself he did and that they would all be together); but that once coming back—hurrying back late, almost dark, in the cold with the stars flickering above her—she saw little Polly wandering toward Arron Brook, trying to find her mommy, and she thought: *What if she falls in—what if? There will be no more little Polly and he will marry me fer sure! We would be so happy together and he is so kind.*

She stood as if transfixed as the child called "Mommy," getting closer to the edge of the falls—

The child held the small doll she had loved, called Mo Mo, in her hand. The night was brimming with the stars from other worlds, and yet in those stars the very notion of what was good or what was evil was ever present, through the clear blackness that now surrounded the earth.

And suddenly, a feeling like a gust of wind came into her soul, and she rushed forward and picked the child up in her arms, bawling like a child over what had flickered in her mind. For it had only been one second. But that second could never be erased.

She was not vain about her looks, but she knew she was extremely desirable, and not only Raskin but a dozen other men, at least a dozen, and not only Sackville but certain other women (yes, she knew this too) seemed captivated by it. Seemed, as Sackville seemed, to want her to disrobe.

In fact perhaps this proved beauty like hers was cruel. That is, perhaps it wasn't even their fault.

If I had not been a desirable woman, the loan would not have been given. He did this to sleep with me. It came to her suddenly, and with such force she had to sit down in the chair. But still she realized she was pleased she had been desirable to him. So now she would do what he wanted because she detested, and wanted to devalue, herself as a human being. This would be the way out—and lessening herself seemed almost sacrosanct.

In fact what did it matter if she was a human being? For Sackville, that woman she once admired who took her for drives— once all the way to Point aux Carr for a picnic, and pleaded with her to let her brush her hair—no longer thought she was.

She held the note from the bank in her hand, the number she was to phone, from his lawyer, the idea of payment to be worked out with his lawyer. Albert could clear it all—he had that much power over them, if she did what he asked.

And as she was sitting there, her father came in, his motions like that of a nervous, despicable little animal, shrugging and smoking and asking if she hadn't twenty dollars to spare.

That was September 15, a Saturday. On the news she heard Princess Diana had a baby boy, and mother and child were doing well.

Shamefully she had taken the contract to Clara, who had looked over it for two days. This was just before Clara wrote the appeal to Albert.

"I am not a fan of his lawyer—he should have made some token gesture to allow you to know what you were signing. We might be able to use that as a wedge, and you did not have a lawyer present. But, as stated, his lawyer also acted on your behalf, and you signed to allow him to."

"Is there any hope?"

"Sure. We can fight to the end. And we will."

She went to a book on the shelf, and bringing it forward—it was beginning to rain hard against the stone outside, and against the lawn and into the cement birdbath—she opened it to a page. The page showed a print from 1867, which showed a painting from an age before. The print had been done in celebration of the forming of the Dominion of Canada, and showed various ancient families who arrived on our shores. And in this print, at one corner, the painting of a boy now hanging at the end of some dark hallway in Montreal, a boy from an ancient family who had made their escape.

"That is Albert's ancestor," Clara said. "It is strange how I came across this quite by accident when all of this trouble seemed to explode. And now I know like a revolution it will be almost impossible to stop."

"It is my fault," she said.

Clara looked at her. She was not given to lying. "Ah, sweetie, yes of course. But maybe somewhat less than you think."

And then Clara said: "A revolution large or small always ends in outrage, torture and blood."

Torry had gone to church. He was rarely a churchgoer; still it was the third time that month. He had no hope unless he did so. He prayed so his house would be saved.

And so she was alone, on September 16. She telephoned Clara but there was no answer. No doubt she had gone to church as well.

She said to Polly, "Here, darling, take this medicine and you can have some ice cream."

She had dressed the little girl in her blue dress with all the buttons. By the time they got to button thirty the child was asleep. She laid her on the bed and put her doll Mo Mo, with the big floppy blue eyes, beside her.

Then she dressed, the way she was told to dress *by him*. Without knowing its implication she wore the watch on her wrist.

Then she walked down to the cottage. Albert let her in. But he told her first to come around the back. He told her he was sorry. He told her he would do everything he could to protect her. She said nothing.

He told her to take the cocaine. She didn't want to, but no, he said, it is the best thing to take. And so she did.

Shane was already there. She could smell his body, as she had the night she was a girl of sixteen.

"Hi," he said. He was nervous, already drunk. "Remember me?"

She had taken pills too. Her eyes closed and opened slowly.

"I want a drink," she said.

"Oh—oh, of course," Albert said.

He went to the kitchen and poured a gin and tonic. He set it on the table, and then running his hands down his cotton pants, he left the room.

"Come here. Don't be shy," Shane said. "It's just me, silly. You remember me. I offered you a watch and you didn't even take it. But now, you are wearing it—yes." He stumbled, and looked at her almost terrified, and then took her arm in his hand and looked at the watch.

"Ahh," he said, as if still frightened, of some omen he did not understand.

He scratched the top of his head, and he lighted another cigarette. Now he was frightened of something beyond him—and he led
her to the room. The same room she had first gone into with *him*,
when it was raining. On that day she had entered a new world, a
new portico. She just didn't know then what world it was to become.

She stared at the ceiling, and did not move. He took her clothes
off, and even before he took her blouse off she was saying: "Please
hurry up."

Shane could not get it up and he got angry and hit her, and then
he could.

Raskin, who had gone into the upstairs sunroom, came back
and stood at the door, and told Shane to stop. But it was now too
late. Raskin held the knife the Nova Scotian had taken off him
years before. Yet seeing the mole on Shane's left shoulder made
him hesitate and he could not thrust it. That tiny mole, that sign
of humanity, saved Shane's life.

"Stop trembling," Stroud kept saying.

Then after, after it was over, after he came inside her, Shane
fled, he ran, he ran like a bad little animal out into the day and
disappeared.

She refused to look at either of them.

Raskin looked at her. Her nose was bloody, her left eye black,
the inside of her left thigh had blood smeared on it and her right
breast had been bitten.

He was crying. He held the knife limply in his left hand.

"Do you want to go to the hospital?"

"Go from me now—be gone, invalid. Be gone always from me.
Don't you dare cross my path again."

Her voice horrified him, chilled him to the soul, and he too
ran away.

———

Then there were a variety of ways to do it. First she took a knife from the barn. But she didn't have the nerve to cut herself deep enough. So she decided to jump into Arron and down she went. She went down to Arron on that Sunday morning, and she could hear the church bells when she did. And then Torry would be home, and find the little girl sleeping—and she would be gone. And then, yes, after she was gone, dead as a nit, all would be fine. And no one would torment Torry again, because she had tormented him. She remembered now his sad face, his sad lonely face, and she walked down over the bank, toward Arron Brook, toward its incessant eddies and whirlpools in the morning sunlight.

No, she wouldn't undress, that was not what she would do. Too much had happened to her to ever want to be naked again. She loathed her nakedness like Eve after she had taken the apple.

She would simply wade into the water and yes, with rocks in her pockets. For that's what she had heard a great woman writer did, rocks in her pockets.

She picked up rocks, and broke a nail doing it. She put them into her dress pocket, and down the bib she wore over her blouse. Yes, no problem to drown now. Mr. Raskin wouldn't plague her anymore.

And here she sunk. She slipped the bounds of earth, as she remembered someone told her about flying. She too would fly away. Then suddenly she wanted to live—suddenly she held her breath and struggled, suddenly she felt herself fall into Glidden's Pool— that is, she had not sunk but was carried downstream almost two hundred yards, and she went over a falls, a falls of thirty-nine feet, and that is how all the rocks fell from her bib and her pocket except two—and she looked down below her, and saw her little feet—one sneaker had fallen away and was floating down and then up past her, to the top with all the bubbles, and so was she—she came up out of the water and found herself next to the shore.

It was at that moment she decided her destiny was going to be very different. And then when she lay on the shore, looking at the heavens, she smelled smoke.

35

NO ONE KNEW HOW THE BLAZE STARTED. IT WAS CERTAINLY a mystery, so therefore as with all mysterious events everyone had an opinion. But it was Torrent Peterson charged with the arson. He said he would burn the house before he lost it.

He had come back from church, an hour after church was over because he had been at the grave of his mother—for the very first time, at the grave of Mary Lou Toomey. He had decided when he was in Saint John that he would visit her grave.

Then he walked up the path alone, in the early afternoon. It was funny—he had not been to church in months and had gone back in the last few weeks.

His best cabinets had been hauled outside, so people said he made sure his work was safe before the fire. She was away, Eva, and was seen earlier going somewhere. But where was Polly?

The varnish, the paint, the boards all in a heap on the floor, and one match was all it took. Once that started it spread to the back of the house. People ran up from the beach near the Arron Tickle— but not many, for it was September, everyone had gone.

Torry and Eva fought desperately to save the house. Becky did as well, and some neighbours, both white and First Nations—they fought desperately to save the barn, but the dry season and the dried timber he had cut for his great cabinets and clocks made a mockery of his life.

Then there was nothing at all left.

They lost the house and barn, four chairs, three secretary desks, four cabinets, and a settee that had been delivered back to him by people who couldn't sell them. He had lost three acoustic guitars that he had secretly been making for musicians in Saint John (one of the reasons he took the trip down there).

It was soon recognized as arson. It only took two days for the report to come back, but they waited two weeks, for the coroner's report on Polly.

As Torrent tried to get the best pieces he had done away from the flame, he heard a small voice behind the locked door. Eva had locked it, so Polly would be safe.

"Hello—Hello—Hello—Daddy, hello. I'm going back upstairs to get my dolly and then will get Peaches, okay?"

He believed she had been with her mother, who arrived just as the girl started calling. He didn't even realize Eva was soaking wet, with one sneaker on. When Torry discovered she was inside, the child was calm. But the whole house was on fire. He had no key on him, and neither did Eva. She had lost it, not in the water but on the bed in the bedroom, at the cottage.

Polly said: "Daddy, I will go around the back—"

"Yes. Go to the window around the back," Constable Donaldson said, and she ran in that direction.

"Wait till I find Peaches."

"No—don't find Peaches! Go around to the window. I will go there and break it."

And both the constable and he ran to the window—smashed it, and flame and smoke billowed out, and Becky fell backwards because of the heat, and the little girl said:

"Oh my dress is caught—wait—I am undoing—my dress—I am going to take my dress off—it's my blue dress—"

Then she said: "Buttons, Daddy, please help me—I have too many buttons."

Eva tried to get into the house, and Becky Donaldson had to grab her—she simply picked her up and tossed her like a doll— and Gordon Hammerstone managed to break into the back door but he was too far away and could get no further.

Eva screamed like no one had ever heard when Polly said: "Mommy put on too many buttons."

And these were four-year-old Polly Peterson's last words.

Oscar the evening after they buried the child took the pistol to Eva, wrapped in cloth. He handed it to her.

"For Torrent's defence," he said. "Sell it to someone, and get all the money you can."

Clara took his case. She wanted no money. But Torrent said he had lighted the fire, to get the insurance money. She said she did not believe him. Polly had been given two sleeping pills. That she had even woken up was surprising.

"I gave them to her too," he said.

Eva said she did not believe him. She said she gave the sleeping pills. But Torry said that was a lie, and he would not stand for it.

Clara asked him to change his plea. He did not want to live, and Eva said he must, he must live, there was too much goodness in him not to.

The prosecutor hated him—it was very evident that this case of greed, intended or not, caused the death of a sweet child. A child it seemed from and because of her progenitors no one seemed to want in the first place. They had a video of her singing in playschool, and one of her playing with her cat Peaches, which survived the fire.

Why then, if he could not care for her and did not want her, did they have her in the first place? Better to have aborted her.

Eva went to the courthouse every day—the picture of the burned farmhouse on an easel in the centre of the courtroom, near the court secretary and the bailiff who weighed two hundred and eighty pounds and stood with his arms folded. It looked in its ruined dimensions like an eerie remnant of some Civil War battle with a beautifully pristine grandfather clock standing alone behind a house of ruin. Some farm after the Battle of Gettysburg.

The prosecutor laid out his reasons for the fire and the reason he was asking for twelve to fifteen years in jail, because of the death of the child.

Torrent was found guilty, sentenced to six and a half years—which was reasonable—by Judge Lampkey, the man, his grandfather, who had given Torrent's mother the six hundred dollars years before because of certain actions at his house, with a naked girl, Torrent's long-lost mother.

"I can sell something I have and get you money," Eva told Clara. "I know Torrent would want me to."

"No. You will not ever do that."

"And we will pay off Raskin," Darren said.

"No," Eva said, startled and ashamed. "No."

"Why not?"

"It is done. He is paid."

And that's how the pistol came to be in her possession. She tucked it in the cloth and put it under the bed, in the small apartment on Layton Street. Someday she would sell it for money for Torrent. And then she would go away—far away. She would kill herself, she was sure. She would not bother anyone again. She wouldn't fall in love with anyone else. She might decide to drown.

Yes—if she had to die, she would drown. That was the only way. Though twice now it hadn't worked.

It was known she attempted suicide twice more. Both times she ended in hospital, both times she was under psychiatric care, both times she was released from hospital. Both times people prayed for her, sat with her, loved her back to health.

She continued to work at Zellers, and she visited her husband three times a month in jail.

She was hit upon by many men, for she was beautiful and alone, and her apartment light shone in the night and so many men wanted to *protect* her. But she walked by them like stone. Yes, she would protect herself. Shane came back once more. She glared at him as if she was made of stone, told him she had informed the police, and he left before they arrived. For the first time in his life, the way she looked at him made him deeply frightened, and he drew his hand back—it was an inch from touching her—and walked as if on eggshells down the stairs.

"What a terrified demon you are," she said, laughing hysterically. She suddenly believed in demons once again.

He did not know how lucky he had been that night. She had the pistol under her coat, and the determination to pull the trigger if his hand touched her. That is why there was a slight smile of acrimony on her face as his hand reached out toward her coat.

"I am not frightened anymore. I will never again be frightened of demons," she said.

Henrietta Saffy waited in the corner of the apartment building. And far after dark on November 2 a man approached from the old railroad track, from the direction of Oscar Peterson's. He had been hidden in the wood behind there most of the afternoon, and now a cold spell had entered, the frost made the ground hard, the trees stood tall and empty on all sides of him, and he never liked the woods. People were on his trail too, people like Constable Becky Donaldson, who had reopened the long-dead cold case of Arlo and Arnie. You see, that's why the man was in back of Oscar Peterson's trailer. Oscar was a blabbermouth and things had been taken away from the trailer over the course of the afternoon—clothing, and dishes—why, one might never know—and a box. What was in that box? Letters Mary Lou had sent her son? He didn't know. He only knew that Oscar told him he no longer had the pistol. Mel was obsessed with getting it.

He yawned, fidgeted and waited for them to go away so he could speak to Oscar politely. But then, worried, he turned and made his way home in the dark.

He had changed his looks, dyed his hair, and possessed an identification that claimed his name as a Mr. White.

Two months before, he had already been paid for the pistol by Albert, who was frightened not to pay him—paid him in an out-of-the-way Catholic churchyard, near the graves of Arlo and Arnie Toomey. It was a cold rain that was falling too and Mel had a heavy heart when he noticed those little graves.

Mel had convinced himself that he already owned the pistol and had convinced Albert to give him the money. But when Albert came that night Mel did not have the pistol on him—nor had he seen it himself in years.

The rain lashed their faces as they stood in the dark. Albert was giving Mel fifteen thousand dollars to start his bottle exchange. He waited to be handed the pistol.

"No worries. I know where it is," Mel said, and he simply took the money and left.

And Albert, who had thought he would get the pistol that very night, was once again left empty-handed, and without the money he had brought. He even cursed Mel for the first time. For the very first time he stood his ground.

"Oh come on," Mel said, "I'm your friend—"

Mel Stroud didn't tell Henrietta about this meeting or the money. Oh, he was going to.

Someday soon.

But now our newly minted Mr. White believed he could get much more by taking it to the States and selling it there. That is, once he had it. That is, once he convinced Oscar to give it to him. In his mind it had already gone up past a million dollars, and the price was climbing.

36

BINGO YEARS AGO AT THE CATHOLIC CHURCH CENTRE. Donaldson knew she would be hard-pressed to solve the case of Arlo and Arnie, two boys he had known—hard-pressed as well to solve the insulin death of little Mary Lou Toomey, their sister, who was three months pregnant.

But she might find something in a batch of letters to implicate a man in the death of a Mrs. Wally who had her bingo winnings stolen and was left dead on the old apartment's back steps years before.

Yes, that was an old, old, old case for sure. But Donaldson believed that was money that this man first used to offer to buy the pistol from Oscar Peterson. She did not think it was Mel's crime. She believed it was his brother's.

So she went into the office, and went back over the effects, in an old brown bag, of Mrs. Jack Wally. Purse was there, money was missing, two brass buttons torn from her Navy Reserve jacket as she fought for her life that cold night. Her son had stated her silver strapped watch that she had won in the raffle at the Mott wedding was missing. It had been an old watch even then, but it was beautiful and she wore it, and kept it in pristine condition.

She discovered over the next few days the watch had been innocently given as a present to Eva Mott. That night she went to collect it.

"It is such bad luck, I think, that watch," Eva said.

"This will be good news for you sooner or later," Donaldson said, putting the watch in a plastic bag. She smiled at the young woman, hoping against hope she would heal.

She and her girlfriend, who had opened up a veterinary clinic, had moved in together. Sometimes Ms. Sackville came in with her calico cat.

"Do take care of Simone," she would advise. "I would be terribly lost without it."

Henrietta opened the back door, and cold autumn air mixed with the stale smoke of the building.

He nodded to her and she let him in, and up the back stairs, and he entered apartment 27, the apartment above the Motts.

"We will have to get a car," Mel Stroud said. "We will have to get a car."

"Does he have it?"

"Sure, but he will never sell it. We will just go in and take it. I am not thinking so much of Raskin now. We will sell it to the Chinese, or the Japanese—they are the ones with the money now."

"Is it really worth something?"

He took out an old magazine page, that had been folded and refolded, spread it on the small table under the light and pointed it out. There were four pistols on the page, from an 1880 Smith and Wesson, to this 1908 model. They ranged in price from twenty thousand to sixty-nine thousand dollars.

He tapped the magazine, smudged with dirt, and then folded it again, and smiled at her.

"Canada-wide warrant on you," she said. She smiled.

"I've had them before," he said. "But it's Shane. You see, Shane is the real trouble-maker in the family. Can't do a thing with him, was always a momma's boy, so the less we see of him the better."

He took out his knife, opened it, cut a piece of hash. It was the same knife he had drawn on Packet Terri.

"It killed Jesse James," he said, "that pistol. I figure it's really worth two hundred and thousand."

"Two hundred and thousand?"

He always exaggerated the importance of everything around him.

"Sure. So we will go to Argentina with the money—get away from all this racket."

There was noise in the apartment below. He went down and knocked on the Mott door for the very first time. It was simply because he had learned Mr. Mott had a job at the car dealership—his eleventh job in eleven years.

"Could you keep it down," he said pleasantly. "My wife is ill. Very ill."

"Oh sorry," said the man, "sorry. We usually don't make noise. It's just the movie. Why, I have been known to hide for weeks and not make a peep."

"Hey, that's just like me," Mel Stroud said. "In fact I used to live in an apartment that used to be here—one they tore down long ago. I miss the old times, don't you?"

"Yes," Mr. Mott said.

"Like King Cole tea!"

"Yes, that's what I have. How did you know? Would you like a cup?"

"Maybe—maybe some other time," Mel said. "Maybe I'll take one up to my wife someday."

"What's wrong with her?"

"Nerves. She just lost a child. She was three months pregnant, but diabetes and she lost it."

"We lost our grandchild a little while ago," Mr. Mott said. The man seemed visibly shaken, even changed by this coincidence. Mel put his hand on Mr. Mott's shoulder and there were tears in his eyes. Tears came to Mr. Mott's eyes too.

"I am so sorry," Mel Stroud said. "I am so, so sorry, sir. I bet she was a nice child."

"Thank you. She was the best," Mott said. "Thank you."

"Sometimes tragedies in life bring us all closer together."

He left.

"I have finally met a nice man in this bugger of a place," Mr. Mott said, going back to his wife. "Someone who won't make fun of me. Maybe give me a loan now and then when I need it."

"Why did you bother them?" Henrietta Saffy asked.

Mel Stroud put the hash on a pin and lighted it with his lighter. "Because he is working at the Chevy dealership—I saw him there today. His brother-in-law must have got him the job; and I think we will test drive a car of his. Not for a while, but after a while. In a while—go for a ride. So he has to trust me."

"The kind of car that will take us out of this dump?"

"Precisely. Precisely," Mel Stroud said, and held the smoke deep into his lungs. "Precisely so. But remember—you have diabetes. If he asks, tell him you're two shots a day and trying for another child. And cry—cry about it awhile. You should learn how to cry and have some feeling."

He handed the hash over, to wild, crazy and dangerously brilliant Henrietta Saffy.

All violence is mimicry, and she was a grand mimic.

They gathered in a group of fifteen kids, macabre-looking in the twilight air. One would think he had fallen into a stage of mimes, so choreographed it all seemed.

So they picked the closest target. Two old men who had committed errors in their lives, trusted the wrong sources, but had never intended in their lives to commit a crime.

It was a crisp, clear starry night just after Halloween and many were wearing masks from the Halloween dance. Some threw firecrackers and others lighted flares. Then a torch flared; the black smoke of burning oil went up against the red night sky when they lighted a truck on fire. It was in fact an accident.

But when they saw it, children cheered, the pit, pit, pit of fire engulfed the black night, and all those students, many richer than Torrent Peterson could ever imagine, most who would never worry about an oil bill, why guess what? After dancing a bit, they all ran away.

Yet a whole section of forest toward Riley Brook burned, and more oil went into the water than had gone in over the last five years.

It spread toward Oscar Peterson's junkyard and he stood out against it with a small hose. The children all scattered. And an investigation into all of this happened.

Mel Stroud watched from his apartment building in awe. If that could be done and justified by middle-class kids of middle-class parents, stealing a pistol would be nothing.

"Fuckin crazy cocksuckers," Henrietta said, taking a sniff of cocaine. "We gotta get outta here—people like them are dangerous. Yes sir, dangerous fuckin sons of bitches."

37

A BOOK CAME OUT CALLED *LEAVING CRUELTY BEHIND: The Story of Systemic Rural Abuse.* It came out that autumn and that's why Eva's light was on at night. It was published by the university and fifteen hundred copies were printed.

The main contributor was Faye Sackville, *with* Albert Raskin. The picture of their farmhouse was on the cover. Eva read the book.

Everything was silent, except the pain, the pain of someone taking over her husband's role, even saying he loved her child in a book, and how they had tried to do right by the child.

At dawn she would dress and go to work. She would do her work and walk home in the cold night air. Then she would eat a cold supper and go to bed.

I will kill Professor Raskin. I will kill him. I will, she thought one day. It simply flashed through her.

It was almost as if the thought was a knife that pierced the centre of her brain. It was so forceful she almost fell over. She looked at her small right hand, red from the cold, with chipped red fingernail polish on it, and when she closed it, it was as if she was closing it on a knife.

Clara asked her to sue him and Sackville.

"No, I will not sue," Eva said. It would cost too much of her soul.

She looked strangely at Clara as if trying to make her cousin, the one she had once wanted to be like, understand. Yes, if she had not wished to be like the talented Clara Bell, whose grandfather might have been the greatest premier in our province, she would not have ended up the lonely, humiliated Eva Mott.

"No," she said again, "I will not sue. I had everything, blueberries and our horse Pete and Peaches the cat, and old Matilda and poor brave little Polly—and he took it all, and I will die."

"No, you will not die. You will not die. I promise, you will not die."

And Eva smiled like a lost little girl.

"Remember we went to the grade nine dance, and danced and danced together because all the boys were too shy to ask us?" Eva said. "Remember that?" And she began to laugh hysterically as if in distress for a time now gone. "And my father—remember he picked us up in that old car? I was so embarrassed!"

"Yes," Clara said, "I remember, sweetheart. I remember."

"Remember our wedding? Torry was some nervous at the altar—and my father whispered to me, 'Do I have to pay for it all?' So Torry and I tried to scrounge up the money—and Oscar— poor old Oscar paid for it without batting an eye. I was so scared something would go wrong!"

"Yes, Love"

"And remember you had to buy me a brassiere because your dad was some embarrassed by me and I didn't have one! What did Torry ever see in me—I was so, so—silly." And she still laughed and laughed.

"Shh. Shhhhh."

She wrote Becky Donaldson a letter thanking her for saving her life that awful day: "*You are as strong as a man,*" she wrote "*But far prettier, and kinder than most. And you burned your hands, and poor*

THE TRAGEDY OF EVA MOTT

Mr. Hammerstone got smoke in his lungs all trying to save my little girl—I am so, so sorry."

Torrent had pleaded guilty to save her. He was sure Eva had lighted the fire.

In prison he heard about the murder of his two uncles, in detail.

"It was Mel," a man told him. He said that Mel followed behind the boys with his lights out.

"He's a real prick," the man, Gary Percy Rils, said, troubled by it all. "Hey Torrent, he's not the nice guy everyone says."

Then he said: "*But his brother Shane is worse."*

Of course Clara and Darren Howl and Torrent himself thought little Eva had lighted the fire in the barn for the insurance. But they were wrong. And Gordon Hammerstone knew they were. His nephew had lighted the fire. He had tried to steal a grandfather clock with the backing of his new best friend Henrietta Saffy. She had watched them come and go, knowing their farmhouse was often empty, their barn locked with a simple padlock.

She had befriended Roderick in August and by September he was doing exactly what she said. He was a little elf with a strange old face and flashing pretty eyes. She laughed at his antics because he had no mental capacity to control himself. From the time they left the hospital and went in different directions, Torrent's and Roderick's lives were destined in this small place to meet again. It only took Henrietta Saffy to enter the apartment building with one Mel Stroud. Mel Stroud told her a dozen times not to have anything to do with him, that he didn't want Roderick around, that he was a nuisance and would bring too much attention.

"He's such a cute little guy."

"Keep him away from here."

"He's my pet," Henrietta said.

So she and Roderick decided on robbing the farmhouse for Native rights.

They were hauling chairs and settees and clocks out of the barn, and were going to put them on Torry's truck and steal it all, and go to Saint John and sell them, but Roderick for some reason simply decided to light the entire barn on fire. One never knew what he was going to do from one moment to the next. No one knew this better than Gordon who had loved and protected him. But who would protect him if he ever went to jail?

Gordon had a terrible moral decision to make, and he wondered if he could. And time, time was passing. But yes, he knew he would have to. When he did, not only would they be looking for Mel Stroud but they would be looking for Roderick as well.

It took a few weeks, but this is exactly what happened.

Mel Stroud had no reason to burn that house or draw attention to himself. But now police were everywhere, the case was being reopened, people were being interviewed. And it was not only the local Corporal Becky Donaldson but the RCMP. That is why he went to the back of Oscar's trailer and watched. Yes, all of this had come about because of the fire.

That is, though Torrent was in prison, Becky Donaldson, after speaking to Gordon Hammerstone, who told her about poor Roderick coming home in soot and paint, was certain Mel and his brother were at the root of it all, and she would not give in. Now he couldn't even go out to a store without worrying.

So he would never trust Henrietta for doing this. He wanted to retrieve the pistol, sell it and leave, and he wanted to leave now and he planned to do it without her.

Now that the police had taken things from Oscar's trailer he realized it had to be things Mary Lou might have sent to her son.

"What things?" Henrietta asked.

"Oh nothing—"

"We can see to it all tomorrow if you want."

"No. You and that little Indian nutcase of yours are out of this. You're a jail cell waiting to happen. I've put up with him for weeks—ketchup on the couch and everything else, dirty dishes. Peanut butter left open on the counter. Pick up after him."

"You're a fuss-budget. A terrible fussy man. You brought me here. You told me to come, so don't blame me. Roderick's a bit unhandiable," she said. And she was unmoved when he said he might not trust her again. She shrugged when he brought out his knife and put it to her face.

"It's because of you every squad car in the fuckin province is here searching for me. They know Torry is innocent or something and they are trying to find me and prove it—and if they do I will give you up."

As Henrietta spit a sesame seed she said: "So unfriendly over a little fuckin barn."

"What do you think?" Chester asked, about the old woman who had caught Albert Raskin with his hand in the till, the morning after her funeral.

"She was a nice enough lady. Blue hair at the end. Lots of the ladies end up with blue hair at the end."

"I know. But sometimes she acted like she had just been hit over the head with a paddleboard."

"I know, but it wasn't her fault."

"No. She was religious—so she will probably go straight to heaven."

"Yes, straight up the stairway. With her can of Pledge."

"Dusting the stairway—up to heaven?"

"Oh yes, I do think so. Her husband was an invalid after the war."

"Which war?"

"The big one. The big one."

"The First World War?"

"No, the Second."

"Oh yes."

"No one answered us from Ottawa. No one seems to know anything about us anymore."

"Remember when the elderly tried to explain their dealings when we were young—when Beaverbrook did? With that investigation? Who believed him? Who ever believes anyone like us?"

"So let us be unmoveable. Let us in the end stand up, together, and say nothing."

"Yes. Let us do that, then."

"Like we did when we were young. We stood against so much when we were young. 'Member?"

"Yes, I 'member."

"Against the takeover bids from Thetford."

"Oh yes."

"No one believes us."

"No, they do not."

Then they began to complain like old men will about what new men didn't seem to know.

"They plan to march against us here soon."

"I know. I thought it would all come after that truck got burned—"

Chester, sitting in an expensive orange sports coat, and wearing a white silk shirt and bowtie, while his brother Dexter wore a pair of Humphrey pants and a woollen shirt, waiting for the cataclysm to trench against them across a field they could just make out from the top window of their house. They just were not too sure when it was coming.

"Damn them," Chester said.

"Damn them," Dexter said.

They sat there. It was pissing down rain, and in the afternoon the first sharp pickaxes of snow began to fall against the window. Their little maid was moving about them with the earliest of Christmas decorations. Sometimes they took sneak peeks up her dress when she was on the stepladder, even though they knew it was wrong. And she worked on the ladder even though she knew they did.

There would be a protest near the statues I had helped carve with the sculptor Jonathan O'Dell. I was commissioned with him to do so, and it took us two years to get it done. I worked them through sketching, he carving, and then in the fall of 1973 he cast them in bronze and they were placed at the front of the Raskin gates, the two men standing side by side, their heads turned in opposite directions, a little smaller than they were in real life, though they had shrunk some by now.

Now these two grand statues were going to be at the epicentre of something the old men did not fully comprehend.

The students and the university professors were coming out in support of the First Nations because the courts said the Wigwam Blockade was unlawful twice in the last year.

Tracy McCaustere wanted Albert to carry a sign. It would show solidarity by a man standing morally firm.

"You're just like Trotsky," Dykes told him. He was tired of Dykes now. He was tired of them all. When he passed bridges he couldn't help looking up at their highest point. If truth be known every morning he arose, dressed impeccably and wanted to die.

Nothing interested him now, even the fact that he had bought a new Mercedes, Sackville demanded it be sky blue, not the baize one they had on the lot, so they had to order it all the way from Toronto. At times she wore a gold coloured hijab when she drove it to town. In fact he hardly drove it at all.

The death of little Polly had shaken him to the core. He knew it bothered Sackville as well. He was old now, and great things were involved in the world he had not thought of before. Guilt and love and sin and soul. In some way he had given up his soul in order to carry a briefcase with important papers and remain well adjusted. He knew this now.

Twice he had tried to commit suicide in secret. Both times as far as he knew, he had failed.

He waited in his grand house on Water Street. He waited for some impossible moment he himself never wanted to happen.

38

DECEMBER 8. SO SACKVILLE, McCAUSTERE, McLEISH AND Raskin were the real vanguard. The renegade professors and McCaustere the student. Professor Dykes too, the old Bolshevik he likened himself to, to the few remaining students who knew of his fervid exploits in 1968.

Joining these people would be three union men who had worked inside the asbestos mine trying to get better rates for their workers. They had been fired for vandalism some years before and made an impression on both McLeish and Ms. McCaustere.

Two had stolen large industrial batteries to sell, and were fired. The third, a tall, hard-boned man of fifty named Clement Ricer, had claimed land belonging to the Raskin works. But he said he was forbidden to access it. He was also the man who had sold the acres on the ridge to Torry Peterson. Besides that were the pensions. The dividends had been paid out to men in Montreal who had helped the company years before. They were paid up until a few years before. They did not know that Albert was paid from the trust fund set up for him when he was a boy, and that he too collected the very dividends he said he was against.

Ricer and the First Nations needed to demand the rest of the land they both now claimed from Raskin works. And the press needed to be there to vouchsafe this demand, to be sympathetic, for the press is always sympathetic over scandal.

McLeish was a union Scotsman, hating all the upper classes, and never tiring of attempting to initiate dissent and strikes in the university itself. Small of stature but robust, red-haired and vainly offended, he had alienated himself with Tracy McCaustere. McLeish was really offended by the way he was not accepted as a visionary; that there was an old class system still in place in Canada. And he saw this horrid class system most deliberately in the Raskin works.

He had never been to Canada before he stepped off the plane, and he did not know that the university he came to would be over a thousand miles away from the centre of the country where he thought he would belong. He often thought of entering politics and running, without bothering to take up Canadian citizenship.

Albert wore a new winter coat, with the hood fur-lined, winter boots and thick white mitts.

So they came together now, in comprehensive solidarity with the students and Natives.

But as always everything would be decided by things very much out of their control, things they did not know about until all things were over.

December 7. Henrietta Saffy picked up the car, to take for a test drive, though the snow was blowing across the road, and a watery blue sky filled with ice pellets seemed to materialize when you stepped out of any building here. The buildings were dull green, the marquee waved, the hedges were covered in sacks of dark burlap. Beyond them across the iced-over parking lot, in a ridge of indigo, the shadowy outline of the barrens were seen. It was as if those boys, Arlo and Arnie, were still walking there, somewhere on that ribbon of snow-covered road that cut through all the way to Chaleur Bay. They were walking and holding on to each other and never, never letting go.

"And your husband, is he coming along?" Mr. Mott said, all his features a nervous jumble, with a black cap with black earflaps and blue borders pulled down over his ears, rushing back and forth. Other than his black cap over his narrow little head, that seemed to be even more pointed, he wore a pair of rubber boots with his suit pants tucked into them, and a suit jacket with a blue shirt and yellow tie. He wore the rubber boots because he had to go out and check the car they wanted.

He had worked here three or four weeks. His brother-in-law had gotten him the job.

This would be his very first sale. Today, late on a Saturday morning, he was the only salesman in the shop. But she had been so nice, talking to them about her lost baby, bringing his wife King Cole tea, and yes, Mr. Mott, a nervous jumble, did hit them up for thirty dollars and heaven forbid they took out forty and gave it to him.

"Yes, I am picking him up. We'll just drive it along Arron Road and bring it back—and I'm sure he'll want to buy it. He's been looking at this car for weeks now."

"Yes, yes. Well then, this is the one you want to test, the sky-blue Corvette. You know the new models will be in soon?"

She nodded, looked down at the paper he was filling out. "This one is fine—is fine. Time passes."

"Yes," he said, looking up and smiling, so you could make out two big buckteeth. "Time passes. Not long ago I was your age."

"There you go," she said. It was the third time he had tried to fill out the forms and got mixed up. His pleasantries she found offensive. So her patience was worn. She often had no patience with dull people. Her eyes were small and her face had a fierce aspect to it, her hair pulled back from her forehead and tied in a small ponytail. And who could blame her for being somewhat impatient. She had things to do. When he asked for her licence she took it out and handed it to him. So he could put it on file.

Glena Brewer. Her sister's picture was close enough—and if he had questions he did not wish to be impolite. Besides, they lived right above him, so there was never a worry about her taking the vehicle.

"There we go," he said. "You'll like it, I'm sure."

"Absolutely I will," she answered.

"Oh, don't forget the temporary licence. Just put it on the dash."

December 8. The little porch light reflected on the snow. The dog was sitting up on top of his house. The barn light was also on, and shone down directly to the ground. Oscar Peterson lay halfway over the porch rail, his arms outstretched as if he was about to pick up something that had fallen. His ears and face were covered in hoarfrost; his feet were bare and covered in a smear of blood. His eyes were half-opened.

Two police officers, Darren Howl, who arrived late, and a group of bystanders who had been told over a dozen times that there was nothing to see here but kept crowding up the old drive toward the lot, were there to witness the aftermath of the murder of Oscar Peterson.

The gun cabinet was opened by Becky Donaldson and another constable with a torch, and the pistol, which Becky had been told about by Darren Howl, was gone.

Only a shotgun, a .22 rifle with the bolt missing and a .308. There was also a fairly decent bow. But no pistol. So who had taken it? When Donaldson got to the trailer the cabinet door was locked, but the place inside was even more of a shambles than previously. And there was blood, all along the floor, and on the door handle from when Oscar was trying to escape.

To both her and Darren, Oscar seemed to have run around the table, initially in a clockwise direction and then a counter-clockwise direction. But they decided that he had been stabbed as soon as he had opened the door. By the first person to enter. The second person, a female, entered a moment later. She must have been surprised because she stood where she was—her footprints in the blood showed this—perhaps startled at what was happening. Then she picked up a steak knife and came forward.

Oscar tried to make it out the window, where he was again stabbed—he had been stabbed in the counter-clockwise direction; and then he tried to make it to the door again. There was a smear of his blood on the handle, so he been stabbed many times by then.

But the cabinet was closed. Which meant Donaldson decided, after an initial inspection, that those who murdered Oscar very likely did not take the pistol. For if they left the place like it was, and the body in its frozen repose, why then did they close and lock the cabinet door so graciously?

There was a picture of the pistol tucked on the top shelf of the cabinet, and it was an authentic police issue six-inch Colt .45, made in 1908. There was even a document on how it was manufactured, and how the early 1895 version had the sanction of Teddy Roosevelt to be used as the New York City Police issue. In the small cramped space of that small cramped trailer, that pistol had sat for many years. Corporal Donaldson was certain the murderers did not take it, but they had ransacked the place for the key. And they had hit the cabinet with a hammer and an axe, so Corporal Donaldson knew they were looking for it and were amateurs. So Mel Stroud was not here. She decided this almost instantly. The key was in a cup in the cupboard.

The idea of the pistol gave her a strange feeling—that odd felt sensation of something immaculately kept, pristinely fussed over, in this disorganized backwoods place. And it gave her a deep, deep sadness for crazy brilliant Oscar Peterson who had mourned Mary Lou for years. Who in fact had predicted his own murder, from a packet of tarot cards.

Darren and Corporal Donaldson had spoken over the weeks about Arlo and Arnie and how they might make an arrest in the case of Mrs. Wally. Mel and Shane could be linked to both now, with the silver watch, the photo from Saint John and the belated testimony of the mechanic Mr. Benson.

Donaldson then went over and spoke to the Raskin brothers about Torrent. Did they believe he lighted the fire?

"Not a word of it. A lie for sure," Dexter said.

Chester said Torrent worked hard. His wife had borrowed money to help him start a little business.

"What happened to the business?" Donaldson asked, startled that there was someone named Torrent.

But she never got to know what happened, because a bell rang, the dining room door opened outward, and a maid stood at the table, with the white tablecloth, holding a ladle, ready to serve them soup, and the two of them got up, cast a suspicious glance at the corporal in her big hat that came over her ears, and the flip of blond hair under it, and on tottering legs left the room.

So she left the old men and went back to Peterson's junkyard.

Donaldson now walked out over the yard, Oscar's grim dynasty, ambivalent to his death in the weak sun, the dog now whining in the scowl of wind, jumping from the top of the doghouse to run on its heavy chain. Across upper Arron Brook the land went flat, and was covered in ice and snow—and far away, some trail of white smoke came up and dissipated in the flat white sky.

Oscar had been stabbed multiple times and had lost two fingers. They lay in the snow just at the bottom of the porch. A knife the man used was in the kitchen. The steak knife she felt the woman used was left on the porch, covered in blood. Then the two, a man and a woman, went back inside and began to hammer the gun cabinet. But they could not get it opened, could not free it from the floor, and left in a hurry, startled by a man who pulled his truck up near the gate.

She had the first direct inkling that Mel Stroud was not involved in this, because he wouldn't have hammered the gun cabinet like that. He would have found some way to unhinge it from the wall and carry it away.

She went and looked at the body again.

There were heavy stab wounds on his neck and back, and lighter ones on his arms and buttocks. He had stopped bleeding three hours before.

Donaldson spoke to the coroner, a Mr. Whittaker, who then phoned the undertaker.

Darren Howl had been alone in the university. The entire building had stopped. Exams were over. The offices were empty, the desks bare, the lights on in only one corridor, the students gone, most gone home. One of the students had come to him to tell him of the protest the students were organizing in support of the First Nations. It was the fourth anniversary of John Lennon's death, so they had to take action.

"I see," Darren said.

"Are you coming with us, Professor? We can have someone to push you along with us?"

"No, I don't think I am," he answered.

The young woman smiled at him and disappeared down the corridor, whispering to another young woman: "No, he isn't coming with us tonight."

Strangely, from his window he saw a brand-new Corvette rushing through the slush, and glancing off a telephone pole, without stopping, disappearing toward the road that led to the barrens. He watched it disappear.

He had been waiting for a telephone call. It was the young man from Newcastle they had teased for not celebrating Karl Marx. He was home from the States for Christmas for the first time in years.

At first he didn't know what Darren was so insistent about. Then he began to remember.

"Oh, that stupid party. I hardly remember it. There was a lot of people there."

"A young girl?"

"Oh—well, yes. The one with the headache. That's what I remember."

"Did she have a headache?"

"Yes."

"Did someone give her aspirin?"

"Well, someone gave her something."

"But you don't know what?"

"Oh yes. I'm pretty sure it was Albert."

"Pretty sure?"

"Yes. Pretty sure. She said, 'Why are you naked?'"

Winston (his name was Winston) did not know the girl had died; he was certainly incensed that she had.

Donaldson got a call at ten after five at night that a Chevy Corvette had not returned from a test drive, and a certain Mr. Mott was involved. She arrived in the dark. The snow was wisping down over the lighted lot; the cars sat apathetic with frozen windows and doors. The little man Mr. Mott was rushing about, here and there, back and forth, stopping in the middle of the office to take a dressing down from Bruce Fletcher, then nodding and continuing to pace, stopping again to nod while he was called a nincompoop, and then pacing again.

"That is a forty-thousand-dollar car, you nincompoop."

"Yes, I know, I know, yes."

When Donaldson entered he stopped, looked and continued to pace, his grey suit pants pushed into rubber boots covered in salt.

"You have to help us," Mott said hysterically. "They took our car—they did—they took our car!"

"Shut up," Fletcher said.

"Who took the car for a test drive?" the corporal asked.

"A woman name Glena Brewer."

Donaldson said nothing, looked over the papers that were signed, looked at the man with his thin head and blue hat, with his rubbers and his mildly naive expression, and said: "You sure her name isn't Henrietta Saffy?"

"No, she lives right above us," Mr. Mott said. "Her name is Glena Brewer."

"Where does she live?"

"Right at our apartment near Dunn's Crossing." Here he looked at Mr. Fletcher and smiled weakly and nodded.

"How long has she lived there?"

"Oh, a few months, I think." Again he looked Mr. Fletcher's way and nodded.

"Is there a man with her or does she live alone?"

"Kindest man you would ever want to meet. Gave me forty bucks when I was short."

Becky went back to the police car, brought forward the picture and said: "Him?"

"Yes. A little different but I think that's Mr. White."

"Mr. White?"

"Yes. Mr. White."

"Mr. White is Mel Stroud."

"Oh. Well who is he?"

"I think he is a serial killer, Mr. Mott—a serial killer." Then she said, "But since this afternoon, I am not at all sure if he is still alive."

Eva Mott was now moving along Connell Street.

All was silent in the wisping snow, all was bleached, with mounds of ploughed greying ice; the trees waved at their very tops, there were frozen lights on the porches of houses. Her cousin, the cousin who had bought her the brassiere because they were embarrassed by her, the woman who had her doctorate, who had married into the local Howl family, was waiting for her. She was on her way to visit that cousin but later she had something else to do.

It was snowing again. A numb, penetrating cold seemed to sit on the air itself.

How she had wanted to love. But the world had gone on. It all became clear when Ms. Sackville met her two days before. It was then, after Sackville simply glanced at her seductively and walked by, that she knew what to do.

Eva did not know that travelling by train to that house, to that party, would make her feel left out in the great world (it was such a pinprick of dissatisfaction, she did not notice it right away), and yet everything she tried to do, to make *restitution*—to allow herself that grand *portico* to happiness—seemed unfulfilling. She, you see, had tried to be perfect. She had followed in the footsteps of others, and she loved—yes, she did love, many people.

The strange embarrassment she felt over her parents had started then. It would last a lifetime. And then she found little Albert (this is what she called him now) or he found her. Each was the other's victim. She knew this, remembering his angular smile, and his talk. All his illusive vanity which she did not understand, did she listen to and believe?

No, she could not *liveth* another day. The delayed reaction to her daughter's death had immobilized her now, except for one part of her, a part that was not evident in anything one might notice. She was in a world where little Albert had put her—a world of *terror*. All she heard now in her ears—and since the trial was over—was the little girl speaking to them through the doorway:

"I have a lot of buttons on my dress—help me, Daddy—I have too many buttons on my dress and it is caught—so I have to get my new dress off."

It was the dress Eva had made for her. And yes, it had forty little blue buttons. That's all she heard now, those words. All she would ever hear for years to come.

Too many buttons because she had made a dress with them. Dread: it seemed the world wished that for others. It is what Albert had given to her, what she had in turn given to Torrent, and what he faced now in jail.

It was the same *dread* those who were marching on the Raskins wanted to create. The truth is, most of the First Nations marching were like people everywhere: they had no will to stop themselves from doing what the majority told them was in their best interest, even when they saw it was not. But for many years they had been given dread as well—for centuries they too had faced dread.

They were all gathering at the end of Bloody Field. Old Professor Dykes the blind activist being supported by the fresh young rugby student with the exhilarating beaming look. And Eva was heading toward them, as soon as she delivered her letter.

Her cousin had started a foundation, to help children, and this is why she had called Eva to her tonight. It was because of little Polly.

Nor did she have to put the slightest bit of money into it. Her cousin and her husband had seen to it. This would allow money to help children who were sick or injured in accidents. Of course other children would be helped as well, Clara assured her. It would be named the Polly Peterson Children's Foundation.

The little doorway beyond the streetlight looked rust-coloured. That is where the kind and good Clara Bell Howl lived, whose own grandfather had risen to rule the province for nine years.

But she was not going there to visit. Nor to see anyone ever again. She was going there to deliver a letter. She would say in the letter exactly what she intended to do. She carried the old pistol in the pocket of her coat. She had not even fired a pellet gun before. But she realized she had only now to pull the trigger and her life would be altered forever. But you see—one must see it already had been.

Tonight Eva wore a tweed hat pulled down over her forehead. She wore a greatcoat to her ankles and high soft leather boots. Clara and her husband had felt an obligation, a responsibility, or both to her. They cared for her and her husband. They had told her this for the last nine months. Eva did not know why, except that Clara was a decent human being. Since the fire started in the barn, the reasoning was they were burning the barn for insurance. Of course she, Eva, was the only one who knew she herself had not lighted the fire. The theory was that she too was complicit in it, and that in the confusion when the fire jumped to the house itself little Polly was left inside, with the front door locked.

She looked up at the frozen trees, the black wind coming over the river ice and catching her still cleverly beautiful face and seeming to pierce her skull. The one thing in her life she must forget she could not. How her beautiful body still moved others to desire.

"I am sorry for what I am about to do," she had written on a piece of scribbler page. "God if there is one forgive me. Clara say a Hail Mary for me please, at the church of Saint Peter and Paul near the black Madonna that you donated last year, and tell Her I believe in Her now more than ever before. I haven't been to Mass in a long time. But I know you still go. Tell Her I weep before Her and ask Her to forgive me"

She went toward that door, that portico of the inner circle, which is so desirable until one finds themself inside. There she placed the letter in the mailbox, and turned and hurried into the dark black night.

39

DECEMBER 8, 1:05 P.M. YOU DON'T MEAN TO DIE BUT YOU do. Everyone does. It is strange that one has no way of knowing the consequences of meeting a young woman at Market Square in Saint John the day it was raining and you had nothing but a rail-thin jacket, and went inside. They were there, Henrietta Saffy and her sister. So he was taken with them and they with him.

Soon in the darkness of the apartment in the quietude of afternoon when her sister was working Henrietta and he were left alone. He would tell her of his life, and she was impressed but not too impressed, and then one night, oh it was during Lent sometime, in the winter, when the snow was dark and filled with gas and soot and crusted along the damp uneven streets, she walked out of the bedroom and sat beside him, and he made her naked and took her on the couch or they slipped off it, and she came twice.

She had been in and out of foster homes and juvenile detention since she was eleven years of age, lost her virginity at thirteen.

How had his death happened? She had sent Roderick in to see if he was asleep, so they could leave, and Roderick, who had heard him yell at her and call her a little cunt, and heard her say "I wish someone would do something about that lad," took Mel's knife and stabbed him in the heart. Then he came out and sat in the chair grinning.

"You stupid dumb fuck," Henrietta said.

But at his end flashes came back to Mel Stroud, of who he was, and what he might have done in his life. He remembered a squirrel trying to climb a tree with rocks tied to its tail, and he wanted desperately to reach out and take those rocks away, to relieve its suffering if only for a second, but he could not.

He tried to sit up, but he had been stabbed by Roderick. The worst of it was he didn't even know why. He had just gone to lie down. He had told her the night before to send Roderick away, but he was still here.

"He's my slave," Henrietta said.

"Send him away," he told her.

The day was getting on, and the snow was wisping in the parking lot. For some reason he saw the same rainbow the snow flurries made across it that he had seen when Arlo and Arnie were cleaning their fish tank. So then he lay back and was drifting to sleep.

But it was immeasurably desolate in front of him at this moment. Remorse like a black funeral cloth surrounded him.

Suddenly you see you are dead, and all of that lack of wisdom comes flooding across your last moments. A deep, dark sadness penetrated him, a deep, deep sadness he could not overcome. Arlo and Arnie—do you think he did not love them? Hell, they were his pals. He now tried to say *help me* but could not.

Worse, though he took it as almost nothing then, he heard the heart of Mary Lou's fetus stop beating. It just stopped. It had gone on beating after she died, for almost an hour—and then it weakened, and went silent. And in his mind as he was reaching out to Mary Lou he begged it begged it to continue beating on—but it did not. Then there was this conversation in a tavern that he had overheard when he was twenty-two. You know, when he was living at the Toomeys'. He heard people speaking. Who was the most dangerous man on the river?

"Everette Hatch." "No, Daryll Hatch." "No, Jerry Bines." "No, Gary Percy Rils." "No—Mel Stroud is worse than them all."

And he remembered smiling at that. And now he begged in his dying moment for his name to be erased from that horrible list but it shone before him in a haze of grey. He thought he could get up and run away but his blood had seeped all over the floor.

His would be the first of three murders this horrible day, the day when Satan wishes for terror to be performed in the name of man.

His name was Mel Stroud. He was murdered by Henrietta Saffy and Roderick Hammerstone, over a squabble that meant absolutely nothing, except that Henrietta said to her slave that she had to do something about that *meddlesome old woman* Mel Stroud or he would ruin her plans of going away to Florida for Christmas vacation.

Then when she discovered what Roderick had done she said: "Cripes Kate, I didn't mean for you to murder him. Son of a bitch, you can't seem to listen to reason."

"I love you," Roderick said. "I would do anything for you."

Henrietta smoked a cigarette and wondered what to do. They would cover him in a blanket and rush to visit Oscar. They had to now that they had the car. One deed propelled the second, the second the third.

They didn't even know what the pistol looked like or why they were doing it anymore.

Mel Stroud would be the last body discovered, covered in raw snow out on the barrens, near Mile 17, a day later. That's where they were heading to when Darren Howl saw them clip the pole.

Interview with Henrietta Saffy, December 20, 1984

"Where did you get the wine?"

"At Oscar's."

"Did you plan to go there?"

"Yes—planned to go. Not really planned to go but yes, planned to go. If Roderick wouldn't have been there, if he hadn't been at the farm, the apartment or the trailer—you get my drift?"

"*Yes, but you were the driving force?*"

"*Maybe—don't know. Oscar didn't suspect him. And perhaps he did not suspect either—that is Roderick—his mother drank all the time she was pregnant, two bottles of wine a day, almost two I heard, so he was born without any way to stop his impulses, that was what I discovered at the house when he lit the fire. You see it goes to show.*"

"*What goes to show?*"

"*It should show what we do.*"

"*I don't understand.*"

"*Well, you might think I don't care for people but I have a lot of compassion. It goes to show what we have done to the Indians—it does show—years of torment and abuse and desolation, and terror and being treated like animals, and given curfews, and forbidden to work in town. And there you have it, you see?*"

"*I see.*"

"*Well, you might say I see and not believe you do, but I have a lot of compassion. That's why I took him under my wing—that is why I tried to help him. But as soon as you mentioned something he would be up and do it. So you couldn't say anything. He was a product of the womb.*"

"*I am not sure I understand.*"

"*He was/is a product of the womb, a fetal alcohol syndrome baby, you see, so in the womb was where he was created, not outside. In his own way, he is the signature of life development. That pregnancy is sacred—he is the lesson to us. And that is why Oscar felt sorry for him, helped them, gave them money, bought him birthday presents. You see, Mel told me to befriend him. And then realized we couldn't control him, that there was no way to control him, so wanted him to go. Oscar had a soft spot for Roderick because he was born the same day as Torry, and he was born with a brain injury because of his mother he had, so you had to talk him out of doing anything. But then he fell all in love with me and I showed him my boobs just to tease him. I used to walk out of the shower naked.*"

"Mel used to tease him about that. But then Mel was right—the little lad was dangerous and he told me to send him away. Roderick must have overheard it all. So he goes at Mel."

"Did you know of the money under his mattress?"

"What money?"

"Almost fifteen thousand dollars—"

"What?"

"Where did he get it?"

"Where would he get it? I didn't know he had it."

"No? Do you think he may have gotten it from someone he was black-mailing?"

"No. Well he didn't tell me a thing—not even a little bit."

"And then?"

"And then?"

"After Roderick came out of the bedroom."

"So off we went."

"And you hid outside the trailer."

"Yes I did, when Roderick went in."

Then she said, *"And within five seconds the place erupted."*

When Henrietta entered, Oscar was backed up against the wall, and had been stabbed twice in the abdomen.

"What did you do that for?" Henrietta yelled, but she knew going in that this would have to happen. And so she picked up the knife on the table, and when Oscar swung the frying pan she stabbed him in the lungs. He tried to get out the window, and then he ran to the door with Roderick yelling and slashing him. He severed his fingers when they were on the handle. Oscar made it outside, to the porch, and Henrietta came out and continued stabbing. Finally he said: *"You don't need to stab me again. I am dead now."*

And that would haunt her life forever. It would actually turn her life around after many years when she recouped and regained her soul.

Once the terror was over, Oscar felt so sorry for her as she stabbed him. He was rising up, he could feel it—and he saw his dog watching him and he smiled, and then he heard little Mary Lou Toomey and turned to her.

"Yes, hurry, come with me. Come with me, love. Come."

Up he went with Arlo and Arnie, and the pain of his wounds seemed to melt away, and he was finally free.

They never found the pistol, and couldn't break into the gun cabinet. They tried to haul it with them but they finally left it where it was.

They went out along the highway toward the barrens with Mel Stroud in the back, covered in a blanket, his face contorted and purple, his large hands stained by swollen blood. They threw him out somewhere in the barrens and made it back to town where they were stopped by the police.

"All that shit for this," Henrietta said. But by the grace of God, the love of her sister, the help of a United Church minister, Reverend Bessie Cortes, she would someday, after many years, radically change. But it would be a struggle, a terrible battle against the odds. She would be let out of prison in 2007. She would live in Saint John and work at a halfway house. All the figures that anyone ever needed and the dates and times of special occasions she would keep in her head. She would read Sophocles and read about Socrates, she would read Milton and Tolstoy, the Brontë sisters and Emily Dickinson. She would speak to assemblies, visit prisons, and hold hands with First Nation women incarcerated for being outcasts.

When someone told her what her IQ was, she would simply say:

"I am not that bright anymore."

And in the end her smile would return.

Two days later, when Gordon got to see his nephew, Roderick jumped up, hugged him and said "Why hello Gordon good old Gordon, my best old Gordon, how are you?" and was concerned that he had lost his Team Canada hat somewhere in the snow while he was running round and round in circles to escape the police. Roderick was never blamed. No blame was ever attached.

December 8, 9:45 p.m. She had to walk many streets, and the streets were dark, shadows played, and at the end of each street a snowdrift sat under the glow of a streetlight and snow fed up off it into the air. Her hat did not keep her warm, the wind pulled at it, her coat did not soften the wind but it hit her with a gale force.

The field that led up to Raskin works was through a stand of dark small spruce. You came out into a soft meadow and along a path, and then the field, Bloody Field, opened a quarter mile long and a half mile wide. Almost no one knew what was happening in town, for the news had not hit anyone here. They were concerned only in their exhibition. Many of these demonstrators were in fact true exhibitionists. In a way they had always been.

Eva had in fact become aware of this so painfully since the expunging of her only child that she hesitated to act out anything. But yet the pistol told her she should.

Vengeance is mine, saith the Lord. She knew this, she had read it, she had a priest who she disliked because of his clever sociability tell her this when she sat with him for an hour.

"Now my dear," he said, "just go home and try to be a better person."

And the priest had that down to an art form, the pretence of new faith, and he smiled at her, touched her hand with his soft lily hand, and she felt ill. She felt he, that priest, had become Albert in his own way—both males who, though on opposite ends of the question of God, used their comfortable theories to hide.

So there was no God. Or was there a God who was angered with both men.

So she ran away from that priest yesterday afternoon. Her head was spinning; she could not eat or sleep. She thought of only one thing: to destroy *him* who had caused her so much pain.

And yet amid all of this was a voice that asked: *Who, Eva, caused you the pain? You alone.*

Yes, she knew, and she loaded the pistol with the shells that came in the black bag with it and headed out toward the field. She even giggled a little when a man she worked with, a man who wore the awful suit and tie at work and lingered in her section of the store after lunch hour, offered her drives home, stopped and grabbed her arm.

"Where are you going, love? Let's get a drink. I've been wanting to take you for a drink for ages. We can celebrate Christmas tonight."

"Oh," she giggled, "is that right? Well you don't want me tonight."

"I want you any night, any night in the world. I would pay to have you." (He knew he took a chance saying this but he would be more than willing to.)

"Ah, but tonight I really might kill you."

And amid his chortles she moved off into the wind and around a corner near the centre snack bar. She remembered the letter written to her by her mother last week:

Oh you know Eva I will always love you—it's not your unfaithfulness—it's why you were unfaithful you must recognize—not some flight on one sweet night but a calculated betrayal of a man and little girl, who I think, and forgive me for saying both suffered agony on your behalf.

And she moved around the corner and came to a group of middle-aged men and women, who were leaning over a man on a park bench. He was a small man with a balding head, little owl-like glasses, and he looked distraught. He had been coming home, walking along the street with a book on Chatterton and two small goldfish in a plastic bag—the progeny of Arlo and Arnie's fish tank, a hundred generations removed, in warm water—and he had been carrying them home for his niece Priscilla who was visiting, and when he asked earlier in the day the one thing she would like, little Priscilla said: "Fish—golden fish. I love to see golden fish."

Amid the howls of wind he went downtown and happened to find in the pet store two wonderfully alive golden fish. He was bringing them home, around the corner, when a group of students and their professors walking to their destination saw him, and some animosity that had lingered in those sallow classrooms took hold against him. There he was, pudgy little soft-faced Eliot Slaggy. And they then ran over the little man on their way to Bloody Field, as if no one had more right than they to do so. The fish fell from his pocket but lay in the bag on the cold street, flapping their tails, and the students stepped over him and around him on their way to exercise their right of assembly and their privilege of dissent.

Now seated on the bench, holding the goldfish in his hand—only one seemed to be alive, the other seemed to have died in the altercation—his eyeglasses askew, he kept searching for his book on Thomas Chatterton. His nose was bleeding. The people, most of whom had never heard of little Chatterton, comforted him in worry and concern, and tried to find his book.

Eva looked at him, turned and continued her walk up the long hill toward Raskin works. Far behind her a siren bleated a moment and was still. They had pulled over a Corvette, its four-way flashers emitting a yellow light through the haze.

Now she remembered the train she was on, and how the nice Negro man (yes, she still thought of Black men that way) gave her the 7Up, and the crossroad lights shone through the bottle like those flashing four-way flashers. How strange to remember that now.

But you see, she did not know who that Negro man was. He was the man who listened to Mel Stroud berate little Mary Lou Toomey one day when she told him she was pregnant, and went over to them and said:

"You wish to come with me, young lady?"

"She won't be going with no one like you," Mel laughed.

"Oh, if she wants she can. And I would not berate her for being with child." The Black man had fought middleweight and was once Canadian champion, and had no fear of Mel Stroud. "No, I would never berate a young lady for being with child," he said.

"Being with child," Mel laughed, taking Mary Lou by the arm.

So the man came back three times to that apartment, bringing her coffee and asking her if she was well.

And that was why Torry heard his mother had run away with "a porter from *darkie* town in Halifax." Because a gentleman had taken up for her on the street and came to her house to see how she was.

And that man was now in touch with Corporal Donaldson about the woman named Glena Brewer, who had contacted him about the death of Mary Lou Toomey.

It was strange because six hours earlier at his last moment, Mel Stroud remembered that incident so clearly, of the man meeting them at the mall.

Yes, this Black man, Tom, if he was here now, what would he say to Eva, "the little lady" as he had called her when he had given her the chicken sandwich? He would say, "My dear girl, those who torment you only torment themselves."

How sad her parents were, how she thought of them, how she remembered her uncle's words. How sad the world as she heard the hopeful students begin their march. She pushed on toward the frozen barrens, toward the field where that ignorant army was ready to clash by night.

40

OLD PROFESSOR DYKES, HOLDING THE RUGBY PLAYER BY the arm, led the way. Albert pushed on as well, caught somewhere in the middle of the crush, and as he tried to manoeuvre others came behind him, and his sign said: *Equality for Native peoples. Stay off our land.* He slapped his Laplander white mitts against his white coat for warmth.

Nor could he see Ms. Sackville. Perhaps he didn't know she had stayed home. She had started out with all the black-clad students and then her feeling of elitism took over and she slipped away into the coffee shop on the corner and then went home. She was reading a book at this time, by Anaïs Nin, and folded neatly on the couch with a glass of red wine.

Albert wanted to drop the sign, and yet he couldn't; he was compelled by all of those singing and holding hands to go forward, to push forward toward Raskin works. The place he grew up and the place they all now hated.

At this moment he felt terrible and he realized he, more than others, was actually being used. He was on display—a Raskin.

Looking at the others as they flashed their eyes his way, he saw a sudden triumph over him.

It was in a way like an army going forward until exhausted and not understanding why.

Really there were only twenty Native men and women, and two dozen students. There was McLeish, and there was Tracy McCaustere, and Raskin asked himself *Are their faces now changed, are they somehow hilarious? Do they look frenzied, and why is that? Why is their smell so suddenly noticeable? Why do I feel like I am no longer a human being? For here I am in the midst of some mob.*

And he thought that and wanted to get out, onto the side, to the edge where he could breathe. But others were pulling them along, demanding to tear things down, demanding that their grievances be heard. Ah yes, a grievance, and he looked and saw McLeish elated somehow, his small muscular body moving forward as if he was in a wrestling ring, and happy that there was a grievance, that there was an injustice, so he could partake in this, and with this vanity he strode.

"Yaahh," he said, and Tracy McCaustere, whose arm McLeish held on to, looked at him and yelled, almost in elation, "Yahhh."

And the young girl who had asked Professor Howl earlier that day if he was going to join the protest fell, and people began to trample her, but she was lifted up, and she yelled "Hurrah!" and moved forward, her shirttail out, her black coat unbuttoned, snow down her pants, and the wind howling against her young, impetuous face.

Albert found himself crying too, and the raw-boned men who had worked in the yard and had been fired were here now to make their case and people were led by them toward the statues. And one man seen earlier talking to the students, and because of the cold slightly squatting up and down on his legs as he spoke, with his hands in his pockets, Clement Ricer, who said he owned the land beyond, had moved to the far end of the field as if he was creating his own pincer movement. Here the snow was deeper, here Clement Ricer followed the shouts with shouts of his own, here he raised his fist in solidarity. Then he lighted his cattails, and his face took on an oily, hardened glow where his chin and cheekbones seemed smeared in red.

"Goddamn you!" he yelled, and then coughed and burst out laughing. He stopped a second, opened a pint bottle of rum, had a drink and continued on.

Except Albert had seen it before; he had seen it all before when he protested in Washington, when he went with Professor Dykes. Now he was forced on toward the statues, and already men seeing them were shouting, "Tear them down! Tear them the fuck down!"

No one had intended to tear them down until that moment. Now one could think of nothing else.

And already the women were shouting, "Native—*land*," though in truth if this land was unceded, where they lived was unceded as well—but have them give up their land, their flower gardens and houses?

The mob no longer thought. Except some thought of the young girl who had fallen and was lifted up, and how her shirt was opened, and her breasts almost visible, in the flashes from lights and cattails, realizing this did she mind it now, her benediction toward *proving some greater cause?*

"*Hurraaaaay!*"

He looked around at all the dark howling and mesmerized faces, but when the crowd yelled "Yaaaah!" he did too. And he reached the young woman who had fallen earlier and putting his arm around her said, "Stay with me. I am here to protect you."

"*Hurraaaay!*"

———

Dexter had said to the maid, "You can go now, dear. It will not help if you are here. Chester and I will dine alone tonight."

"But what about your medicine?"

"We will take it."

"What about the police?"

"We will phone them if we need them. They patrol here every night, so they will come sooner or later."

"What about the letters? Did you get those letters? They will help you."

"No, we did not. But you go now because it does not matter," and then he added, "it does not matter, my dear." And he patted her hand.

"But they called you monsters in the paper and that isn't fair," she said. She started to cry. "What a thing to say. It is not fair."

"I have discovered in this life that nothing is."

"I can't just abandon you."

"That is so brave of you, my dear, because everyone else has. But you go home."

The lights were on outside and snow had drifted up against the porch, and a very cold moon shone, its light like splinters against the window, and the chimes in the back tinkled briskly and the inordinate muffled sounds of people came from somewhere beyond the trees. They wanted to show that they were happy, so as Chester said, they were "hamming it up."

Dexter did not know if they were, if they were hamming it up. He just hoped, prayed a little, that Albert wouldn't be among them. Would not have given in to it all.

There was nothing wrong with having a protest. People had been protesting against them since they became independent enough to buy their own socks. They had fired more men over the years than most companies had ever employed. They had made more money than most too.

But now they were sick and old, and they told the maid to go. She left, but first she laid out their pills, Dexter's on one side of the table and Chester's on the other.

They knew who they were going to face; they had faced men like this before. They knew there would be no pleasing the Native men and women against them no matter what they said or signed or did not sign.

The nurse as well they told to leave. She said she wouldn't but as far as they could tell she too had gone.

"What do they want?" Dexter said when he heard the noise approaching and saw the lighted torches.

"They want our blood," Chester said. "They might say they do not, and pretend that they don't."

"Ten years ago a hundred men would have put a stop to this."

"Yes."

"But now there is no men . . . How many men do we have now?"

"No men, really."

"No men?"

"No, the men are gone. The place is shut. We have ourselves."

"Well then, we must go meet them."

"Yes. We must go out and meet them."

Both these men had fought at Vimy, both had suffered wounds, both had received commendations. And so when they dressed tonight, long after the maid had left, they put on their suits, and ties, and jackets with the Order of Canada, the Order of Merit and the Royal Victorian Order, pinned exactly alike on both men. They sat down to the soup that had been prepared, both of them supping with a large spoon, with three crackers beside each plate and a glass of sparkling water.

They then sat in the dark and waited, both ruffled up a bit, while they heard the crowd gather. Both of them stood, each of them took their canes and put on their woollen hats, but they went to the window and waited.

"You'd better take your pills, Chester. I took mine."

"Are you sorry about the letters?"

"No, I am no longer sorry about anything I have ever done. I will when my end comes stand on the fuckin principle of being a man."

She, Eva, had entered the field at the back, and saw the mob ahead of her. She moved along the perimeter to catch up but slipped over bared branches and fell. She stood, realized the pistol had been cocked and one bit of pressure on the trigger would have shot her through the groin. She had a terrible urge to shoot now—like someone who sees game in the distance—but she knew she was far too far away.

But then she began to trudge across the field itself, moving diagonally to the men and women. One of the women from the reserve had a blow horn and was yelling: "This is not Raskin property! This is our land—been our land for three thousand years!"

"Five thousand," one of the other women corrected her.

"Five thousand," the woman said. "You have poisoned our land and our people."

Then someone who was standing beside Albert yelled: "Kill all the Raskins!"

And all the students joined in, even the girl whose shoulders he protected.

The great surge of men and women pressed ahead. There were lights on everywhere it seemed now—from old cattails that had been lighted, to flashlights, to the floodlights of Raskin, to the television camera that seemed to come out of nowhere, interviewing Tracy McCaustere who stridently moved along as she spoke, her long thin legs in high black boots. Beside her was a man she did not at all like but was desperate to show off at the moment, Albert Raskin, and she put her arm through his, as he with his other arm about the young half-naked woman.

McLeish like a pit bull had run ahead of McCaustere, had bullied people out of the way with his strength, and now seemed in competition with the tall, raw-boned red-headed man Clement Ricer who was striding in with a few stragglers from the far side, yelling now and then as he held his cattails aloft.

Really, if one thought of it, McLeish he had no connection to this place, went back home every April to Scotland where he spent his summers hiring out his prize bull and making light of the primitive Canadians, had never spoken to a Native man or woman until four years before, had never had one in his house, nor ever hunted game with one. He knew nothing of the internecine battles that went on, on the reserves, the fights for power among band members, the misuse of money. He knew not a thing of this.

Unfortunately what had started here two years before as just, was perhaps no longer so.

Onward they went.

Now everyone realized that they were here seeking to tear the eroded statues down, and it had turned blisteringly cold. Now they picked up their pace to get to the statues first, pushing ahead of one another, and others pushing back.

Here was Dan Fournier, part First Nations, and Giles Mallet, First Nations and Acadian, both of whom had been fired for vandalism. What they could not believe was that so many students were with them tonight;

"Tonight we are the professors, we will teach you tonight." And they smiled at this brashness, and Dan Fournier felt vindicated for all past losses, tests that he did not know, and grades that he did not pass. He moved toward the statues with the students suddenly and spontaneously yelling: "Tear them down! Tear the statues down!"

When they started yelling "Tear them down!" it seemed as if this was the only reason they had trudged across Bloody Field in the wind. "Tear them down, tear them down!"

Standing under the grand floodlights in front of their industry, in the howling wind and under the cover of large pine trees, were the two old men, off a little to one side watching the people approach, their Distinguished Service Medals and the Order of Canada on their lapels, the medals from the First World War on their chests, standing amongst people who no longer knew their world and some who didn't even know there was a First World War.

Eva made it to the front just as they started mocking the sculptures, jeering and laughing, swearing and calling names like children do.

The old men, however, walked toward the statues, and turned to face the mob. Eva was five feet from them, looking in astonishment at all the people. Her nose was bleeding from her fall, her hair was wet with snow and sweat, and still her face held beauty and innocence looking awestruck at all those coming toward her. Yet nothing seemed strange to her, even the young girl with her shirt opened and one of her breasts visible. At the moment this did not matter.

Eva kept looking at all the faces, but as Tracy McCaustere had ordered when they had turned the cameras on, "Cover your faces— cover your faces!" and so, so many had done so on her behalf.

"Old white bastards!" the white students were yelling now. "Old white fuckers!"

There was a ringing in her ears, a buzz that did not go away. Far down the hill two RCMP cars were approaching, but even coming onto the property would take time. Looking at the young woman whose breast was visible she thought of the bra that Clara had bought. Strange how that had started it all, she thought.

People stood around the old men yelling; the old men stood their ground with their last bit of strength, stood solid on their canes. For a moment or two everyone and everything became quiet. It was as if in their presence the mob did not now know what to do.

The two old men searched the faces, and looked at Albert and simply passed on to others.

"Spit on them," someone finally said. But far from making the old men turn or run, or whatever might have been intended, they stood side by side, seeming in their feeble stances more deter- mined than an army. Then two or three men from the mob of men and boys started to rock the statues back and forth. One wearing woollen gloves slipped and fell on his back, others yelled that someone had hit him. Albert went forward with McLeish and Fournier because he must.

He looked at his uncles and saw in them more dignity than he had ever seen before, and tears from the bitter wind came to his eyes. Suddenly both statues fell. They simply fell and people were yelling "Hurrah!" and others were saying, "Let them fall. Let the statues fall."

And Chester bent over to pick Dexter up, as men and women rushed about them. He grabbed the hand of his brother like he had on the second day of Vimy Ridge when they were going up the hill attacking the place the Canadians called "the Pimple," and Dexter managed to stand just like he did that day almost seventy years before. Out from the left rushed Clement Ricer, his cattail gone out, his gloves damp and his floppy hat covered in snow.

And then the gun went off. Three shots went off and people began to run.

McLeish screamed: *"They have a gun! They have a gun!"* And he began to run over people to get away. He knocked McCaustere down, and the young girl who had earlier fallen, and ran. McLeish was halfway down the field by the time the echo from the gunshots faded. He had fallen three times and his hat had come off. The rugby player ran as well, leaving old Professor Dykes stunned and alone, turning in circles as people rushed by him.

Eva wasn't trying to save the statues, as was later stated by people. She was trying to kill Albert Raskin. But she missed him and killed the raw-boned man, Clement Ricer, who had said he owned the property.

They said it was her ultimate act of revenge perpetrated on Clemet Ricer. They said she had a long-standing affair with Shane Stroud.

"Of all people," they said.

41

STILL, THINGS WOULD COME OUT LITTLE BY LITTLE about Stroud. Henrietta's sister said that Mel Stroud had given the injection, and she was present when he did. But Mel simply sat there in the corner playing solitaire.

Over the next three years Clara Bell, under the auspices of Chester and Dexter Raskin, would take charge of the monies of Raskin Asbestos, and they along with the government would give out close to thirty-five million dollars to those families who had suffered.

The old men died within hours of one another in 1992. Chester first, and then Dexter.

The property was sold for condominiums, and a new park on Good Friday. The statues were put into storage, and the old building Eva Mott had lived in that fateful summer with her parents was torn down.

The local Native band in contract with a Finnish company took over the remaining logging interests on Good Friday. But Torrent Peterson was left his stand.

Professor Eliot Slaggy had his book on Thomas Chatterton published. He and his friend Mr. Beansworthy took their long-waited trip to England, Scotland and Wales.

The world changed. It changed dramatically when DNA became widespread in legal opinion. One week in 1993 a test was done on the ancient articles of Mrs. Wally, and a database was searched and a match was found.

It was not Mel Stroud. It was, however, as far as 89-million-to-1 ratio was concerned, his younger brother Shane. He was convicted of second-degree murder.

He asked for Constable Donaldson, and told her he needed a deal.

"What deal?" she said.

"I don't want to go to Renous. There are too many there I don't get along with. And I need a chance at parole. I need a chance at parole. I don't believe in this DNA anyway, so you should help me put in a request. You have an Indian guy killing my brother and he is away in some nuthouse—but look where I am."

"I can't promise anything, but I will speak on your behalf."

So Shane told her about the mescaline, and how Professor Raskin had given the girl what she thought was an aspirin, with, he said, criminal disregard.

"Are you sure?"

"Yes, I am, That's exactly what caused her death."

For weeks Albert, who had become our MLA, had heard of an impending arrest.

And one day just as he was leaving, he was arrested on the steps of the legislature building and put in handcuffs. He was charged with criminal negligence causing death. This time Donaldson didn't smile, though her hair flipped under her hat the same way when she walked, and when she took him by the arm her hand was like a vise, she was that strong.

Just before the trial he resigned and pleaded no contest in court. Out of a four-year sentence he had to serve eighteen months in jail. He was released because of ill health. His health was not at all what it used to be. He often complained he had measles in prison or maybe the mumps—he was sure he might have had a few mumps—and couldn't eat the food.

Sackville stuck by him. Her hair was grey now and made her look very dignified. But by 1996 she too resigned from the university after some upset with a female student, and both of them lived on pensions and his endowment. They played bridge for money at the golf club. They walked together along the shore hand in hand, and were seen in the summer playing croquet at Lampkey's. He seldom spoke.

Sometimes Sackville went away for a week or so, and would not tell him where. She had a female companion. He was often alone.

She would say, "Wait exactly where you are, my dear, and I will be back to you if you do. Don't worry my little Canuck I will always come back to you."

Once I had to visit them. It was strange how her little black boots sitting in the corner closet made an impression. Little black lace boots. Such a remarkable impression I painted them from memory, and the painting hung for half a summer in the Beaverbrook Gallery.

After that I saw Professor Raskin only once more. He was walking toward me, but he didn't recognize who I was. It was in the autumn and very cold. I was surprised to see he was wearing a poppy.

Things had come out in a book about Raskin Enterprises published in Toronto. Letters had been found at Parliament, redacted though they were—the money Albert had received while he marched against them revealed at over a million dollars. The press began to hound him, young fresh-faced reporters who loved scandal.

Once he picked up his cane and yelled at one. "I am Albert Raskin. Do you even know who I am!"

The reporter laughed, something like the reporters once had at his uncles.

He had gone away, he was forgotten, and no one seemed to care.

People teased him now, and he often looked distracted, puzzling over some problem in his head.

One night people saw him in the upstairs window of his house. He was writing a letter to someone, or somebody. He looked quite dignified, and quite old.

Four days later a lone figure in a bright brand-new suede jacket and brand-new fedora, and a gold wristwatch, was walking on the bridge. People said they saw him looking into the water for many moments. Then he simply got onto the rail at the highest point. He placed his fedora on the ledge beside him, and after a few moments, as if he was saying a prayer, fell, like a stone. An off-duty police officer tried her best to rescue him. Her name was Becky Donaldson. Tears actually came to her eyes.

The bridge is high, and his body was washed away. It was November 11 and already snowing. Sackville herself stood on the prow of one of the boats, looking for his body, a resolute old woman with a resolute life. Though it was minus ten, and the spray splashed over her, she refused to shiver. She was the first to spot his body, far out in the bay. There was a letter in his pocket. But the water had diluted the ink, and no one knew who it was addressed to or what it said.

"We have lost Albert Raskin," she told the press. "Do you understand? We have lost our Albert Raskin. He would make ten of any of you."

And she never spoke of him again.

Shane Stroud died in prison twelve days later.

McLeish is in Scotland, at Edinburgh where he teaches and helps organize the writers' festivals. And keeps a breeding bull. He does help the poor—of that he should be commended.

Tracy McCaustere is the first name in legal assistance for First Nations rights in our province. She is well known here.

Dennis Howl was appointed to the senate in 1995. There was an uproar over this by some, and that is always to be expected.

Clara Bell and he adopted two children.

The Polly Peterson Children's Foundation continues today.

Torry Peterson was released from jail after Roderick's confession. He returned to Arron Brook where he rebuilt his house. He was seen at times fishing far away on late summer afternoons, taking trout from those deep hidden pools. Eva would not accept his visits, so he stopped seeing her years ago.

He did what he had always done: he went back to making tables, and cabinets and chairs, and when the timber was right a grandfather clock. Half the land he had bought from Mr. Ricer the First Nations bequeathed him, and they kept the upper half, which was closer to Riley Brook.

Gordon continued to work with him, and they sold enough. He and Gordon did not become wealthy, but neither was poor.

I used to sell my paintings at the fairs alongside his work, and at the Chatham exhibition, and help both him and Gordon in the junkyard that he never relinquished, a memory of the father who loved him in spite of the odds.

I painted Arlo and Arnie for Torrent, and his mother Mary Lou. From a picture where they are all together laughing, as if the world was filled with love. I suppose in a way it is.

One evening close to Christmas in the year 2003 I saw Gordon as I left the shop. I was looking for Torrent but he was away.

Gordon had a huge basket filled with chocolates and candy, cigarettes and smoked salmon. He was heading off to the institution where his nephew was incarcerated. At this time his nephew had little memory of Henrietta or the events of that day.

42

THAT SAME DAY TORRY PETERSON TRAVELLED DOWN TO Fredericton. On the way back he picked up a hitchhiker. She had a small white suitcase, wore a light blue dress, with a thin jacket, and high heels though there was snow on the road. She got into the back seat with the suitcase beside her. He drove off and she sat silently, staring out the window. Her face looked resigned and toughened through resignation; a strange beauty still pervaded her. He asked her her name.

"Eva."

"Eva what?"

"Eva . . . Mott."

"Oh! Are you related to Ben Mott?"

"Yes."

"How are you related?"

"He's my father."

"Oh! Is he still alive?"

"Last I heard."

Silence followed for quite a while. The sky was bright blue.

"So where are you going, Eva Mott?"

"Going to Arron Brook Road."

"Arron Brook! All the way there. Why?"

"Tipping," she said. "I could make up some money tipping if I can get there."

(Tipping was the art of collecting boughs for Christmas wreaths, and it was already the second week of Advent.)

"Well," he said, "maybe we could do it together this year. Then we could sell them at the market next week. You could if you want have lunch with me. Just up here at Burke's Diner."

"I don't think so, no, no."

"Why not, Eva Mott?"

"I just got here from Ontario. I just got out of jail, if you wanta know," Eva said. She seemed distracted now. When he caught her eyes in the mirror she looked away in fear.

"Yes. I am aware of that. You got your BA in jail. I am very proud of you. Today you had a plane ticket. I knew that too, I didn't expect you to be hitchhiking with high heels back to the Miramichi in winter."

"Well then, tell me this. Who in hell are you?"

"I'm your husband, Eva. My name is Torry Peterson. You remember me?"

"Yes. I'm sorry, I didn't recognize you. You got older some. You didn't get married again?"

"No. I did not."

"Have any other women?"

"Of course—"

"Not one to marry?"

"There is only one girl for me."

He stopped the car, he got out and opened the back door, took her by the hand and put her into the front seat. Then he spontaneously kissed her on the forehead, and gently closed the passenger door.

As he walked to the front of the car he looked in at her and smiled. She smiled just so slightly back.

"It is you, Eva," he said when he got into the driver's side again. "It has always been you, Eva—always you."

"Why?"

"Ha! What a question—why? It's what Oscar said, when asked by the miserable Dews why he brought me up alone, when I wasn't his son and tormented him, and tried to shame him as they called him down for not doing a good enough job, as if any other had ever done a better one."

He paused, tears came to his eyes, and the highway spread before them.

"Well whatever did he say, Torry? Whatever did he say?"

"*Love*, Eva. Oscar said, with his voice I remember, both humble and shaking, *love*."

"You still even love me?"

"As the sky is blue, Eva Mott, as the sky is blue."

She glanced at him, saw tears running down his face.

"Oh please," she said, and reaching out took his rough and time-worn hand. "Please don't cry."

Then she looked up. Yes, the sky was indeed so very blue, and too those trees stretched with the afternoon light across the snow-packed highway. She was no longer cold, for the car was warm, and forever and ever there was a fulsome chance at a new life, a new beginning, a new and holy destiny, here as well as in all the world.

And Torrent and Eva were going home.

ACKNOWLEDGEMENTS

I would like to thank my editor Tim Rostron; thank copy editor Shaun Oakey; thank Amy Black and Kristin Cochrane—thank my wife and my two sons—and anyone else over these many years who has stood with me.

Once a professor I believed was a friend, doing work on my novels, phoned and said that he knew more about me than I knew about myself. I realized we both had made a terrible mistake about who both of us were. Later after his work on me was complete he said I should quit writing, and his friend, another worthy professor, said he worried that I was no longer revolutionary.

Safe it is to say I did not quit writing all those many years ago, and do believe my work is in the most important ways as revolutionary as any of the writers I know.

A NOTE ABOUT THE TYPE

The Tragedy of Eva Mott is set in Monotype Van Dijck, a face originally designed by Christoffel van Dijck, a Dutch typefounder (and sometime goldsmith) of the seventeenth century. While the roman font may not have been cut by van Dijck himself, the italic, for which original punches survive, is almost certainly his work. The face first made its appearance circa 1606. It was re-cut for modern use in 1937.